Dudley Bernard Egerto ... ...25 into an ancient Cornish seafaring family. He joined the Merchant Navy at the age of sixteen and spent much of his early life at sea. He was torpedoed during the Second World War and his resulting spinal injuries plagued him for the rest of his life. Towards the end of the war he turned to journalism becoming the Naval and Defence Correspondent for the London *Evening News*. Encouraged by Hornblower creator C S Forester, he began writing fiction using his own experiences in the Navy and his extensive historical research as a basis.

In 1965 he wrote *Ramage*, the first of his highly successful series of novels following the exploits of the heroic Lord Nicholas Ramage during the Napoleonic Wars. He continued to live aboard boats whenever possible and this was where he wrote the majority of his novels. Dudley Pope died in 1997 aged seventy-one.

RAMAGE AND THE DRUM BEAT

DUDLEY POPE

HOUSE OF
STRATUS

This edition published in 2001 by House of Stratus, an imprint of Stratus Books Ltd., 21 Beeching Park, Kelly Bray, Cornwall, PL17 8QS, UK.

www.houseofstratus.com

Typeset, printed and bound by House of Stratus.

A catalogue record for this book is available from the British Library and the Library of Congress.

ISBN 1-84232-473-X

For Bill and our baby Jane
who sailed across the Atlantic with us

CHAPTER ONE

The heat and humidity of a Mediterranean summer made the watermark in the paper stand out like a fading scar, and traces of mildew left a tarnished gilt outline round the edges. The orders, in a clerk's careful handwriting that was sufficiently faint to indicate he was short of powder to make the ink, were dated 21st October, 1796, headed 'By Commodore Horatio Nelson, Commander of His Majesty's ship Diadem and senior officer of His Majesty's ships and vessels at Bastia,' and addressed to 'Lieutenant Lord Ramage, Commander of His Majesty's ship Kathleen'. They said, with a directness reflecting the Commodore's manner:

> 'You are hereby required and directed to receive on board His Majesty's ship under your command the persons of the Marchesa di Volterra and Count Pitti, and to proceed with all possible despatch to Gibraltar, being careful to follow a southerly route to avoid interception by enemy ships of war... On arrival at Gibraltar you will report forthwith to the Admiral commanding to receive orders for your further proceedings.'

And be told, Ramage guessed, that the Marchesa and Pitti would go to England in a much bigger ship. The Kathleen would then almost certainly be ordered to rejoin the

Commodore's squadron, which should have finished evacuating the British troops from Bastia (leaving the whole of Corsica in rebel and French hands) and have sailed back to the island of Elba to salvage what it could as General Bonaparte's troops swept southward down the Italian mainland like a river in full flood.

Genoa, Pisa, Milan, Florence, Leghorn and by now perhaps even Civitavecchia and Rome... Each city and port that was beautiful and useful to the French would have a Tricolour and a wrought iron Tree of Liberty (with the absurd Red Cap of Liberty perched on top) set up in its main piazza, with a guillotine nearby for those unable to stomach the Tree's bitter fruit.

Yet, he thought ironically, it's an ill wind... Thanks to Bonaparte's invasion, His Majesty's cutter Kathleen was now the first command of Lieutenant Ramage; and thanks to Bonaparte – an unlikely enough Cupid – one of those who had fled before his troops was on board the Kathleen and the said Lieutenant Ramage had fallen in love with her...

He scratched his face with the feather of his quill pen and thought of another set of orders, the secret orders which had, like a fuse leading to a row of powder kegs, set off a series of explosions which had rocked his career for the past couple of months.

On 1st September, the date those orders were issued to the captain of the Sibella frigate, he had been the junior of three lieutenants on board. The orders, known only to the captain, had been to take the Sibella to a point off the Italian coast and rescue several Italian nobles who had fled from the French and were hiding near the beach.

But a chance evening meeting with a French line of battle- ships had left the Sibella a shattered wreck, with himself the only surviving officer, and as night came down he'd been able to escape in the remaining boats with the unwounded men. And before quitting the Sibella he'd grabbed the dead captain's secret orders.

Supposing he had thrown them over the side in the special weighted box kept for the purpose? That's what he should have done, since there was a considerable risk that the French would capture him.

Well he hadn't; instead he'd read them in the open boat – and found that only a few miles away the Marchesa di Volterra and two cousins, Counts Pitti and Pisano, with several other nobles, were waiting to be rescued. The fact that the Volterras were old friends of his parents hadn't influenced his decision (no, he was sure it hadn't) to take one of the boats and carry out the rescue.

And everything had gone wrong. Only the Marchesa and her two cousins had finally risked escaping in the boat, and he'd bungled the whole business. Surprised by French cavalry, Pitti had apparently been killed by a shot which destroyed his face, and Ramage had been lucky to get the Marchesa and Pisano away safely.

Lucky...it was an odd word for him to choose; the Marchesa had been wounded and Pisano, who'd behaved in a cowardly fashion – so much so that the seamen in the boat were shocked by what they saw – had suddenly accused him of cowardice. And when he'd got them safely to Corsica, Pisano had repeated the accusations in writing.

He shivered as he thought of the resulting court martial. It was bad luck that the senior officer ordering the trial had been an enemy of his father's; it was almost unbelievable how the Marchesa had suddenly thrown aside all loyalty to her cousin and given evidence on Ramage's behalf, not only denying that he'd been a coward but declaring that, on the contrary, he'd been a hero...

And at the end of it all, with the wretched Pisano discredited, Count Pitti had suddenly arrived in Bastia. Far from being shot in the face, he had twisted his ankle while running alone to the boat and, rather than delay his rescuers, hidden under a bush.

Although both the Marchesa and Antonio Pitti had subsequently been fulsome in their praise to Commodore Nelson (who'd arrived in Bastia while the court martial was in progress) Ramage admitted to himself the trial had been more of a blow to his pride than anyone (except perhaps Gianna) had guessed. The proof was that he kept on thinking about it.

He sat up impatiently: the devil take it, the whole business was over and done with now and this was no time for sitting here like an old hen brooding over it. He folded the Commodore's orders, which he now knew by heart, opened his log book, and dipped the pen in the ink.

Against the time of nine o'clock and under the columns headed COURSES and WINDS, he wrote with a petulant flourish of his pen 'Becalmed'. In the next column headed REMARKS he noted, 'Sunday, 30th October 1796. Ship's Company employed ATSR. 10 o'clock Divisions. 10.30 Divine Service. 11.30 clear decks and up spirits. 12 dinner.'

He disliked the abbreviation ATSR but it was customary: 'as the Service required' usually appeared at least twice a day in a log book.

Since it was still only half past nine he'd anticipated the rest of the morning's routine, but his temporary cabin was dark, hot and airless and he hated it. He wiped the pen impatiently, smearing ink on his thumb, locked up the log and his orders, and went up on deck, acknowledging the sentry's salute with a curt nod.

The discontented scowl on his face warned the men to keep clear as he strode off. He always detested Sundays at sea because of all the rigmarole it entailed for the commanding officer of one of His Majesty's ships of war, even if he was but a very junior lieutenant and the ship of war a very small cutter armed with only ten carranades.

But even more he detested being becalmed in the Mediterranean on a late autumn day when the long oily swell waves gave no hint of a breeze arriving in the next hour, or even the next week. Purgatory must be something like this, he thought wrily, though he had the advantage over everyone else on board since he could display his irritation and they could not.

Leaning over the taffrail he watched the crest of each swell wave coming up astern to see-saw the cutter, lifting first her buoyant counter and then sweeping forward to raise the bow and let the counter drop into the trough with a squelch like a foot in a sodden boot.

It was an irregular, unnatural and thoroughly uncomfortable motion, like dice in a shaker, and everything on board that could move did move: the slides of the heavy, squat carronades squeaked and the ropes of their side-tackles groaned under the jerky strain; the halyard blocks banged and the halyards themselves slatted against the mast. And – the last straw as far as Ramage was concerned – the headsails were lashed down to the foot of their stays, the big mainsail furled and the wind vane at the masthead spun round and round on its spindle as the mast gyrated, instead of indicating the wind's direction.

Because of light winds and brief thunderstorms the Kathleen had covered only four hundred miles in the past eight days – an average of a couple of knots, less than the pace of a child dawdling to school. It was more than eleven hundred miles from Bastia to Gibraltar, and he was only too conscious of the phrase 'with all possible despatch' in the Commodore's orders.

An occasionally outraged growl from behind him told Ramage that Henry Southwick, the elderly and usually almost offensively cheerful Master and his second-in-command, was making a last-minute search before reporting the ship and ship's company ready for inspection. With a Master like Southwick the Sunday inspection was merely a routine; Ramage knew not a speck of the brick-dust used to polish brasswork, nor a grain of sand lurking in the scuppers after the deck had been holystoned and washed down with a head pump would escape his eye. The cook's coppers would be shining and each mess' bread barge, platters and mugs would be spotless and its pudding cloth scrubbed. Every man was already shaved and rigged out in clean shirt and trousers… Yet for all that Southwick would soon ask permission to muster the ship's company. Then, after the inspection, all hands would be ordered aft for Divine Service, which Ramage would have to conduct himself.

The thought made him self-conscious; he would be taking it for only the sixth time in his life, since he'd commanded the Kathleen for precisely forty-two days and still found it hard to believe that almost the last entry in the cutter's muster book said, 'Lieutenant Nicholas Ramage…as per commission dated 19th September 1796…' The sixth Sunday – and he remembered that under the Regulations and instructions, the captain had to read the thirty-six Articles of War to the ship's company once a month. Since it could replace a sermon he might as well read them today because the sun was shining, and next Sunday it might be pouring with rain and blowing a gale of wind.

After three years of war all but the most stupid seamen knew by heart the Articles' forthright exhortations warning everyone in the Fleet, from admirals to boys, of the perils and punishment for the sins of treason, mutiny, blasphemy, cowardice and drunkenness; and they knew in particular the thirty-sixth, nicknamed 'The Captain's Cloak', which was so phrased that it enabled a captain to word a charge to cover any other villainy that the wit and ingenuity of errant seamen might devise. Still, as long as they could then bellow a few hymns to the fearful tunes John Smith the Second scraped on his fiddle, the men would listen patiently enough. After that they'd be piped to dinner and those off watch would spend the rest of the afternoon skylarking, dancing, mending clothes and, Ramage thought gloomily, before sundown – unless they were an exemplary ship's company – one or two who had hoarded their grog or won extra tots from their messmates, would be brought before him blind drunk...

The Marchesa di Volterra stood under the skylight of the captain's cabin, which was hers for the voyage, twisting the looking glass in her hand first one way and then the other to make sure no stray locks of hair had escaped from the chignon that she had spent the last ten minutes trying to tie. Her arms ached. She was hot, and for the first time since the Royal Navy, in the shape of Ramage, had rescued her and her cousin from the mainland as they fled before Bonaparte's cavalry, she wished herself back in her palace at Volterra, where her merest frown would bring a dozen maids running. For the first time in her seventeen years of life (nearly eighteen, she remembered proudly) she really wanted to make herself look beautiful to please a particular man, and she was having to do it in a tiny cabin without a maid, a wardrobe, or jewellery. How did Nicholas ever manage to live in such a cabin? She was much smaller – his chin rested on her head when she stood close – yet the ceiling, or whatever Nicholas called it, was so low that even now she had to stoop to hold the looking glass high enough. Impatiently she flung the glass into the swinging cot and sat down in the single chair in front of the desk which served as a dressing table. Accidenti! What was the use? If only her hair was blonde! Everyone had black hair, and she wanted to look different. Did he like high cheekbones? Hers were much too high. And the mouth – hers was too big and she wished the lips were thinner. And her eyes were too large and brown when she preferred blue or grey-green, like a cat's. And why was her nose small and slightly hooked, when she wanted a straight one? And her complexion was shaming – the sun had tanned it gold so that she looked like a peasant girl instead of the woman who ruled a city and a kingdom (even if the kingdom was small the city was big). She ruled twenty thousand people, she thought bitterly, and not one of them was here now to help her dress her hair – except her cousin, Antonio, and he'd only laugh and tease.

Well, Antonio could laugh, but he must help. When she called, a heavily built man with a short, squarely trimmed black beard came into the cabin, shoulders bunched to avoid bumping his head on the low beams.

'Well, well! And whose garden party is my beautiful cousin gracing with her presence today?'

'There's only one, my dear Antonio. Hasn't Lieutenant Ramage invited the elegant Count Pitti? Everyone will be there – Nicholas makes them put on their best clothes and sing hymns. Perhaps he'll flog some of them with a cat of seven tails just to amuse you.'

'Cat o' nine tails,' Count Pitti corrected in English.

'Nine then. Antonio, help me tidy my hair.'

'It doesn't need it. You're beautiful and you know it and if you want compliments...'

'Will you help me tidy my hair?'

8

'You love him very deeply, don't you?'

The question was sudden and unexpected but she neither blushed nor glanced away, Instead she looked directly at him, and said with awe, almost fear, in her voice, 'I didn't know it was possible. I was a child before I met him; he's made me feel a woman. And he – he's a man, Antonio; everything a man should be. I know only one other man like him.'

'And he is?'

'You, my dear cousin. One day a woman will feel for you as I do for him.'

'I hope so,' he said soberly, 'though I won't deserve it. But you have known him – three weeks, a month?'

'Does that matter?'

'No – but never forget you met him in romantic circumstances. It's the stuff of story books – the dashing young naval officer sweeping in from the sea to rescue the beautiful Marchesa from beneath the feet of Napoleon's cavalry and...'

'I know. I've thought all about that. But I've also seen him dirty and stinking and exhausted, seen him fighting Napoleon's cavalrymen with only a knife, seen him unjustly court-martialled on a trumped-up charge of cowardice... Is this the stuff of story books as well?'

Pitti shook his head. 'No, but when you're parted? When he's at sea for months, perhaps years, what then? You've never had patience, Gianna. Since you inherited Volterra you've been able to have everything you wanted – at once.'

'That's true,' she admitted. 'But they were material things: jewels, gay balls, excitement. I think perhaps I wanted all that so urgently because I hadn't met him. When you've no one to love, to confide in – to live for, in fact – you get bored; you need entertaining. When there's no sun, you need many candles everywhere.'

'Tell me more about this English chandelier!'

Even as she smiled she realized she knew very little about him in the conventional sense; but in the past month when the two of them had together faced so much danger, adventure, death and intrigue she'd learned things about him that in normal times a woman might live with a man a lifetime without discovering. And apart from the times of immediate danger she'd seen him in the secret agony of making decisions on which his men's lives depended. She'd seen what probably none of his men ever saw, that command was desperately lonely, particularly for someone as young and sensitive as Nicholas. He'd been given command at an early age and it hadn't yet (nor, she knew, would it ever) brutalized him so he became callous about his men.

'He was twenty-one years old a few weeks ago and he's been at sea since he was thirteen; the scar on his forehead is a sword wound from when he was boarding a French frigate last year, and when he's nervous or under a strain he rubs it and blinks and has trouble pronouncing the letter "r". I don't really know why he never uses his title – as an earl's son he has one, and the Navy uses it in official letters – but I think it makes social difficulties with superior officers if he is called "Lord". His parents knew mine, Oh, Antonio, I sound like a catalogue. I can't describe him!'

'Wasn't there some trouble about his father?'

'Yes. Perhaps you can remember the famous trial of Admiral the Earl of Blazey? I was too young. No? Well, anyway, that was Nicholas' father. The French sailed a large fleet to the West Indies and the Earl was sent out much too late with a tiny British fleet. He fought them bravely but he didn't win; nor did the French. Then the English people, who didn't know how few ships the Earl had – and they were old and decrepit anyway – made a terrible fuss and the Government got frightened. Like all Governments it wouldn't admit its mistake, so it court-martialled the Earl because he didn't capture all the French ships.'

'And he was found guilty?'

'Yes – he had to be, to save the Ministers. He was the scapegoat. If he'd been found innocent then obviously the Government was guilty. Apparently the judges in a naval court martial are naval officers, and since many of them are mixed up in politics it was easy for the, Government – the Admiralty, anyway, which is the same thing – to choose officers supporting its own party for the court martial, Commodore Nelson told me it often happens. He says politics are the curse of the Navy!'

'So the Earl must still have many enemies in the Navy, and this affects Nicholas. A sort of vendetta...'

'Yes, very much so. That horrible man who had Nicholas court-martialled at Bastia after he had rescued me was the protégé of one of them, but luckily Commodore Nelson knew all about that.'

'If the Earl still has enemies among the admirals, Nicholas will always be in danger,' reflected Antonio. 'You can always put someone in the wrong if you want to... Nicholas realizes that?'

'Yes I'm sure he does, though he's never mentioned it to me. But I often sensed, when he was making some important decision, that – well, he knew that even if there were only two alternatives, his father's enemies would say whichever he chose was the wrong one. It never affected his decisions – just that I felt there was always something lurking in the shadows, threatening him. As if he knew he had the Evil Eye on him...'

'You've discovered a lot about Nicholas in a month!'

'Jackson told me some things, and so did the Commodore.'

'This seaman Jackson – isn't he an American?'

'Yes – a strange man. No one knows much about him, but he has a great respect for Nicholas – even though he's twice his age. It's curious – when they're in danger they seem to be able to read each other's thoughts.'

'Well, he saved my life,' said Antonio, 'and that's enough for me!'

Just then a shrill warbling note of a bosun's call echoed through the ship, followed by shouted orders. 'Time for church,' Antonio grinned. 'Your Nicholas makes a good priest!'

Southwick was glad the inspection and Divine Service was over, and watching a handful of men dancing on the fo'c'sle as John Smith the Second perched on the barrel of the windlass scratching at his fiddle, he was thankful the Kathleen had such a good ship's company. Out of the sixty-three men on board he'd like to change only a couple, whereas most ships he'd previously served in had only a couple of really good men out of five score.

But trust Mr Ramage to spot something, he thought ruefully. Every captain he'd ever served under looked for brick-dust, sand, dirty coppers or a bit of mildewed biscuit in a bread barge. But not Mr Ramage. Out of nearly two hundred round shot in the racks beside the carronades he'd spotted two that had sufficient rust scale under the black paint to make them no longer completely spherical, so that they might stick in the barrel while being loaded and also wouldn't fly true. The man who noticed that without passing each one through a shot gauge could see through a four-inch plank. Yet Southwick readily admitted, although he was only a youngster, Mr Ramage was the first captain he'd ever served under who was more concerned with the way a ship could fight than the way it could be scrubbed and polished, and that was a dam' good thing since there was a war on. And in twenty-six years at sea he never thought he'd ever daily see men actually enjoying three solid hours of gun drill in the hot sun of the forenoon followed by two more before hammocks were piped down. Still, a lot of it was due to the Marchesa. Southwick didn't know whether it was her idea or Mr Ramage's, but having her standing there with Mr Ramage's watch in her hand timing them certainly kept the men on their toes. And it rounded off the day nicely when she awarded the prize tots of Mr Ramage's brandy to the crew of the gun that had been first to report 'Ready to Fire!' the most times.

But Southwick was certain the Kathleen was a happy and efficient ship simply because, young as he was, every man on board trusted Mr Ramage as their captain. His twenty-six years at sea had taught the Master that that was the only thing that mattered. Certainly, under the regulations they had to salute the captain and call him 'Sir'; but they'd have done so anyway. Although he was quick enough to rub 'em down for slack sail-handling or slowness in running out the guns, the ship's company knew Mr Ramage could do most things better than they and he had a happy knack of proving it when necessary with a matter-of-fact smile on his face, so that the men, far from being resentful, took it as, well, a sort of challenge.

Suddenly remembering he was still holding his quadrant, Southwick picked up the slate and went down to his cabin to work out the noon sight he had just taken. Mr Ramage would soon be calling for the day's reckoning, since at sea the new day began at noon.

Ramage felt like singing. He'd watched a tiny wind shadow dancing over the sea to the north; then more appeared and closed with the Kathleen. Within a minute or two he had the men cheering as they heaved down on the halyards, hoisting the great mainsail, then the largest of the cutter's jibs and foresails. A few moments later the maintopsail was set, followed by the jib topsail, and while the men afted the sheets under Southwick's orders, Ramage looked at his watch and then at the luffs of the sails.

When the Master saw the last sail trimmed properly, he bawled 'Belay that' to the sheetmen and swung round to Ramage, an inquiring look on his face. Ramage, noticing the men had also stopped to look at him, put his watch back in his pocket with deliberate slowness and shook his head.

Southwick looked crestfallen and he sensed the men's genuine disappointment so that he was slightly ashamed of his deception and called with a grin, 'All right, all right, you've just beaten the record – by half a minute!'

Southwick slapped his knee with delight – he'd obviously been thinking of a few seconds – and the men were laughing as the Master dismissed them. Southwick and all except those on watch went below. Ramage, disappointed Gianna did not stay on deck now the Kathleen was under way once again, decided against sending for her to enjoy the breeze with him because she might be sleeping. Then for no apparent reason he suddenly felt uneasy, and he remembered how his mother sometimes shivered and said, 'Someone's walking over my grave!'

CHAPTER TWO

When he was sober, John Smith the Second looked sly and foxy, an impression heightened by his small, wiry body; but once he had sunk his tot of rum – and any others he'd won by gambling – his features softened and the shifty eyes settled down so his drink-mottled face had the blissful look of a poacher after a successful night's raid on the squire's game preserves. Rated in the muster book as an able seaman, and listed as 'the Second' to distinguish him from another seaman of the same name, Smith was also the Kathleen's band. He had a fiddle which, as long as he was not sober, he enjoyed playing, and Sunday was his busy day. He played hymns for the service in the forenoon, and in the afternoon sat on the barrel of the windlass scraping away as the men danced.

Ramage had been on watch for half an hour and although he valued Smith both as a seaman and a means of keeping the men happy, the sawing of the fiddle was an outrage to a musical ear; so much so that Ramage felt he could cheerfully shoot the fiddle out of John Smith the Second's nimble fingers.

Suddenly he remembered the case of duelling pistols which the Viceroy of Corsica, Sir Gilbert Elliot, an old friend of his family, had sent on board at Bastia as a present when he heard Ramage had been given his first command. He had not yet had time to try them out, and now was a good opportunity. He passed the word and a few moments later Jackson had the brass-edged mahogany case open on the cabin skylight, wiping off the protective film of oil from both the pistols. They were a beautiful matched pair made by Joseph Manton, whose lion and unicorn label was stuck inside the lid of the case. Each gun had a long hexagonal barrel and a rich-grained walnut stock.

Ramage picked up one of them. It was perfectly balanced. The stock fitted into his palm as though the pistol was a natural extension of his arm; his index finger curled round the trigger as if the gun had been specially made for his hand. And the mahogany case was fitted with a mould for casting shot, a stamp for cutting out wads, flasks of powder and a box of extra flints. The set was, Ramage thought, a credit to the gun maker of Hanover Square, and he richly deserved the proud announcement on the label, 'Gun Maker to His Majesty'.

In the meantime Jackson had loaded the other pistol.

'It's a lovely piece, sir,' he said, handing it to Ramage. 'I'll go down and get some bits of wood from the carpenter's mate to use as targets.'

'And pass the word to ignore the sound of shots!' Ramage said.

A few minutes later Jackson was back with a bundle of wood under his arm. Ramage, who had loaded the second pistol, climbed up on to the breech of the aftermost carronade, balancing himself against the roll of the ship. He sighted with the pistol in his right hand, then tried the left.

'Right, Jackson, throw over the largest piece!'

The wood arched up into the air and splashed into the sea several yards off and began drawing away as the ship sailed on.

Ramage had cocked the pistol and brought up his right arm straight from his side, sighted along the flat top of the barrel, and squeezed the trigger. A tiny plume of water, like a feather, jumped up two yards beyond the piece of wood.

'All right for traverse but too much elevation sir!' Jackson called.

Almost at once Ramage fired the second pistol with his left hand. The wood jumped and the shot whined off in ricochet.

'Phew,' commented Jackson. 'Left-handed, too!'

Ramage grinned. It had been a lucky shot because usually he had a tendency to pull a pistol to the left when firing with his left hand.

He gave both pistols back to Jackson to re-load and as he jumped down from the carronade he saw Gianna coming up the companionway.

'Accidente!' she exclaimed. 'Are the enemy in sight?'

'Target practice – I'm trying out the pistols Sir Gilbert gave me.'

Southwick came up, and then Antonio joined them and watched Jackson as he rammed the shot home.

'Duelling pistols, Nico? Surely they're rather long in the barrel for use in a ship?'

'Yes – but a pleasant change. Our Sea Service models are so heavy on the trigger you need to jam the muzzle in a man's stomach to be sure of hitting him. But these – just a touch on the trigger.'

Gianna took the pistol Jackson had loaded.

'Careful,' Ramage warned.

She looked at him scornfully, lifted her skirts and scrambled on to the carronade.

'Look, you see that bit of weed? I'll hit it! You'll wager me?'

'One cestesimo.'

'More. Two – hurry!'

Without waiting for a reply she cocked the pistol and fired. The shot sent up a tiny spurt of water several feet beyond the piece of floating weed.

'The ship moved!'

'You didn't allow for the roll!'

'It's not fair. I do not pay. Let's have a proper match. You and your knife and me with this pistol.'

'Match or duel?' Ramage asked wrily.

'Match – to begin with.'

'Be careful, Nico,' warned Antonio. 'Don't forget her mother wanted a son and brought her up as a boy! She shoots like a hunter, rides like a jockey and gambles like a fool!'

Gianna gave a mock curtsy from atop the carronade. 'Thank-you, cousin Antionio. You see, Nico how close are the family ties among Italians!'

'Tell me, Nico,' interrupted Antonio, 'surely throwing a knife isn't part of a sailor's training?'

Ramage laughed. 'No – that's Italian training! When my parents lived in Italy – they did for a few years – we had a Sicilian coachman. He taught me.'

'Come on,' Gianna exclaimed impatiently. 'Jackson will throw something into the sea and I hit it at the count of ten. You, Nico,' she looked round, 'you have to hit the mast with your knife while standing by that steering stick thing.'

'The tiller.'

'Yes, the tiller. That's fair, I think. And the stakes?'

'Un cestesimo.'

'You are a gambler. Can't you afford more?'

'I'm only a poor lieutenant, Ma'am!'

'You can afford more, though.'

Although her voice was still bantering he knew she was not joking. He looked puzzled and she pointed to his left hand. When he lifted it she indicated the gold signet ring with the rampant griffin crest on his little finger.

'All right, then,' he said reluctantly, 'my signet ring against – '

Still holding the pistol, she had turned her right hand just enough to let him see the heavy gold ring she was wearing on the middle finger.

' – against the ring you are wearing.'

'Oh no!' she exclaimed. 'That's not fair!'

He knew her too well. 'That or no match.'

Shrugging her shoulders with apparent ill grace she said, 'Very well. But if you win the first time you give me another chance.'

Ramage was just going to refuse when he realized her subtlety: if she lost and then won, they could exchange rings without anyone knowing. It was childish but he felt elated: their secret was a secret yet they took pleasure in almost flaunting it.

'All right, but Antonio must hold the stakes,' he said, pulling off his signet ring. He turned to call for Jackson and saw he and Southwick were standing nearby, Southwick holding a small wooden cask.

'This do as a target, sir?'

'If it's half full of water, yes.'

'It's empty, sir.'

'So it floats high in the water, eh? Has the Marchesa bribed you?'

'Deck there! Deck there!'

The shout from aloft suddenly reminded them that for the last fifteen minutes everyone except the lookout and the two men at the helm had forgotten the Kathleen was a ship of war.

'Deck here,' bellowed Southwick.

'There's a hulk or summat – maybe a small island – fine on the starboard bow, sir.'

'What d'you mean, a hulk?'

'Well, sir, no masts nor nothin', yet looks like a hull. S'just lifting over the horizing, sir.'

Southwick handed his telescope to Jackson. 'Here, get aloft with this bring-'em-near and see what you make of it.'

This aspect of commanding a ship annoyed Ramage: a few weeks ago when he was junior lieutenant in a frigate he'd have been up the ratlines in a moment, having a look for himself. Now, as captain of the tiny Kathleen but with the same powers of life and death over his crew as the captain of a great three-decker, he had to maintain an appearance of calm detachment – at least, he thought ruefully, he would if Gianna was not on board, cheerfully turning a dull voyage into a fête.

The lanky, sandy-haired American ran up the ratlines as effortlessly as if hauled up by an invisible halyard. Once astride the cro'jack yard he paused to pull out the tubes of the telescope and then looked in the direction the lookout was pointing.

Henry Southwick, whose cherubic face and flowing white hair gave him the appearance of a benevolent parson, would celebrate his sixtieth birthday in a few weeks' time, a fact he remembered as he glanced at Ramage. Although the young captain was a year or two over a third of his age and they'd served together for little more than five weeks, Southwick sensed that given a long war and that Ramage survived the intrigues of his father's enemies and the efforts of the French and Spanish, every man that ever sailed with Mr Ramage would spend his dotage boasting about it to his grandchildren, and Southwick admitted he'd be no exception. Young captains usually annoyed him. He'd served under too many who had been given commands because their fathers owned enough cash and countryside to ensure their own nominees were elected to Parliament. All too often, when grumbling about the blatant inexperience of some young puppy in command, he'd met with the reply, 'Well, his father's worth a couple of votes to the Government.' (What's the ratio of pastureland to patronage? he wondered sourly.) Anyway, none of that could be said about Mr Ramage, since the Government had tried to get his father shot, like poor old Admiral Byng.

Southwick saw Ramage was blinking again, as though looking at a bright light, and rubbing the scar over his right brow. Although recognizing the warning signal, Southwick wondered what had caused it and, glancing at the Marchesa, saw she too had noticed and was watching with anxiety and affection in her face.

A well-matched pair, he thought, and he could well understand her love (although he was sure Mr Ramage was quite unaware of the depth of it). Sentimentally, picturing the Marchesa as his daughter, the old Master tried to see Ramage through her eyes. He had that classical build like the Greek statues he'd seen in the Morea, with wide shoulders and slim hips, light on his feet and the kind of walk that'd betrayed him as a man born to lead, even if he was dressed in rags. But as far as Southwick was concerned the eyes revealed most: dark brown, deep-set over high cheekbones and slung under bushy eyebrows (which met in a straight line when he was angry or excited), they could look as cold and dangerous as the muzzles of a pair of pistols. Yet he had a dry, straight-faced sense of humour which the men liked, although Southwick admitted that often he only realized he was having his leg pulled when he noticed the tiny wrinkles at the corners of the eyes.

'Deck there,' hailed Jackson. 'A hulk, for certain.'

'Can y' make out her build?' yelled Southwick, suddenly jerked back into the present.

'Not yet. She's stern on but yawing around.'

Southwick knew it couldn't have been an island – there was no land for miles; but what was a dismasted ship doing out here? Suddenly he remembered the previous afternoon's squall. At first he'd taken it for just another Mediterranean autumn thunderstorm, one of the usual couple a day. But as it approached Mr Ramage had come on deck, seen it and at once called to him to get every stitch of canvas off the ship, and as Southwick had passed on the order he'd been hard put to keep the surprise and doubt out of his voice. But Mr Ramage had been right; three minutes after the last gasket had been tied, securing the furled sails and leaving the ship rolling in a near calm, a seemingly solid wall of wind had hit the Kathleen and, with only the mast, spars, furled sails and hull to get leverage on, heeled her right over until water poured in at the gun and oar ports, and it had taken extra men at the tiller to get her to bear away under bare poles.

Southwick had expected her to capsize and knew he'd never fathom how Mr Ramage guessed there was so much wind in that particular thunderstorm. It'd seemed no larger and its clouds were no blacker than any of the others. But a ship whose captain hadn't known – well, even if she hadn't capsized, her masts would have certainly gone by the board.

He looked at Ramage and as their eyes met he knew the lieutenant had worked all that out even before Jackson had started up the ratlines.

'One of ours, sir?'

'I doubt it; not in this position.'

With that Ramage went below to use the desk in his own cabin, ducking his head under the beams and acknowledging the sentry's salute. Even with his neck bent he could not stand upright, although it hardly mattered since the cabin was too small to walk around. And at the moment there could be no mistaking it was temporarily the quarters of a young woman accustomed to having several servants running around after her: flimsy and intimate silk garments edged with delicate lace were strewn on the desk, others tossed into the cot. As he lifted several from the desk he saw one still held the shape of Gianna's body; she must have flung it off when she changed for lunch. Quite deliberately Ramage pictured the naked Eve carved by Ghiberti on the east doors of the Baptistry in Florence – an Eve for whom Gianna might have been the model: the same small, slim, bold body; the same small, bold breasts, flat belly... He swept the clothes aside, unlocked the second drawer and took out a thick book with a mottled brown cover labelled Signal Book for Ships of War.

Towards the end he found some handwriting on pages left clear of print which listed the numbers and positions of the various rendezvous for ships of the Mediterranean Fleet. He noted the latitude and longitude of the nearest, Number Eleven, and pulled a chart from the rack above the desk. The rendezvous was seventy-five miles to the eastward of the Kathleen's present position – and with the wind they'd been having it ruled out any chance the dismasted ship was a British frigate waiting like a sentry at the rendezvous with fresh orders or information for ships ordered to call there.

He put a finger on the chart. The Kathleen was here, about a hundred miles due west of the southern tip of Sardinia, because he was going well south to skirt the

African coast, at the same time giving a wide berth to Majorca, Minorca and the south-eastern corner of Spain. The ship ahead was much too far north to be British and bound from Naples, Malta or the Levant to Gibraltar. He glanced at the top of the chart. Toulon – yes, a French ship from the eastward and bound for the great naval base could be here. But he saw Barcelona to the west and, farther south, Cartagena, were also possible destinations for Spanish warships whose captains would be anxious to keep to the northward because of the shoals and unpredictable currents along the low-lying African coast. A ship returning after rounding Corsica and Sardinia (as he knew several Spanish ships had done recently watching for the British Fleet) might also be here.

He heard Jackson shouting from aloft but could not make out the words, and after replacing the chart and locking up the Signal Book, turned to leave the cabin just as Southwick came down the companionway.

'Jackson says she's a frigate sir,' the Master explained, following Ramage up the ladder. 'Swept clean and not a stick set as a jury rig. Says she looks Spanish built.'

'Very well, Mr Southwick: continue heading up towards her until we can be sure.'

Gianna and Antonio both looked excited as they walked over to meet him. 'If she's Spanish, we can pull her to Gibraltar,' Antonio said.

Ramage shook his head. 'There'll be no towing, unless she's British.'

'Oh!' exclaimed Gianna. 'Why not?'

'I – '

'Deck there!' hailed Jackson. 'She's definitely Spanish built.'

24

Southwick acknowledged the hail and Ramage turned away to avoid answering Gianna's question, but she repeated it.

'Because, madam,' Ramage said heavily, 'we have a ship's company of sixty-three and we carry ten carronades, each of which fire a 6-pound shot for less than five hundred yards. If that ship over there is a Spanish frigate, she has about two hundred and fifty men on board, and probably soldiers as well, and carries at least thirty-six guns which fire a 12-pound shot for fifteen hundred yards. Any one of those shot could cripple us – they're more than four and a half inches in diameter – and if we were hit on the waterline by a couple of them we'd sink!'

Antonio stuck an arm out sideways. 'But don't their guns point out at right angles, like ours? Surely they can't shoot straight ahead or behind?'

'Yes, they're broadside guns, and we could keep out of their arc of fire. But they could use their bow and stern chasers.'

Antonio looked puzzled.

'Most ships have two special ports aft and two forward. You just haul round a couple of broadside guns and aim 'em through the ports,' he explained, gesturing aft. 'That's what those two ports are for.'

'But can't we risk being shot at by just two guns?' Antonio persisted. 'After all, they'll be rolling, and without sails they can't swing the ship round to aim a broadside, can they?'

'No, but even if she had no guns, how can we possibly capture two hundred and fifty men who'd strongly object to us boarding the ship, let alone take them prisoner?'

'Well, if they haven't any guns,' interrupted Gianna triumphantly, 'why can't we just keep shooting at them until they surrender?'

'I didn't say they haven't any guns,' Ramage said, fighting to conceal his exasperation. 'I simply said "If they hadn't" – but they have.'

'Oh well, it's a pity. We should cut a fine figure towing that big ship into Gibraltar.'

'If you can imagine a little donkey pulling a large cart loaded with blocks of Carrara marble all the way over the Alps, that's about how we'd be towing that. She displaces – if you put her on the scales you'd find she weighs about 1,300 tons against our 160 tons.'

'Less the weight of her masts!' Antonio exclaimed.

'Masts, spars, bowsprit, jib-boom, rigging, blocks, sails and boats. Yes,' Ramage conceded ironically, 'you can deduct about a hundred tons – a little less than the weight of the Kathleen…'

Southwick called. 'You can just see her now, sir.'

Ramage spotted the small black shape just beginning to rise over the curvature of the earth as the Kathleen approached; and pointed her out to Gianna. The frigate was about eleven miles away. He glanced astern at the cutter's wake; she was making between five and six knots, so it would be nearly two hours before they'd be within gunshot. Close enough, rather, to make out her name.

He wondered afterwards why he corrected himself and why he went below and changed from his best uniform into an older one that bright sun, salt spray and his steward's constant spongings and brushings had reduced to the pleasantly faded blue that he preferred to the original colour.

CHAPTER THREE

Ramage's cabin for the time being was Southwick's, who in turn had taken over that of the next senior, John Appleby, the Master's mate. He had just finished changing when Gianna called from her cabin. Her face was serious as she motioned him to shut the door and, not knowing what she was going to say, Ramage first told the sentry to station himself a few feet away, out of earshot.

Sitting at the little desk, the chair swung round to face him, she reached up with her right hand and traced the scar over his brow. 'Nico…?'

'Marchesa…'

'My Lord…?'

They both laughed with embarrassment over her difficulty in starting whatever she wanted to discuss, and he said: 'Clench your hands, shut your eyes, and say it!'

'It isn't my business, Nico, but…'

'But…?'

'…but is it wise to leave this Spanish ship with – '

'Without letting you leap on board, capture her single-handed and hoist the flag of Volterra?'

'Be serious, Nico! I mean, couldn't people say you ran away – that you refused to try to capture her?'

'Some may, and probably will. Others will say it'd be madness even to attempt anything against a ship eight times the size of the Kathleen. Others – and they'd include

Admiral Sir John Jervis and Commodore Nelson – would say I'm already disobeying orders even by going close enough to identify her. You realize the Commodore ordered me to take you and Antonio to Gibraltar as quickly as possible by the safest possible route? That means whatever we meet I have to run away, not fight.'

'Yes, but Antonio's afraid that since neither Sir John nor the Commodore are at Gibraltar, one of your father's enemies might be there to make trouble, as they did at Bastia. After all, who knows what might have happened there if the Commodore hadn't arrived in the middle of that mockery of a court martial?'

Since he'd been thinking of all this long before Jackson identified the ship as Spanish, Ramage knew Gianna's fears were well-founded. It was difficult being in the Service as the only son of John Uglow Ramage, tenth Earl of Blazey, Admiral of the White, Cornish landowner, man of honour and bravery – and also, after Admiral Byng, the most celebrated political scapegoat of the century; a man whose honour and career, and almost his life, had been snatched away from him by the Government to use as props to keep itself in office. Yes, it was difficult and at times seemed impossible; but...

'What are you thinking, Nico?'

For a few moments he'd forgotten she was there. 'Just something my mother once said – that I had the same fault as my father.'

'What is that?' she asked quickly, revealing a sudden fear.

'That neither of us will bother with an easy problem – someone has to say it's impossible before we make any effort.'

'I'd have thought that's half-way between a fault and a virtue.'

He kissed her and led the way up on deck, walking to a carronade away from the rest of the men. While he stood with one foot on the slide facing outboard she leaned back against the bulwark, the sunlight on her hair making it glint blue-black like a raven's feathers, and as she turned to look at the strange ship Ramage wished he was a painter to capture on canvas the splendid, patrician profile outlined against the almost harsh blue of the sea and sky. The small, slightly hooked nose and high cheekbones, the large brown eyes and delicate ears revealed by the swept-back hair gave her features the classicism of a Roman bust but belied the warm, generous lips.

Deliberately he turned away and looked round the cutter. It was in his power to have this deck swept by enemy shot, their impact gouging out swathes of great splinters and sending them scything through the air, slicing off limbs and stabbing men. Within a couple of hours, at a word from him, the newly scrubbed decks he'd just inspected could be daubed with the blood of these men now standing round laughing and joking, no doubt repeating every witty jeer they'd ever heard against the seamanship, courage and sexual prowess of the Spaniards.

Gianna said softly, 'Can you hear what the men are saying?'

'I wasn't listening.'

'Listen now then.'

Ramage did not know whether to tell them in anger to be silent, shake them by the hand with pride, or to stop listening in shame. Every man was speculating about the prize money they'd receive when they towed the frigate into Gibraltar. For them it was a foregone conclusion, Ramage realized bitterly, that their captain would capture the ship, but none seemed to realize it'd require magic to make the Spanish ship surrender...

'You see?' she said.

Southwick came up rubbing his hands and mustering a laugh so bloodthirsty that Ramage thought the villain in a melodrama at a Haymarket theatre would have been proud of it. Gone was the Master's look of a country parson; despite the chubby face and mop of flowing white hair, the prospect of battle had transformed his appearance from a benign curer of souls to a dedicated and ruthless curer of skins; his face was flushed, his hair seemed to bristle, and his eyes were bloodshot.

'I thought it'd be a good idea to start the men rousing out one of the thirteen-inch cables, sir,' he said briskly. 'It'll take a bit of time, and though the eight-inch'd be easier because it's not so heavy, I thought it might part and still leave us with having to use the thirteen-inch.'

Ramage began rubbing his brow, caught Gianna's eye, and instead of ordering Southwick to leave the cable stowed said lamely, to give himself time to think, 'Very well, Mr Southwick.'

The Master was too excited to notice the lack of enthusiasm in the flat voice and trotted off forward to supervise the shifting of more than two tons of heavy, stiff and immensely strong cable.

Gianna had heard Ramage make that formal response: 'Very well' dozens of times; but there had never been that undertone of – well, almost despair. His face betrayed nothing; but that instinctive rubbing of the scar warned her his mind was in a turmoil. She guessed he was being tugged this way by the precise wording of his orders, another by the shadow of his father's trial, yet a third by the assumption of Southwick and the crew that they'd capture the frigate. And perhaps duty and honour told him to steer yet a fourth course.

She knew instinctively that if he obeyed his orders and left the frigate alone he would probably be safe; but that lean and tanned face, those deep-set eyes, naturally proud bearing, also told her that whatever he did, he had to live with himself afterwards; that while others praised his bravery he could condemn himself for cowardice simply because at some point he felt a moment of fear. She knew this only because she too had experienced it: she recalled setting her horse at an apparently impossible fence and successfully clearing it to the almost hysterical cheers of her family, but she had ridden on to avoid facing them because she knew she had failed herself; because, in the instant before knowing whether the horse would jump or refuse, fear had paralysed her. Ruefully she reflected the price she'd paid to learn that if you were to lead successfully, whether a kingdom or a ship's company, the only standards worth bothering with were those you set yourself; those of others were, well, those of the mob; those who were led, who had neither the ability nor the courage to sit alone and make the decisions.

Cramp in the foot resting on the carronade slide reminded Ramage time was passing quickly; he had to make up his mind in the next few minutes, before the ox-like enthusiasm of Southwick and the ship's company swayed his judgement. The situation was simple enough – once you stripped away the details (and left out any thought of the consequences and the orders locked in the desk).

He could leave the Don severely alone after identifying her, note her position and pass it to the next British warship he met. Or he could – well, easier to see first what he could not do. Obviously he couldn't capture her by boarding because his men were out-numbered at least four to one.

Nor could he sink her by gunfire. So Southwick's preparations for towing were laughable.

Yet...he had to admit frightened men bolted from shadows; drowning men clutched at straws. From bitter experience he knew the next most alarming thing to water flooding into a ship faster than the pumps could clear it was to be dismasted; the ship was utterly helpless and at the mercy of wind and current. Without the steadying effect of masts and spars the ship rolled like a pig in a midden, and as the Spaniards hadn't rigged jury masts yet, perhaps they couldn't. They were hundreds of miles from the nearest Spanish or French port, and well off the normal routes, so only a miracle could send another Spanish ship their way.

And not a hundred miles to the south was the African coast, where almost every bay was the base for the Barbary pirates who'd cut their throats just for the fun of it and whose fast galleys rowed by Christian slaves often frequented this area... Yes, the Spaniards would be frightened men, frightened where the whims of wind and current would take them; frightened that a dozen Barbary galleys would get alongside in the dark and put several hundred pirates on board. But at the moment they probably weren't frightened enough to grasp at a straw. They'd need just a little extra, just enough to turn fear into panic...

If he only could bluff the Dons into believing he could destroy their ship if they didn't accept his alternative – to surrender and be towed... But having achieved that piece of wizardry, was the little Kathleen capable of towing the hulk? He couldn't remember a precedent, and there was only one way of finding out.

Ramage looked across at the hulk yet again, cursing the fate that had left it within sight of his lookout, and conscious the seamen round him were still laughing and joking, and that Gianna was watching. Southwick's cheerful curses were streaming up from forward, hurrying the men rousing out the cable.

Then Ramage looked at every alternate seaman on deck. He knew them all by name, knew most of their faults and merits. He'd promoted several and liked them all. Then he glanced at Gianna and Antonio and deliberately forced himself to imagine them all sprawled on the deck dead, lying in pools of their own blood, as the Kathleen tried to claw away from the frigate's broadsides because he'd miscalculated and the Spaniards had called his bluff.

He had everything to lose – his ship, his life, Gianna, the ship's company who blindly and cheerfully put their trust in him – and, by comparison, very little to gain if he succeeded. Perhaps a few grudging words of qualified praise from Sir John and the Commodore, but no more since he'd have paid scant attention to his orders. Certainly he wouldn't get a Gazette letter because, although success avoided awkward questions being asked, he could hardly expect a reward for virtual disobedience.

An admiral's dispatch to the Admiralty praising an officer and subsequently printed in the Gazette was the dream of everyone, from a midshipman to a senior officer, since it meant a lot in gaining promotion (providing, he thought ruefully, the person mentioned survived the action the letter described).

Why even think about trying to tackle the frigate? Was he juggling with the stuff of dreams? Or – and it was a sobering thought – was he becoming a compulsive gambler, like one of those pale, twitching, glassy-eyed men who haunted White's, driven to that fashionable gambling den by some inner demon to risk half a fortune on the night's turn of the cards or roll of the dice? Risking a well-loved estate, wife, children, position in society, for an urge about as noble – and apparently as hard to resist – as the need to relieve himself?

Ramage was surprised how dispassionately he saw the situation. His father would be proud if he succeeded – and just as proud if he failed in the attempt, because above all he'd want him to try. Gianna really knew nothing of the problems and was young and impulsive, yet she wanted him to try, perhaps for the same reason as his father, but also because she enjoyed adventure. His rescue of her from under the noses of the advancing French had also rescued her from the prison that was the life of a young woman heading one of the most powerful families in Tuscany, and whose mother had brought her up as a boy in a desperate attempt to fit her for the task of ruling that turbulent little state.

Ramage suddenly turned and walked towards the fo'c'sle, trying to break away from the torrent of thoughts and misgivings. Ahead lay the hulk, placed there by the vagary of a single thunderstorm. But before he was abreast the mast he suddenly knew that whatever happened he was going to try to do something, for the simple and singular reason that like those contemptible and pallid creatures at White's, he couldn't resist the challenge, and the thought made him feel guilty.

Southwick hustled up the companionway buckling on a sword – or what passed for a sword, Ramage thought wrily, since the cutler who'd fashioned it must have drawn his inspiration from a butcher's cleaver, a Saracen's scimitar, an overgrown claymore and a West Indian machete.

'Glad she's a Don, sir,' the Master grunted, drawing in his bulging stomach to hitch in the belt buckle another notch. 'Easier to deal with than Frogs, 'ticularly as they've only been in the war a few weeks. They'll be jumpy, and I bet the

Fleet was manned with a hot press o' yokels who still don't know a yardarm from a farmyard.'

'Maybe, but don't forget she's probably carrying a lot of soldiers as supernumeraries.'

'The more the better,' Southwick said cheerfully, attempting yet another notch in his belt, 'they'll get in the way o' the sailors.'

'I hope so, but unless you're a betting man, never forecast the result on the day of the race.'

Southwick looked up in surprise. 'Why, I suppose not, sir, but,' he added with a grin, 'I'm a betting man today!'

'Very well,' Ramage said ironically, 'if you've placed your wagers and the jockeys are booted and spurred, we'll get ready for the first race. Beat to quarters, Mr Southwick.'

As Jackson from his position high up on the cro'jack yard heard the staccato but rhythmic beat of the drum sending the men to quarters he felt a considerable relief. He'd kept one eye on the wallowing hulk and one eye on Mr Ramage standing at the carronade below, and he wasn't sure which worried him most.

For once the American was glad he was only a seaman. He knew better than most of the ship's company Mr Ramage's loneliness in deciding what to do. Jackson admitted he didn't fancy the idea of tackling the Don because he firmly believed Nature intended that only knaves and politicians should be forced to risk their lives unnecessarily. Yet at the same time he didn't fancy leaving the hulk just wallowing there, like a ripe peach waiting to be plucked (although by a bigger hand than the Kathleen) and turned over to the prize agent.

Yet for the life of him he couldn't see how they'd get her to surrender and be taken in tow. However, the drum was beating to quarters so obviously Mr Ramage had finally thought of a way. That scar on his forehead must be

burnished by now, the way he'd been rubbing it. Jackson
tried to think what the plan could be, failed, totted up the
weight of the frigate's broadsides – or even just her stern
and bow chasers – and finally decided miracles were
needed rather than plans.

He steadied himself against the occasional wild, inverted
pendulum swing of the mast as the cutter heeled to heavier
gusts of wind, and looked again at the hulk ringed in the
lens of the telescope. A sudden movement and flurry of
colour at her taffrail made him grip the brass tube tighter.
Hmm, they were hoisting a flag on a pike, or something.
The wind caught it and blew it clear. Horizontal stripes of
red, gold and red!

'Deck there!' he yelled. 'The frigate's showing Spanish
colours. Using an oar or a pike as a staff.'

'Very well, Jackson,' he heard Mr Ramage reply, as though
he'd known she would eventually. 'Can you see if she has
any boats at all?'

He trained the telescope again. The deck was bare, so
she'd lost the boom boats. Ah, a sea was pushing her stern
round. Yes, there was one in the water – they probably used
it to cut away the wreckage.

'Deck there! I can only see one – lying astern to its
painter.'

What on earth was Mr Ramage worrying about boats for?
Oh yes – if they had three or four boats, they could tow the
hulk's bow or stern round to train the broadside guns. He
shrugged his shoulders; it was a small thing yet it showed
Mr Ramage was thorough. But come to think of it, he told
himself ruefully, it wasn't a small thing; the Dons' ability to
train their guns meant all the difference between tackling a
couple of stern chasers or a full broadside.

Below him the boy drummer was still rattling away, his
drum seeming as big as he was himself. Watching from

such a vantage point as the men went to quarters, Jackson realized the value of the last fortnight's constant training: no man took an unnecessary pace nor got in anyone else's way; no one ran or shouted. Yet already the lashings had been cast off the carronades, gun captains had collected their locks and trigger lines and were fitting them, with horns of priming powder slung around their necks, and the sponges, rammers and wormers were beside each gun. The head pumps were already squirting streams of water across the deck ahead of four men walking aft in line abreast and scattering handfuls of sand as though they were sowing corn, the sand ensuring no one should slip, the water ensuring no spilled gunpowder would be ignited by friction.

Five men were hoisting up the grindstone from below while several more stood waiting to use it, arms laden with cutlasses, pikes and tomahawks taken from the racks. Other seamen rolled small wooden tubs into position near the guns and half-filled them with fresh water from the scuttle-butt, so the guns' crews could refresh themselves in action. Other wider but shallower tubs were being dragged between the guns and filled with seawater to wet the 'woolly 'eaded bastards', the sponges which would swab out the barrels and douse any burning residue left behind after a round had been fired and also cool the barrel. Several tubs with notches cut round the top edge were in position and the long, worm-like slow matches, already lit, had been fitted in the notches with their glowing ends hanging down over the water out of the way of stray powder, but ready for use should a flint in the lock of a gun fail to spark.

The American pictured the scene below deck round the magazine: screens would have been unrolled, hanging down like thick blankets, and soaked with water to prevent the flash from an accidental explosion from getting into the magazine itself, where the small cylindrical bags of gunpowder for the carronades were stacked. Outside the screens all the young powder boys would be waiting. They'd be chattering with excitement and waiting to be handed the cartridges, which they would put into their wooden cartridge boxes, slide the lids down the rope handles, and scurry up on deck to their respective guns, dreaming of glory, fearing death, but more scared of a gun captain's bellow should they delay reloading for a second.

A rumbling noise made Jackson think of Mr Ramage, who could not stand the scraping of metal on stone. The men had the grindstone turning and he saw Mr Southwick, a great curved sword in his hand, gesticulating to a man to pour more water on the spinning wheel and then begin to hone the blade with the skill of a butcher, pausing every few seconds to sight the edge against the sun and finger it gently.

Catching sight of Ramage looking up at him, Jackson hurriedly raised the telescope to look at the frigate.

'Jackson! If you're so interested in what's going on down here you'd better leave the telescope with the lookout and reload my pistols.'

'Aye aye, sir.' Thankfully the American started down the ratlines.

Southwick cursed as the reflection showed he'd honed a slight flat into one side of the curved blade, but that bit of carelessness would have to be removed later because the men with the cutlasses were impatient to get at the stone. Southwick loved his sword and as he slid it into the rawhide scabbard, which was itself stiff enough to break a man's arm with a single blow, he reflected that it was a real fighting sword, heavy yet balanced, and the rasping of the shagreen covering on the handle against the palm of his hand reminded him he personally caught the shark, cured the skin and fitted it on himself. No, his sword wasn't one of those strips of tin decked out in pinchbeck wire that was only fit to wear on ceremonial occasions; it was a man's sword.

Unaware of the effect his own enthusiasm had had on his captain's thoughts and decisions during the past fifteen minutes, Southwick would have given anything to know what was in Ramage's mind; what his plan was to capture the frigate. To the Master the whole thing looked impossible, and he'd been in half a mind to tell Mr Ramage so but couldn't think of a tactful way of saying it. Anyway, the captain had looked confident enough from the time the hulk first hove up over the horizon, and had guessed she was a Don long before she'd shown her colours. So obviously he had a plan, though Southwick admitted that if it'd been up to him he'd have squared away for Gibraltar by now, merely noting in the log the time the Spaniard's colours had been hoisted, and her position.

Standing to weather of the men at the tiller, Ramage appeared confident enough in his faded blue uniform and a battered hat, whose silk cockade was so frayed that it looked like a black dahlia. He sensed from the way the men bustled about that they thought these were the first moves in some brilliantly simple scheme to capture the frigate. But his mind had never been so barren of ideas, and the Kathleen was closing rapidly with the hulk – hell, how the scraping of that grindstone grated on his nerves.

He needed a red herring to draw across the Spaniards' bows to occupy their attention while he conjured up some plan to force them to surrender – but it'd need to be an explosive red herring to do any good, he thought gloomily. An explosive red herring! 'Gunner's mate!' he bellowed. 'Mr Southwick, pass the word for the gunner's mate!'

CHAPTER FOUR

George Edwards, the gunner's mate of the Kathleen, had issued the gun locks, spare flints, trigger lines and other equipment for the carronades from his store, and then gone to the tiny lead-lined magazine. After taking off his boots and putting on a pair of felt slippers, he emptied his pockets of metal objects that might make a spark, unlocked the door with a brass key and entered to issue the waiting gun captains with powder horns containing the fine priming powder for the locks.

The fire screens round the magazine had already been unrolled and were hanging down like thick blankets and dripping with water. By the light of the lantern placed outside and illuminating the magazine through a glass window, Edwards inspected the magazine men as they trooped in, stripped to the waist, bare-footed, and with rags tied round their heads to stop perspiration running into their eyes – heaving out the cartridges in the magazine was hot and exhausting work. As Edwards looked slowly round the dimly lit magazine, methodically checking what he saw, the magazine men lined up ready to hand the neatly stacked cartridges from the racks out through the scuttle to the waiting powder boys.

Although he had not been back to his native Kent for more than a few weeks at a time in the last thirty years, Edwards had lost little of the Kentish burr in his voice and none of the slow, thoughtful, almost cautious habits of the fisherman, painfully learned during a boyhood spent in his father's fishing boat working among the treacherous shoals of the Goodwin Sands from Deal beach.

In build he was like one of the guns to which his life was devoted: slightly round-shouldered, barrel-chested with narrow thighs and long legs. From his shoulders to his feet his body had the same taper as a gun, his head forming the knob-shaped cascable at the end of the breech, his body the barrel.

For once Edwards was satisfied with what he saw in the magazine: thanks to the captain he'd been able to exercise the men so they could be trusted to pass the cartridges to the boys with the minimum of fuss and movement; in fact they could do it blindfolded – that was how they'd been exercising for the past week.

For all that, Edwards was puzzled when he heard the word being passed that the captain wanted to see him at once, and the sudden bright sunshine made him blink as he emerged on deck to find Mr Ramage and the Master waiting.

Ramage said abruptly to him and the Master: 'We have to make the Dons think we can destroy their ship.'

Southwick said 'Aye aye, sir,' in a matter-of-fact voice, but Edwards thought of the row of gun ports along the frigate's side.

'How do you propose we should do it, Mr Southwick?'

Both Master and gunner's mate knew by now this was the captain's way of testing them, and while Edwards pondered carefully Southwick admitted frankly and characteristically: 'Haven't thought about it, sir. Must be some way, though…'

'Listen then, particularly you Edwards. I want you to be able to blow the stern off that ship.'

Ramage, nettled by Southwick's easy-going attitude and disappointed that neither looked surprised at what he'd just said, mistook their confidence in him for indifference and snapped at Edwards: 'Any ideas?'

The gunner's mate shook his head. 'Sorry, sir, it's a bit – well, sudden, as you might say.'

Ramage nodded, realizing that resentment from either man at the present moment would mean he'd lose their co-operation.

'Well,' he said, noticing both Gianna and Antonio edging closer to hear, 'if the Dons can get a broadside into us, we'll soon be down there,' he pointed towards the seabed, 'where the chart says "No bottom at ninety fathoms". So we've got to tackle her from ahead or astern, risking only her bow or stern-chasers.'

Ramage saw both men nod warily, obviously expecting another question to be shot at them.

'Now then, you can see she's lying with the wind fine on her starboard quarter, which means, Mr Southwick?'

'That we can run across her stern, rake her with one broadside and luff round and rake her again with the other without getting into the arc of fire of her broadside guns!' the Master answered promptly.

'We could. Now supposing she was one of our own ships – on fire, perhaps, and we wanted to get the men off?'

Southwick thought for a moment, ruffling his hand through his hair. 'We could heave-to the Kathleen to windward and drift a boat down on a grass warp, sir.'

'And how does all that help us with our present problem of capturing an enemy ship?'

'Fill the boat with boarders?' Southwick asked hopefully.

'And have them picked off one by one by musket fire?'

Edwards' eyes narrowed. If it'd been a question of seamanship alone, Mr Ramage would have sent for the

Master's mate and the bosun's mate as well as the Master, but certainly not the gunner's mate. Since he had been sent for, it must be something to do with guns – or powder. Well, there was no harm in guessing.

'Powder, sir? A few barrels in the boat and a long fuse?'

He was a man who spoke slowly and deliberately, as if every word was a shot to be aimed without haste and, when fired, to have the maximum effect on the target.

Ramage nodded and unexpectedly felt relieved. Perhaps his idea wasn't so wild after all if Edwards could guess it. He took a piece of paper from his pocket, unfolded it, spread it on top of the binnacle and sketched with a pencil as he spoke. 'Precisely. An explosion boat. I want a big enough explosion to damage her stern and spring the butts of the planks – just a couple on the waterline would be enough; the pumps couldn't keep up with that. And she may be leaking already. So how much powder do we need in the boat?'

'No idea, sir,' Edwards admitted frankly, making no attempt to avoid Ramage's eyes, which seemed to bore right through him. 'Never heard of a thing like that before. No experience of powder exploding in an unconfined space. Lose p'raps two-thirds of the effect.'

'If you loaded up a boat and saw it explode, do you reckon you could then judge how much more or less powder you'd need in another one to damage the frigate?'

Edwards paused, his eyes almost closing with concentration. Then with complete confidence he nodded. 'Yes, sir.' He remembered how the captain hated anyone adding 'I think so' to a statement.

'Very well, you'll have the chance of seeing one. I want to force the Dons to surrender and take a tow. I don't want to sink 'em unless we have to.'

'Indeed we don't,' Southwick exclaimed, 'think of all that prize money going to the bottom!'

'So,' continued Ramage, 'first of all I want to explode a boat about fifty yards away. The Spaniards will have been wondering why the devil a boat with a canvas cover over it was being drifted down towards them. When it suddenly blows up they'll get the shock of their lives. So I want a big bang and lots of smoke. Then, while they're still feeling shaky, I shall send a boat over with a flag of truce, warn 'em the next explosion boat will remove their stern, and suggest they surrender.'

'And if they don't, sir?'

'We blow their stern off,' Ramage said grimly, rubbing the scar on his forehead.

Neither man said anything and Ramage, knowing speed was now essential, snapped, 'Now look at this sketch. Here is the Spaniard. We approach like this and lower the boat here, and tow it on a long warp – a grass warp because it must float. Then we carry on towards the Spaniard, making sure we keep out of the arcs of her broadside guns, and begin to turn here, and then we heave-to to windward. The boat should drift round like a tail, and I want it to explode about fifty yards from the Spaniards.

'Your fuse, Edwards, will be lit when we get to there and must fire the powder when we are there. We're making about five knots. I want at least a mile to get the boat into the right position. Say fifteen minutes from the moment you light the fuse.'

'Right, Mr Southwick, prepare the boat and a long grass warp. Use the jolly boat and we'll have to lower it loaded. Edwards, decide how much powder you want, how you'll fire it, and get it all loaded into the boat. Any questions?'

'Yes, sir,' said Edwards. 'The fuse. Fifteen minutes is a long time.'

'Yes, but I daren't risk less. Hadn't you better use a portfire?'

'I was just thinking that, sir. Safer than fuses. I'll use two, in case there's a dollop of spray or one goes out. They burn for fifteen minutes anyway so I don't have to cut 'em.'

'Don't forget we'll be towing the boat at five knots: there'll be more than a dollop of spray flying over it.'

'Aye aye, sir. How much time have I got to prepare?'

Ramage looked at the frigate. 'A quarter of an hour. And Mr Southwick, make sure the deck is thoroughly wetted round the jolly boat. A few loose grains of powder...'

Edwards went down to the darkness of a magazine. He could think better there. It had the same peace as the fish cuddy in his father's boat when the wind howled on deck, because the lead lining of the magazine with the dampened fire-screen hanging down deadened the noise. He sat down on a stack of cartridges, feeling the flannel of the bags coarse against his hand, and went through every point.

First the powder. Should he use it in its special barrels or in cartridge bags? It'd have to be cartridge bags because barrels would need separate fuses and they probably wouldn't explode simultaneously.

How much powder? Well, to breach a wall you generally reckoned on fifty to a hundred pounds, depending on its thickness, and that had to be tamped down with a covering of ten times its own weight of earth. Each flannel cartridge weighed just half a pound, and he finally decided on a hundred. It was only a guess, but anyway he daren't use more for the first boat because if he had to increase the quantity for the second one he'd be left very short of cartridges for the guns, since the rest of the powder was still in the copper-hooped barrels.

Edwards stood up and told the magazine men to pass a hundred cartridges out through the scuttle, calling to the powder boys to carry them up on deck and stack them near the jolly boat in the stern davits. After sending a man to warn the Master that the powder was on its way up, he sat down again. How was he going to fix the portfires? There was no question of just making a hole in the flannel bag of a cartridge and jamming one in – that would be a quick way of blowing up the Kathleen! No, he'd have to use a barrel, jamming the long cylindrical tube of the portfire into the bung-hole, then wedging each barrel among the bags of powder.

He ordered two of the magazine men to get a couple of small barrels and then fill them with powder; another to get a lump of pitch and a ball of caulking cotton from the carpenter's mate, and two pieces of leather and some marline from the bosun's mate and bring them to him at the main hatch. With that Edwards went to see the captain.

He saluted Ramage and said apologetically: 'I know we are at quarters, sir, but I need to heat up some pitch.'

Ramage knew the man too well to question the necessity, but for safety the galley fire had been doused immediately the drum beat to quarters. The only light left in the ship was illuminating the magazine. He remembered the little oil-lamp left behind by the Kathleen's previous captain.

'The oil-lamp for heating my tea urn will do. Get my steward to bring it up from the cabin. You've thought of a way of securing the portfires?'

Edwards nodded and pointed to the paper and pencil on the binnacle. 'May I just show you, sir?'

He drew a quick sketch and Ramage nodded. 'Wedge it among the bags so there's no chance of it moving. And make sure the canvas over the boat is wet so it doesn't catch fire.'

Edwards nodded. 'I'm afraid we'll probably lose three minutes on the portfires, sir: I hadn't allowed for the base going into the barrel. Difficult to know exactly when the burning part will reach the powder. I can't guarantee anything more than twelve to fifteen minutes.'

Ramage thought quickly. The boat would be drifting for perhaps three minutes. Well, the first one was only a demonstration, so whether it exploded fifty or a hundred yards from the hulk wouldn't matter much.

'Very well, you can't help that. Carry on, then.'

Within a couple of minutes Edwards was sitting on the coaming at the forward side of the main hatch with one small wooden barrel filled with powder held between his knees, bung uppermost, and another nearby. Beside him on his left were two portfires – fifteen-inch-long cylindrical tubes filled with a composition of saltpetre, sulphur and gunpowder mealed by treating it with spirits of wine, and which when lit burned steadily like a large Roman candle at the rate of an inch a minute.

On Edwards' right were a pair of scissors, a brass pricker looking like a large darning needle stuck into a wooden handle, two squares of soft leather, a ball of marline (the light tar on the line mingled curiously with the cobbler's shop smell of the leather) and a chunk of pitch chipped from a large piece, black and shiny like coal but already beginning to dull and soften slightly in the sun, and a battered saucepan in which to heat it.

Three men stood round the gunner's mate holding leather buckets of water and each with strict orders to douse the powder-filled barrels at a word from Edwards, who picked up one of the pieces of leather and, standing a portfire on it, marked out the circular shape of its base using the tip of the brass pricker. He cut out the circle with the scissors and then with the same preoccupied air of a schoolboy pushing a pencil through a square of paper, slipped the portfire into the hole, making sure it was a tight fit.

At that moment a seaman came up to report the captain's oil-lamp was lit, and went away with the pitch and saucepan with orders to start heating it. 'Just runny,' Edwards said, 'don't let it start bubbling.'

With a warning glance at the men standing round, Edwards gently drew the bung from the barrel, carefully folding the cloth in which it had been wrapped so that none of the slate-grey grains of powder still adhering to it should fall on the deck, and handing it to one of the men to drop in a bucket. Then he worked the piece of leather with the hole in it into the bung-hole, flattening it out with his fingers inside the barrel and over the top of the powder to act as a washer so that it covered the powder except for the hole he had cut out.

He worked his index finger in the powder until he made a cavity three inches deep, picked up the portfire and pushed it through the leather washer and into the powder until the portfire stuck up out of the bung-hole like a candle on a cake. Taking up the roll of marline he tucked an end between the leather and the inside of the barrel and began to wind it round and round the base of the portfire, as though rewinding a cotton reel, pausing every now and again to push it down until the portfire was a tight fit in the bung-hole, and leaving a shallow depression all round.

He called for the hot pitch and the seaman came running from the fo'c'sle with the old saucepan. Edwards inspected the pitch in case it was too hot, then gently poured some on to the marline wound round the portfire in the bung-hole, filling up the circular depression, He then wound on more turns of marline, pushing them down with the pricker, and poured on more pitch, using the pricker to shape it so that when it set there would be a little mountain of pitch stuck up on the barrel with the portfire sticking out in place of a peak He inspected it carefully, waiting for the pitch to cool, then gently pressed the portfire. It was firmly seated.

Motioning to the man to take the pitch back to the lamp and keep it hot, and telling another to hold the completed barrel, he then set to work repeating the whole operation with the second one. He had just finished when Southwick came bustling up.

'Well, Edwards, have y' got those boxes of fireworks ready yet? The cartridges are stowed in the boat the way you said, and the boat cover's rigged and ready to be secured. We haven't much time left y'know. Look!'

Edwards glanced up and was startled to see how near was the frigate. He ordered the barrels to be carried aft. 'Handle 'em gently,' he warned the men. 'If you knock those portfires I'll personally dry your corpses in the sun and sell the meat to the Dons as prime jerked beef.'

The tone of his voice warned them he was only just joking, and as soon as they were by the taffrail, holding the barrels as though they were glass, Ramage walked over and carefully inspected each one.

'You've done a good job, Edwards. Let's hope the portfires burn true. You'll see the boat cover's rigged so that once you've lit the portfires and got from under it, that line has only to be drawn taut and belayed and the cover's snugged well down. Don't rush things when I give the word, but remember that even if the portfires burn the full fifteen minutes, we can't afford to lose a moment from the time you light them.'

'Aye aye, sir,' said Edwards and climbed up on to the taffrail and out to the boat slung in the davits. 'You,' he said to a seaman, 'come and give me a hand in here.'

The two men almost disappeared under the canvas cover and then took the first barrel as it was handed to them. Edwards lifted out some of the stacked cartridges to make two separate gaps for the barrels to be wedged in. As soon as he had fitted them he put a square of canvas over each one, the portfire sticking up through a slit in the centre. The canvas was thick enough to protect the flannel of the cartridge bags from the sparks thrown out by the sputterings of the portfires. He told the seaman to get back on board and crawled to the opening in the boat cover.

'Ready now, sir.'

'Very well, but you might as well stay there for a few minutes,' Ramage said, and turned to look once again at the frigate.

Although the curvature of the earth just hid the waterline – indicating she was still more than four miles away – her roll was so violent he frequently glimpsed the copper sheathing on her bottom. His telescope clearly showed the discoloured reddish-yellow of the metal and Ramage noted there was no green streak of weed or patches of barnacles.

That told him a great deal – the frigate had been docked in the last month or two and, more important, since Spain came into the war only a few weeks ago, was almost certainly newly-commissioned with a raw crew and probably unseasoned officers and captain as well, if ships were being rushed into commission. And even trained guns' crews would be hard put to hit anything from a ship rolling like that – anyone peering along the barrel of a gun would sight the sea a hundred yards away one moment and the blue sky the next, the horizon flashing past in a split second. For a few moments he pictured the Kathleen with the explosive 'red herring' towing astern at the end of the floating grass rope. For the demonstration, time was not so important. But if his bluff was called and he had to try to sink her, the boat must be in position under the Spaniard's stern just as the portfires exploded the powder; a minute too soon and the Spaniards would have time to drop round shot through its bottom. A minute too late might not be so disastrous: much of the explosive effect would be lost, but it'd probably be enough to start some planks. How about musket fire? Well, it'd take a lot to sink the boat or make it leak enough to spoil all the powder. What were the snags then? It was late in the day to start thinking of them, but why hadn't anyone used an explosion boat before? After all, fireships had been used against the Armada...Would powder exploding in an unconfined space do much damage? Well if he didn't know, presumably the Spanish didn't either; but since the first boat was bound to make a splendid firework display the Spaniards, as the potential victims of a second one, would be more nervous than he was. And in his experience the bigger the bang the more frightening the weapons, irrespective of the damage – which was why he'd been training the Kathleens to avoid shouting unnecessarily when working the guns, but scream like madmen if they ever had to board an enemy ship or repel boarders.

But whatever the effect of the explosion boat, Ramage thought inconsequentially, one thing was certain: afterwards the gunner's mate would need a certificate signed by him to send to the Board of Ordnance explaining why so much powder had been used up in such a short time... And he visualized the letter he'd probably receive later from the Admiralty expressing Their Lordships' 'displeasure', the result of a peevish protest from the Ordnance Board. Bureaucrats thrived on war – to them the smoke of battle transmuted itself into hundreds of orderly piles of forms and certificates, affidavits and letters, neatly tied with the familiar pink tape, and men killed in battle were swiftly disposed of by two strokes of a pen – simply a two-letter entry against each name, 'DD', the official abbreviation for 'Discharged Dead'.

Realizing he was rubbing his forehead again, Ramage turned away. 'Mr Southwick, make sure the jolly boat is ready to be hoisted out, and have a white cloth lashed to a boarding pike as a flag of truce. And I'll have all the guns loaded, if you please.'

In a couple of minutes the little Kathleen would be ready for bluff and for battle. Divisions, Gianna's shooting match, the men dancing to John Smith's fiddle – all seemed to have happened days ago. Even now splashes of spray had mottled the polished brasswork with patches of dried salt. And, he reflected ironically, the decks are thick with wet sand where, only three or four hours ago, Southwick methodically searched for even one dry grain.

Another three minutes and he'd head directly for the frigate, which was now fine on the starboard bow. He looked significantly at Gianna and then turned to Antonio. 'I'd be grateful if you'd both go down below in a few minutes.'

The Italian nodded and stretched out his hand. 'Gianna told me to return your stake.'

Ramage took the ring, saw it was not his own and glanced at Gianna. Her right hand was instinctively clasping the middle finger of her left, where he guessed she was wearing his. She looked as if – with a sudden shock Ramage saw that Antonio had the same expression – as if they were saying a silent farewell to a condemned man. Turning away, slipping her signet ring on to the little finger of his left hand, he felt cold, as if the warmth had suddenly gone from the sun. The frigate was black and big; she seemed to roll much less now and her ports were open and the guns run out.

CHAPTER FIVE

The Spanish frigate was La Sabina. She was lying almost stern-to fine on Kathleen's larboard bow, and her name in bold letters right across her transom was picked out with too much gilding and red paint. Ramage looked impatiently at his watch, the vane at the masthead to see if the wind was constant, and then at the boat towing fifty yards astern. Thin wisps of smoke from the burning portfires were seeping out from under the canvas cover.

With the telescope he could clearly see the stubby black gun barrels poking out of the ports on La Sabina's starboard side. Presumably they were trained as far aft as possible, and as soon as he got nearer they'd make good leading marks – by keeping this side of the line of the barrels he'd be outside their arc of fire.

As the men reeled in the log Southwick reported the Kathleen was making just over five knots. The easterly wind was right aft, and with the ship on the larboard tack the great boom of the mainsail was swung right over, blanketing both jib and foresail which, with no wind to keep them full, slatted with the cutter's roll. Ramage glanced at his watch again. If the portfires burned evenly, he had eight minutes to go – barely enough.

Inexorably the seconds sped by. The black paint of the frigate's hull was shiny and the over-elaborate ornamentation

DUDLEY POPE

on her transom stood out boldly. Many pounds' worth of gold leaf on the quarter galleries alone showed the captain to be a rich man, since he'd have paid for it with his own money.

How far now? Without the telescope he could just make out men on her decks, so she was less than half a mile ahead – about six minutes at the Kathleen's present speed. The hands of his watch showed the portfires should fire the powder in five minutes. He was running it close; much too close.

Glancing round the cutter, he was surprised how cool and detached he felt. Or was it resignation? His father had often said, 'If you can't do anything about it, don't fret about it!' A dozen seamen were aft, waiting to pay out the rest of the grass warp: waiting to lengthen the monkey's tail at the last moment to give it a longer reach as the cutter turned. Southwick gave him an inquiring look, anxious to put more distance between the Kathleen and the bags of powder in the smoking jolly boat, but Ramage shook his head.

The two men at the helm were having a hard time. The pressure on the big mainsail was not being balanced by pressure on the flapping headsails forward so the cutter was trying to come up into the wind, with the result that she   was edging herself up to larboard. Ramage snapped an order to the quartermaster and in a few moments the frigate was once again fine on the larboard bow. She was growing noticeably larger and he could distinguish individuals among a group of men standing at the taffrail (just over seven hundred yards away, he noted). Some were much taller than the others. No – a quick glance through the telescope showed the smaller ones were leaning on the taffrail holding muskets to their shoulders. Sharpshooters, with orders to pick off the officers and men at the helm…

Ramage called to Jackson and told him to hold the watch.

'For the next four minutes read out the remaining minutes and half minutes starting…now!'

The Kathleens were silent, all looking ahead at the squat stern of the frigate. Hell! The barrels of the aftermost broadside guns began to foreshorten, and now Ramage could see farther along her starboard side. She was yawing and if the wind and sea continued to swing her round a few more degrees her aftermost three or four guns would be able to fire into the Kathleen. Then slowly she paid off and the gun barrels lengthened.

The wind began to strengthen – he felt it on his face – and the cutter picked up speed, pitching rhythmically, and the boom rising slightly as the wind bellied the mainsail. Six knots now? No time for another cast of the log.

Tiny puffs of smoke along the frigate's taffrail, barely glimpsed before the wind dispersed them, and faint popping noises – musket fire – at that range a nuisance but no more.

'Three minutes and thirty seconds,' said Jackson.

Ramage guessed the distance at six hundred yards and signalled to Southwick. At once the seamen began paying out the rest of the grass warp and the jolly boat dropped farther astern, the warp floating on the water like a long thin snake. Southwick swore as a bight of the rope twisted into a figure of eight, knowing a sudden jerk on the boat might shift the casks and snap the portfires, exploding the powder prematurely, but a seaman untwisted it before the weight on the boat came on.

Many more puffs of smoke along the frigate's taffrail

'Three minutes,' Jackson chanted gloomily.

Two stern chase guns were poking out through the ports like accusing black fingers. If they hadn't fired by now they never would – the Spaniards must have decided that with the rolling it was a waste of powder.

'How much more to run?'

'Nearly all gone,' Southwick called. 'Five fathoms or so left… There, that's the lot. Steady lads, take the strain now. All hundred fathoms out, sir!'

So the jolly boat, the explosive red herring, was towing astern on the end of a two-hundred-yard rope tail.

'Two minutes and thirty seconds,' said Jackson, excitement beginning to show in his voice.

About four hundred yards, Ramage noted.

'Mr Southwick! Overhaul the mainsheet. Stand by to bear up. Not a moment to lose when I give the word.'

Yards mattered now as he sailed the Kathleen right down to the frigate's starboard quarter, carefully staying just enough   to windward so the wind would blow the jolly boat down to the frigate when, fifty yards away, he turned the Kathleen round to larboard to head back the way she came for a moment – giving the tail a flick, in fact – and hove-to. Then, stopped with her stern to the frigate and the grass warp floating in her wake in a huge crescent, if he'd judged it correctly the wind would slowly blow the boat down towards the frigate, and if the portfires burned true… If, if, if!

'Two minutes, sir,' said Jackson, his voice revealing tension for the first time.

Spanish officers were standing among the men with muskets on the taffrail – he could distinguish their uniforms. Not even a stump of the mizzen left; it must have been a fantastic squall that hit her – or else, for all that new paint, her rigging was rotten.

Yet again Ramage glanced astern at the boat. She was towing beautifully, bow riding high but the stern not squatting so much that water slopped up over the transom.

No sign of even a whisp of smoke: he swore – had the portfires gone out? A quick glance with the telescope did not reassure him. More popping from ahead and a man at the second carronade on the Kathleen's larboard side screamed with pain and another dropped silently to the deck. Ramage stared curiously, trying to recognize the sprawled figure.

'One and a half minutes!' Jackson said.

Startled at the realization he had only ninety seconds left, Ramage looked again at the frigate. She had suddenly become enormous and even as he shouted to Southwick to put the helm down it seemed impossible for the Kathleen's enormously long bowsprit to miss swiping the frigate's starboard quarter as she swung round to larboard.

With all that preparation, Ramage swore to himself, he'd let a wounded man divert his attention long enough to wreck the whole bloody manoeuvre. He rubbed the scar on his brow, fighting back the panic trying to get him in its grip.

For a moment as the tiller went over there seemed total confusion on the Kathleen's deck; one group of seamen sheeted in the mainsail at the run; others hardened in jib and foresail sheets and both sails filled with a bang as the cutter's bow swung to larboard and brought them out from under the sheltering lee of the mainsail. The sudden weight of wind in both sails tried to push her bow off to starboard and the quartermaster ran to help the two men hold the heavy tiller.

'One minute to go,' bawled Jackson, dodging round the busy men as he tried to stay within earshot of Ramage and yet still keep an eye on the watch.

He'd overshot by – oh God! As the Kathleen's turn brought the frigate's great squat transom flashing down the starboard side, Ramage found himself looking up at a row of faces, some half-hidden by muskets, and just had time to notice several of the men were wriggling and jabbing with their elbows to get enough room to aim as they were jostled by some officers trying to peer down at the cutter.

Little flashes of flame, puffs of smoke and that ridiculous popping. More shouts of pain on the Kathleen's deck and he was conscious of falling men. A glance back showed that by some miracle the jolly boat seemed to be in roughly the right position. Musket balls whined close in ricochet. Every musket seemed to be aimed at him. The frigate swung round to the quarter as the Kathleen continued turning; then she was astern.

'Mr Southwick! Back the jib and let fly the foresail sheets! Keep the helm hard down!'

Swiftly the men hauled the jib to windward so it tried to push the cutter's bow to starboard but was balanced by the mainsail and rudder trying to force the bow round to larboard, like two children of equal weight at either end of a seesaw. The Kathleen began to slow down. As she stopped she began to roll, the noise of rushing water ceased, and the popping of muskets was much louder.

Jackson shouted 'Thirty seconds!' just as Ramage looked for the jolly boat.

The wind was drifting it swiftly, the drag of the grass warp turning it broadside on to lie parallel with the frigate and perhaps fifty yards away. Ramage wasn't sure how it happened, but the boat was in exactly the right position, the warp linking it to the Kathleen making an almost perfect crescent superimposed on the smooth water of her wake.

'Time!' bawled Jackson, and nothing happened.

For several moments hope clouded judgement in Ramage's mind; after all that, he thought wearily, surely at least one of the portfires must be still alight, but he felt too sick with disappointment to look again with the telescope for a wisp of smoke. Fifteen minutes was the maximum burning time for a portfire, and fifteen minutes, sixteen by now, had elapsed.

Southwick was steadily cursing in a low monotone; Edwards, white-faced, watched the jolly boat as if stunned; Gianna stood unconcerned, looking astern at the frigate curiously; and Ramage, conscious of yet another fusillade of musketry, was deciding he'd better get the Kathleen under way again before the sharpshooters picked them all off.

It was only then he registered that Gianna was standing near him amid the thudding and whining of musket balls and instinctively gave her a violent shove that sent her flat on her face, hard up against the taffrail. At the same moment Edwards clutched his arm, obviously hit by a shot and Ramage heard a curious clang beside his leg.

Suddenly a blinding flash from the direction of the jolly boat was followed by a deep, muffled explosion, and a blast of air. The flash turned into a billowing mushroom of smoke, and jagged pieces of wood – the remains of the boat – curved up slowly through the air in precise parabolas before spattering down on to a sea across which concentric waves rolled outwards from where the boat had been, like the ripples from a rock flung into a pond.

'Half that amount of powder would do the job for you, sir,' Edwards said quietly.

'Yes. And I hope our friends over there haven't missed the point.'

'The bang was a bit late though, wasn't it, sir?' Jackson said with a grin.

'Aye,' said Edwards, 'but if you'd been a friend of mine you'd have flogged the glass.'

Ramage laughed rather too loudly. Flogging the glass – turning the half-hour glass a few minutes too soon to shorten a watch on deck – was an old trick.

'Never mind, Edwards, it worked perfectly.'

Edwards gave Ramage an odd look as though he was drunk and had difficulty in focusing his eyes, nodded and collapsed at his feet, still clutching an arm from which blood spurted. In a moment Gianna was kneeling beside the man ripping away the sleeve.

CHAPTER SIX

Ramage was just going to climb down the Kathleen's side to the waiting boat when Jackson pointed at his sword and offered him a cutlass. Ramage pulled the sword and scabbard out of the belt and flung it down. That explained the curious clang – a musket shot had hit and bent the blade and ripped away part of the scabbard. Still, better to be unarmed when boarding an etiquette-conscious Spaniard than have a cutlass, which was a seaman's weapon, and Ramage waved it away. The fact that he boarded completely unarmed would not be lost on the Spanish.

The boat shoved off and Jackson looked like a lancer in the stern sheets, tiller in one hand and in the other a boarding pike to which a white cloth had been lashed as a flag of truce.

The men rowed briskly and as smartly as if going alongside a flagship, and soon the boat was under the lee of La Sabina. As Ramage looked up at her, realizing it was not going to be easy to board because she was rolling so much, he was surprised to see water running out of the scuppers and down the ship's side. How on earth could she be getting sea on deck?

While Jackson was giving the last orders which would bring the boat alongside, Ramage looked back at the Kathleen and felt his confidence ebbing fast as he saw how tiny the cutter appeared, even though she was hove-to barely a couple of hundred yards away. From the deck of the frigate she must seem about as threatening as a harbour bumboat.

The bowman hooked on with a boat-hook and Ramage jammed his hat on his head, waited a moment until the boat rose on a crest, and jumped on to one of the side steps – the thick battens fixed parallel, one above the other, up the ship's side. The Spaniards had been thoughtful enough to let the manropes fall so that he had handholds.

He hurried up the first three battens in case the frigate rolled to leeward and a wave soaked his feet, then slowed up to avoid arriving at the gangway hot and breathless. While climbing he decided that if he did not reveal he spoke Spanish he might learn a lot from unguarded remarks. If none of them spoke English – which was unlikely – he'd use French. Faces lining the bulwark were watching him, and as Jackson shoved off with the boat, leaving him alone on board, for a moment Ramage felt a loneliness verging on panic; he was away from the ship with whose command he had been entrusted; he was – and now he had to admit it – completely disobeying orders; and he was at the mercy of the Spaniards. If they chose to ignore the accepted behaviour governing flags of truce and make him a prisoner (or, more likely, a hostage) Southwick was unlikely to have the skill to drift down another explosion boat and successfully blow off the frigate's stern even if he had the nerve to sacrifice his captain's life.

Well, it was too late to fret about a situation he couldn't change. But as he climbed he realized it was a situation he could have changed.

At last his head was level with the deck at the entry port and he looked neither to the right nor the left as he passed through until he was standing on the gangway. His hat was straight and surprisingly he suddenly felt nonchalant, as if he was walking into the Long Room at Plymouth. With the memory of the size of the Kathleen only seconds old, he was almost light-headed with the ludicrousness of what he was about to demand.

A Spanish officer to his right straightened himself up after an elaborate bow, hat clasped in his right hand over his left breast.

Ramage returned a polite but less deep bow.

'Teniente. Francisco de Pareja at your service,' the officer said in good English.

'Lieutenant Ramage, of His Britannic Majesty's cutter Kathleen, at your service. I wish to speak with your captain.'

'Of course, Teniente. Please come this way. My captain asks me to tender his regrets that he speaks no English.'

'If you would be kind enough to translate,' Ramage said politely, 'I am sure we shall all understand each other perfectly.'

'Thank-you. I am at your service.'

Without letting his eyes wander too obviously, Ramage saw the frigate's deck was indeed swept clean. The remains of the masts, like stumps of clumsily felled trees, were monuments to a fatal combination of a powerful squall and bad seamanship. But however long and strong the squall had blown it failed to remove the usual smell of boiled fish, stale cooking oil and garlic which permeated most Spanish ships, and there was a smell like a bonfire just put out by a rainstorm. Ah! Suddenly he realized why there was water running from the frigate's scuppers: some of the burning wreckage from the exploding boat had come on board and started several small fires... He mentally noted that a few signal rockets and blue lights put on top of the powder next time might yield good dividends.

Waiting aft by the big double wheel, but deliberately looking away, stood a portly man of perhaps forty, resplendent in a uniform almost entirely covered in gold braid. The thick jowls hanging over the stock betrayed a professional gourmet. The pinkness of the face, the slackness of the mouth, protuberant belly, shifting and watery eyes that could not refuse food... Ramage guessed the Spanish captain regarded his cook as the most important member of the ship's company.

Deep bows, exchange of names – the portly man was Don Andreas Marmion – more bows, and both Ramage and Marmion turned to Pareja, waiting for the other to begin. Suddenly Ramage realized he had a chance of seizing the initiative and announced with all the confidence of a man stating something obvious and indisputable:

'I have come to make arrangements for passing the tow.'

Pareja paused for several seconds, then prefaced his translation into Spanish with an apologetic, 'I am afraid the Englishman says...'

Ramage watched the captain's face. The pink turned red and, as the neck swelled, deepened to purple, and he replied in an abusive torrent of Spanish which Pareja translated as tactfully as he could, 'My captain says you can't tow us and anyway you are his prisoner and he will send your ship to Cartagena for assistance.'

Since Ramage had understood even before Pareja spoke, he looked Marmion straight in the face, his eyebrows a straight line, hard put to stop rubbing the scar, and answered.

'You are under a misapprehension. Apart from the fact I boarded under a flag of truce, this ship is our prize. You obey our orders. The tow is prepared and will be passed to you as soon as I return to the cutter.'

Pareja waited, but Ramage's expression was cold and formal and the Spaniard was frightened by the deep-set brown eyes. 'Translate that. I haven't finished yet, but I do not want any misunderstanding.'

Like a dog on a leash, Marmion took half a dozen paces one way and half a dozen paces the other as Pareja translated. Suddenly he stopped and snapped a few phrases, emphasizing some of them with a petulant and rather comical stamping of his foot, but avoiding looking at Ramage as he spoke.

Pareja said lamely: 'My captain says it is ridiculous; you have a tiny ship; you cannot possibly take a big frigate like this as a prize. But he respects the flag of truce and grants you permission to continue your voyage.'

Ramage tensed. This moment was the climax; instead of a battle of broadsides, it was a swift battle of wills. So far he'd kept the initiative; now, faced with a flat refusal, he was on the verge of losing it. Yet Marmion had avoided his eyes, and Pareja was doing his best as he translated to soften both Ramage's and Marmion's phrases, as if he felt Ramage still had some trump card. Then Ramage guessed the reason for Marmion's attitude – pride. It was as simple – and as complicated – as that. Marmion could see how Spain would receive the news that La Sabina had surrendered to a tiny cutter. He'd be disgraced among his brother officers; a laughing stock. And Ramage knew he now had to give Marmion a way out: a way of backing down gracefully, an excuse acceptable to the Spanish Ministry of Marine.

'Tell your captain,' he said, 'that he is in an unfortunate situation. His ship is absolutely helpless and he cannot make repairs. He has only one boat – insufficient to tow the ship round to aim a broadside. All of this will be made clear in our report. His ship is at the mercy of any enemy

– whether a three-decker, a cutter, or a dozen Barbary pirates – and the four winds. He has limited food and water and little sea room. If a northerly wind blows for a couple of days his ship will end up on the beaches over there' – he gestured towards the African coast – 'and he and his ship's company will end their days as slaves rowing in Barbary galleys...'

Pareja translated but Marmion argued violently. As soon as Pareja finished translating Ramage, knowing this was the moment for the real threat, said harshly:

'Tell your captain he knows as well as I do that we can destroy his ship, smash it into driftwood. And we cannot be expected to take nearly three hundred men on board as prisoners – even if they survived the explosion.'

'What explosion?' Pareja asked, after translating and getting Marmion's reply. 'My captain says you cannot destroy us, and it is only a matter of time before our fleet finds us. We have plenty of provisions, and the weather is good.'

'Your own fleet,' Ramage said, taking a chance, 'is not within three hundred miles and won't come this way. And we can destroy you. You saw the explosion boat.'

'But the boat exploded fifty yards away! We were not damaged in the slightest!'

'It exploded fifty yards away because we intended it to: you saw how we manoeuvred. We were simply showing you how easy it would be to tow a second boat and place it under your stern. We are in agreement, are we not, that such an explosion would remove your stern? Surely you don't dispute that? And a second boat would also carry a considerable amount of incendiary material...'

As soon as Pareja related this, Marmion swung on his heel and began to walk to the companionway to go below.

Ramage felt himself going cold at this insult and snapped:

'Tell him to come back here at once. He is my prisoner, and I've seen no reason so far to show him any more mercy than he'd receive from the galleys!'

Pareja obviously sensed this was no idle threat and hurried after Marmion, repeating Ramage's words in a low voice. He then beckoned to Ramage, who ignored him and Pareja came back.

'My captain wishes to continue the conversation in his cabin.'

'Your captain will continue the conversation on board the cutter. He has five minutes to pack a bag. In the meantime your first lieutenant and I will discuss the details of towing.' Once again Pareja went back to Marmion and reported Ramage's words. The captain went below and Pareja told Ramage:

'He agrees under protest and only to save the lives of the ship's company. He regards an explosion boat as a barbarous and dishonourable method of waging war and unprecedented in history. He says that in the face of such barbarity it is his duty to protect his men.'

'Very well,' said Ramage. 'Now, you are the first lieutenant? Very well, these are your orders for the tow.'

As Marmion followed him on board the Kathleen, Ramage was pleased to see that in his absence Southwick had been busy. He'd changed into his best uniform and the rest of the ship's company were neatly dressed and, apart from those standing to attention at their carronades, drawn up on the quarterdeck. There was no sign of a wounded man nor a trace of blood. Every rope was neatly coiled; match and sponge tubs were spaced at geometrically precise intervals with sponges and rammers in their racks.

The impression of smartness and, compared with the Spanish ship's company, the natural confidence and determination showing in the men's bearing, would not be lost on Marmion, who was looking round carefully as he slowly unbuckled his sword.

When Southwick saluted Ramage, Marmion turned in surprise and exclaimed involuntarily, 'You are the captain?' Ramage nodded since there was no further need to pretend he did not speak Spanish, and said, 'Yes, I am in command. You surrender your sword to me.' The hard note in his voice left no doubt that it was an order and Marmion gave it to Ramage, who accepted it without comment and passed it to Jackson as if it was dirty.

Although Ramage felt contempt for the Spaniard because he had made no attempt to brazen it out and had accepted all the terms, he was wary. Those little watery, shifty eyes... He wished he hadn't left Marmion and Pareja alone while he inspected the frigate.

Southwick, although still standing to attention, showed by his attitude and expression that he still did not know exactly what was happening, and Ramage said, 'This gentleman is the captain of the frigate. He is a prisoner. Detail two men to guard him. Rig up screens to make him some sort of cabin, and get a cot slung. Now, all the Spanish ship's company are prisoners on parole. They've given their word to obey my orders – which are to haul in and secure the cable, and then do all they can to safeguard the tow. They were impressed with the explosion...'

Ramage broke off because the Spaniard's eyes were popping. He was staring at Gianna, who had just emerged from the companionway. Ramage guessed it wouldn't hurt to create a bit of a mystery and ignored her.

'Take the boat and pass the cable,' he continued. 'The frigate's first lieutenant speaks very good English. And make sure they have lights ready. At night they're to burn three white lights, one on either bow and the third on the centre line amidships but high, so we can always see how they are heading. Is that quite clear?'

'Aye aye, sir,' Southwick said and added with a grin, 'Shall I take our colours over, and hoist 'em over the Spanish?'

Ramage laughed. He had forgotten all about that. 'Yes, but you'll need something to rig 'em on – they've nothing longer than a boarding pike left!'

With that Southwick turned away and began giving his orders.

'Thirsty work, sir,' Jackson commented.

Ramage eyed him. 'Yes – for me. I've been doing all the talking. Tell my steward to bring me some lemon juice and water.'

Jackson looked crestfallen and Ramage relented. The capture of a frigate was worth an extra tot for all the men.

'Remind me again at supper time how thirsty you are.'

'Very good sir. You can rely on me.'

Two seamen with cutlasses left Southwick and came over to Ramage, who said: 'As soon as his cabin is prepared, the Spanish gentleman is to be taken below, under guard. For the time being keep him forward of the mast.'

As seamen lowered into the boat the messenger, the light line which would haul across the heavy cable, Ramage walked over to Gianna, who was talking to Antonio.

Her eyes were bright with excitement she was finding hard to control.

'Nico – who is that funny man?'

'The captain of the Spanish frigate.'

'But why did you bring him over here?'

'He is our prisoner – a hostage, in fact.'

'But how can you control all those men in the frigate?' Antonio asked. 'Why, there are hundreds of them. Mr Souswick let me look with the telescope.'

Ramage shrugged his shoulders. 'We have to continue to bluff.'

Antonio said eagerly, tugging his beard, 'Nico – let me take a dozen men over to the ship. I'll make sure they behave!'

Ramage shook his head. 'But for one thing, I'd have asked you to do that.'

'What is the one thing?'

'Antonio – you and Gianna are the reason for the Kathleen going to Gibraltar. You're in my care. If anything happened to you...'

'You and your orders,' Antonio said gloomily. 'It's hardly worth having escaped from Italy.'

'Antonio!' exclaimed Gianna. 'After all Nico has done for us!'

'No,' Antonio said hastily, 'no, I didn't mean it like that. You know I'm grateful, Nico; but those Spaniards – they're worse than the French. They've only come into the war because they think the French will win.'

'A successful man has many friends,' Ramage said wrily. 'But a failure is very lonely.'

Southwick came up and saluted. ''Scuse me, sir. All ready. I'm just going off in the boat.'

'Very well. Don't stand any nonsense over there. Make 'em jump about, flagship style.'

Ramage silently cursed the frigate towing astern and then realized it was as stupid as cursing fame and riches because they led innkeepers to double your bill. But the sun dropping over the horizon took most of the wind with it and now, with the sky changing from purplish-mauve to the chilly and impersonal grey of dusk, the cutter was making barely two knots. He had four men at the helm to counteract the drag on the Kathleen's stern from La Sabina's occasional sheer one way or the other.

Gianna and Antonio were standing at the taffrail with him, and Gianna shivered. 'I never like this time of the day and it's always worse if there's anything worrying you, because it's cold and grey.'

Antonio asked, 'What's worrying you?'

'Oh, nothing really – except that great thing,' she said, pointing at the frigate. 'I have a premonition…'

'Of what?' asked Ramage.

'That…it's silly, Nico, but I feel she will bring bad luck.'

Ramage laughed. 'You must ward off the Evil Eye for us, then!'

'Don't make jokes about the Evil Eye, Nico…'

'Then don't be so serious. I noticed our Spanish friend couldn't keep his evil eyes off you!'

'He makes me feel unclean, the way he looks at me,' she shuddered. 'I don't trust him.'

'I should think not,' Ramage said. 'Nor do I. That's why two seamen are guarding him. After all, he is our enemy!'

'An enemy,' she mused, 'that fat man down there…'

Antonio said coldly, 'That fat man down there would strangle you slowly – and everyone else too – if it would get him his ship back.'

'I'm feeling cold,' Gianna said. 'I am going to bed.'

Ramage and Antonio kissed her hand, and she called goodnight to 'Mr Souswick', who gave his customary bow. When she had gone down below, Antonio asked, 'Do you expect trouble?'

'Well, I can't see what they can do – apart from cast off the tow. That wouldn't help them because we'd obviously wait until daylight and sink 'em.'

'But do you – how do you say – do you "have a feeling"?'

'Yes – probably just a reaction from the excitement.'

'I expect so,' Antonio said. 'Well I'm tired, too, so – buona notte, Nico. This has been a day to remember!'

A few minutes later Ramage suddenly felt weary too and decided to get some sleep in case he was called frequently during the night.

'Mr Southwick, I'm going below for a couple of hours. Observe the usual night orders. If there's anything suspicious – even the faintest hint – call me. And issue pistols and muskets to the steadiest men, and cutlasses, pikes and tomahawks to the rest.'

Ten minutes later Ramage was sprawled fully dressed in his cot in a deep sleep, his two pistols, both at half-cock, tucked against the canvas sides.

Jackson had been tired, but as darkness came down an indefinable uneasiness drove away all thoughts of sleep. He watched idly as the Master walked round the deck, speaking briefly to the lookouts amidships and on either bow. The old boy was thorough – at each of the carronades, which had been left run out, he checked the tackles and breeching and made sure the canvas apron covering the lock was secure so the damp night air should not get at the flint. As he came aft he saw the American.

'Well Jackson, a busy day!'

'Aye, sir, and likely to be a busy night, too.'

'You think the Dons'll try something, eh?'

'Well, we would if we were them!'

'Quite so, but that's the difference. Looked a pretty sheepish bunch when I was on board.'

'Hope you're right, sir. Still, if they started something…' Southwick's grunt indicated he thought the possibility remote, and then he said, 'By the way, Jackson, are you really American?'

'Yes, sir.'

'When were you born?'

'Not sure of the exact date, sir,' Jackson said warily.

'Born English, tho', I'll warrant; before '74, when all you folk revolted!'

'Maybe sir. But I'm American now, for all that.'

'You've got a Protection?' Southwick's voice was flat, as though he was stating rather than asking, and Jackson said slowly 'Yes sir. I've got a duly attested Protection.'

'Why haven't you used it, then?'

Jackson shifted from one foot to another. The Master's persistent questioning didn't anger him. Most people were curious, which wasn't surprising since the Protection, signed by J W Keefe, Notary Public and one of the Justices for the City and County of New York, certified that Thomas Jackson, Mariner, had been sworn according to law, deposed he was a citizen of the United States and a native of the State of South Carolina, five feet ten inches high and aged about thirty-seven…

Mr Keefe further certified that the said Thomas Jackson, being a Citizen of the United States of America and liable to be called in the Service of his Country, is to be respected accordingly at all times by Sea and Land. Whereof an attestation being required, I have granted this under my Notarial Firm and Seal.

That piece of paper, headed by the American Eagle with United States of America in bold type beneath it, meant he could not be forced to serve His Britannic Majesty and, like anyone else possessing one, could get his discharge any time he liked – any time, rather, he could get in touch with an American Consul.

What was more, unlike many in circulation, the Protection was genuine. But Jackson tried to imagine the Master's reaction if he knew he also had another genuine one, attested and signed by a notary but with the spaces for the name and details left blank. It had cost ten dollars – and was worth twenty times as much.

'Well, sir,' Jackson said, after an appreciable pause, 'my own country's at peace, but I don't like missing a good scrap.'

'So you've decided to give us a hand.' Southwick said with a chuckle, and his last doubts about the American disappeared. He'd never questioned Jackson's loyalty – from all accounts he'd saved the lives of Mr Ramage and the lad and both were obviously very fond of him – but nevertheless Jackson was a Jonathan, and he couldn't forget many American merchants and shipowners were making their fortunes trading with the French.

Southwick's attitude to the rest of the world was uncomplicated and uncompromising: in war, those who were not openly his friends were his enemies. Neutrals were at best a nuisance, always pettifogging about their rights, and at worst a conniving bunch of crooks selling their wares to the highest bidder without regard to the consequences.

Jackson, sensing Southwick was lost in his own thoughts, excused himself and picked up the night glass.

Balancing himself at the taffrail against the Kathleen's uneven roll, he had a long and careful look at the frigate towing astern, blinked his eye to make sure he wasn't mistaken, had another look and hurried over to where the Master was standing.

CHAPTER SEVEN

Southwick jumped down the last three steps of the companionway, snatched the sentry's lantern while hissing at him to make no noise, and ducked his head as he hurried into Ramage's temporary cabin.

'Captain, sir!' he whispered as he shook the cot, and Ramage woke in an instant. Southwick's face, heavily shadowed by the lantern's glow, warned him of danger.

'What is it?'

'The Spaniards, sir. They've got their boat and are rowing towards us, keeping close along the cable.'

'Many in the boat?' Ramage asked as he scrambled out of his cot.

'Seems packed.'

Ramage pulled on his boots, flipping back the little strap over the sheath in the right one to expose the throwing knife.

'They'll row to within twenty yards then swarm up the cable to board us.'

'S'what I thought, sir.'

Ramage picked up his pistols, tucked them in his belt and sat on the swinging cot for a full minute. Then he gave Southwick a string of orders.

'Wake the Count and send him up to me. Tell the Marchesa she's to transfer to this cabin – it'll be dangerous for her with that skylight overhead. Tell the sentries on the

Spanish captain's door to lay him out with the flat of a sword if he shouts. Then rouse the watch below. I want all of them waiting at the bottom of the companionway. They're to seize and secure anyone who's thrown down. No pistols or muskets to be fired – I want absolute silence the whole time. Understand? Absolute silence from everyone.'

'Aye aye, sir.'

Southwick hurried off forward and Ramage made his way up the companionway. Only a few patches of stars were showing; high clouds hid the rest.

'Who's here?' Ramage hissed. 'Keep your voices down.'

'Quartermaster, Jackson, and twelve men, sir: four at the tiller, four lookouts, three topmen and the man watching the cable.'

'Right, keep quiet, behave as though you haven't seen anything. Topmen – get forward and stay there for the time being.'

Ramage knelt down and peered through the stern-chase port. He could just make out the boat about forty yards astern. It had twenty or so yards to go before reaching the point where the sagging cable came up out of the water in a gentle curve to the Kathleen's starboard stern-chase port. A gentle curve which would be an easy hand-over-hand climb for nimble seamen.

Jackson appeared in the darkness beside him and after Ramage whispered orders disappeared down the companionway.

Ramage then told the quartermaster and the other men at the tiller: 'No matter what happens around you, don't leave the helm. Keep the ship on course – that's your only concern.'

The man who had been watching the cable was told to warn the lookouts forward and the topmen to disregard anything that happened aft unless they received direct orders.

Jackson came back with Antonio, Southwick, Appleby, the Master's mate, and Evans, the bosun's mate. While Jackson went off to collect some belaying pins, Ramage looked at the boat again with the night glass.

The Spaniards were holding on to the cable where it stayed a steady three or four feet above the surface, apart from an occasional wave crest which reached up to touch it. The Spaniards would not risk using pistols – there would be misfires due to wet priming.

'Ah, Jackson,' he whispered, 'give us all one.'

Each took a belaying pin and Antonio, who had never held one before, tried it for balance, giving some imaginary blows. Then Ramage whispered his orders to the group of men.

'They'll crawl up the cable, so they'll have to come in through this stern-chase port. You can see it's only just large enough for a man. We'll knock them out one by one as they come on board – but without the next astern on the cable knowing. So no noise. One man bangs him smartly on the head and catches him and the next hauls him to one side out of the way and tips him down the companionway. No mistakes though – one bang has to do the job. Understood?' The men whispered agreement.

'Antonio,' Ramage said, 'your Spanish is good?'

'Reasonably so.'

'Well, in case I'm – er, busy, or anything – we've got to find out the signal these men are supposed to make to the frigate when they've captured us. So as soon as you can, get hold of one of them below and make him tell you. I'll try to get it out of the last one as well. Now, into position!' With the exception of Southwick, they all crept to the taffrail, bent double, and grouped themselves on either side of the port.

The Master began carrying out Ramage's orders, calling in a loud voice, 'Forward lookouts – anything to report from ahead?'

'Nothin' to larboard sir,' came back one voice, followed by 'Nuthin' to starboard, neither, sir.'

'Very well. Keep a sharp lookout.'

The normal hails made every ten or fifteen minutes; nothing to indicate to the Spaniards that they had been spotted.

'How are you heading, quartermaster,' Southwick asked in a quieter conversational voice.

'Due west, sir.'

'Very well.'

Ramage glanced out of the port. The thick cable now had men swarming along it, like monkeys on the bough of a tree. The nearest man was fifteen yards away.

'Mr Southwick,' he whispered, 'show yourself above the taffrail. Just glance over the stern but don't stare at the Dons. When you know they've seen you, just walk about as though you haven't seen them.'

As soon as Southwick began pacing the deck again, his orders completed, Ramage whispered, 'Ask the lookouts how the headsails are setting.'

The Master hailed, and a puzzled lookout answered they were setting well enough. Again the normal shouts and replies which would reassure the Spaniards that they hadn't been spotted – and perhaps make them over-confident.

'Quartermaster,' hissed Ramage, 'luff up for a moment so your leeches flutter. Mr Southwick, curse him as soon as they do.'

The tiller creaked and from ahead the headsails flapped, while overhead the mainboom swung inboard a foot as the pressure of the wind eased, and then went back with a bang. Southwick swore violently and Ramage peered through the port. The Spaniards hanging under the cable had stopped crawling, but as he watched they began again. The flap of sails and the resultant cursing from the officer of the watch was an international language.

Fifteen feet to go. Ramage saw the dull gleam of metal in the darkness – a knife or cutlass. Each Spaniard would have to sit astride the cable for a moment and grasp the edge of the port before coming through because it was only just a little wider than his shoulders, partly blocked by the cable itself and the rope keckling wrapped round it to prevent chafe. Ramage indicated to Jackson that he would deal with the first man but the American must catch the body as it fell. Southwick was standing still, and Ramage whispered, 'Mr Southwick, walk around a few paces, then stand a couple of yards ahead of this port and act as the live bait.'

Ramage saw the first Spaniard was a slim, agile man, climbing easily and being careful not to get out of breath.

Twelve feet…nine… The man paused to let go with one hand and transfer a knife from his belt to his teeth. Six feet…five… Ramage, sure the Spaniard would hear his heart beating, gripped the belaying pin.

Three feet…one foot… The Spaniard swung himself up astride the cable, gripping it with his legs, and reaching out with his hands for the sides of the port. Ramage could just see him, and suddenly realized it was Pareja. He prayed the lieutenant would not first poke his head through the port to peer to his immediate left or right, but instead crawl straight through and make for Southwick who, from his stance and the night glass glinting under his arm, was clearly the officer on watch. The men following would be much less careful because as far as they were concerned the coast would be clear.

Pareja was so quick, coming through the port like a snake, that Ramage was only just in time to hit him. Jackson caught him as he fell and pulled him to one side and left Appleby to get him to the companionway. They all waited for the next man, who could suspect nothing. He was through in a moment and Antonio's blow sent him sprawling into Evans' arms.

Jackson was ready again to catch the third man as Ramage hit him. The fourth, fifth and sixth men followed at close intervals and ended up unconscious. Not one groaned. The seventh man's knife fell with a clatter, but the eighth took no notice.

As soon as the twelfth man had fallen to Antonio's belaying pin Ramage glanced through the port and saw there were three more to come. He motioned to Antonio to go below – the first victim should be fit for interrogation by now. The thirteenth and fourteenth men were also knocked unconscious, then Ramage motioned to Jackson to take up his position for securing the fifteenth and last man, who was heavily built, the biggest and the clumsiest of them all. He had to struggle through the port and in a moment Jackson's hands were round his throat while Ramage tried to pinion his arms and Evans grabbed him round the legs.

But the man was too strong for Ramage who, realizing that in a moment he would break free and tear Jackson's hands from his throat, jerked his knee into the man's groin, and he collapsed groaning. Ramage bent down, drew the knife from the sheath in his boot, and held the blade an inch from the man's face.

'Look!' he hissed in Spanish. 'If you shout, you will die.' The man mixed a few words of prayer with his groans.

'Drag him clear of the port,' Ramage ordered, keeping his knife in position as Evans pulled the man's legs.

'Now,' Ramage continued in Spanish, 'tell me the signal you are to make when you have captured the ship.'

'Never!'

'The other man also has a knife,' said Ramage harshly. 'He will use it. When he has finished, you will no longer be a man.'

Ramage, almost laughing at the melodrama in his voice, told Jackson, 'Rip his belt open; I've threatened to emasculate him.'

The Spaniard's eyes were wide open and there was enough light to show the terror in them as he stared up at Ramage, gasping and reeking of garlic. Jackson sat astride the man's stomach, facing his feet.

'I count ten,' Ramage said in Spanish. 'If you haven't told me by then – pouf! Now, uno, dos, tres...'

He counted slowly. At seven the Spaniard begin to wriggle his hips, and Ramage tapped Jackson on the shoulder. The American ripped at the man's trousers.

'Ocho...neuve...'

'Senor – I tell.'

'Tell, then!'

'We had to show two lanterns – that was all.'

'If you lie...'

'No, no, senor – I swear that was all! Two lanterns, one on each quarter, and leave them there.'

'All right. You go below without a noise. Remember...'

'Yes, yes, senor!'

'Get him below,' Ramage snapped, and Evans dragged the man by the feet diagonally across the open companionway and then let go, so he slid down below head first.

'Jackson – two lanterns, quickly. Light fresh ones – don't leave 'em in the dark below. Mr Southwick, get down there and sort out the prisoners.'

Suddenly he remembered more men may have been left in the boat, but a quick look round showed it was empty. Should he make a noise to show the frigate there had been a struggle? No – men with knives in their backs died quietly. Antonio was beside him.

'The signal the ship is captured is two white lights!'

'Good – that's what my man said.'

'And as soon as the frigate removes the upper of the three lights she's showing,' Antonio continued, 'we alter course to the north-west.'

'Good for you,' Ramage said ruefully, 'I forgot to ask that!'

'My man was only too anxious to talk,' Antonio said.

'What did you do to him?'

'Nothing – I merely threatened this.' Antonio made an unambiguous gesture. 'And you?'

'The same.'

'It never fails.'

'Apparently not,' Ramage said drily, 'though it's the first time I've tried it.'

'And me, but – well, how would you like it if…'

'Please!' Ramage said hurriedly, 'it's bad enough threatening someone else!'

As soon as the lanterns were in position, the course altered and the frigate signalled, and some seamen had gone down the cable to retrieve the Spanish boat, Ramage went below to Marmion's cabin and without any preliminaries demanded, 'You knew this attempt would be made?'

The Spaniard glanced from side to side, avoiding Ramage's eyes, his fat face glistening with perspiration.

'Captain Marmion,' Ramage said in a deceptively calm voice, 'Your officers were on parole. They gave their word of honour they would obey my orders.'

'It seems they disobeyed them.'

The Spaniard's tone was defiant now.

'They obeyed your orders, then.'

'Yes, it was my idea.'

Ramage gripped the sides of the doorway so hard the battens began to bend, but a moment later his anger was under control.

'Earlier today I could have sunk your ship and left you and your men swimming. By now you would all be dead.'

'And why didn't you?' Marmion sneered. 'Because you want the honour and glory of capturing a frigate.'

And of course Marmion was partly right.

'That has nothing to do with breaking parole.'

'It is ridiculous,' Marmion exclaimed. 'A cutter capturing a frigate! Whoever heard of...'

'But we have, my dear Marmion, we have. A cutter has captured a frigate. And, I haven't changed my mind, at dawn you will be put back on board and, to save myself the bother of towing, I shall demonstrate how a cutter can sink a frigate. How many in your ship's company? Say three hundred? Think of three hundred survivors – if all of them survive the explosion I shall have arranged in the magazine – clinging to the wreckage, and the sun rising and getting hotter and hotter and all of you thirstier and thirstier... By tomorrow night, you'll have all been driven mad – except those who were too weak to hold on and drowned. Goodnight, captain. I wish I could send you a priest; you won't have much time to make your peace in the morning.'

CHAPTER EIGHT

By the time Ramage was called by the Master's mate just before dawn he had decided how to avoid a repetition of the previous night's antics, and as he shaved he took malicious pleasure in the thought that Captain Marmion would have spent a sleepless night anticipating an unpleasant death. The pleasure was only slightly marred by the fact his steward had not stropped his razor properly and the water was almost cold, and he winced at every stroke of the blade.

On deck it was cold; dawn warned of its approach by a dimming of the stars and the hint of grey in the black of night. Appleby reported the Kathleen's speed – still only a couple of knots – and that the wind had not changed.

Then Ramage realized he had forgotten something which might – apart from the attempt at boarding – have led to the Kathleen's capture during the night. If the wind had dropped there would have been no strain on the cable, which would have sunk, and its enormous weight would have pulled the cutter and La Sabina together. The frigate would probably have ranged alongside and one broadside would have destroyed the cutter – or a Spanish boarding party would have overwhelmed the ship's company… He felt sick at his foolhardy over-confidence; it was the worst peril after winning the first round of a battle.

The sky to the eastward was lightening perceptibly.

'Beat to quarters, Mr Appleby, if you please.'

It was routine in wartime to meet the dawn with the ship's company standing to the guns and ready for action.

After the excitement of the last twenty-four hours, Ramage wanted to hear only one hail, 'The horizon's clear', and that would not come until it was light enough to send a lookout up to the masthead. For once he was looking forward to breakfast. He remembered just in time to tell Appleby to send the men to quarters quietly. The rattling of the drum would give the game away.

In quick succession, he was joined by Southwick, Antonio and Jackson. The Italian knew the dawn routine, and betrayed no anxiety at the order.

'Good morning, Nico. You anticipate any excitement?'

'No – at least, not from the frigate, but there may be another ship in sight.'

'Have you thought of a suitable punishment for the Spanish lieutenant, and the rest of the gentlemen over there who broke their parole?'

'Not yet. Make 'em scrub the deck on their knees, perhaps!'

Antonio laughed. 'But the prisoners we have on board need many of our men to guard them.'

'I know; I shall be disposing of them shortly.'

Ramage chuckled as Antonio, Southwick and Jackson all stiffened, obviously misinterpreting 'disposing'.

'I shall dispose of them, Mr Southwick, by sending them back in their own boat.'

The Master shuffled his feet, and then said apologetically, 'If you'll forgive me, sir, but is that wise? After all, they'll have seen how short-handed we are…'

'They must have guessed that from the start. But think of the surprise when all their boarding party led by their first lieutenant row back with bruised heads! Don't forget that at this very moment everyone on board that frigate thinks the Kathleen is a prize, that the boarding party has killed most of us.'

'By God, I'd forgotten that,' Southwick exclaimed gleefully, slapping his thigh.

'Yes, and before they recover, our gig will be alongside to take off all her officers, except the Master.'

Antonio drew his hand across his throat.

'You cut off the snake's head.'

'Precisely.'

'Unless, of course, the snake strikes first, and refuses to have its head cut off. In other words, the officers refuse to leave the ship.'

'We have their captain, don't forget,' Ramage said. 'He's our hostage. By the way Mr Southwick, we'll have Spanish colours run up over ours, if you please.'

As soon as the lookout climbed the shrouds and reported the horizon clear, Ramage told Southwick to get the prisoners over the side into their boat. Once they were sitting on the thwarts, bruised, bleary, frightened and bewildered, Ramage ordered them to row to La Sabina, snubbing Pareja by giving the order to a seaman.

Five minutes later, after protests from Southwick, he handed him the telescope. 'They're on board. I can just imagine the look on Teniente Pareja's face as he describes what happened. Right, if the gig's ready it's time for me to join them.'

'Let me go, sir!'

'Please, Mr Southwick, don't let's go into all that again. Apart from anything else, you don't speak Spanish and you'd probably miss some significant remark.'

'Aye aye, sir,' the Master said with as much disapproval in his voice as he dare express.

The crew were already in the gig as Ramage climbed down. Suddenly he realized that with the Spaniards' boat already alongside the frigate and the Kathleen's only remaining boat going alongside in a few minutes, the Spaniards could (if they thought of it) capture both and by risking their captain's life scupper his only weapon, the explosion boat.

'Mr Southwick,' he called. 'I want a dozen more men. I'll send the gig straight back and bring the Spanish officers over in their own boat.'

A group of Spanish officers were waiting at the gangway for them to come on board, but Jackson put the gig neatly alongside the other boat and, with Ramage and the dozen extra seamen, leapt in, leaving the gig to drift clear and row back to the Kathleen.

The whole manoeuvre had taken place so smoothly and quickly that Ramage knew the Spaniards had either been taken by surprise or had not realized the importance of boats. Lieutenant Pareja was waiting for him as he reached the gangway, followed by Jackson.

As the Spaniard began his long formal greeting he gingerly removed his hat, revealing a plaster stuck on the crown of his head. His face was white and he winced in pain as, his bow completed, he stood upright again. Even as he winced he saw the scar over Ramage's brow was now a white slash against the tan, as if the skin was too taut, and the eyebrows were drawn into a straight line. Then he looked into the deep-set eyes.

Since Pareja's voice had trailed off for no apparent reason, Ramage said icily, 'You broke your parole.'

'Sir! How can you suggest...'

'You broke your parole, and there is no basis for discussion. Please present your officers to me.'

Pareja shrugged his shoulders and called to a small group standing by the wheel. They came at once, four young men with barely a couple of years' difference in their ages, and lined themselves up like nervous schoolboys, although Ramage knew they were all about his own age. He was careful to stand three or four paces from them to avoid any handshaking, and Pareja introduced them as the second, third, fourth and junior lieutenants and each bowed in turn.

'And the Master?'

Pareja waved to an unshaven man, perhaps five feet tall but looking more like a weather-stained barrel with legs. Ramage turned to catch Jackson's eye, glancing meaningfully at the pistol tucked in the American's belt and then at Pareja, who missed the byplay.

While the Spanish Master waddled over, resentment, hatred and contempt showing in his face, Jackson moved casually so that he was standing a couple of paces behind Pareja.

As the Master was introduced Ramage knew he could not be left on board. He too would have to be a prisoner; he was obviously a tough, brutal man and capable of any treachery or crime that came into his greasy head. In his place Ramage decided to leave the fourth lieutenant, a willowy and weak-faced youth, foppish in his manner and obviously someone who had more 'interest' at Court than interest in seamanship.

Ramage turned to Pareja.

'With the exception of this gentleman,' he said in English, pointing to the fourth lieutenant, 'you will all go into the boat at once.'

Pareja, dumbfounded by the unexpected order, stared at Ramage, and then stuttered, 'But...but...'

'Translate the order, please.'

'No, I refuse.'

Ramage looked at Jackson over the Spaniard's shoulder and nodded.

The muzzle of the American's pistol pressed into the back of Pareja's neck. He stood as if paralysed and Jackson, with a neatly timed sense of the dramatic, cocked the pistol so that Pareja must have felt the click all the way down his spine. Ramage could see beads of perspiration on the man's forehead and upper lip, but because he looked as though he would remain silent, Ramage suddenly snapped out the order in Spanish himself. The suddenness of Jackson's movement and Ramage's unexpected ability to speak Spanish sent the second, third and junior lieutenants walking to the break in the bulwark, but the Master stood firm.

'You, too,' Ramage said.

'No, I stay.'

Ramage was determined not to argue; but he did not want to spend life unnecessarily, so he turned to Pareja with what he hoped was a ruthless expression on his face, at the same time drawing his own pistol and pointing it at the Master.

Speaking in Spanish he said coldly, 'Lieutenant, until yesterday I did not know you existed. Today I do not care whether you exist or not. The same applies to this man. If he does not get into the boat I shall kill you both. It is a matter of no consequence or significance to me or my plans, so please yourself whether or not you give him a lawful order as his senior officer; it is his last chance – and yours, too.'

Pareja now looked as if he would faint before he had a chance to speak: Jackson was pressing the muzzle of the pistol so firmly into his neck he was having to brace himself to avoid being forced to take an undignified pace forward.

Finally he whispered to the Master: 'Do as you are told. Get into the boat.'

The Master seemed about to disobey, but after glancing at the muzzle of Ramage's pistol and then at his eyes, he shuffled after the others. Ramage then spoke to the fourth lieutenant, standing by himself and obviously scared at having been singled out.

'You are now appointed temporarily in command of La Sabina. You will follow in my ship's wake, day and night. Burn three lights at night, as before. Make sure your men steer carefully. Don't make any mistakes. The first one you make will cause the death of the Master – you'll see his body float past. Then the junior, third, second and first lieutenants. Your sixth will send your captain to perdition. You understand?'

The man nodded, unable to speak.

Ramage motioned Jackson to remove his pistol and Pareja walked to the bulwark.

'You are a barbarian,' he half-whispered in English. 'No better than a pirate.'

'You flatter me,' said Ramage coldly, enjoying himself in his temporary rôle and hard put to stop laughing, and he could not resist adding, 'My pastime is murder. Legally, you understand; it must be done legally – that's half the fun. That's why I enjoy war – don't you? After all, His Most Catholic Majesty declared war on us. We didn't start it, you know. We are just heretics – you remember how your priests used to burn us to save our souls? Since you've shut the gates of Heaven to us we're eternally damned and have nothing to lose. But you, why, if I kill you, you are bound to go to Heaven – aren't you…?'

CHAPTER NINE

Ramage looked through the telescope with as much nonchalance as he could muster, forcing himself not to rub his brow as he put the telescope down. Instead, he picked some fluff off the sleeve of his jacket.

The two ships whose sails were now lifting over the horizon to the north-east were frigates, probably out ahead of the Spanish Fleet, though the ludicrous mirage effect which made them appear upside down also made it hard to identify them.

But a few minutes after being sighted by the Kathleen's lookouts they'd altered course towards the cutter, each diverging slightly, so that if Ramage cast off the tow and ran either could cut him off. They obviously had more wind up there and were probably bringing it down with them.

Ramage's face was slack with weariness; his bloodshot eyes seemed sunken now, rather than deep-set. Yet he was freshly shaven, his uniform newly pressed, and without seeing his face one might have thought him an elegant young officer on board a flagship at anchor at Spithead.

He snapped the telescope shut, rubbed his brow for a moment before snatching his hand away, and repeated to himself once again that his duty now was to destroy La Sabina. Yet he knew the Spanish crew, with help at hand, would never let his men get on board to scuttle or burn her, even if it meant the death of their officers held as hostages in the Kathleen. And there wasn't time to rig an explosion boat.

Gianna said in Italian, and it made her voice more intimate. 'We haven't much more time together, caro mio…'

Ramage was startled because he had not seen her and said without thinking, 'No, I'm afraid not,' then added quickly, 'don't worry – you'll probably be rescued again before they get into port. They're bound to be intercepted.'

'Shall we be left alive to be captured?'

It wasn't really a question, and she said it so simply that for a moment he missed its significance.

'We don't fight,' he said almost harshly.

'Why not? Or let's use the hostages. Why not threaten to kill them unless the two ships let us go – we can make a bargain and leave them the wrecked ship.'

'My dear,' he said gently, 'we can't.'

'Why? Why not?' she asked fiercely.

'Because – well, we can't murder prisoners. And we'd have to if they called our bluff.'

'Why can't we? It's war. You once gave us a long lecture about how we Tuscans let Napoleon walk through our country without fighting. Now you have the faint heart. Don't forget the Spanish officers broke their word of honour and sent men with knives to try to murder us last night!'

There must be an answer but he was too weary to think of it, and she added, 'If they capture Antonio and me, we shall be executed.'

'You won't! They've no idea who you are.'

'They'll guess. The Spanish captain heard a sentry use my title this morning. I saw the look on his face.'

And this, Ramage thought to himself savagely, is what happens when you gamble. Capturing La Sabina hadn't really been a gamble – he'd been reasonably certain the explosion boat bluff would work because he knew enough of the Spanish mind to be sure of the outcome. But he'd thought no farther than having La Sabina safely in tow astern of the Kathleen; he hadn't thought of the consequences. In halving the Kathleen's speed he'd doubled the time for the voyage to Gibraltar, and that doubled the chances of being intercepted. And doubled the chances that Gianna and Antonio would end up on a French guillotine.

Gianna glimpsed the agony in his mind and touched his arm.

'Nico – neither Antonio nor I would have changed anything that's happened, anything, do you understand?'

He was too distraught to answer for a moment and she said fiercely, 'Nico – I talked with Antonio. You were right – we now realize we Tuscans did let that Napoleon walk over our land. But you've given us the will and the chance to regain our pride. We're proud, Nico – proud of the Kathleen, of you, of all those men, and proud of ourselves. Antonio asks only one thing – that we fight those two ships. He'll be killed, but we'd die anyway – the French would see to that. We've nothing to lose. Except,' she added quietly, 'for you and me. We lose each other. So, caro mio, if it's your duty to fight then…'

Then, Ramage said bitterly to himself, let's all die in the coffin that Lieutenant Ramage has so carelessly constructed. His eyes were fixed on the tight spiral of metal that was the elevating screw of a carronade. If he surrendered without a fight, the Kathleens would rot in a Spanish prison and Gianna and Antonio would end up on a French guillotine. There was no choice. He swung round to the Master and called, 'Mr Southwick, clear the ship for action!'

Southwick rubbed his hands as he bellowed the order, not waiting for the bosun's mate to pipe it first. Not content with that he went to the hatchways and bawled down each of them in turn.

As soon as he returned aft, Ramage said, 'Double the sentries over the prisoners. Warn 'em if they move an inch they'll be shot. Have we any musketoons on board? If so, see the sentries have them, and make sure they understand my orders.'

'Aye, aye, sir!'

Antonio came over, grinning happily and tugging his beard.

'So we fight after all, Nico!'

'Yes.'

'Good. I was afraid you'd...' he stopped, embarrassed. 'For the best possible reasons...'

Ramage laughed. 'Antonio – you worry more about my reputation than your own neck.'

'My neck keeps getting caught up in your reputation,' Antonio retorted. 'And this time I join in the battle, whatever you say!'

Men were running along the deck, placing sponges and rammers ready beside the carronades, undoing the canvas aprons protecting the flintlocks and snapping them to make sure the flints were sparking well. Others were flinging buckets of water over the deck and sprinkling more sand. And Ramage sensed every man knew that this time it was a fight to the death; a fact and not an empty phrase, and he was humbled by their cheerfulness. They were too busy to dwell on what might have been; too busy for morbid thoughts.

Jackson, standing to one side, coughed discreetly until Ramage was sufficiently irritated to look at him.

'Wondered if I might borrow the "bring-em-near" for a moment, sir.'

Ramage gave him the telescope and within a few seconds the American was scrambling up the ratlines.

Then Ramage went below, put his secret papers in the lead-weighted box which had holes drilled in it so that it would sink quickly, brought it up and put it by the binnacle, warning the quartermaster to keep an eye on it. By then Jackson was coming down from aloft. With a grin on his thin face and waving the telescope with one hand as he ran the fingers of the other through his thin, sandy hair, he trode across the deck.

'Beg pardon, sir, but I'm pretty sure of the two frigates.'

'Well, out with it, man, who are they?'

'I'm positive one's the Heroine, sir. I was in her for six months. Or she's one of that class. The other – the one to windward – is the Apollo.'

'You're absolutely sure?'

'Yes, sir.'

It made sense. Both ships were in Sir John Jervis' squadron. Ramage saw Gianna was looking at him, a curious yet happy look in her eye. In Italian she murmured, 'So we'll share another sunset.'

Antonio heard and growled. 'To the devil with your sentimental sunsets. Once again I miss my own personal naval battle. Nico, you might ask if I can transfer to one of the frigates; to the one commanded by the most bloodthirsty captain. Otherwise what tale shall I have to tell my grandchildren about how I fought in the Royal Navy?'

Captain Henry Usher, commanding His Majesty's frigate Apollo, was a large, ruddy-faced and cheerful man with a ready laugh, and as senior of the two captains sat in his cabin listening to Ramage's story with open admiration.

'Explosion boat! By Jove, a splendid idea! That accounts for it!'

Ramage looked puzzled and Usher explained, 'When you hove in sight we recognized the frigate as Spanish but couldn't think how you'd managed to capture her, so we suspected the Dons were setting some sort of trap for us. By Jove, and not a bit of paint scratched on your own ship. By the way, you have your orders with you?'

Ramage gave him the folded paper signed by Commodore Nelson and as he read a new interest showed in Usher's face.

'This Marchesa – is she old?'

Ramage said warily, 'She's fairly young, sir.'

'And pretty, no doubt?'

'Fairly sir, but a tiresome woman. Never satisfied with anything – always grumbling. You know the type...'

'And this Count Pitti?'

'Cousin of the Marchesa, sir. A chaperon,' he added hopefully, 'he never lets her out of his sight.'

'Yes – well,' Usher handed back the orders to Ramage, 'since the Commodore places such importance on the safety of your passengers and they're cramped in the Kathleen, I'll take them on board the Apollo. They'll be more comfortable, and safer, too – the Dons are out in force.

'I must say you can hardly be accused of obeying your orders, Ramage; you've taken just about every possible risk with this young lady. I can't help feeling the Commodore won't be very pleased. Yes, she must come on board the Apollo for her own safety. My mind is made up. And her cousin, too,' he added hastily.

'May I – '

'And I have to make all speed for Gibraltar, so I'll leave you to try to get the frigate in. Discretionary orders, of course – you can cast her off if you meet bad weather, and no one'll think any the worse of you.'

'Perhaps I – '

'I'll help you out by taking off all the Spanish crew and the officers you have on board and split 'em up between the Apollo and Heroine, so you won't have prisoners to worry about. And I'll give you twenty hands to man the frigate. That's the wisest plan.'

Ramage knew Usher was right. Gianna would be safe and, with twenty British seamen in the frigate, towing would be much easier. And Usher was being very generous; he could have taken the frigate in tow himself, or ordered Ramage to scuttle her, which would have meant the prize money would have to be shared or lost altogether. Usher must have read his thoughts.

'Won't affect your prize money; I shan't put in a claim because of my men – by Jove, no! That'd be dam' unsporting. My clerk'll have your orders ready by the time the Marchesa comes on board. It's a pity we both have so much to do, otherwise I'd ask you to join us for dinner.'

He shook Ramage by the hand. 'Stout effort, m'boy. I'll tell 'em in Gibraltar. Of course, I'll be making a report to Sir John and the Commodore, too. Best of luck.'

Ramage went down into the boat knowing he was sulking like a schoolboy, and he knew Jackson was curious to know what was happening, but he was in no mood for talking. Gianna met him as soon as he climbed on board the Kathleen. 'All went well?' she asked in Italian. 'They're pleased with you?'

'Yes – they are taking off the Spaniards and sending English seamen across to the frigate.'

'Oh good – we'll get her to Gibraltar yet!'

'The captain of the Apollo, a Captain Usher, is very concerned about your safety – and rightly so.'

Gianna looked at him suspiciously. She recognized the slightly pompous tone he used when he was about to tell her something he knew she would not like. 'And…'

'And so you and Antonio will go in the Apollo to Gibraltar.'

'We shall not!' she retorted.

'Gianna – you must.'

'No. We stay with you. You have the Commodore's orders. You must obey them and take us to Gibraltar. I insist. Antonio insists, too. We both insist. I shall tell this Captain Ushair!'

'But Captain Usher can give me new orders in the circumstances. My job was to get you both to Gibraltar safely. Captain Usher can do that better. And,' he warned, knowing it was the only thing that would end her defiance, 'if he wanted to, he could get me into a great deal of trouble over the frigate. Instead he's writing a favourable report.'

Antonio, who had heard most of the conversation, took Gianna's hand. 'It's the best way,' he said reluctantly. 'We are a – a preoccupazione for Nico. He must concentrate on towing his prize; but with us here, he's thinking always of our safety.'

Southwick came up and saluted. 'Lot's of boats putting off from the Apollo and Heroine, sir. Look as if they are pulling for the Spaniard.'

Ramage outlined Captain Usher's orders.

'Ah – so we can sleep o' nights without worrying what the Dons are doing at the other end of the cable!'

Gianna said, 'I'll go downstairs and pack.'

'Down below,' corrected Antonio.

'Humour me,' she said, 'I'm doing my best to be obedient. But I am on the verge of mutiny.' She looked at Ramage and said coldly, 'This Captain Ushair – he is handsome? Yes, I am sure he will be. I think I shall enjoy myself.'

CHAPTER TEN

Every man of the Kathleen's crew missed Gianna's lively presence. The ship was as dead as if lying to a quarantine buoy at The Nore. Already the Apollo and Heroine had disappeared into the broad purple band of haze joining sea and sky on the western horizon and in an hour it would be dark. Astern the prize was towing in the Kathleen's wake like a docile cow following a dog back to the farmyard.

For the first time in his life Ramage discovered loneliness was a many-sided thing; not simply being alone. And its worst side was being parted from someone who – and he'd only just acknowledged it – was part of himself. Now she'd gone, he knew that without Gianna he was incomplete: there was no one to share the secret joys of a glorious autumn sunset; no one else who saw the usual, almost prosaic spray sliced up by the bow as flying diamonds forming the Kathleen's necklace; her excitement had exhilarated him and her zest had put new life into the ship's company.

As he watched La Sabina, Ramage saw a boat pull towards the cutter. Southwick must have completed his work, leaving behind the Kathleen's Master's mate, Appleby, to the responsibility of his first command – if that was not too grandiose a description of being the senior of twenty men in a towed prize.

Southwick was soon reporting that in obedience to Ramage's orders all casks of wine and spirit in the frigate had been staved and the liquor poured over the side, to avoid the seamen getting drunk. There was plenty of water and ample provisions but, Southwick said with disgust, 'The state of the ship, sir! Don't think she's had a scrub for weeks. Not just scraps of food on the mess decks and the galley, sir, but chunks; just like a piggery!'

'Quite,' Ramage said hastily to interrupt the recital. He could visualize it and guess Southwick's reaction to a ship which was not spotless.

With that Ramage went to his cabin (at the bottom of the companionway he almost walked forward to his former temporary berth) and slumped in the chair, staring at the dim lantern. Weariness numbed him; he seemed to exist only in his eyes while his body remained remote and detached. Yet with Appleby away in the prize, he and Southwick would have to stand watch and watch about.

As the cutter rolled, the cot slung from the beams overhead, swung from side to side and he saw something dark lying on the pillow. It was a long, narrow silk scarf in dark blue embroidered with gold thread. The tiny patterns were all the same, delicately sewn designs of a mailed fist holding a scimitar. Instinctively Ramage touched the heavy gold ring which – from the time the two frigates came in sight – he wore slung by a piece of ribbon round his neck, beneath his shirt. The same design was engraved on it, Gianna's family crest. She had left him a memento – or, remembering her last remark and chilly farewell, had she just forgotten it? – and he wound it round his neck, half-ashamed of his sentimentality, and sat back and thought of her and fell asleep.

Ramage paced up and down the quarterdeck in the darkness: ten paces forward, turn about, ten paces aft and turn again. He had taken the first watch, from 8 p.m. until midnight, slept soundly until 4 a.m. while Southwick stood the middle, and now with dawn not far off he was shivering with cold an hour or so through the morning watch.

The wind had backed until it was on the beam and the down-draught from the mainsail was chilly. Ramage's clothes felt damp and smelled musty – spray had so often soaked the material that it was impregnated with salt which absorbed the damp night air, and he made a mental note to get his steward to rinse them if there was enough fresh water.

He shook his head violently, banged his brow with his knuckles, but still sleepiness came in waves. Using the old trick of licking a finger and wetting his eyelids to refresh himself, he cursed as the salt in the spray which had dried on the skin made his eyes smart.

But with a tremendous effort he listened carefully because the distant shouts had finally penetrated his drowsiness. He heard them again: a series of calls, very faint and up to windward on the starboard beam. A seaman padded up to him in the darkness.

'Captain, sir,' the man whispered.

'Yes – who is it?'

'Casey, sir, lookout in the starboard chains. Reckon I just heard shouting to windward and some blocks squealing, like a ship was bracing up her yards. Thought I'd better come aft instead of hailing you, sir.'

'Quite right. I've just heard it myself. Warn the other lookouts. And report anything else you hear – but keep your voices down.'

A ship close to windward – and the Kathleen advertising her presence by burning a lantern on either quarter and the prize three more.

Ramage turned to the quartermaster standing beside the two men at the tiller, 'Douse the lanterns, pass the word for Mr Southwick, the bosun's mate and my coxswain, and send the hands to quarters. But be sure no one makes a sound. There's a ship close by up to windward. And sling a jacket over the binnacle to shield the light.'

He prayed the prize crew would hear the shouts and snuff out their lanterns as well.

It'd begin to get light in ten minutes or so. At that moment he heard another shout – to leeward this time, close on the larboard beam, and then a deep creak that could only be the rudder of a big ship working on its pintles. She must be very close for that to be audible. Southwick, Evans and Jackson arrived in quick succession and men were gliding past him bare-footed on their way to the carronades, which were still run out.

Southwick left and after a quick inspection of the men at the guns returned to report the ship ready for action. Once again he was rubbing his hands and Ramage guessed he had the usual expression on his face, like a butcher well-satisfied with the meat on a newly slaughtered carcase.

'Just because we're ready for 'em, they'll probably turn out to be British. You think so, sir?'

'No,' Ramage said shortly. 'I couldn't make out what was being shouted but I'm sure it wasn't English. Anyway they must have seen our lanterns and one of our own ships wouldn't make such a noise if she was going to clap herself alongside as soon as it's light.'

'Hadn't thought of that,' Southwick admitted. 'Which of 'em will you have a go at first, sir?'

'Neither.'

'Neither?' Southwick could not keep the surprise out of his voice.

'Mr Southwick,' Ramage said sourly, 'don't let's make a habit of attacking frigates with a small cutter. We've been lucky so far, not clever.'

'Quite, sir. Then why don't we – ?'

Ramage snapped, 'Think man! If we cut the tow and drop astern or draw ahead we lose the prize to them. If they're British we won't get a penny. If they're Spanish – which is more likely – it'll be light enough for 'em to see us in' – he glanced eastward – 'four or five minutes, and with this breeze they'd soon catch us. And anyway, I doubt if they're alone.'

'So what do we do, sir?'

'We've no choice. We wait, Mr Southwick, and hope. Those who wish can pray as well.'

'The prize has doused her lanterns, sir,' Jackson reported. Ramage thought he could see a vague, blacker outline in the night, showing where the prize lay, but he was far from sure. 'Very well. Keep a good lookout; I'm going below for a few moments.'

In his cabin, the sentry shielding the lantern with his hat, Ramage unlocked the drawer in his desk and once again put his secret papers in the lead-lined box. Suddenly he remembered a conversation with a midshipman who'd once been prisoner in France: it was essential to have strong boots and warm clothes – the French marched their prisoners hundreds of miles north to such camps as Verdun, and presumably the Spaniards did the same. And you needed money to buy food on the march.

Ramage was already wearing boots and breeches. He took some guineas from a drawer and tucked a few into the lining of his hat, dropping the rest down his breeches. He waved the sentry away and as the man left with the lantern he thought he could detect the night turning grey at the skylight overhead. As he took a last glance round the cabin he remembered the ring round his neck: that would be stolen from him. He knotted it into a corner of Gianna's scarf and put them both in his pocket. He'd feel a damned fool if the ships turned out to be British, and they probably would, after all these precautions.

He took the weighted box up on deck and gave it to the quartermaster beside the binnacle, 'You know what this is by now. Keep it beside you.'

As soon as Southwick saw him he reported: 'Sound a rum lot, sir: make as much noise as if they was beating through a convoy anchored in a thick fog off Spithead.'

The cries from to starboard were musical. Even though the words were blurred, Ramage was sure he could detect a certain sibilance, an emphasis of certain vowels. The ship was a good deal closer now and from the shouting and subsequent noises, he was certain her sails were being trimmed constantly to edge her slowly down to leeward, to where they thought the Kathleen was. He walked over to the larboard side and could hear more voices from the second ship, even closer, and thought he could make out the hiss and bubble of the water being thrust aside by her stem.

The two ships obviously knew they were converging on the Kathleen but did each know the other was? Were they working to a pre-arranged plan or had they been sailing in company and both separately spotted the Kathleen in the darkness? Did they know their intended victim was only a small cutter? Unlikely. Was there a chance, therefore, of playing one off against the other?

For a wild, almost ecstatic moment he thought of manoeuvring the Kathleen until she was precisely midway between the two frigates and then, as they closed in on either side, drop all sail. The weight of the tow would act as an anchor and the Kathleen would stop as suddenly as if she'd run up on a sandbank.

Then, with a bit of luck, the two Spanish ships would crash alongside each other in the darkness, each thinking the other was the enemy. The chances were that each would have fired at least one broadside into her consort before realizing the mistake.

But a glance round the Kathleen's deck and up at the sails showed him the attempt would be hopeless: it was too late.

The black of night had gone, the grey of dawn was already here. In a few minutes both Spaniards would be able to distinguish the outlines of the cutter. A pity; the prospect of provoking a brief outbreak of fraticidal warfare between two of His Most Catholic Majesty's ships of war appealed to him. But he was wasting valuable time even thinking about it.

'Evans.'

The bosun's mate appeared beside him.

'Send the ship's company below – two at a time from each gun, and the rest take it in turns – to get shoes, a couple of shirts and any warm clothing they can sling round their neck. Don't put the shoes on,' he added hurriedly, 'in case there's any powder on deck.'

Evans paused a moment; although he had heard, he did not understand.

'Prisoners have to march, Evans. Probably through thick snow over mountain passes...'

'Oh – aye aye, sir!'

Jackson handed him his pair of pistols. 'Sound like Dons for sure, don't they, sir?'

Ramage grunted as he tucked them into the top of his breeches.

'Their fleet's at sea, isn't it! sir?'

'Yes.'

'Hum, wouldn't surprise me if – '

'Nor me,' snapped Ramage, who wanted time to think. 'They're probably about five miles astern, twenty sail of the line, and Admiral Don Juan de Langara sound asleep in one of them. Now, go below and get yourself shoes, warm clothes and money, in case we become prisoners.'

'Prisoners, sir?' Jackson exclaimed involuntarily. 'Aren't we – '

'Get below, Jackson. This isn't a debating society.' He felt ashamed at the snub; but all the Kathleens seemed to be off their heads, unable to distinguish between capturing a dismasted frigate and engaging a pair of them. He pictured himself and his Kathleens trudging first under a blazing sun along a track shimmering with heat, trying to breathe while the stifling air was thick with white dust thrown up by dozens of other prisoners being herded along by dull-brained shuffling, Spanish soldiers. And then dragging one foot after the other across mountain passes almost blocked by snowdrifts, the wind so cold that every indrawn breath was like a knife in the chest and against which no clothes could protect them.

The shouts this time were unmistakable: they were Spanish and he almost sighed with relief. Fear was not knowing. Once you knew, you weren't frightened – or at least there was a limit to it. It was not knowing that made fear depthless.

'Dons, sir; I can hear 'em clearly,' said Southwick.

'I know.'

'The prize, sir?'

'Keep her in tow: there's no point in letting her drift and Appleby hasn't time to scuttle her.'

'Shall we give each of 'em "one for the flag", sir?'

'No,' Ramage said sharply. 'Leave that sort of thing to the French.'

Pour l'honneur de pavillion: the French ritual of firing a single broadside and then hurriedly hauling down their colours, so they couldn't be accused of surrendering without firing a shot. Who cared? If the odds were that great no one blamed you anyway; if they weren't one broadside was not enough. Why for the sake of vulgar pride risk a return broadside which would kill your men unnecessarily?

When would he see Gianna again? Years rotting in some Spanish prison, and she in England, fêted by all the dandies of London Society. After a few gala balls at St James's, at the Duchess of This' and Lady That's, she'd forget (gladly, probably) the brief days in the smelly and uncomfortable little wooden box that was the Kathleen. Yet oddly enough he didn't feel bitter: indignant because it was his own bad luck, but not bitter. Perhaps a sign of old age, he thought wrily; perhaps even maturity. Attempt the impossible but accept the inevitable – if you can't work miracles. Thank God she wasn't with him now: in his imagination he saw them being parted outside some reeking Spanish prison, watched by the bloodshot eyes of Spanish guards and of lethargic disease-ridden dogs slowly dying in the sun. Surrender. He felt sick. It seemed that for the last few days everything he'd done had been without a thought of the consequences. Without any damned thought at all.

Just before the boat pulled away from the Spanish frigate lying hove-to to windward, Jackson came up to Ramage and said excitedly: 'Sir – change into seamen's clothes quickly!' Ramage looked so startled that Jackson added: 'I've a plan, sir: no time to explain now, but you must pretend to be a seaman. I've explained to Mr Southwick and he'll say the captain died some days ago and he's been left in command. Please go and change sir – ' he held out some clothes ' – I'll tell the men you are just a seaman.'

The boat, full of Spanish seamen, and some soldiers too, was ready to cast off. Ramage hesitated, unable to guess what Jackson was planning.

'Oh, sir,' Jackson exclaimed impatiently, 'you've got to say you're an American pressed into the Navy, if anyone asks. They won't for a few hours. Think of a name for yourself so's I can tell the crew and add it to the muster book. And I've got to enter your death, too.'

When Ramage did not move Jackson realized he would have to explain. 'I've got a blank Protection, sir. I'll fill it in so you can prove you're an American. But what name? Think, sir – what about that artist chap that draws the cartoons? You know – the one who always has sailors in his pictures, and the women always have a bosom hanging out of their dresses.'

'Gilray,' Ramage said automatically, still looking for any hidden snags in Jackson's scheme.

'That's him. "Nichlas Gilray" – how about that, sir?'

'Not "sir", Jackson, "Nicholas Gilray, able seaman",' Ramage said, finally grasping the full significance of Jackson's scheme and realizing it might remove the threat of a Spanish prison.

'Well, hurry up, Gilray,' Jackson said with a grin.

Ramage grabbed the proffered clothes and ran to his cabin, calling to the quartermaster to throw the lead-lined box of papers over the side. He slipped off his clothes, guineas cascading from his breeches, and pulled on the trousers and shirt Jackson had given him. Then, taking Gianna's silk scarf with the ring knotted into one corner, he tied in the sovereigns and secured the scarf round his waist, beneath the shirt. He decided to risk keeping his boots, which were partly hidden by his trousers, but pushed his uniform into a locker. Then wrenching open the door of the lantern, he smeared some of the soot on to his face. He put the pistols in their box, opened the little hatch leading to the bread-room, and pushed the box down on top of the bags, securing the hatch again.

A thud warned him the Spanish boat was alongside and he ran up the companionway and walked to the nearest gun. The men glanced at him and grinned.

He looked at the nearest of them. 'How do I look?'

'Fine, sir – er, fine, Nick!'

'Yes, belay the "sir".'

Ramage watched Southwick at the gangway receiving the Spanish officer, who spoke English and nodded sympathetically as Southwick explained how the captain had died after a painful but mercifully brief illness. The Master seemed so sorrowful that Ramage had an uneasy feeling that he was already dead. And for the purpose of Jackson's plan Lieutenant Nicholas Ramage was.

Jackson joined him at the carronade and whispered: 'You're down in the muster book, sir: last name on the list: transferred at Bastia from the Diadem. You come from New Milford, Connecticut. Aged twenty-five and rated able seaman. And you'd better have this.'

Ramage took the proffered piece of paper, unfolded it, and in the half-light saw it was a printed form with the American eagle at the top: a Protection carried by most American seamen (and many British, too, since false ones could be bought without much difficulty). He could just make out the handwritten name of the person to whom the Protection allegedly had been issued, 'Nicholas Gilray', and said to Jackson: 'You haven't left the pen wet with ink, have you?'

'No – I used Mr Southwick's, and wiped it dry.'

CHAPTER ELEVEN

Herded below the Spanish frigate, the Kathleens stood in a group surrounded by Spanish seamen and soldiers armed with muskets. A small cannon had been hauled over and trained down the hatch at them, and standing at the breech were two Spanish seamen, each holding a slow match in case the flintlock misfired.

'They aren't taking any chances,' muttered Jackson.

'I don't blame them: we didn't – ' said Ramage but left the sentence unfinished as two Spanish guards threatened him with their muskets.

It was hot and the ship stank: bilge-water, sweat, garlic, stale olive oil, rotting vegetables and ordure from the animals kept forward all added their quota to the stench. Finally, they heard sounds of the yards being braced round as the ship got under way, and the Spanish guards signalled they could sit down.

A few minutes later they had to stand again as a Spanish officer came down the ladder holding the Kathleen's muster book in his hand. Ramage wondered for a moment if Southwick had told a convincing story, then felt angry with himself: he'd put an unfair burden on the old Master's shoulders. If the Spaniards found out, Southwick would suffer as well, and Ramage felt ashamed at having embarked on the deception by merely following what Jackson had told him to do. Yet Southwick seemed to have accepted everything with his usual cheerfulness; indeed, Ramage sensed he and Jackson must have discussed it earlier.

The Spanish seamen stood to attention as best they could, shoulders and necks bent because there was little more than five feet headroom. At the foot of the companionway the Spanish officer held up the muster book to catch the light and read out the name of one of the seamen. The man looked startled.

'Over there,' said the officer, pointing to one side. He then read out more names, each time motioning the particular man to leave the group. Suddenly Ramage realized he was sorting out the foreigners – a Genoese, two Americans (at least, they were so listed in the muster book but Ramage knew both were English), a Portuguese, a West Indian and a Dane. Then he called for Jackson and Ramage, and as soon as they had joined the others, beckoned them to follow him up the companionway.

On deck the sun was rising and, glancing round, Ramage was startled to see they were in the midst of a large fleet – six great three-deckers, more than a couple of dozen two-deckers, one of which had the dismasted frigate in tow, and five or six frigates, one of them towing the Kathleen, which was flying Spanish colours. Seeing her a prize, picturing a Spanish officer in his cabin – Gianna's cabin – left Ramage feeling almost faint with dismay and anger.

As they lined up along the gangway under the direction of the Spanish officer, he realized he was the only one who had shaved within the last twenty-four hours and promptly rubbed his face to spread the dirt and perspiration more generously.

As the officer walked towards the captain's cabin Jackson whispered: 'Guessed as much: now we just swear we were pressed from neutral ships and forced to serve.'

'What good will that do?' said Ramage. 'They'll just press us into their service.'

'May not. If they do, it'll be easier to escape from a Spanish ship in port than from a Spanish prison. But we start off claiming our freedom as neutral subjects.'

'Yus,' said one of the others, Will Stafford, whose Cockney accent belied the entry 'America' in the 'Where born' column in the muster book. The entry had probably been made in deference to the fact he had purchased a Protection.

'Yus,' Stafford said almost to himself, 'we must 'ave our rights: we 'adn't oughta bin pressed in the fust place. Free men we are.' He sucked his teeth, as if appreciating his own declaration of independence, and added 'and that goes fer Nick 'ere, too.'

The rest of the men giggled self-consciously, but Jackson hissed at them, 'For God's sake don't forget it, lads; he is Nick to us now!'

The Spanish officer came back with the captain, a tall, slim young man with black, carefully combed curly hair. Ramage guessed that while his friends called his features aquiline, his enemies said he had a hatchet face.

The man stopped a few paces away, looked them up and down as though they were cattle in a market, and said in perfect English, 'So – men who are traitors to five different countries!'

Jackson quickly asked: 'How so, sir?'

'None of you is English?'

'No, sir.'

'Then by fighting for the English, you betray your own country.'

'We had no choice, sir!' Jackson said so indignantly Ramage knew he'd be believed.

'Why?'

'We was just kidnapped out of our own ships by the English. We had to serve – they'd have hanged us if we didn't.'

'Is that true?' he asked Ramage.

'Aye, sir. These English just come on board, take off the men they want – the best, usually – and that's that.'

'You are American?'

'Aye, sir.'

'But you have a Protection, no?'

'Yes, and I showed it to the officers, but they don't take any notice.'

'But you can insist.'

'S'no good, sir: we all did at one time or another. The only way you can get released is to get on shore somehow and find an American Consul who'll lodge a complaint. Then they have to free you.'

'Why did you not do that?'

Ramage gave what he hoped sounded like a respectfully cynical laugh. 'Never given a chance of going on shore in port, sir. I've been allowed on dry land only twice in two years an' that was for wooding and watering.'

'Wooding and watering?'

'Aye, sir: cutting wood for the cook's boilers, and filling water casks. Always in lonely places.'

'Of course, I understand. Well now, I am sure all of you wish to enter the service of His Most Catholic Majesty?'

'Who?' asked Jackson, with such surprise in his voice it obviously was not feigned.

'My Master, the King of Spain.'

'Well, thank-you very much, sir,' Jackson said, 'but we'd all much rather be allowed to go home.'

'Very well,' the Spaniard snapped, annoyed at having lost the chance of getting eight prime seamen. 'You'll be transferred to the flagship. You may eventually wish you'd decided to serve with me.'

With that he went below, leaving Ramage wondering whether it was an idle remark made in a fit of pique or if anything else lay behind the words.

The Spanish admiral sat at his desk in the great cabin and looked closely at Ramage and Jackson. He turned and spoke rapidly to the translator who said, 'His Excellency wishes to know when you last saw British ships of war?'

'Two weeks ago,' said Ramage.

'Where?'

'Off Cape Corse – a frigate.'

With this related to the admiral the translator asked several more question designed to find out where the British Fleet was, sometimes asking Ramage and sometimes Jackson.

Suddenly the admiral asked Ramage, in poor English, 'You seem to be a man of superior intelligence: how many sail of the line and frigates do you think the English have in the Mediterranean?'

Ramage pretended to be counting on his fingers while he thought of an answer. Should he exaggerate to frighten the Spanish admiral back into port, or say fewer, so the Spanish would seek out the British Fleet and thus give Sir John Jervis a chance of trouncing them? Then, remembering that the evacuation of Corsica – which meant protecting large convoys of merchantmen – was Sir John's prime consideration at the moment, he decided to exaggerate.

'Reckon about fifteen ships o' the line, sir. Frigates – I can only guess. 'Bout thirty.'

The surprise showed on the admiral's face: this was bad news.

'Fifteen? Name them!'

Ramage listed all those he knew had been in the Mediterranean and to the Tagus in the past few months, although many had subsequently left again.

'That makes twelve,' the admiral said.

Jackson promptly added three more names, saying he had seen one off Bastia and two off Leghorn less than a month ago.

'Why did you not know of these?' Ramage was asked.

'I was in another ship; I wasn't sent to the cutter' – he could not bring himself to say 'Kathleen' – 'until two weeks ago.'

'Very well. Your cutter – she was taking part in evacuating Corsica?'

Ramage just avoided falling into the trap and answered before Jackson could speak. 'No, sir, we was going to Gibraltar for orders, so I heard at the scuttlebutt: but I never heard any talk of 'vacuating Corsica. Why would they want to do that?'

Jackson was shaking his head, as if equally puzzled.

'You may go,' the admiral said abruptly.

Ramage turned, but Jackson asked: 'Sir, none of us – that is, the ones sent over from the frigate – is English, so will we be set free when we get into port?'

The admiral said pompously, 'We are not kidnappers like the English. If you do not wish to serve the King my Master and I am told you do not, which is ingratitude since his servants were your rescuers – I will consider your applications.'

'Thank-you, sir,' said Ramage. 'We are most grateful. When your ships came alongside, we all guessed we'd be delivered.'

It was spreading the jam thickly, but Ramage could see that profusely thanking the admiral for doing something he had not yet done – had simply said he would consider doing – would ensure his vanity did the rest.

The admiral held up his hand deprecatingly.

'It is nothing. My officers will see you are fed and clothed.'

Ramage gave a clumsy salute, followed by Jackson, and they both left the cabin. They found the other men lounging about on the gangway chatting as best they could with the Spanish seamen. There seemed to be a complete lack of discipline: men were sleeping beside the fo'c'sle guns; others were on the hammocks stowed in the nettings along the top of the bulwarks.

'What's the news, Jacko?' asked the Cockney seaman.

'The admiral – ' he caught sight of the translator approaching, and raised his voice slightly ' – the admiral has promised that we are free men and we can go on shore as soon as we get to a Spanish port.'

The men gave a cheer and Ramage suspected it was in response to a wink from Jackson, but it was effective: the translator, who was probably the admiral's secretary and clerk, gave an ingratiating smile as he passed, and Ramage knew Jackson's announcement and the men's cheer would be reported back to the admiral.

The main things that interested Ramage now were to discover the strength of the Spanish Fleet and the admiral's plans – both the original one, which presumably would now be abandoned, and the new one taking its place. He'd have plenty of time to see how he'd get the intelligence to Gibraltar…

A glance round the horizon answered the first question: there were exactly thirty-two sail of the line – at least six of them three-deckers – and a dozen frigates (and three or four more presumably over the horizon). The Cockney seaman, Will Stafford, provided some of the other answers, after pointing out that the frigate towing the Kathleen had left the Fleet (to avoid delaying it, Ramage guessed).

'They've been telling us they 'aven't 'ad much luck this cruise, Nick.'

'Is that so?'

'Nah – bin chasin' Old Jarvie all rahn the Meding-terraneang, and never did see 'im. They reckon he's too scared to show 'isself.'

'They're right, Will,' Jackson said, conscious two or three Spanish officers had apparently casually walked into earshot 'Old Jarvie wouldn't want to meet this Fleet.'

'Nah – well, anyway, the admiral's goin' to Carthygeeny for water and vittels, so I reckon 'e'll put us on shore there.'

'Don't care much where it is,' Ramage said, 'as long as we can get a ship home.'

'Aye,' echoed Jackson, 'as long as we can get home.'

Four days later the smell of scorching rope as the anchor cable raced out through the hawse hole drifted back to where Ramage stood on the starboard gangway looking at Cartagena. He could see, even though it was almost dark, that Spain was lucky to have an almost land-locked naval base where Nature provided such high cliffs and mountains as powerful defences against its own onslaught and the attack of enemy fleets.

As usual Ramage dreaded going below. He had no illusions about conditions below decks in a British man o' war in port: the regulation space allocated to every seaman was six feet by fourteen inches: in that space he slung his hammock. A man every fourteen inches. At sea, of course, each man had double that space because most of the ship's company was divided into two watches, arbitrarily called larboard and starboard. Usually a man in the larboard watch slung his hammock next to one in the starboard watch, and since one was always on watch the other had an empty hammock on either side of him. In harbour though, with both watches sleeping, it was a different story, and with the low headroom (usually five feet four inches or less) the whole deck would be packed solid with sleeping, snoring and sweating men (and, all too often, women). The air was frequently so foul the candles guttered in the sentries' lanterns and men woke with a taste in their mouth as if they'd been sucking a copper coin and a headache which affected their sight. But for all that, in a British ship the decks were clean, spotlessly clean, and the bilges were kept fairly sweet by frequent pumping.

But as far as Ramage was concerned, the lower decks of all Spanish men o' war were worse than the manger of a British ship when it was full of pigs and cattle: they were, as far as he could see, scrubbed but rarely, and pieces of vegetables and particularly tough meat the seamen could not chew were tossed over their shoulders and left rotting in odd corners. And always the reek of garlic – bad enough if you stood too near a Spaniard – grasping you with invisible tentacles if you went below.

Ramage had, therefore, been relieved to hear the outraged complaints of his men the first night on board: Jackson swore he'd never ever had a nightmare in which a ship was so filthy, and Will Stafford swore in his broad Cockney that by comparison the Fleet Ditch smelled like a young maiden's boudoir, even if it did carry most of London's muck and ordure into the Thames. From then on he had always referred to going below as 'visiting the Fleet'.

Jackson came up and said, 'Guess what's for supper.'

'Bean soup.'

'How did you know?'

'Well, we've had it for every meal so far.'

The admiral's secretary called them over and with him was the flagship's first lieutenant, who did not speak English.

'The captain has given orders that you are free to go on shore as soon as a boat is available – as soon as the admiral's suite and certain officers have left the ship,' he said.

'Please thank the captain – and the admiral.'

'Of course. You will all stay at a particular inn for the time being.' He paused. 'It is a condition of your release that you stay at this inn until you leave Spain.'

'Certainly, sir,' said Ramage, 'but how can we pay an innkeeper's bill? We've no money – the English haven't paid us for months.'

'I know that: I read the ship's books. The admiral has generously given orders that you'll be given the equivalent of the pay owing to you. The lieutenant has the money and I have a copy of the amount due to each of you. I shall give you the copy and you will issue it to the men. This,' he said to Jackson, 'will be agreeable to you and the others?'

'Oh yes, sir,' Jackson said respectfully, 'we all trust Nick.'

'Very well.' He gave Ramage a slip of paper, and spoke to the lieutenant, who handed Ramage a small canvas bag which, from its weight, obviously contained the money, and held out a piece of paper.

'The receipt for the money. You will sign it,' said the translator. 'Come to my cabin. I have a pen there.'

Ramage would have liked to have counted the money to see how much less there was in the bag than stated on the receipt, but decided not to in case it delayed them getting on shore.

An hour later the eight former Kathleens stepped out of a boat on to the quay and followed a Spanish seaman to the inn – a typical crimp's establishment. If it had been at

Portsmouth, Plymouth or in the Medway towns, a seaman using it would have been on his guard against the innkeeper seeing him and his mates to bed drunk and calling a crimp (if he wasn't a crimp on his own account) who would then sell the drunken bodies to the skipper of a merchantman short of crew, or if times were hard, to a naval press gang.

The eight of them were given two rooms, and Ramage gathered them all in one of them to issue the pay.

'I signed a receipt for the Spanish dollar equivalent of the pay owing,' he said. 'But there won't be that many dollars in this bag.'

'No,' said Stafford. 'The purser, the officer who gave you the money, and that translator... That makes at least three of 'em who've already took a reef in it.'

Ramage counted out the coins. Exactly a third of the amount had been abstracted.

'They're as bad as our chaps,' Stafford said bitterly. 'Every – oh, beggin' yer pardon, Nick...'

'Don't worry,' said Ramage, 'I wasn't born yesterday. But everyone has to take a third less than is due to him.'

With that he shared out the money then said, pointing to the door, 'Jackson, just check...'

Jackson whipped the door open, but no one was eavesdropping.

'Right,' said Ramage. 'For a moment I am your captain again and I must tell you that although the Spanish have freed you, you are still subject to the Articles of War: you are still under my command. Now, any one of you can sneak off to the Spanish authorities and reveal who I am. No one can stop you. The Articles of War can hardly be enforced here, so only your personal loyalty can make you obey my orders. Yet we all have a duty to perform, and I for one propose doing it. But I'm not forcing any of you to follow me: all I ask is that those who don't want to come with me – those who wish to stay in Spain or go elsewhere – I want those men to say so now, and do nothing to give me away. As soon as it's safe to do so, I'll free them from their obligations. Now – who wants to go?'

The Portuguese seaman looked shamefaced.

'I haven't seen my family for three years, sir, and the frontier...'

'Very well, you can go.'

'You understand, sir?'

Ramage held out his hand as an indication of his sincerity and the Portuguese gripped it eagerly. 'I promise you, sir, I shall never say anything.'

'I know,' Ramage said.

'Will you have to – '

'Put you down as "Run"? Officially I have to, but I've a bad memory for names, Ferraro. When the time comes it'll be hard to remember who were prisoners and who were taken to the flagship.'

He looked round. 'Anyone else?'

No one moved. It was hard to be sure. Among the remaining six men was there just one crafty enough to realize that by feigning loyalty and discovering Ramage's plan, he'd have useful information to sell to the Spanish for a high price? It was hard to be sure; very hard.

'Very well. Now, all of you go off and get your supper. Go steady with the liquor – remember it loosens tongues: a quart of red wine could put Spanish nooses round all our necks.'

The men trooped off, jingling their dollars, but Jackson stayed behind.

'Well, Jackson, can we trust them all?'

'Every single man, sir – including Ferraro. You can't blame him for wanting to go.'

'Of course not, and I don't.'

'Would it be impertinent if I asked about the plan, sir?'

'You may, but there isn't one yet. Obviously I've got to pass all we can find out about the Spanish Fleet to Sir John as soon as possible. At the moment I don't know how.'

'It's not far to the Rock, sir. We could get horses…'

'Too dangerous – and too uncomfortable. A long ride and then the risk of crossing to the Rock. If the Spanish didn't shoot us our own sentries would.'

'That leaves the sea, sir.'

'Yes,' said Ramage. 'We're sailors, not cavalrymen. Ships don't need sleep or fodder. But I need both at the moment. We'll have a look round the port in the morning and see what it has to offer.'

CHAPTER TWELVE

A good night's sleep had not refreshed Ramage: he had been at sea so long that lying in a bed that did not move in a room that did not creak was both unnatural and disturbing, and wakefulness had only emphasized that he shared the straw mattress with a number of small creatures entirely un-Spanish in their persistence and capacity to cause irritation.

He looked round the room at the seven men and nodded to the Portuguese. 'Since you are leaving us, Ferraro, what I have to talk to these men about doesn't concern you; but you can lend a hand by sitting in the parlour and watching the stairs so no one can listen at this door.'

As soon as the Portuguese left Ramage looked back at the remaining six men. Motley, cosmopolitan…the words hardly described them. Well, he'd better get started, although he was going to sound like a pompous parson. The men watching saw only the deep-set brown eyes glancing keenly from one to another. Although he did not know it such was the strength of his personality that not one of them noticed that instead of wearing the blue, gold-trimmed uniform of a lieutenant, their captain was dressed in trousers and shirt even more faded and worn than their own.

'Men, you know the position because I explained it to you yesterday. You are free: you never need serve in the

Royal Navy again. You are all foreigners or, like me,' he smiled, 'you have documents declaring you to be foreign subjects. But despite my splendid Protection, I'm still a King's officer, there's still a war to fight, and I've my duty. Yesterday, with the exception of Ferraro, you all said you wanted to continue serving with me. You've had a night to think it over. Has anyone had second thoughts? If so, speak up now. You've all served me well, so I'll never remember names, and you'll never be marked down as having "Run". But I warn you if you stay with me, you'll be no safer than you were in the Kathleen.'

No one spoke; no one looked uncomfortable, as though he wanted to leave but dare not face the others. Jackson had been right. Then Will Stafford finally sucked his teeth – an inevitable preliminary, Ramage realized, before he ever made a remark – and said with a broad grin, 'Beggin' yer pardon, sir, but yer can't get rid of us as easy as that!'

'Thank-you,' Ramage said almost humbly. Because he was young, he thought the men must be crazy to miss such an opportunity; but at least he had been fair in twice offering them their freedom.

'S'just one fing, sir,' Stafford continued, and the tone of his voice made Ramage's heart sink: here was the catch, here was the condition, the pistol at his head.

'Well?' he tried to sound amiable.

'Our pay, sir, 'Ow do we stand abaht that? We've got some dollars, but I've 'eard it said yer pay stops if yer gets captured. Don't seem fair on a man, but that's wot I've 'eard.'

Although Ramage didn't know the answer, he tried not to let the relief show on his face. But the more he thought about it, the more he thought it was stopped, and anyway, with the last muster book lost, it'd be hard for a seaman to claim his pay from those scallywag clerks at the Navy Board office. Still, he had money of his own, and he said: 'You'll get every penny owing to you: I'll see to that. At the moment you're paid up to date, thanks to the Spanish admiral – minus the Spanish purser's deductions!'

This raised a laugh, since pursers were notorious for their ingenuity in finding reasons for deducting odd amounts from the men's pay.

'The deductions wasn't too bad, sir,' Stafford said philosophically. 'We gets a quarter knocked off when we sells our tickets; sometimes more. Just depends.'

And that, Ramage knew, was only too true: one of the more glaring injustices in the Navy was that the seamen were normally paid at the end of a commission, and then usually in the form of tickets which could be cashed only at the pay office of the port where the ship commissioned. This was rarely the port at which they were paid, so the men frequently had to sell their tickets to touts on the quay who paid only a half or three-quarters of the face value and then took them by the bundle to the appropriate port office and cashed them for the full amount.

Six men – three with genuine Protections 'proving' them to be Americans (but only one of whom, Jackson, really was); a Genovesi, whose loyalty belonged to the Republic of Genoa (although Ramage remembered that after overrunning it, the French had renamed it something else fairly recently); a Dane whose country maintained a wary neutrality, with the Czar of Russia watching from the east and the French from the south; and finally the West Indian lad.

Although he hadn't the slightest idea what he was going to do, Ramage knew that all their lives and the success of the plan might eventually depend on the bravery, skill or loyalty of one man; so it was vital he knew more about each of them – except for Jackson, who had more than proved himself already.

Will Stafford, the Cockney with the American Protection, had been one of the liveliest of the Kathleen's crew. The snub nose stuck on a round face, stocky build and the cocky walk reminding him of a London pigeon, left Ramage wondering about those delicately shaped hands. The man had a habit of rubbing his thumb and forefinger together, as though feeling the quality of a piece of material.

'What were you before you became a seaman?'

'Locksmith, sir.'

'Did you work on the locks at night or in the daytime?'

'Ah!' Stafford laughed, 'always in the daylight sir, nothing unlawful. Me father 'ad a locksmith's shop in Bridewell Lane.'

'So you were apprenticed to him?'

'Father learned me the job, sir, but I wasn't apprenticed. That was the trouble – the press couldn't 'ave took me if we'd signed the papers.'

So, thought Ramage, Will Stafford is a seaman simply because he had not signed the indentures that made him an apprentice to his father, and by law apprentices were exempt from the attentions of the press gangs. A locksmith – that perhaps explained those hands. Hmm.

'Tell me Stafford, could you pick a lock?'

'Pick a lock, sir?' he exclaimed indignantly. 'Make, pick or repair – it's all the same to me.'

Henry Fuller, the tall, angular man squatting untidily on the floor next to Stafford and reminding Ramage of a lobster thrown carelessly in a corner, was a man who thought of little else than fish: to him the sight of a good-sized fish swimming round the ship, easily seen in the clear water of the Mediterranean, was considerably more tempting than a pretty girl on the quay or a pot of ale in a tavern.

Ramage knew from Southwick that when in harbour Fuller regularly asked for permission to fish from the fo'c'sle, and had often heard him cursing gulls or exclaiming at the sight of fish. Fuller rarely spoke: his long thin body, narrow angular face, grey spiky hair and a thin-lipped mouth in which remained only a few tobacco-stained teeth growing at different angles, might have been one of the fish stakes along the coasts of Norfolk and Suffolk. Ramage could not distinguish from his accent which of the two counties the man came from.

'Were you ever a fisherman, Fuller?'

'Aye, sir.'

'From where?'

'Born at Mutford, sir; just the back o' Low'stoff.'

Lowestoft, one of England's biggest fishing ports, its entrance almost surrounded by sandbanks which shifted with every gale. Yet as a fisherman Fuller too would have been exempt from being pressed.

'Did you volunteer?'

'Aye, sir. Bloody Frenchies – a privateer out of Boolong – stole m'boat. T'was only a little 'un an' all I 'ad. I 'ate 'em, sir; they stopped m'fishing for good an' all.'

Ramage looked next at the sallow, black-haired young man of about his own age who came from Genoa. Handsome in a coarse, full-blown way, he was getting fat – no mean feat considering the food served in a King's ship. Alberto Rossi – he was glad he remembered the name, since the man was always known as 'Rosey' – spoke passable English and, next to Stafford, had been the most cheerful man on board.

'How does a Genovesi come to be in the English Navy?'

'I am in a French privateer, sir. An English frigate make the capture. The captain say, "Rossi, my man, you'll get very little food and no pay in a prison hulk, so why not take the bounty and volunteer to serve with me?" He explain the bounty is a special present of five pounds from the King of England, so – ' he shrugged his shoulders.

'Don't you want to see Genoa again?'

Rossi tapped the side of his nose with a forefinger, knowing Ramage understood the gesture. 'For me, sir, Genova has the unhealthy climate.'

'What did you do before you became a privateersman?'

'My father have a share in a schooner, sir. A small share. My five brothers and I are the crew. The captain is a bad man: he have all the other shares.'

'And…?'

'He cheat us, sir, and one day he fall overboard and we take the ship into La Spezia. Then we hear by some miracle he is not drown: he swam and is rescue, so we sail very quickly. We sell the schooner to a Frenchman who is wanting to become a privateersman. I stay with the ship.'

'So in Genoa they tell lies about you: that you're a pirate and tried to murder your captain?' Ramage asked ironically.

'Yes, sir: people will gossip.'

There were two men left, a blond with a bright red face and a nose which, broken at the bridge, was vertical instead of sloping, and the dark-skinned West Indian. The blond was a Dane, but Ramage could not remember his name and asked him.

'Sven Jensen, sir. They call me "Sixer".'

' "Sixer"? Oh yes, five, six, seven. Where do you come from?'

'Naerum, sir. A village just north of Copenhagen.'

'And before you went to sea?'

'Prize-fighter, sir. Win five crowns if you can knock me down in less than half an hour.'

'Did people ever win?'

'Never, sir. Not once. I have a good punch. I call it my "Five Crown Punch".'

So apart from Jackson, Ramage thought, I've a locksmith, a fisherman, a pirate who doesn't baulk at murder, a prize-fighter, and the coloured seaman whom he only knew as Max.

'What's your full name, Max, and where do you come from?'

Max grinned cheerfully; he had been looking forward to being questioned and had the answers ready.

'James Maxton, sir. Age, twenty-one years; religion, Roman Catholic; where born, Belmont; volunteer; rating, ordinary seaman.'

Maxton's recital showed he had obviously served in several ships and knew the headings under which a man's details were listed against the name in the muster book.

'Where's Belmont?'

'Grenada, sir. Across the lagoon from the Carenage at St George. It's a beautiful place, sir,' he added proudly. 'And we've got big forts to protect us!'

'And before you went to sea?'

'I worked in a sugar plantation, sir, cutting cane with a machete.'

'So you can handle a cutlass, then.'

Jackson gave a low whistle and Ramage glanced at him inquiringly.

'Toss an apple, sir, and he can slice it in half and then cut one of the pieces in half again before it hits the ground.'

'I was born with a machete in my hand, sir,' Maxton said modestly.

So, mused Ramage, these are my six men. All fine seamen, all with another trade – if that was the right word – at their fingertips.

'Very well, we'll go down to breakfast. Watch your tongues – the innkeeper probably speaks some English and will report everything he understands to the Spanish authorities.'

* * *

The chill in the morning air warned Ramage that December was approaching, although there was enough sun to remind him that Cartagena was in Spain, with the usual piles of stinking refuse lying about in the streets, a happy hunting ground for flies and beggars and packs of miserable, emaciated dogs. The cathedral bells tolled mournfully as he walked down towards the Plaza del Rey where the main gate through the great walls surrounding the city was guarded by bored sentries who did not bother to challenge him.

Immediately outside the gate was another square with a big rectangular dock on the far side which had only one end open to the sea. A long, low building on the nearer side of the dock had piles of cordage stacked outside it and was probably the rigging store, with the sail loft next to it. At the landward end of the dock was a large timber pond in which great tree trunks floated, seasoning or left in the water to stop the sun's heat splitting the wood. Next to that two big slipways sloped down to the dock and on one of them shipwrights were busy with adzes shaping new planks to replace rotten ones in the hull of a small schooner.

Turning left and walking seaward he came to the Muralla del Mar, the long quay forming the landward side of the great, almost land-locked harbour. As he glimpsed the white crests of waves through the narrow entrance he saw he'd underestimated just how much Nature had given the harbour almost complete protection.

To his right a peninsula of high hills jutted out seaward to form the western side of the entrance, the two highest peaks capped by small castles, with several batteries built into natural platforms at various levels on the lower slopes.

On his left, more high hills thrust even farther out to sea to make the eastern side of the harbour, with several more batteries built into them and a fort almost at sea level covering the entrance.

An old Spanish fisherman in threadbare clothes, toothless, tanned and wizened as a walnut, sat on the ground with his back to the great wall, mending a net, and he nodded amiably at Ramage who realized he could be as useful as a harbour chart. Ramage nodded back and then looked at the Spanish Fleet at anchor: so many masts that the harbour looked like a forest of bare trees, so many hulls they overlapped each other.

Carefully he counted them... Twenty-seven sail of the line, and twelve frigates. But there had been thirty-two sail of the line and sixteen frigates in the Fleet a few hours before they reached Cartagena, which was the last time Ramage had been able to count them. Jackson was right after all: the missing five sail of the line and four frigates must have been French. Since they'd come so far to the westward but were not here, they must have gone on through the Strait of Gibraltar and out into the Atlantic. Had they been intercepted? Unlikely, since there were so few British ships in the area. More important, had they found any of the British convoys from Corsica and Elba?

How long was the Spanish Fleet going to stay in port? And what a Fleet it was! Ramage knew that whatever reputation the Spanish had as fighting seamen, they built splendid warships. There was talk than many of them had been designed by a renegade Irishman named Mullins, but whatever the truth of that, the Fleet at anchor was one of the finest afloat. And the great ship of the Fleet – the greatest in the world, in fact – was the four-decker Santísima Trinidad, the flagship, and conspicuous because of her red hull with its white strakes as much as for her sheer size. She carried 130 guns – some people said 136 – compared with the 112 guns of each of the six three-deckers anchored near her.

Ramage knew that until the end of his days he would carry in his memory the sight of those ships, and even now he felt a spasm of fear when he thought what they could do. What could England match with them? Her Navy was scattered half-way round the world – blockading the French Fleet in Brest, protecting the Tagus against any Spanish attacks on the Portuguese, guarding the Indian Ocean and the Cape of Good Hope for the Honourable East India Company ships, watching over the West Indies from the Windward and Leeward Island stations, and Jamaica and covering dozens of convoys… And here, anchored in one harbour, were one 130-gun ship, six of 122 guns, two of eighty, and eighteen seventy-fours.

Several of the big ships and some of the frigates were showing the effect of their recent cruise: many had yards sent down on deck while others were lowering them into the sea, indicating they were sufficiently badly damaged to need towing to the dockyard for repairs. And he suddenly realized neither the Kathleen nor her captor was in the harbour yet.

He turned to greet the old fisherman who put down his net and the long wooden needle and, apparently noting his accent, asked: 'Are you French?'

'No, American. I came in yesterday with the Fleet. You have a fine harbour here.'

'Indeed!' exclaimed the old man. 'You can get in with most winds. Just watch out for Santa Anna, that's all!'

'Santa Anna?' inquired Ramage.

'Over there,' the old man said, pointing to the eastern ridge of high hills and cliffs jutting seaward to their left. 'You see the guns at this end – that's the San Leandro battery and then farther along another, the Santa Florentina battery. Then the fort low down on the small point you see it? That's Fort Santa Anna on Point Santa Anna. Just off the point is Santa Anna Rock – very dangerous. You can't see it now because the flagship is in the way. Beyond that is Trinca Botijas Point with another battery on it. Those guns! Bad for fishing, you understand? The noise drives away the fish. They swear it doesn't, but why aren't there any fish after they fire them for practice? You tell me why not, if it isn't the noise.'

'It's the noise all right,' said Ramage hastily. 'But do they fire them often?'

'No,' said the fisherman, 'mercifully not. Did you ever hear of a Government spending money? No! Collect it yes. Taxes, taxes, taxes. But spend it on powder and shot? No! And it's poor powder, too. Why, when the Santa Florentina battery last fired you know what happened? It was laughable. All ten guns should have gone off at once, but bang! Only one gun fired. When they drew the shot and powder from the other nine they found it was bad powder. Damp and poor quality. Good thing, otherwise we fishermen would starve.'

'Bad powder means good fishing, that's certain,' agreed Ramage. 'What about over here – ' he gestured to the hills on the right. 'Any rocks to worry about there?'

'No, not one. But these nearest hills,' he gestured to the right, towards the two small sugar-loaf hills with a steep one behind (Ramage guessed it was more than six hundred feet to the castle on the top), 'they make the wind fluky when it's from the north-west. I've seen many a three-decker get caught a'back there and almost go on to Santa Anna before they could brace round.

'Then they built that big castle on top, too: that makes the wind even crazier. Castillo de Galeras they call it, but I can think of a better name. And that battery below there, almost on the beach. You know what they call it? Apostolado Battery. It's blasphemy, no less: no Apostle would harm a fisherman – think of St Peter. But those damnable guns…

'And you see the big hill beyond, at the entrance? That's Punta de Navidad, and you can guess – another battery of guns. The blasphemous pigs,' he grumbled. 'I've told the priest many times that it's sacrilege to call batteries after saints and holy things when all the guns do is drive away the fish and leave honest folk like me to starve after a day hauling nets.'

Ramage nodded sympathetically as he looked at some of the small coastal craft alongside the quay unloading their cargoes. The nearest one, La Providencia, was a zebec, a fine example of one of the most beautiful vessels in the world, and, for her size, one of the fastest.

She had the narrow, sleek hull of a Venetian galley but more beam, and her long graceful stern and slender bowsprit was emphasized by comparison with the clumsy, applecheek bows of the ships of war near by. Her stern sloped aft in a gentle curve, narrowing all the time, so it overhung the water by several feet. But to an eye unused to Mediterranean craft, the most striking feature was her rig: she had three masts and lateen sails. Although the mainmast was vertical, the foremast raked forward and the mizzen aft. Each mast had a long, thin yard slung fore and aft from it, hanging diagonally with the fore end down at deck level and curving gently from its own weight. The triangular sails were furled at the moment, and all Ramage could see confirmed its reputation of being one of the simplest and most efficient rigs afloat.

La Providencia was the only vessel alongside the quay that was not unloading cargo. She had ports cut into her bulwarks on either side to take her guns, and abaft each of them was a much smaller oar port, so that in a calm she could be rowed. La Providencia, Ramage guessed, was probably a privateer at the present moment: she had new sails and her rigging looked new. And her paintwork was too elaborate for a vessel constantly loading and unloading cargo.

He nodded farewell to the old man and strolled along the quay for a closer look. Yes – through the ports he could see that the ropes of the breechings and tackles of the guns were all new. Obviously the owners had decided that now Spain had entered the war there was more money to be made from privateering (since the British merchantmen from the Levant had to pass only a few miles south of Cartagena to get through the Gut – as the Strait of Gibraltar was known to generations of sailors) than from carrying cargo. And they were right.

There was only one man on deck, and Ramage sat down on a nearby bollard and mopped his brow as if hot and in no hurry to go anywhere. Slowly and carefully he examined the zebec, familiarizing himself with the position of every sheet, halyard and brace. He'd seen zebecs tacking into harbour enough times to know how the great lateen sails were handled, and as soon as he returned to the inn he would make some sketches, and he'd also send the men down to walk along the quay and study the ship.

While Ramage had been inspecting the harbour and the zebec La Providencia, Jackson had found the American Consul's office and made an appointment for the four possessors of Protections to see him at four o'clock that afternoon. The booming of the cathedral clock was just filling the whole port when Jackson led them to the Consulate building just inside the main gate in the Plaza del Rey.

Ramage was thankful the Consul, unlike Spanish and Italian officials, did not find it necessary to keep them waiting half an hour to demonstrate his importance. Instead, as they entered the hall a quiet voice called them into a large room. Ramage made a conscious effort to appear as nervous as Stafford and Fuller, hoping to leave the talking to Jackson.

The Consul was a tall, grey-haired man with twinkling blue eyes, and as the four men came through the door he was collecting up some playing cards which had been laid out on the desk at which he sat.

'Good afternoon,' he said cheerfully, 'you've interrupted my game of patience, but fortunately I'd reached the point where I could only win if I cheated. Now, what can I do for you?'

'Seamen we are,' said Jackson. 'We...'

'We thought,' Ramage said equally as nervously, 'that...'

The Consul shuffled the cards and began setting them out for a new game. Ramage, guessing he did it to lessen their embarrassment, continued in a hesitant and uncertain voice, 'The Spanish rescued us from a British ship of war, sir. We were all pressed a long time ago. The Spanish – well, we showed them our Protections, sir, and they – well, as soon as we got here they set us free.'

The Consul picked up a sheet of paper. 'Nicholas Gilray, Thomas Jackson, Will Stafford and Henry Fuller?'

'Why, yes, sir!'

'Yes, the admiral wrote to me about you. He even had you paid up to date, I believe.'

'Yes, sir – well, more or less.'

'How much less by the time the money reached you?' the Consul asked shrewdly.

'Only about a third, sir.'

'You were lucky. They're a sticky-fingered nation.'

A curious expression, Ramage thought. Did the Consul dislike the Spaniards? If he did – and it was a distinct possibility if he had been in Cartagena for a long time – he might be of some use.

'So we gathered, sir. Tried to make us serve in the Spanish Navy, they did; but we insisted on our rights.'

'Yes, of course,' the Consul said drily. 'Perhaps I could see your Protections?'

The four men fumbled in their pockets. Jackson was the first to find his and, after unfolding it and smoothing out the creases, put it in front of the Consul, who read aloud from it, half to himself. 'Thomas Jackson… Charleston, South Carolina…about five feet ten inches high…' He held the paper up to the light to see the watermark, then folded it and gave it back to Jackson and picked up the other three, reading out the details. 'You are Stafford?'

When Stafford replied the Consul's eyebrows lifted. 'You were born in America?'

'No, sir. Taken there when I was a baby.'

'Indeed? And you must be Fuller?' he said, turning to the Suffolk man, who nodded. 'No doubt you, too, went to America as a baby?'

'Aye, sir!' Fuller said eagerly. 'Just a tiddler.'

Ramage almost laughed aloud at both the accent and the inevitable allusion to fish.

'And you, then, are Gilray.'

For a moment Ramage looked at the Consul blankly then said hurriedly, keeping his voice as flat as possible, 'Yes, sir: Nicholas Gilray.'

The Consul handed them back the Protections and asked: 'What do you want me to do for you?'

'If you could help us get a berth in a ship going to America, sir?'

'Not too difficult, but you might have a long wait, though.'

'Oh,' said Jackson sadly. 'Haven't seen my home for three years.'

'Have you enough money to live on while you wait?'

'Depends how long we wait, sir.'

'Of course, of course. But anyway, for the time being you have enough Spanish money. By the way. Stafford, how much did you pay for that Protection?'

'Two pounds!' exclaimed Stafford and then looked down at the floor, realizing he had fallen into a trap.

'Don't sound so indignant,' the Consul said, smiling, 'five pounds was the current price when I sailed from New York two years ago. I imagine Gilray and Fuller probably paid more.'

Ramage knew that with the exception of Jackson, the only genuine American, they were now at the Consul's mercy. He also knew, since the man was at least fifty years old and American Independence had been declared little more than twenty-five years ago, and the accent sounded familiar, he might well help them. Clearly this was no time for evasion.

'I don't know what Fuller paid, sir, but mine cost more. This doesn't mean that you'll...?'

'No, don't worry, you're not the only Englishmen with American Protections. And I was born an Englishman too, only I took the precaution of becoming an American citizen by lawful means.'

Ramage couldn't resist the impulse. 'Cornish, sir?'

'Yes, Cornish,' the Consul said, almost wistfully. 'Cornwall...the finest county of them all. I want to walk again on Bodmin Moor...and yet here I sit playing patience in an odd corner of an alien land.'

The man was talking to himself now, reviving old memories and longing to see once again his birthplace. 'Yes, to get away from this heat and stink and walk across Bodmin as the sun comes up and melts the mist. To hear the church bell of St Teath ringing out again...'

The name of the village startled Ramage into a sudden movement which broke the Consul's reverie and made him look up inquiringly. St Teath – the next village to St Kew, where his father and mother lived at the Hall: St Teath, every square inch of which had been owned by the Ramages since the days of Henry VIII, and father was also the patron of the very church the Consul remembered, and probably paid for the very bell he longed to hear ring again. Why did the Consul leave England? Had he been a debtor – perhaps to father even? What would be his reaction if he knew that the son and heir of the Lord of the Manors of St Kew and St Teath stood before him, at his mercy?

Because Ramage's first impulse was to tell him at once, he deliberately said nothing: it could wait until tomorrow, by which time he would have slept on it.

'Well,' the Consul said, 'I'll do what I can to find you a ship. Don't spend all your money on wine and women, because I've no funds to help you, and there's not enough work round here for the Spaniards, let alone Americans who don't speak the language. Which inn are you staying at?'

Jackson told him, and the four men saluted and left the room after thanking him profusely.

Back at the inn Jackson waited until they were alone, then said to Ramage, the concern showing in his voice: 'Was there anything wrong, sir? You went white as a sheet when the Consul mentioned that village – St Teath, wasn't it?'

'My family owns it,' Ramage said sourly. 'My home is in the next village. Obviously he left there before I was born. But why did he leave? Most people leave in a hurry for America because they're in debt or wanted for some crime. Debt usually means rent. Rent may well mean my father. But – ' No, rent wouldn't mean his father; the low rents on the Ramage estates were a sore point with neighbouring landowners. But the Ramages were rich and the old admiral saw no reason to charge his tenants more than was required for the upkeep of the cottages. He always maintained there was no such thing as a bad crew, only a bad captain; and as a landowner he lived by the same principle, that there were no bad tenants, only bad landlords.

Jackson realized Ramage was not going to finish the sentence and said, 'He seemed to have happy memories of the place, sir: the church clock and the walks and the morning mist. Doesn't seem at all bitter. If I'd left because of some landlord, or because I was wanted for some crime, I think I'd be bitter about a place, not sentimental.'

And Ramage knew that Jackson was right. But since the American Consul in Cartagena was the personification of neutrality, was he likely to do anything more than give the statutory assistance to four men claiming to be United States citizens and wishing to return home? They could be fairly certain he'd do nothing to harm them. Should he reveal himself as the Earl's son in a gamble to get more help, at the risk of getting none?

CHAPTER THIRTEEN

Next day, while Ramage walked out along the hills forming the bay and examined the batteries protecting it, the six seamen sat chatting with their backs to the Muralla del Mar and, without the Spaniards realizing it, studied the zebec La Providencia until they knew they could board her – or any other zebec – in the dark and set all sail without a moment's delay.

'It ain't a seamanlike rig,' concluded Stafford. 'Might do fer a lot o' 'eathen Moors, but wot, I hask yer, 'appens to those yards in a gale o' wind? I'll tell yer: they whip like a master-at-arms' rattan.'

'But each one's got a vang at the lower end and another near the top,' Jackson interjected mildly.

'Yers,' jeered Stafford, 'they'll be useful when you want to 'aul 'em back in again after they've gorn overboard.'

'But very fast ships,' Rossi interjected. 'The fastest. That's why the Moorish pirates use them.'

'And that's why Mr Ramage is interested in them, Rosey,' said Jackson. 'When we leave here for Gibraltar we'll be in a hurry.'

'Like as not there'll be a Spanish three-decker chasin' us,' Fuller added gloomily.

Stafford laughed. 'If they get close, yer can 'ave a boat and row over to the Spanish admiral wiv a big plate o' fish and tell 'im we was really only 'avin' a nice day's exercise wiv rod an' line.'

Fuller grunted contemptuously: he couldn't be bothered wasting his breath on a man who talked like that about fishing.

'She's fast enough,' said the Dane. 'And she's not too big for us to handle.'

'That's the point, Sixer,' said Jackson. 'Four of us could, if necessary.'

'When do we sail Jacko? Tonight?'

'No – at least, I don't expect so.'

'Why not? No point in 'angin' about. Two weeks in that inn'll cost us two years' pay.'

'What are you worrying about? You're sitting here chatting, you're not standing watches, you'll sleep soundly tonight in a bed with no chance of being roused out to take in a reef, and there's no deck to holystone tomorrow morning. And Mr Ramage is paying you all the time.'

'Mr Ramage? Oh, yer mean for and on be'alf of 'Is Royal Majesty King George, an' all that.'

'No – Mr Ramage is paying out of his own pocket.'

'But – '

'You asked him about pay, didn't you,' Jackson continued. 'You said you'd heard our pay stopped the day we were captured. Well, he waited a moment before answering. 'I saw he'd heard the same thing and didn't know for sure. But straight away he said, "You'll get every penny owing to you: I'll see to that." Well, I know your pay does stop. So in fact what you got was a guarantee from Mr Ramage that he'll pay you.'

'Cor,' exclaimed Stafford. 'Why didn't yer tell 'im?'

'No point,' Jackson said impatiently. 'He'd still have paid you out of his own pocket.'

' 'Ow d'yer know?'

Before Jackson could answer Fuller said flatly, 'Because he's Mr Ramage, that's why.'

'That's right,' said Rossi. 'If he say he pay, he pay.'

Jackson suddenly asked Stafford, 'Why did you stay with him? You didn't intend to when the Spaniards sorted out the foreigners, did you? You reckoned this was your chance to say goodbye to His Royal Majesty King George, didn't you?'

'Not "Royal" Majesty,' said Fuller. 'Just "His Majesty".'

'Yers,' Stafford ignored Fuller and admitted, 'Yers, to begin with I intended to be quit of His Royal Majestic Highness King George.'

'But why – '

'Well, later on it didn't seem right to leave Mr Ramage,' Stafford said almost defiantly. 'What about all of you? You intended to quit too – not you Jacko,' he added hastily, 'but the rest of you.'

'Not me!' Rossi said sharply. 'After how he rescue the Marchesa when she is a stranger, and after he is a good captain to us – no! At first I do not know why the Spanish pick me out, but when I see Mr Ramage comes with us, I am not frightened.'

'And that goes for me too, you miserable little pick-lock,' Fuller growled at Stafford.

'I wasn't a pick-lock, you fathom o' fish bait.'

'Steady now,' said Jackson, running his hand through his sandy hair, 'the only thing that matters is we're still with him. And all that matters to him is that those ships out there – ' he nodded towards the Spanish Fleet at anchor across the harbour, ' – can do a terrible lot of damage when they sail, unless Old Jarvie knows they're at sea.'

Jensen glanced at Jackson. 'Do you mean that we'll...?'

'I don't mean anything, Sixer; I'm just telling you what I think matters to Mr Ramage.'

* * *

The long, many-arched balcony on the first floor of the American Consul's house was large and overlooked the Plaza del Rey. The apex of each arch was high, which added to the feeling of coolness. Ramage sat in a comfortable cane chair which had a small oleander plant growing in a tub beside it, and reflected that his impulsive evening visit to the Consul was proving interesting, if nothing else.

The Consul was in an expansive mood. He had loosened his silk stock, apologized for discarding buckled shoes in favour of embroidered Moorish slippers and now that four glasses of brandy had followed a good dinner eaten amid a gentle flow of sentimental reminiscences, he viewed most of the world with favour. The exception, Ramage was surprised to learn, was France.

'I think you'll agree, Mr Gilray,' he said, holding up his brandy glass against the light from the chandelier, 'that although in general the Italian people have a certain shallowness, a certain insincerity, they make up for it by their artistic nature and gaiety. The Spanish, in my experience, are also rather an insincere people, yet in compensation they have a natural dignity, and a personal sense of honour – although not a national one – and this reflects in their fighting ability. But the French…'

The Consul drained his glass, saw that Ramage's was also empty, and rang a little silver bell on the table beside him.

'The French – well, their present behaviour frightens me. They've grown greedy. It's only seven years since the Bastille was stormed, and when they executed their King four years ago last January they made fine speeches about liberty and equality. Then, already at war with Austria, they declared war on Britain, Holland and Spain. They've butchered their own people by the thousands, and Spain has since changed sides.

'I agree it's not our business what goes on in France while they try to establish a better system of Government. That was long overdue. But how does declaring war on everyone else help? Now, still talking of liberty, they've over-run half of Europe. Since this – ah, liberation – has simply replaced the previous misrule with French misrule, I think we're entitled to ask the Directory if one inch of the foreign lands captured by General Bonaparte has helped give France a better Government, put more bread in the French people's larders, or helped the peoples of the foreign lands. From what I hear, Bonaparte charges them a pretty penny.'

A servant came on to the balcony and poured more brandy.

'Since I'm here solely as the Consul of a neutral country, I suppose I should guard my tongue; but I keep on asking myself whether Spain has just entered the war against England of her own free will, or because France has given her no choice. I'm certain of one thing, though: the French consider the Spanish Navy as being virtually under the Directory's command.'

Ramage felt the Consul had a good reason for saying that, and wondered how to discover what it was.

'Surely, sir, the King of Spain is too proud a man to take orders from men like Barras and Carnot? Surely he isn't at the Directory's beck and call?'

'He has no choice,' the Consul said drily, and as he looked out across the Plaza del Roy. Ramage took the opportunity of pouring most of his brandy into the oleander tub. 'No more choice than you'd have if a footpad stuck a pistol in your back on a dark night and demanded your purse. I suspect the Directory have been more responsible for Langara's replacement than the King.'

'Langara's replacement?' Ramage exclaimed. 'I've heard nothing of that! Why, he's been back in port only two days.'

'Langara himself heard only when he arrived in Cartagena. In fact,' the Consul could not help adding, the brandy getting the better of discretion, 'I was in the curious position of knowing even before the admiral.'

Ramage nodded knowingly and said, 'You obviously have influential friends in Madrid – and a fast messenger!'

Would the Consul fall into the trap and, in correcting him, reveal his source?

'I have influential friends in Madrid, yes; but I don't need my own messenger,' he said enigmatically, then deliberately turned the conversation by adding, 'Aren't you interested to know the name of the new admiral, and why Langara was replaced?'

'Of course, sir.'

'Langara has gone to Madrid to be the new Minister of Marine: I assume to liven up the Navy. The new admiral is Don Josef de Cordoba.'

'Has he arrived here yet?'

'No, and I doubt if he'll hurry himself.'

'Why, isn't the Fleet going to sail again soon?'

'No – they've been given at least four weeks in which to refit, and from what I hear they need every minute of it. Anyway, I'm sure Admiral Cordoba won't want to arrive here until his house is prepared for him!'

The Consul spoke ironically and Ramage laughed. 'Yes – they must air the bed, polish the silver and stock the cellar. Is he going to be a neighbour of yours?'

'No – he's taken a house near the Castillo de Despenna Perros. But my dear young man, forgive me: your glass is empty!'

Again the servant was called, and again the glasses were filled.

'Your health, Mr Gilray.'

Ramage raised his glass. The risk involved in calling on the Consul and revealing, by inference rather than a direct statement, that he was not simply a seaman, had so far been more than worthwhile. But he was curious to know if he'd been right in not risking telling the Consul his real name. If the old chap knew, would it lead to him sharing more of the information he was getting about the Spanish Fleet, or throwing Ramage out of the house?

'You spoke of Cornwall yesterday, sir. You were born there?'

The Consul put down his glass and settled more comfortably in his chair. 'Yes – I spent the first twenty years of my life there. Or most of it, anyway. My family were Bristol merchants and shipowners trading with America. My father went to Bristol once a week, otherwise we lived – well, in some comfort, at St Teath, while his partner, my uncle, lived in New York running affairs there. And then the War came... Soon we had lost all but one of our ships, and all our American market, so we could not do business elsewhere. Naturally we were quickly impoverished. Fortunately my uncle had foreseen much of what would happen – I fear   my father tended to ignore his advice – and had begun other commercial enterprises in America which were not so badly affected by the war and increased considerably at Independence. He had no children, and I had no inheritance to come from my father...so I joined my uncle in New York.'

'So you are an American citizen by accident, almost.'

'Yes – but when I see a young Englishman like you, with your life of adventure, I think I envy you. Mainly, of course, I envy you your years!' he added with a smile. 'Yes, if I was twenty now, I think I'd like to be English again.'

Ramage knew at once there was nothing to be gained by revealing his real name; the Consul would help as much as he was inclined without that.

As if reading his thoughts, the Consul said quietly, 'You still have your duty to do, I suppose, hence the – ah, gentle subterfuge. Are you alone?'

Ramage shook his head. 'Mercifully, no.'

'But with three men…'

'Six – I have a Dane, a Genoese and a West Indian as well.'

The Consul laughed. 'The world – in a microcosm – in arms against the Directory! These men are reliable? They won't disappear in an emergency? After all, not one of them owes you any loyalty as far as the Spanish authorities are concerned, although you personally are safe enough while you have that – that, ah, Protection. Without it you could be shot as an English spy – you realize that?'

'Yes, but I think they are loyal. I hope so. The one real American, Jackson, certainly is.'

'I trust you'll forgive this question,' the Consul said, looking into his glass. 'You were genuinely captured? I mean, it was an accident of war? Your Protection…?'

'Or are the English deliberately planting spies in Cartagena?' Ramage said with a grin. 'No, I'm afraid it was all too much of an accident: we were caught by the whole Spanish Fleet: I have a Protection simply because one of the seamen had prudently acquired an extra one without the details filled in.'

'A wise move. All the Protections are genuine documents, incidentally, although I noticed the details of yours were written in a different ink from the notary's. I asked that man how much he paid for his merely to see his reaction. It was clear only one man was a genuine American.'

Again Ramage laughed and as the Consul joined in, looking up at the ceiling, Ramage emptied his glass into the tub. At this rate he'd soon be able to see the oleander growing – or swaying.

By the time Ramage left, to be back at the inn before curfew, the Consul was happily drunk and insistent that Ramage soon paid him another visit. All the men appeared to be asleep, but as Ramage crept to his bed he heard Jackson whisper, 'Everything all right, sir?'

'Yes – he's friendly enough.'

The small amount of brandy Ramage had drunk was not enough to soften the mattress. He tried to sort out from the rambling conversation exactly what the Consul had revealed. Admiral Cordoba had been given command of the Fleet and a house was being prepared for him. Typically Spanish, that: too fond of comfort to live on board his flagship, even though it was the largest ship of war afloat. With four weeks to refit, the Fleet would be ready to sail, allowing for a few delays, by mid-January. The admiral wouldn't be concerned with the refitting, so could arrive in early January.

The Consul's source of information was not from friends at Court and he'd given a curious answer when Ramage had referred to 'a fast messenger'. What had the old man said? – 'I have good friends in Madrid, yes; but I don't need my own messenger'. There'd been a slight and probably unwitting emphasis on 'my own', as though he relied on someone else's messenger. He wasn't relying on a spy close to Admiral Langara since he'd known of the replacement before Langara.

Ramage knew instinctively that the Consul had told him more than he intended and more than Ramage himself yet realized, and a little thought should reveal what it was. Not the Consul's messenger, but someone else's, and not a spy in Langara's staff: that much was certain. So – how did the information come to Cartagena? Start at the beginning. Probably the King decided. He would tell the Minister of Marine that Cordoba should replace Langara. Normally the minister would write to Langara – and to Cordoba, if he was not in Madrid. That letter would be sent by messenger here to Cartagena and given to Langara, or kept here until he arrived with the Fleet. Of course! Sent by a messenger... 'I don't need my own messenger!'

Yet a messenger of the Ministry of Marine could not be in the Consul's pay because messengers would change: there was obviously a regular messenger service between Madrid and the main ports, Cadiz, Cartagena and Barcelona, just as there was between London and Chatham, Portsmouth and Plymouth. It must be all of two hundred and fifty miles to Madrid from here, mostly across the province of Murcia, which was fairly mountainous, with a high range running parallel with the coast. The condition of Spanish roads was notorious, so the messenger would ride on horseback rather than by carriage, and would probably stay at least two nights at regular inns. Could the Consul have someone at one of the inns who abstracted letters from the messenger's bag, opened, read and re-sealed them?

As the seamen sat on forms round the bare, grease-stained table eating a breakfast of hard bread and highly spiced blood sausage, Ramage found himself listening to Stafford's cheerful chattering. A lad trained as a locksmith in Bridewell Lane and by chance swept up by a press gang and sent to sea was now sitting in a Spanish inn, armed with an

American Protection, and just as at home as if the inn had been next door to his father's shop. Yet had he signed the indentures or stayed at home the day – night, more likely – that the press gang was out, he might well have died of old age without going farther than Vauxhall Gardens, a mere five miles from his birthplace...

Well, Ramage thought as he bit savagely at the stale bread, at least Admiral Don Josef de Cordoba will have better bread to eat when he arrives, and there'll probably be plenty of bustle near the Castillo de Despenna Perros as the house is being prepared.

Seeing Jackson had finished eating, he decided to take the American with him when he went to inspect Don Josef's house. He asked the men what they had learned about the zebec's rig and, satisfied they had studied it well, told them they could spend the day wandering round the town.

Don Josef's house was an imposing building; one that befitted an admiral commanding such a large fleet. Painted white, with a flat roof, it was entirely surrounded by a covered walk formed of graceful arches, like a cloister, and standing in a couple of acres of gently sloping land, most of which was covered with trees and flowering shrubs. Even the gardener's shed was made of stone, but, Ramage noted thankfully, unlike most large Spanish houses, it was surrounded by a low hedge, not a high wall.

From what he and Jackson could see in an apparently casual stroll past the house, the preparations for Don Josef's arrival had hardly begun. Most of the windows had the green shutters closed, and except for a gardener hoeing round a double row of shrubs lining the road up to the front door, there was no one else in sight.

For four days Ramage and Jackson took a stroll past the house, and apart from the gardener slowly moving from one shrub to another, there was little to indicate that new residents were due. But on the fifth morning, a dull overcast day with a bite in the wind, showing the snow in the high mountains inland wanted to remind them of its presence, Ramage and Jackson found the great iron gates flung back, the wide, double front doors gaping, all the shutters latched back and the windows open, and signs of movement inside the house.

The gardener was still hoeing and had progressed to the shrubs just inside the gate. As the two men passed he looked up and painfully straightened his back. A shrug of his shoulders and a quick glance at the sky indicated his disapproval of whatever was going on, and Ramage called, 'Looks as if you've finished the weeding just in time!'

The old man carefully propped his hoe against the shrub and walked over to them. Ramage guessed he must be nearer eighty than seventy: his eyes were such a light brown it seemed they had faded with the years, and although the face was lined it was contented, as if a lifetime sowing seeds, nurturing them, reaping their harvest of food or beauty and then, their life over, cutting them down and planting them again, had taught him a philosophy rarely understood by other men.

'Yes, both rows finished, and now I have to trim them into shape – the sap has stopped rising now,' he explained. 'You must never trim them when the sap is rising.'

'Is that so?'

'Yes, never when the sap is rising. In the winter they sleep, and when they sleep they do not bleed their sap.'

'Does the owner of the big house like a fine garden?'

'Don Ricardo? Yes, both he and his wife love it, but they rarely come: they spend most of their days in Madrid, or wherever the Court is.'

'But now they pay you a visit?'

'Oh no – Don Ricardo has lent his house to someone: an admiral, they tell me. I don't think an admiral will worry much about a garden – he'll be used to the sea. But perhaps,' he said hopefully, almost wistfully, 'perhaps he'll find the garden a change from always looking at the waves...'

Ramage only just stopped from commenting that Spanish admirals seemed to spend more time in Madrid than at sea, and said, 'Everyone seems to be bustling at the house: the admiral is due soon?'

'In a few days. Julio – the major-domo – has just heard the admiral is sending down some of his own furniture and silver from Madrid and it has made him angry: he regards it as a criticism of Don Ricardo. But a man likes to have his own things round him – I told Julio that, but he just blasphemes.'

'It seems a lot of trouble, sending furniture from Madrid at this time of the year. After all, there's rain and snow in the mountains and it could get spoiled.'

'Yes, that's what Julio said. Anyway, the carts are at Murcia already, so they'll arrive tomorrow and we shall see. Well, now I must start over there – I don't know where all the weeds come from.'

Ramage bid him goodbye and as they walked on past the house explained to Jackson, who commented, 'Must be fine to be rich. I wonder what he's sending down – more than his favourite armchair sir, that's for certain.'

Yes...sending down his own silver Ramage could understand, but furniture! Suddenly he had a picture of an admiral sitting at his desk, reading official – and secret – letters and writing them. He'd spend much of the day at a desk with a secretary, and clerks would be there to make dozens of copies of every order to the captains of all his ships. And Don Josef de Cordoba would assume, probably quite correctly, that his friend Don Ricardo would be unlikely to have a sufficiently large desk; a desk with drawers which could be locked...

The two great carts with wide wheels which were carrying Don Josef's furniture rumbled and squeaked their way along the last couple of miles of rutted and dusty road into Cartagena with Ramage and Stafford sitting with the driver of the first one and Jackson on the second. Without any prompting from Ramage, Stafford picked up the tin mug, half-filled it yet again with brandy, and handed it to the Spanish driver with a knowing wink.

The Spaniard was already sufficiently drunk to pause for a moment before taking it; then Ramage realized the poor fellow was hard put to distinguish which of the three or four he saw was the actual mug. Finally, with a desperate lunge, he grasped it and with an appreciative grunt bent his head back and poured it down his throat. His head continued going backwards until it was hard up against the side of the cart; then, with a contented belch he fell asleep still grasping the mug.

'Wish we could pump out bilges as easily as that,' Stafford said, awed by the man's capacity.

Ramage glanced back at the second cart and Jackson saluted twice – the signal that his driver was also too drunk to know which tack he was on. Ramage nudged the Cockney.

'Carry on, Stafford. Take your time, but don't forget if I slap the canvas, stay inside until I call.'

'Aye aye, sir.'

With that Stafford quietly jumped off the cart, waited until the tail end drew level, and scrambled on board again, climbing under the canvas canopy. Ramage kept a good lookout ahead and behind, but the road was empty.

In two or three minutes Stafford was out again, walking beside the cart. 'Not in this one, sir. I'll try Jacko's.'

Ramage nodded. So far it had been all too easy: a dawn start from the inn and after only five miles they had met the two carts coming towards them from Murcia. The drivers were only too glad to give them a lift; only too glad to accept a mug of brandy and soon unable to refuse more. Now Stafford, with several pieces of soap in his pocket, was searching for the desk and, Ramage prayed, would find the keys in the drawers. The only thing that could possibly go wrong was that the admiral had decided to make do with one of Don Ricardo's tables.

Stafford climbed up on to the cart beside him, saw the Spanish driver had woken and was trying to focus his eyes on the bottle and, holding the tin mug steady in the man's hand, poured in more brandy. Ramage, almost shaking with impatience and anxiety, swore he'd wait for Stafford to report, instead of asking him at once.

The Cockney watched with admiration until the Spaniard had swilled down the drink, then took the mug and looked inquiringly at Ramage, who nodded, unsure for a moment whether Stafford was asking for a drink himself or offering Ramage one. Stafford poured a small amount into the mug and drank it, sucking his teeth appreciatively.

The horse stank, and Ramage's head ached from the sun glaring on the bleached rock lining the road and the white dust covering its surface. What little wind there was came from behind and kept the dust cloud raised by the horse's hooves just where the three men sat.

'Cor, me froat was parched, sir,' Stafford announced.

He glanced at the Spaniard who was still holding the reins but had fallen asleep again, and pulled a small box from the front of his shirt. He showed Ramage two pieces of soap, each of which bore the impressions of one large and two small keys.

'Lovely desk, sir: solid me'oghny. Four men could sleep on it. Free drawers. Top one's big – them's the impressions of each side of the key,' he said, pointing to the upper marks on the pieces of soap. Other two drawers is smaller. I reckon 'e'd keep letters and secret fings in the top one 'cause the front of the drawer is much ficker wood. Bottom two is just fick enough to take the lock.'

To Ramage, the designs on the soap seemed more beautiful and infinitely more valuable than if they had been castings of silver inlaid with gold.

'You're sure you can make keys from those impressions?' Stafford gave a contemptuous wave. 'I can make perfect keys usin' just the impression left on the back o' me 'and ten minutes after I pressed it, sir,' he said, and then looked away quickly as Ramage glanced round in surprise.

'I thought you always worked by day?'

'Only worked at night when times was 'ard, sir. Difficult not to when y'ain't got even a crust in the 'ouse.'

'I suppose not,' Ramage said noncommittally, knowing that faced with the choice he would do the same. 'But you're sure you'll be able to tackle the door locks?'

'If I can get a sight of 'em, yers: don't worry, sir.'

And instinctively Ramage knew he need not worry: a boy who had been forced to burgle to eat and then grown into a man who served cheerfully in the Navy after being swept up by a press gang and become one of the best topmen Ramage had ever seen (apart from standing by his captain when he could have gained his freedom) could deal with most situations he met.

But would the major-domo at Don Ricardo's house accept their offer of help when he found the carters were too drunk to carry the furniture?

Stafford had all the keys made within a couple of days because fortunately the major-domo had been only too glad to have the three foreign sailors help carry the furniture into the house; indeed, he had thanked them specially for driving the carts for the last mile since by then each of the carters had relapsed into a drunken stupor.

Ramage and Jackson had carried in a few chairs when suddenly Ramage had noticed that Stafford was missing and then discovered that the first time the Cockney had entered the house he had seen what Ramage had failed to notice – the key of a side door hanging on a hook on the wall. Within five minutes of first removing the key Stafford had taken it to the cart to make the impression, stowed the two pieces of soap in his little box, and returned the key to the hook.

After that it had been simple: Stafford had told Ramage the few tools he needed, and a blacksmith had been only too willing to sell some strips of metal. During the two days that Stafford had been filing away in their room at the inn, with one or two of the other sailors always lolling about casually, but keeping guard in case the innkeeper or his wife heard the rasping, Ramage or Jackson would stroll past Don Ricardo's house to see if the Admiral had arrived.

On the evening he finished the keys; Stafford came to Ramage and said: 'I'd like to try 'em tonight, sir, just to be on the safe side.'

Ramage thought for a moment. To be sure all the servants in Don Ricardo's house were asleep, Stafford would have to be out after curfew. Trying the keys meant risking being caught burgling the house and completely wrecking Ramage's plan. But if they didn't fit they'd be useless on the night they were needed – a night when there'd be no second chance.

'Very well. Go carefully, though. If you get caught...'

Ramage tried to think of a tactful way of putting it, then decided Stafford would understand anyway: 'Listen, Stafford – if you're caught, we'll have to swear we know nothing about it.'

'It's all right, sir; I understand, but don't worry. I won't get caught. If I do, I'm all prepared.' He patted the waistband of his trousers. 'Got me file an' a strip of brass, so I won't stay be'ind bars long! I'd like ter go now, sir, an 'ide up near the 'ouse a'fore curfew.'

Ramage nodded. 'Good luck.'

That night Stafford came back to the inn late and crept over to Ramage's bed to whisper, 'Fitted a treat, sir. Didn't 'ave to give even one 'o' them a wipe o' me file!'

'Good! Any trouble getting in?'

'None, sir. I 'id in that little shed place, where the gardener keeps 'is tools.'

'Fine, you can tell me more in the morning.'

Admiral Don Josef de Cordoba arrived several days later in the second of a procession of five carriages. He was spotted by Ramage, whose turn it was to make the evening check on the house and who had decided to have a walk choosing the Murcia road. All the horses were covered in dust, the drivers had handkerchieves over their noses and mouths, and from what Ramage could see of the Admiral sitting back in the carriage, he looked hot and weary.

While walking back to the inn Ramage had to decide whether or not to raid the house that night. The admiral, his staff and family – who appeared to be in the fourth coach – would be exhausted, and no doubt the servants would be too by the time all the new arrivals had washed and supped and had their clothing unpacked and put away in wardrobes and drawers.

Since the admiral had arrived a few days earlier than the Consul expected, had he brought his orders for sailing? Probably not, Ramage finally decided: with Christmas Day only four days off, he might want to be settled in for the festivities.

No, there was no need to pay a visit to the admiral's study tonight: if the sailing date hadn't been decided before he left Madrid three or four days ago it was unlikely the Fleet was intended to go to sea for two or three weeks. A sudden flurry of work would be the clearest indication that the admiral had received orders to sail.

CHAPTER FOURTEEN

Christmas Day and New Year's Day passed with Ramage and his men celebrating at the inn. The surly innkeeper's liking for free wine finally overcame his disapproval of all seamen in general and foreign seamen in particular and he joined in their party at Christmas with wary reserve. By New Year's Eve he had obviously decided the foreigners were more skilled than most in roistering, and an hour before midnight was too drunk to know what they were celebrating.

To Stafford's disgust he never offered a drink in return, so the Cockney, finally nettled by the Spaniard's refusal to pay for even half a bottle of wine, mixed the man's drinks, explaining to Jackson that he wanted to make sure the fellow felt so ill next morning he'd 'think the drummer's using his head to beat to quarters!'

Twice each day Ramage strolled down to the Muralla del Mar to look at the ships, but there was no sign of any hurried preparation for sea. At least two dozen great yards from the three-deckers had been lowered into the sea and towed to the mast house quay, where they had been hoisted up for repairs. Yet there were so few men working on them he suspected the Navy was short of wood or money to pay the men – or both.

He was also puzzled by the convoy of seventy or more transports that arrived from Barcelona the day before

Christmas. They were all heavily laden, and rumours spread through the town that they were carrying large quantities of powder and shot, provisions, a couple of battalions of troops and a regiment of Swiss mercenaries.

Not one cask of cargo nor one soldier had been sent on shore, so obviously the convoy was bound elsewhere. Since it had come from Barcelona to the eastward and was not unloading in Catagena, it must be bound westward, probably for an Atlantic port. Would the Spaniards dare sail such a convoy out through the Strait without the Fleet escorting it? Decidedly not. But where could the Spanish Government be sending troops and munitions? The West Indies? Perhaps round to Cadiz – it was easier to transport materials by sea than land – though risky. Somehow the convoy seemed more significant than the fleet.

The daily walk along the Muralla del Mar became a pleasant habit: the old man fished by night and mended his net by day, and always greeted Ramage with the comment that the guns had not fired so there'd be a good night's fishing.

Then on Monday, 30th January, the first thing Ramage saw as he came past the sail loft and looked across the ropewalk was that at least twice the usual number of men were working on the yards, several of which had already been lowered into the sea ready to be towed back to the ships. A glance at the ships themselves warned him the admiral had received orders – almost every one of them had swarms of men working aloft in the rigging while others were painting the ships from stagings slung over the side. In the Arsenal Dock several lighters were alongside being stowed with casks of provisions; others, flying warning red flags, were taking in powder.

The raid on the admiral's house must be that night. At any moment the admiral might decide to go on board his flagship. That, Ramage had known only too well from the time Stafford made the keys, was the greatest threat to his plan.

Originally he'd assumed the admiral would work at the house, and only when Stafford had left to test the new keys in the locks had Ramage realized that, although the admiral was living in the house, there was no reason why he should not spend the day working in his flagship, returning to the house each night. Fortunately a close watch had shown that although the admiral had gone out to the flagship for two hours the day after he arrived, he had not been on board since. And, significantly, his flag officers and captains, too, were all living on shore in hotels and houses.

However, since the admiral had obviously given orders for the refitting to be speeded up he might well spend more time on board – and keep his documents locked up in the flagship... Ramage hurried back to the inn to check whether the admiral had gone out to the ship. If he had, then Ramage knew his whole plan was wrecked.

The gardener's hut was hot and smelly: obviously a donkey had recently spent several weeks in it, but since there was no window it was easy to shield the flickering candle. Ramage knew that even Jackson was on edge as they both waited for Stafford's tap on the door, signalling that he had returned from his raid on the house.

When the tap came both men jumped nervously and then grinned at each other shamefacedly. Jackson held a tin mug over the candle flame and stood shielding the remaining faint light with his body as Ramage quickly opened the door. Stafford slipped in and blinked as Jackson lifted the mug and the hut lit up. He handed Ramage a small bundle of papers.

'No trouble, sir. All in the top drawer. Only writin' paper, quills, bottle o' ink, sealin' wax, candle an' sandbox in the uvver drawers.'

Hurriedly Ramage glanced through the letters, careful to keep them in the right order. All had been sealed with red wax and several bore the superscription 'Ministry of Marine'. The first two were routine letters telling Cordoba's predecessor, Langara, that his request for more rope was refused because none was available, and he would have to make do with the gunpowder he had because although the Minister knew it was 'somewhat deficient in quality', it was the best that could be obtained. The third letter, addressed to Cordoba and signed by Langara in his new role as Minister of Marine, was brief, and after the usual polite introduction it said:

'His Catholic Majesty has indicated to the Minister of Marine that it is His Royal pleasure that the Fleet under your command should complete its refit with all despatch and sail under your command from Cartagena at the latest by 1st February to join those of His Catholic Majesty's ships already at Cadiz, which you will also take under your command. Orders have been sent ensuring these ships are ready for sea. Immediately upon your arrival at Cadiz you will report the fact to me, keeping your Fleet at twelve hours' readiness to sail, and further instructions will be sent to you...'

1st February – in two days' time. And for Cadiz, one of the greatest natural harbours on the Atlantic coast and Spain's main naval base! There must be quite a few sail of the line there already. Once they were joined by Cordoba's fleet,

His Catholic Majesty would have something like an Armada ready. To do what?

Was this part of a great joint French and Spanish plan to launch an invasion of England or, more likely, Ireland? Would the ships, full of troops, sail from Cadiz and drive off the blockading British squadron at Brest and let out the French Fleet, so the combined fleets could sweep up the Channel to carry out a plan agreed by France and Spain aimed at destroying Britain? It must be something as vast as that for Spain to risk her whole fleet. They wouldn't forget what happened the last time they sailed an Armada...

Ramage suddenly felt chilled as he realized the fate of England might – probably did – rest on how quickly Sir John Jervis received the information written on the piece of paper in his hand, and which he had just read in a stinking gardener's hut by the light of half an inch of guttering candle.

After glancing through the rest of the documents he told Stafford to hold the letter while he unscrewed the cap of a tiny ink bottle, took a short quill pen from inside his hat, smoothed out a piece of paper he had brought with him specially for the purpose, and copied out the exact wording of the important part of the order. He then refolded the original order, put it under the letters relating to rope and gunpowder, and gave the bundle back to Stafford. 'Thanks. Go back to the inn when you've returned them. Right, Jackson, douse that candle and bring it with you.'

Although there was a curfew there were few patrols in the streets to enforce it and the rope which one of the seaman had stolen from the dockyard was ready to be dropped from the window of their room when Ramage and Jackson arrived at the inn, followed a few minutes later by Stafford.

Lying on his bed in the darkness, Ramage had great difficulty in controlling his excitement: he was shivering, although hot from shinning up the rope. His plan had worked perfectly: in his pocket he had a copy of the order to Cordoba. But now he realized he had made yet another mistake. He'd intended to steal a zebec as soon as he knew the date the fleet was to sail, and make for Gibraltar. He should have guessed there'd be no exact date; that Cordoba's orders would tell him to sail by a certain date. Now what the devil should he do? Today was 30th January and he could go to Gibraltar with the bare information that the Spaniards were under orders to sail within two days, even though it was extremely doubtful they'd be ready and the Spanish national habit of mañana and their Navy's tradition of delay in getting to sea made the date mentioned in the King's order more of an optimistic hope than a definite date in the calendar. And what had Cordoba replied to the Minister of Marine? That he could sail by then, or giving a later date?

He sat up suddenly, realizing there was really no problem. Even if he left a couple of days ahead of the Spanish Fleet they could easily overtake him if he ran into a calm or strong headwinds, and anyway it'd probably take several days to locate Sir John Jervis. It was much more important that Sir John should know the Spanish Government's intentions than the precise date they were to be carried out.

'Jackson,' he whispered, 'get dressed, and tell the rest of them to get dressed, too.'

'I haven't undressed, sir,' said Jackson, 'but I'll rouse out the others.'

He felt a moment of irritation. The American didn't know what was written in Cordoba's orders but seemed to have some sixth sense when there was the chance of a sudden emergency.

The men, dressed quickly and gathered round Ramage, who whispered:

'We are sailing for Gibraltar at once. La Providencia is still down at the quay, it's eleven o'clock, and the crew will probably be drunk. We've got to board and sail in absolute silence. If the Spaniards suspect anything, we'll be blown out of the water before we get past the Santa Anna Fort. Use your knives: no shouting by anyone. We'll leave here one at a time and go down to the quay. Watch out for patrols. Meet at the buttress where the old fisherman mends his nets. And don't forget – over the city wall; don't try marching out through the gate!

'When I give the word, we all board amidships: the crew will probably be asleep aft, if they're on board at all.'

Twenty minutes later the seven men were crouching beside the huge buttress in the shadow of the city wall, the three masts and long lateen yards of La Providencia a few yards away jutting at odd angles, black and stark against the southern horizon. The wind – what there was of it – was light and from the north, Ramage noted thankfully. Once clear of the quay and the high land behind him, he'd find it fresher, and the hills flanking the harbour would funnel it at the entrance. He could just make out the dark mass of Punta Santa Anna on his left and Punta de Navidad on his right. He had to pass at least six batteries and two forts. Perhaps the sentries would be dozing...

He looked both ways along the quay and saw there was no one in sight, and as he whispered, 'Now!' the men glided bare-footed across the quay towards the zebec, fanning out slightly so they could all climb over the bulwark at the same time. There was absolute silence except for the monotonous clacking of the frogs, the metallic buzzing of cicadas and the slapping of wavelets against the quay.

With his throwing knife grasped in his right hand Ramage quietly climbed over the bulwark, put his boots down gently, and followed by the rest of the men crept aft under the overhanging quarterdeck. He was frightened now: up to that moment he'd been too busy to think about danger. Now the dagger-in-hand creeping, like an assassin at work, reminded him of the soft days at the inn. Once again sudden death was standing a watch with him, and the thudding of his heart seemed loud enough to rouse out the Spaniards.

It was almost impossible to see, and there was a great danger his men might attack each other by mistake. As his foot suddenly touched something soft he lunged down with his knife and there was a thud and a shock through his arm as the blade pierced a mattress and stuck in the deck. In a moment he'd struck twice more, moving along each time, but there was no one on the mattress. A similar thud to his left warned him one of the other men was doing the same thing. He crept on, and as his eyes grew accustomed to the intense darkness he could make out small, lighter squares on either side, indicating the position of the gun ports. Another mattress at his feet and again he stabbed downwards, but there was no one on it. He passed two ports and was abreast the last one when he felt yet another mattress and again the knife plunged, to bury its point in the wooden deck. Men were moving aft level with him. In a moment his groping hand touched the transom.

'Found anyone?' he whispered.

The men hissed their replies. Mattresses, but no Spaniards. Where the hell were they? Surely not down in the hold or on the fo'c'sle? Hurriedly he ordered Fuller and Jensen to search the fo'c'sle and then stand by the foremast, Rossi and Stafford to check in the hold before going to the main mast, and Maxton and Jackson to cast off the lines – the breeze would blow the zebec clear of the quay.

Ramage then crept out from under the quarterdeck, climbed the ladder and hurried aft to the tiller, which curved up from deck level just abaft the mizzen. A few moments later he heard a heavy rope splashing into the water and saw a man jump back on board.

'All clear aft, sir,' Jackson called in a low voice, and another splash was followed by Maxton's arrival beside him reporting all clear forward.

The zebec's high stern caught most of the breeze and started to swing out while the forward part of the ship, being lower, was still in the lee of the quay. So far so good. The pivoting effect of the stern meant her bow was heading in towards the quay. No problem about that.

'Right, Maxton: get for'ard and tell 'em to set the foresail and sheet it in smartly. Jackson – take the helm. Let her head fall off. Keep over to the eastern side in case the wind backs – I don't want to tack or wear this thing in the dark.'

A flapping from forward and a dark triangle unfolding against the sky, blotting out the stars, showed the foresail was set, and a few moments later there was the squeak of ropes rendering through blocks as they trimmed it.

The quay was now receding fast and the zebec's bow swung seaward under the pressure of the sail. She gathered way and the rudder began to get a grip on the water.

'Stafford!' he whispered sharply. 'Let fall the mainsail. Lively now!'

The mainsail, only slightly larger than the foresail, flopped down like a large sheet being shaken out of a window and began to slat. Once out of the lee of the quay the wind was fresher, as Ramage had anticipated, and while the men sheeted home the sail and braced the yard the zebec gathered way and he could hear the crisp bubbling of the water round the stern.

Ramage hurried to the tiller. 'Right, Jackson: set the mizzen – I'll take the helm.'

The tiller was surprisingly light compared with the Kathleen's. The mizzen suddenly dropping down overhead made him jump but fear had gone: he had too much to think about. High up to starboard, outlined faintly against the stars, he could see the Castillo de Galeras towering over the harbour more than six hundred feet up, with the Apostolado Battery almost at sea level below it. He could see a light at the   Battery – were the sentries alert and even at this moment raising the alarm? Or would they be so accustomed to looking for a ship trying to enter that they'd never think of one trying to leave?

Three minutes since the foresail was sheeted home: more than time enough for the Spaniards to have loaded the guns. For a moment he imagined a dozen gun captains kneeling down, sighting along a dozen barrels, the point of aim being the zebec.

As he pushed the tiller over, heading directly for the entrance, the wind was right aft and the sails trimmed too flat: a fluky puff of wind would gybe the zebec all standing. If the masts went by the board under the muzzles of the batteries...

'Jackson! Ease all sheets and vangs – smartly, now!'

The Apostolado Battery abeam to starboard and a light showing in the window of the soldiers' hut. On the starboard bow he could distinguish the outline of Punta de Navidad sloping from three hundred feet right down to the sea level. No more batteries to starboard until he'd rounded the point, but on the other side of the harbour the San Leandro must be almost abeam now – though he couldn't pick it out – with the Santa Florentina beyond and then the Fort of Santa Anna.

The zebec began to pitch slightly as she met the swell waves rolling lazily into the harbour entrance from the open sea beyond. The three triangular sails seemed enormous against the sky, blotting out whole constellations of stars. For a moment it seemed impossible the sentries at the batteries would miss seeing them; then he realized they would hardly show against the black hills on either side. A sharp-eyed man more than six hundred feet up in the Castillo could see the ship as a dark patch against a shiny sea reflecting the starlight and pewtered by the wind, and he might also see her wake.

Ropes squealing through blocks again, and the three triangles of the sails broadened out and curved, the hard edges rounding as the canvas bellied. Ramage was startled at the way the zebec suddenly picked up speed: already the Apostolado Battery was on the starboard quarter and he realized he'd passed most of the Spanish Fleet anchored over to larboard because they were dark against the shadows of hills behind them. Had they guard boats out, rowing round the harbour? Give me three minutes, he prayed: then it won't matter if the alarm is raised – the artillery men at the barracks wouldn't have time to load and train the guns. But no – with this wind an alert frigate could slip its cable and get out of the harbour only too easily and give chase...

Maxton, the West Indian, was standing beside him. 'Small boat dead ahead, sir! Forty, maybe fifty yards!'

Ramage leaned against the tiller to heave it to larboard. The sweeping sheer of the zebec cocked the bow up so high it was difficult to see anything close ahead, but Maxton, leaning over the bulwark, said 'You'll pass it twenty yards off, sir!'

'How many men in it?'

'Only one, sir – he's fishing, I think.'

The old fisherman! The guns hadn't fired and he'd be out with his nets. There was a cheery hail and Ramage stuck a finger in his mouth so the old man should not recognize his voice. 'Good fishing – see you tomorrow. Save a big one for us!'

'Certainly, I will!' the old man called back. 'It's good fishing – the guns haven't fired, you understand?'

By then the zebec had left him astern, cheerfully unconcerned. Ramage knew he wouldn't raise the alarm, yet the sentries might have heard the shouting. But what if they did?

There was probably an order against ships leaving the harbour at night, but what would they make of a friendly exchange spoken in Spanish between an old fisherman and a zebec? They'd hesitate before raising the alarm – he hoped.

Now he could just make out the Fort at the end of Punta Santa Anna and then Punta Trinca Botijas opening out beyond Cala Cortina, a tiny bay cut sharply into the coast between the two points.

Pale green sparks in the water began to stream outwards from the zebec's hull and, leaving the tiller for a moment, Ramage ran to the taffrail and looked astern. The zebec's wake was a pale green swathe in the water and there was a wide band round the entire waterline. Damn and blast, what a time to run into phosphorescence!

The Fort was abeam to larboard, so he must have passed Punta Navidad and was now in range of the Navidad Battery beyond and approaching the one on Punta Podadera. Those two and the battery on the other headland were the only ones left.

Jackson said, as if to himself, 'They'd never hit us now, even if they knew we were here.'

Ramage was annoyed with himself for having stayed at the tiller when Jackson could have taken over. 'Here – take the helm.'

He sent Stafford to rummage below for lanterns, but in the meantime without a binnacle light Jackson would have to steer by the stars. Once through the entrance the course was west-south-west to cover the seventy-five miles across the huge shallow bay to Cabo de Gata. Gibraltar was 165 miles farther on. They'd cross Almeria Bay, passing three small headlands on the Plain of Almeria, and from there he'd see the six big peaks of the Sierra Nevada bearing due north, the two highest, Pico Veleta and Cerro Mulahacen, reaching up more than eleven thousand feet After that the next sight of land would be the towering rocky mass of Europa Point, the southern end of Gibraltar, with Blackstrap Bay to the north of it on the Mediterranean side, and the rounded hills of Africa across the Strait.

Poor old Blackstrap Bay, Ramage mused: its name was taken in vain by almost every sailor in the Navy. When Spanish wine was substituted for grog, the sailors contemptuously referred to it as 'Blackstrap' – indeed, going to the Mediterranean was often termed 'being Blackstrapped'. And in a calm the strong east-going current always flowing from the Atlantic often carried a ship past Gibraltar into the Mediterreanean, and she had to spend days beating back both against current and wind – unless a convenient Levanter blew. That too was called being 'Blackstrapped', since the unfortunate ship's company spent their time gazing at Blackstrap Bay and Europa Point, getting a slightly different view each time they tacked.

Nevertheless he'd be dam' glad when he could see that view; and La Providencia has such a shallow draught that if the wind was light he could creep close in along the coast, where the current was much weaker and one could some times even find a counter-current.

Stafford came up with a lantern, opened the glass-fronted door in the binnacle and put it inside so its light shone on to the compass.

Punta Podadera was now on the starboard quarter and as they cleared the high land, bringing the wind on to the beam, Ramage gave more orders for trimming the sails. The sea was calm, apart from a few low swell waves, and La Providencia gave the impression of skating along on the water like a flat stone skimmed across a pond, whereas by comparison the Kathleen, with her deeper draught and vastly different rig, ploughed her way through the sea. Ramage looked at his watch. An hour ago he had been lying on his bed in the inn, wondering what to do next. He wished he'd remembered to leave a note for the American Consul.

CHAPTER FIFTEEN

The Convent was a five-minute walk from the Commissioner's office. Ramage raised a hand to hail a passing carriage, realized he had no money and began striding up the steep cobbled slope of Convent Lane. With an irritation verging on petulance he reviewed his meeting with the Commissioner. It had begun with almost effusive congratulations, but the old fool ended up being damned stuffy. After implying that delaying sailing for even half an hour to visit The Convent would certainly let Cordoba's Fleet escape through the Strait, and probably allow Napoleon to cross the Channel as well, he'd even hinted that young officers only visited Gibraltar's Convent 'to keep up with the right people'.

A mixture of excitement and nervousness made Ramage begin a laugh which he only managed to choke when he saw the frightened look on the hideously wrinkled face of an old woman in a doorway. She was offering him a penn'orth of sticky dates from a greasy wicker basket that looked like an asylum for every fly on the Barbary Coast, but snatched it away when she looked into his eyes and hurriedly crossed herself with her free hand.

At the top of the lane Ramage turned left into Main Street and was promptly surrounded by a crowd of ragged higglers who with strident Spanish voices and clutching hands were peddling everything from corn cures and

Crucifixes to demijohns of arrack, their fervour and glittering eyes reminding Ramage of what it must have been like to face the Inquisition.

As he walked through the Convent's big double doors the two sentries rattled their muskets in faultless salutes which nevertheless subtly conveyed that soldiers cared little for naval officers and hardly at all for young lieutenants.

Inside the hall a wizened little man whose ancient wig had for years been a martyr to incipient moulting stood up and cautiously inquired the purpose of the young lieutenant's visit. A lifetime at the job had obviously taught him to take nothing for granted: one elegantly dressed gentleman with languid voice and gold-topped cane might demand an audience with the Governor only to pass a forged letter of credit, while the next could be the Governor's long-awaited cousin. The poor fellow had his carefully enunciated motto written all over him: You Cannot Be Too Careful.

Reluctantly Ramage had to give his name while explaining his business but emphasized it did not matter since he was only a messenger. The old man kept nodding like a pigeon gleaning a newly cut cornfield then, after motioning Ramage to a chair, hurried off down an apparently endless corridor.

Ramage deliberately made his thoughts wander to ease the tension. Why was the Governor's residence called The Convent? He'd always intended to ask someone. The chapel next door was originally a Franciscan friary... In Spanish a monastery usually meant the home of a religious order whose members never went outside, while those free to travel – like the Francisans – lived in a convent. How many governors had bored their guests at dinner with weary jokes about nuns and –

The little man was beckoning him from the far end of the corridor with the nearest he dare get to a show of impatience and Ramage managed to stop himself leaping up like an eager schoolboy. Instead he rose with carefully controlled movements, composed his face in a frown he knew would make his cheek muscles ache within a couple of minutes and walked along the corridor, hat tucked under the left arm, his hand holding the scabbard of his sword. Plonk, plonk, plonk: he walked heavily, hoping the jarring of his heels on the mosaic floor would stifle the inane giggle lurking just under his Adam's Apple.

From the moment the Commissioner had told him, Ramage had deliberately shut the picture from his mind; all the way up Convent Lane he'd forced himself to think of something else. Even waiting there in the chair he'd conjectured about The Convent. And now... The little man scurrying along ahead stopped every few paces and peered back to make sure he was following as though scared he'd bolt through a door. Ramage wanted to give him a hearty pat on the back but instead mustered an even fiercer frown and snarled: 'Don't walk so damned fast, I've only got two legs.'

'Oh, quite, quite sir, I'm very sorry,' the little man said sympathetically as if it was the result of battle wounds.

Up a pair of stairs and the corridor was narrower, the closely spaced doors indicating the rooms were smaller, and he guessed they were now in the private part of the residence.

The little man paused at a door, knocked and before Ramage could stop him walked into the room and announced in a neutral voice that showed he had not bothered to mention the name earlier:

'Lieutenant Ramage.'

After the gloomy corridors the room was almost dazzlingly bright and for a moment Ramage stood blinking as the door closed softly behind him.

'You look like an owl who's just woken up,' she said and ran over to fling herself into his arms. His hat went flying, the scabbard dropped with a clang, and they clung to each other with that desperate urgency reserved for lovers and those who are drowning.

It seemed hours later – hours during which he wanted to tear off the clothes separating their bodies, hours after scores of kisses on her eyes, mouth and brow, hours after he'd wiped tears surreptitiously from his eyes and openly from hers, hours after the waves of exhilarating dizziness had gone, that she looked up at him and whispered.

'My dearest, I thought you were dead – and then that silly man...' she sobbed but there were no tears or sadness now, only wonder, almost unbelief, '...that silly man tells me there's a naval officer to see me and I...'

'You what?'

'I had a terrible premonition he was going to tell me they'd heard you were dead.'

'And when you saw it was me, all you could say was I looked like an owl!'

'An owl?'

He pushed her away and held her at arm's length. There was no mistaking the puzzled expression. Could it...?

'What did you say when I came in?' he asked gently.

'I said nothing. I was so shocked, so – well, I couldn't believe – '

'You don't remember saying, "You look like an owl who's just woken up"?'

'Of course I didn't say that!'

Again the picture came back to him: a picture of battle when a Marine was spun round by a shot which slashed off his hand at the wrist, and as he staggered across the deck holding the stump from which the blood spurted he said to Ramage in a conversational tone, 'I was born out of wedlock, you see, sir; they never knew for certain who me father was...'

The irrelevant remarks of someone experiencing a severe shock. At this revelation of the intensity of her love for him he suddenly felt frightened and inadequate and unworthy, forgetting it equalled his own for her.

'But you look like an owl now!'

He looked down at her smile which was also an impudent grin: happiness sparkled in the large brown eyes and showed in the delicate flush over the high cheekbones. The impudence was in the arch of the eyebrows and the curve of her lips. He held her tightly and at that instant there was a harsh metallic boom above and a ripping noise at his back. Giving her a violent push out of danger's way he spun round, his hand going instinctively to the hilt of his sword. But even before he could draw it she was standing four paces away clapping her hands and laughing until tears ran down her cheeks. 'It's one o'clock, my love!' she gasped. 'The chapel bell!'

'And I think I've split my new coat,' he said ruefully.

She danced round behind him, 'And you have! The stitching of the seam!'

Even as he joined in her laughter he realized within an hour he must sail. Within ten minutes he must say goodbye.

'My lovely little Tuscan czarina, when you've stopped examining the proof of my passion, can you get someone to mend it?'

She eyed him with feigned doubt, hand to her chin, and secretly marvelling that every time she looked at him – a man she loved so desperately and pictured almost every waking moment – his face or body revealed something new – often startling, always thrilling and sometimes frightening. His eyes, set deep under the brow, sometimes let her see into his soul; at other times they were a barrier which shut her out. The scar on his brow was a weathercock to his mood – anger tautened the skin, driving out the blood, making it a hard white line. His mouth – did he realize a slight movement of his lips made him as remote and forbidding as the moon – or so close she felt they were one? A thin face – yes, but the jawbone, like the scar, became a hard, bloodless line when anger tightened the muscles and sharpened the angles so it seemed cast in steel. It was a face a woman could only love or hate with a great passion; the face of a man to whom no one could be indifferent.

She saw he was puzzled, waiting for an answer.

'No, I like your passion as it is, even if it tears easily. But when it does want mending, I'll do it.'

'Gianna – '

'Nee-co-lass,' she mimicked the serious note, 'let's join the Governor: he insists on punctuality at meals. I'll be your seamstress this afternoon. Oh, don't look so worried – it's only the stitching!'

He grinned nervously as he sought a way to explain and then blurted out: 'No, it's not that. I can't stay.'

'Never mind, we'll do it this evening then.'

'I'll be away sometime…'

She took his hand, made him sit in an armchair and curled up at his feet, her head resting against his knees.

'Tell me what happened,' she said quietly, 'and why you have to leave so soon.'

He traced with his finger the line of her eyebrows, the tiny Roman nose, the soft and moist lips and the high cheek-bones, and then she reached up to take his hand and press it to her breast, as if to comfort him.

'Was it too awful, caro mio?'

'No,' he said quickly, realizing she'd misunderstood his silence. 'No, it was perfectly simple.' Briefly he described the Kathleen's capture, the way Jackson had helped him pose as an American, and their release in Cartagena. He omitted the raid on Cordoba's house and the information he discovered, and told her how they had stolen La Providencia and sailed to Gibraltar.

'But why stay so long in Cartagena? Weeks and weeks! Surely you could have stolen a ship earlier?'

'The Spanish Fleet was there: I wanted to find out when they'd sail and where they were bound?'

She spotted the flaw before he did.

'But how could you do that without waiting for them to sail and see which way they went? They haven't sailed, have they?'

Ramage cursed his wayward tongue which was talking him into a dangerous situation: the only other person in Gibraltar who knew of Cordoba's orders was the Commissioner, who'd been emphatic that the knowledge must be kept absolutely secret. The whole of Gibraltar, he'd said bitterly, was swarming with spies and the Governor's circle of friends talked too freely.

'Well,' he said lamely, 'I found out something which will interest Sir John, but you mustn't mention it. Now – and this is absolutely secret too – I must find Sir John and tell him.'

'But, my love,' she said with quiet irony, 'all you've told me so far is that I've got to keep secret the fact you know a secret!'

'And that's quite enough for now!'

She looked up with eyes unnaturally bright with tears, but in them he saw anger as well as unhappiness.

'So even though I am the ruler of a state which has joined England as an ally, I can't be trusted with some silly little secret?'

Anger, bitterness, hurt – yes, and a touch of patrician arrogance. A few moments ago they had been as one person; now a stranger sat at his feet.

'I – well, the Commissioner gave me strict orders. Not even the Governor knows.'

'Very well,' she said coldly. 'You found out this information, so let's not talk any more of that. But why are you the messenger boy running off to find Sir John? Make the Commissioner send someone else. You deserve a rest: for months you've been risking your life – first rescuing me, then capturing La Sabina, then playing the spy at Cartagena. Why,' she added with a shiver, 'if the Spaniards had discovered you weren't an American – '

'I'd have been shot, but I wasn't. And I arrive here to find you waiting for me! Incidentally, young lady' – he snatched the chance of changing the subject – 'why are you here and not in England?'

She shrugged her shoulders gracefully – and coldly and remotely. Her voice was flat and neutral. She was a stranger, the ruler of Volterra and, he thought, no longer a woman.

'Very well, you may change the subject When the Apollo arrived here she had to wait two weeks. By then we heard the Kathleen had been captured. I wasn't in a hurry to go to England so I decided to stay – I was curious to know whether you were alive or dead.'

'Curious'. The word stabbed where he had no protection. Now did it help that he knew she was deeply hurt; unable to understand the demands of the service. And her pose of indifference was truly regal: even though she was sitting at his feet he felt for a moment as though their positions were reversed and he was a humble (and errant) subject kneeling before the ruler of the state of Volterra.

'And Antonio?' he asked, numbed and hardly thinking what he was saying.

'He went in the Apollo. He wanted to stay but I told him to go to London as my Minister Plenipotentiary to your King, so that he can draw up the draft for the alliance.'

It was a proud little speech but the ruler became a girl once again when he pictured Antonio as the Minister of an already enemy-occupied state of 20,000 people arguing the terms and wording of Volterra's treaty with a Britain which was already fighting the combined strength of France and Spain and for whom Volterra was simply another debit entry in an already overloaded budget.

'How could you persuade the Spanish you were an American when you were wearing that uniform?'

She was holding out a very small and rapidly withering olive branch but he reached for it eagerly.

'I was wearing a seaman's rig. I've just bought this one. A lieutenant about my size – a bit narrower across the shoulders, rather! – just had it delivered from the tailor.'

'He was kind to let you have it.'

'He wasn't really; in fact he refused, but the Commissioner ordered him to sell it to me.'

'Your Commissioner is fond of giving unpleasant orders…'

'I'm afraid so,' Ramage said hypocritically. 'But – well, when you had to give unpleasant orders to anyone in Volterra it didn't occur to you they wouldn't be obeyed, although probably you didn't enjoy giving them…'

'That's true, I suppose it's the same thing, really,' she admitted.

'Absolutely the same. The foundations of a navy or a state – or even a family – rests on discipline,' he said pompously.

'Except that I love you.'

There was defiance in her voice and he knew that single fact meant she'd accept neither rules nor obstacles. Fearing she'd make the Governor use his influence to have another lieutenant sent to Sir John, Ramage kissed her and bruised both their lips as the clock struck again and made them jump.

Nearly an hour gone: the Commissioner would be watching the anchorage. He stood up, helping her to her feet, and before she could say anything, kissed her hard again, then gripped her tightly so she could not look into his eyes and began talking quickly in a low, urgent voice, as though he had to compress a lifetime into the remaining minutes.

As he walked down the worn and slimy steps of Ragged Staff Wharf Ramage felt the same emptiness that almost every man experienced when going back to sea in wartime: he was leaving someone he loved, drawn away by some inner compulsion towards – well, duty was a pompous sort of word and only a tenth of it. That there'd be weeks, perhaps months, of discomfort and monotony was so certain that brief moments of danger would come as a relief, like the sharp taste in the mouth after the long diet of dreary, barely eatable salt food that drove seamen to chew tobacco. But no man had ever found anything to shew, drink, do or say that eased the ache of knowing the farewell might also be the final one. It was probably worse for the women who were left behind, never knowing whether, even as they sat with their memories, their men had been left unscathed by battle, disease or accident.

So what was he really looking for out on the ocean? Honour and glory, the power over men that came with command, the almost erotic thrill of fear in battle? He was concentrating so hard on giving himself an honest answer that his heel slipped off the edge of a step and he nearly fell, yet even while regaining his balance he knew the answer was 'No' in each case.

What stopped him from asking to go on to half pay (or resigning his commission) and returning to England, to the life of a gentleman, helping Father run the estates and perhaps dabbling in politics? There'd be no discredit in that (except dabbling in politics, and he rejected the idea) nor difficulty in arranging it. The Navy had far too many young lieutenants – at least a quarter of them were always unemployed, haunting the Admiralty or badgering friends with 'interest' to write to the First Lord to get them a berth. He shrugged his shoulders and felt a few more stitches splitting in his coat. Blast the fool who'd sold it him and triple blast his tailor, and whoever made the thread could rot in hell.

He suddenly realized that for some seconds he'd been standing and staring at a dead cat floating in the water, and glanced up to see Maxton holding the boat alongside, his glistening brown face split with a grin of pleasure. Jackson, watching him curiously and probably trying to fathom his thoughts, was at the tiller and the rest of the men who had been with him at Cartagena were manning the oars. All of them were rigged out in new blue shirts and white duck trousers, and were freshly shaven. He climbed in, nodded, and a few moments later the boat was being rowed briskly across the anchorage.

Perhaps if he knew the answer he could leave the sea. But would finding the answer be like finding the Golden Fleece the very fact of succeeding meant there was nothing more to do with your life: no spur, no goal, no purpose…?

He turned for one last unhurried look at Gibraltar, and for a moment he was a child again, lying flat on his stomach on a Cornish beach staring up at a great boulder only a few feet away. The houses clustered on the steep sides were tiny limpets; the grey defensive walls studded with embrasures just cracks in the rock lined with sea snails. Was Gianna watching from a balcony of The Convent? He wasn't too sure – they'd parted as both lovers and strangers; there'd been no time for the tranquil minutes which –

He glanced up to see La Providencia at anchor a hundred yards away. He hoped Sir John would buy her into the service. Even without him foregoing his share of the prize money, the six men now in the boat would each get a few hundred pounds; more than they'd ever earn in a lifetime as seamen.

'She served us well.'

'Aye, sir,' Jackson said wistfully. 'I wouldn't mind having her as a privateer!'

In taking only three days and four nights from Cartagena La Providencia had made a fast passage in such light winds and Ramage, like the Commissioner, could only pray the Spanish Fleet had been delayed in leaving, then met the same humbugging winds, and found the convoy of seventy transports – if they sailed at the same time – as slow, mulish and stupid as convoys of transports usually were.

But the chances that they'd have a slow passage were slight – the wind had now gone east and was becoming squally, and the wispy clouds beginning to stream westward from the peaks of Gibraltar, like steam from a boiling kettle, were a warning that a strong easterly wind, the Levanter, was already on its way across the Mediterranean.

Bringing heavy rain and poor visibility, it was just the wind to let Cordoba's Fleet scurry through the Strait.

As he'd brought La Providencia round the great craggy Europa Point, close in along Dead Man's Beach and up to Rosin Bay, he'd been startled to see that, with one exception, there wasn't a ship o' war at anchor in the Bay: obviously every available vessel was at sea, either helping Commodore Nelson evacuate the Mediterranean or with Sir John Jervis.

The boat came alongside and the men's grins were wider than ever as Ramage scrambled up the side battens to the trilling of bosun's calls. It was childish, but one of the best things about commanding a ship was being piped on board...

A few moments later he was returning Southwick's salute and shaking him by the hand while the ship's company, drawn up on deck in two ranks, began a wild, spontaneous cheering that Southwick did nothing to stop.

'Welcome back on board, sir: the Kathleen hasn't been the same without you!'

Ramage blinked and thought irrelevantly of the split seam in his coat. Jackson had been the first to spot the Kathleen at anchor as La Providencia rounded Europa Point, and Ramage had been both delighted and nervous until he'd reached the Commissioner's office and been told the frigate Hotspur had recaptured both the Kathleen and the Spanish frigate towing her into Barcelona, and freed all her crew, who were prisoners in the frigate. His nervousness vanished completely when the Commissioner, after hearing about Cordoba's instructions, had ordered him to resume command and find Sir John 'with all despatch'.

But he hadn't anticipated such a home-coming, for his return to the cutter was just that, and stood open-mouthed at the gangway as the men cheered again and again. By now Jackson and the gig's crew had come on board and were standing to one side, and as Ramage waved to include them the ship's company roared their approval.

Southwick said above the din, 'I think they'd appreciate a few words, sir!'

Ramage jumped up on top of a carronade and held up his hand for silence. He tried to look grim and succeeded: the lean face, hard eyes, the diagonal slash of the scar light against the tan, lips compressed and muscles of the jaw taut, made him look both ruthless and determined.

He held up his hand for silence.

'You must be the most stupid ship's company it's ever been the misfortune of any man to command,' he said harshly.

The smiles vanished. Every man looked crestfallen, like an errant schoolboy.

'I've tried to kill you with La Sabina and failed. I thought I'd get a second chance with the two frigates but they turned out to be British. I couldn't be bothered the third time when we met the Spanish Fleet. Now you are so dam' stupid you cheer me when I come back again.'

With that the men began roaring with laughter and, breaking ranks, surged round him, several of them shouting ' 've another go, sir!'

'I'm going to! But this time – and I'm not joking now – we'll probably be playing chase with the Santísima Trinidad.' He paused to let it sink in. 'In case you've forgotten, she carries 130 guns. Once we've dealt with her there'll be six more each of 112 guns, and two with eighty. Then if you've still got any fire left in your bellies, there'll be eighteen more seventy-fours. But don't think there'll be any time for grog after that because you'll still have a few dozen frigates left to bring into Gibraltar or the Tagus!'

If he thought the list would have a sobering effect he was mistaken: the men promptly began cheering again and he glimpsed Southwick rubbing his hands in a familar way. If every Spanish ship's company had even half their spirit, he reflected, Cordoba's great fleet would be invincible. Even as the men cheered, Ramage pictured Cordoba's Fleet leaving Cadiz and joining the French Fleet at Brest for an attempted invasion of England. French troops marching through Cornwall, looting and burning St Kew Hall, and probably guillotining his father for being both an earl and an admiral. The men fell silent and he realized his thoughts showed in his face. Well, despite the need for secrecy on shore, there was no harm in telling them what it was all about, since they'd be at sea in fifteen minutes.

'Now listen carefully. I've told you the size of the Spanish Fleet, and Jackson and the others have probably described what it looked like at anchor in Cartagena. What Jackson and the others don't know is the whole Fleet was under orders to sail the day before yesterday. The Spanish Admiral has orders to make for Cadiz, so any minute you're likely to see 'em pass Europa Point and out through The Gut.'

He gestured towards the grey mountains of Africa, less than a dozen miles across the Strait. 'If they pass through there before we can get out, find Sir John and warn him then only the Spanish and French know what the consequences will be. If a Spanish Fleet that size picks up troops at Cadiz and sails north to raise the blockade of Brest and let the French Fleet join them, then there's very little to stop them invading England: they'd total more than fifty sail of the line. To stop Cordoba's twenty-seven sail of the line getting to Cadiz Sir John has only eleven, as far as we know. There you are, men: our job is to warn Sir John, but since we don't even know where he is, we haven't a moment to waste... Mr Southwick! Let's get under way!'

With that he jumped down from the bulwark feeling as melodramatic as an actor who'd just recited Henry Vs speech on the eve of St Crispin's Day – though omitting the beginning, 'He which hath no stomach to this fight, let him depart...'

As he walked to the companionway, the men still cheering, he thought wrily of an earlier phrase in the play, 'I would give all my fame for a pot of ale, and safety.' His fame was such that he'd need only a small pot of very poor ale.

Ramage took off his sword in the tiny cabin and when Jackson brought down a large leather pouch, he unlocked it and transferred the books and documents it contained to his desk. The key was still in the lock of the drawer – only the little lead-lined box usually kept beneath the desk and now sunk in about a thousand fathoms was missing. He'd have to get another made.

He sat down heavily. It was not just physical weariness: his brain was tired. He longed for a week's rest with no decisions to be made, no need to be constantly goading himself, and free from the constant fear that a moment's relaxation would let the enemy – either Spaniards or weather – get one move ahead. To go to sleep without the fear that he'd be wakened only to deal with yet another emergency.

The Commissioner's words still rang in his ears. 'Yours is the only vessel we can send after Sir John... If I had three frigates, I'd use 'em all: but there's only your cutter. Make no mistake, Ramage, find Sir John you must. You know what's at stake. Drive the ship and drive the men as you've never driven 'em before, even if you get a gale a day. If you see a frigate, give her captain one of the sets of orders I'm having drawn up. Go from one rendezvous to the next. If you find a neutral ship, wring the master's neck if that's the only way to make him say whether or not he's seen Sir

John's squadron. And,' he'd added grimly, 'if you fail, don't offer any excuses.'

Find Sir John's squadron… Ramage reached out for the chart. Precious little he had to go on. Sir John had sailed from Lisbon, leaving the Tagus on 18th January with eleven sail of the line to escort some Portuguese men o' war and a Brazil convoy southwards to a safe latitude. (How far south was 'safe'?)

Having done that, Sir John intended to work his way back to the rendezvous off Cape St Vincent to meet any reinforcements the Admiralty had been able to send from England. He certainly needed them. The Commissioner – who was in a difficult position since officially he had no executive authority over Ramage – did not expect Sir John to be back at the rendezvous before about 12th February.

Once through the Strait and out into the Atlantic, the rendezvous off Cape St Vincent (the south-western tip of Portugal and one of the most forbidding headlands on the Atlantic coast) was 170 miles away to the north-west. With an easterly wind, the Kathleen could be there in about thirty-four hours, assuming an average of five knots.

If Sir John, the reinforcements or a frigate were not there, Ramage decided he would head down towards the Canaries – that would be the route Sir John would take with the Brazil ships – for three days, and then return to the rendezvous. That increased the chances of finding Sir John farther to the south, so the Fleet would have less distance to cover to intercept the Spaniards before they reached Cadiz.

Jackson appeared at the companionway. 'Mr Southwick's respects, sir: the cable's up and down.'

The Master was waiting by the taffrail. 'Very well, Mr Southwick, let's get under way. And remember,' he added quietly, 'with no other ship here, every telescope on shore is going to be trained on us... Jackson, I want you at the helm.'

Southwick nodded, picked up his speaking trumpet and began bellowing orders. Soon the two headsails and the great mainsail were hoisted, the gaff and boom swinging lazily from one side to the other and the canvas of the headsails rippling as the wind blew down both sides of them, finding nothing to exert its force on.

Once again the windlass creaked as men heaved down on the bars (why, Ramage thought idly, don't they fit cutters with capstans?) and slowly the heavy cable came home, water squeezing out of the strands and streaming back down the deck. A seaman watching over the bow signalled to Southwick – the anchor stock was in sight.

'I'll take the conn, Mr Southwick.'

The Kathleen had a little sternway which Ramage used to pay off the bow to starboard. He gave an order to the men at the helm, another to the men at the sheets, and the wind filled the great mainsail with a bang. Slowly she began forging ahead.

Ramage was just going to tell Southwick to set the gaff-topsail when he saw a dark shadow moving fast across the water between the cutter and shore, a shadow rapidly becoming dappled with white-capped wavelets: one of the sudden white squalls for which Gibraltar was notorious.

'Ease sheets, Mr Southwick: smartly now!'

Turning to Jackson and the man with him, he yelled, 'Meet this squall! Here – you two men: stand by the helm!'

Then it was on them: although invisible it seemed solid, snatching their breath and screaming shrill in the rigging, slashing off the wave tops and driving them to leeward like heavy rain. Under the wind's enormous pressure the Kathleen heeled over until the water swirled in at the gunports. Ramage saw that although the helm was hard over in an attempt to keep the cutter on course, she was being forced to round up into the wind and head for the shore. The headsails were beginning to flog: in a few moments they'd probably explode into a dozen strips of torn canvas.

'Let the mainsheet run, Mr Southwick!'

The waves slicing up solid over the weather bow were blowing into spray, sparkling briefly in a few moments of weak sun. Then, after what seemed like hours, with Ramage waiting for the sails to blow out or the mast to go by the board, the big boom moved over to leeward as the men slacked the sheet, easing the pressure on the mainsail, which had been forcing the cutter's bow up into the wind. Almost immediately her angle of heel lessened and as the men eased the helm to bring the Kathleen back on course the headsails stopped their insensate flogging.

Algeçiras, on the Spanish mainland, was five miles away across Gibraltar Bay on the starboard beam; Europa Point was almost on the larboard beam and he could see past it into the Mediterranean beyond. Ahead on the African coast, eleven miles across the Strait, low cloud streaming in fast from the east now hid the great peaks of Renegado and Sid Musa which ranged parallel with the coast like teeth in a petrified jawbone. For a brief moment he glimpsed the isolated summit of Haffe del Benatz, climbing almost sheer to fifteen hundred feet, and then Marsa farther west.

Soon the cutter turned to head out towards the Atlantic and with the wind aft she rolled violently, the end of the main boom occasionally dipping in the water. Ramage could see the tiny island of Tarifa ahead, with the Moorish town of Tarifa on the mainland, high-walled with several towers sticking up like enormous tree stumps.

The current was west-going at the moment and stronger close inshore, and because he was anxious to gain every yard to the westward Ramage kept as near the mainland as he dared. The Kathleen was at that moment in sight of at least half a dozen Spanish watch-towers and a couple of castles. If they knew of the scrap of paper locked in his desk, horsemen would already be on their way to Madrid. The tiny ship they were mercifully ignoring – too lazy, perhaps even too contemptuous, to fire at – had the potential to defeat the objective of the combined Fleets of France and Spain...

On the south side of the Strait the African coast was trending south-west, but it would be dark before they passed Tangier. Now Tarifa was near – he guessed Admiral Cordoba would also be glad to get it abeam. From there, Cordoba would have a short run of about forty miles north-westward along the coast to Cadiz, passing only two capes, de Gracia and Trafalgar with its off-lying shoals.

The Kathleen, however, had 170 miles to sail before reaching the rendezvous off Cape St Vincent, crossing a gulf notorious for its sudden south-easterly gales which could trap ships so they could neither weather Cape St Vincent at one end nor round Cape Trafalgar to run into the Strait of Gibraltar at the other.

By the time Tarifa was abeam and with darkness falling, Ramage saw the weather was rapidly deteriorating so that only a miracle could save them from an easterly gale by dawn, and he had to decide within the next hour whether to get some shelter by following the Spanish coast as it trended round northward to Cape Trafalgar and Cadiz, or steer direct for Cape St Vincent and risk eventually being forced to run westward before the full force of it, a course which would take him well out into the Atlantic, leaving Cape St Vincent forty or fifty miles to the north.

Prudent seamanship indicated keeping in the lee of the Spanish coast, but the scrap of paper locked in his drawer; not to mention the Commissioner who'd emphasized every word by thumping his fist on the deck as he said, 'Drive the ship and drive the men as you've never driven 'em before, even if you get a gale a day...' left him with no choice: he must sail direct and risk the gale. There was some consolation that even if the same gale brought Cordoba's Fleet scudding through the Strait, the Spaniards with their great three-deckers and clumsy transports would have a much harder fight to claw up to Cadiz without getting driven far out into the Atlantic.

The full force of the gale – which was bad even for a Levanter – caught the Kathleen just as she cleared the Strait and entered the Atlantic, with Cape Spartel on her larboard quarter showing where the African coast suddenly swept sharply southward to begin the curve which ended in the Gulf of Guinea, almost on the Equator, while on her starboard beam the mountains of Spain disappeared as they trended north towards Cadiz.

Southwick swore the gale was the worst Levanter he'd ever seen but Ramage, although fearful and yet awed by its majestic, and apparently effortless power, reckoned the Kathleen's smallness exaggerated it. But it could not have caught them at a worse time: the east wind howling uninterrupted for perhaps a thousand miles across the Mediterranean, was now being funnelled through the narrow Strait by the high mountains of Spain and Africa, compressing and increasing its frenetic power just as it met the full strength of the Atlantic current which was flowing into the Mediterranean. Wind against current; the worst combination of all.

Its enormous strength was piling up great waves which rose and rolled and thrust up crests which the wind slashed off in sheets of spindrift and foam, driving it across crest and trough in long angry veins until the whole surface of the sea seemed a mottled, raging cataract of molten green and white marble.

Ramage, standing beside Southwick at the taffrail and looking aft as one wave after another surged up astern, mountains of water, each steeply sloping side threatening to scoop up the ship, each curling breaker atop it apparently intent on sweeping the decks bare of men and gear, was almost too numbed to wonder that a frail box of wood like the Kathleen could ever survive.

On and on came the seas, relentless, seemingly unending, and even more frightening since each contained its strength in itself, in its very vastness, in the smooth, purposeful and powerful way it surged inwards, rising higher and higher until Ramage, his imagination heightened by fear, tiredness and awe, felt he was looking up at the cataract destined to swamp the whole world. The crest of each wave was a curling, hissing jumble of frothing white water broken only by the Kathleen's wake which showed on the wave's face as an insignificant double line of inward-spinning whorls, like the hair springs of clocks.

The hours passed and Ramage was barely conscious of fresh men at the helm as the watches changed. He saw only wave after wave in a wild chase to overtake the cutter. Just as a roaring crest was about to crash down on the Kathleen's deck, the ship's stern began to lift (began, it always seemed, just a moment too late), and the bow dip slightly, as if the ship was starting a hesitant curtsy. Suddenly the crest was right under her counter, first lifting the stern even higher and burying the bow deeper on the forward face and then, as the crest slid forward, tipping the ship like a see-saw in a gigantic pitch which would let the stern sink back on the rear face, the bow lifting high in the air as the crest swept on.

As suddenly as it arrived, that wave would be gone: for a few moments the Kathleen would be almost dead in the water, sunk deep in a trough so her tiny spitfire jib was blanketed, starved of wind. Then once again the next wave would race up astern…

Suddenly Southwick pointed. A couple of hundred yards astern a freak wave was rushing down to them. The crest was solid water, still wedge-shaped and still thrusting itself higher.

Even as they watched the wind's pressure was working on it, and unable to resist its force the crest slowly turned and then toppled to break into a two-foot high rolling, swirling, roaring mass of water sweeping along on the forward side of the wave.

The next moment the cutter dropped into a trough and the wave disappeared from view. Ramage, noting it was the third, saw the first sweep down and pass, turning to make sure Southwick had warned the quartermaster and the men at the helm, banged Southwick on the shoulder and motioned him to grip something firmly, and himself seized an eyebolt beside the stem-chase port. The second wave lifted the cutter enough for Ramage to see the third had grown even larger, rearing up as high as a big house.

In one split second he guessed this time the little Kathleen's stern would never lift in time to avoid being pooped; that the whole wave would crash down on her and then sweep forward, washing away every man on deck, stoving in skylights and ripping open hatches to send tons of water cascading below, and, with no one at the helm, slew the whole ship round so that she broached, lying broadside on to the next wave and probably heeling over on her beam ends.

With the heavy carronades then hanging vertically and breaking loose from their slides and tackles, and bulky casks of provisions and dozens of round shot stowed below smashing their way through the hull planking, the Kathleen would founder.

In the instant before the wave reached the Kathleen, Ramage thought of the scrap of paper on which he'd hurriedly copied part of the order to Admiral Cordoba. Sir John would never see it; the great Spanish Fleet would pass the Strait and eventually link up with the French Fleet at Brest. Gianna would never know of the Kathleen's fate: all the risks of the past few days had been unnecessary: what a stupid, useless way to die...

A moment later there was nothing but sky: a grey, menacing sky across which thick cloud raced in untidy patterns. The Kathleen's stern rose so fast Ramage felt he was being shot up into the air and a moment later dropped just as quickly, and the wave was past.

He glanced round at Southwick and saw the old man, eyes shut, was muttering a prayer – or a stream of curses – and still hadn't realized the wave had gone. Then he looked round at Ramage and making no attempt to hide the relief he felt, shouted: 'I thought that one had our number painted on it!'

Ramage shook his head and grinned, showing a confidence he did not feel. He was thankful he'd reduced sail in time, and housed the topmast, run in the bowsprit and lowered the cro'jack yard – which carried the cutter's squaresail – down on deck to reduce the windage. It had been a slow and tiring business stretched over the past few hours: one reef in the mainsail and changing down to a smaller jib as the wind piped up just past Tarifa; another two reefs in the mainsail, handing the foresail and changing to an even smaller jib half an hour later; then furling the mainsail and hoisting the tiny storm trysail in its place, handing the small jib and hoisting the storm jib.

Still the Kathleen had raced on almost out of control. He and Southwick had watched astern, shouting orders to the four men at the helm and the eight others manning the relieving tackles hooked on either side of the tiller, making sure that each of the seas met the Kathleen exactly stern on. If any one of them had caught her on the quarter she would have been pooped.

Finally Ramage had admitted to himself what Southwick had been telling him for some time – he was driving the cutter beyond the limit of her endurance: sailing so fast that she was as wild and uncontrollable as a runaway horse.

Reluctantly he'd told Southwick to hand both storm trysail and storm jib and set the storm foresail in their place. That had no sooner been hoisted and sheeted home than there was an immediate improvement in the handling of the ship – she was sailing more slowly with less tendency to broach. But it was a short-lived respite: with a bang like a 32-pounder being fired, the sail blew out, scraps of flax flying off to leeward and a few strips still attached to the bolt rope streaming out like tattered banners.

For several minutes it had been touch and go whether they could keep control of the cutter while men scrambled along the deck to bend on and hoist the spitfire jib – a few score square feet of tremendously strong but stiff and intractable flax.

Every time the ship pitched she dug her sharp bow deep into the sea and flung up sheets of spray which hid the men from sight, and as she rose again the water raced aft along the deck in small tidal waves while Ramage counted the men to make sure no one was missing – not that anything could be done for anyone who went overboard. The wind snatched contemptuously at the sail as they hoisted, flogging it with no more effort than a washerwoman shaking a shirt.

Finally the men were safely back aft and although the sail once hoisted and sheeted home seemed ridiculously small, the weight of the wind bellied it out as hard as a board and drove the cutter on again, and Ramage expected any moment to see the material tear out of the thick roping round its edges.

All that was – well, about five hours ago, just after dawn. And now the really great seas were coming: seas that made the earlier ones seem like wavelets. Facing into the wind, he found it difficult to breathe, and the shrill howling in the mast and rigging combined with the actual buffeting of his face and ears left his mind numbed.

Normal thought was becoming impossible; the only way he could keep any control over the situation was to talk to himself – asking a series of questions to make sure he hadn't forgotten anything. Navigation – no need to worry about that now with four thousand miles of open Atlantic ahead and the wind and seas forcing the Kathleen to steer west. Sails – well, the spitfire jib was holding. Leaks – the carpenter's mate had sounded the well fifteen minutes ago and reported only the usual amount of water. Food – the cook and cook's mate were at this moment doing their best to produce something. Sheets checked over for chafe – Southwick had done that, but he must remind him again in half an hour, was there anything else? God, he was cold and wet and tired – so tired he knew he was on the verge of having hallucinations. Always, beyond every one of those seas piling up one after the other astern, he could imagine the enormous blunt bow of the Santísima Trinidad, the red hull scudding along under just a close-reeled fore-topsail, unable to get round to make Cadiz and with the rest of the Spanish Fleet streamed out astern.

By noon two days later the gale had eased slightly but gave no sign of a break. Ramage and Southwick estimated the Kathleen had run more than two hundred miles, which put the rendezvous off Cape St Vincent nearly a hundred miles away to the north-eastward. And, more important, the cutter was probably astride the western-most route by which Sir John would return (even allowing for the gale) to the rendezvous from whatever position he'd left the Brazil ships. Ramage knew that if he could stay in this position there was a chance he'd meet the Fleet on its way back. And that meant heaving-to – if possible.

The only way of knowing for certain was to try it, which meant risking being pooped as the Kathleen rounded up. It also meant risking blowing out the spitfire jib, and also the storm trysail that he'd have to hoist.

Ramage gave his orders to Southwick and then looked aft, waiting several minutes until two large waves were followed by a smaller one. The instant the second wave had passed he yelled, 'Down with the helm!'

The bow began to swing so slowly it seemed impossible the cutter would turn before another huge wave built up astern, and although she was swinging faster than Ramage realized – the horizon was just a featureless line of grey and green – he looked round just in time to notice a large sea coming up on the quarter. The Kathleen caught it just abaft the beam and gave such a tremendous roll that for a moment the four men at the helm could only hold on to the tiller to prevent themselves falling over, but the men at the relieving tackles, bracing themselves against the bulwarks, managed to stand firm. Water spurted in waist-high at the gun ports, raced across the deck and sluiced out through the ports on the other side. Then the Kathleen was round, with the wind on the starboard bow.

Ramage pointed up in the air and he could see Southwick's mouth working as he hurried the men at the trysail halyards. The sail crawled up the mast, slatting with a noise like musket shots and the tiny gaff swinging crazily. Southwick was keeping an eye on Ramage, who pointed at the spitfire jib sheets. By brute force a dozen men hauled on the tiny sail and as soon as it was backed Ramage shouted at Jackson to put the helm down.

How was she going to ride? A glance over the starboard bow showed that there were no particularly large seas coming up for a minute or two. It was a juggling act – the wind on the backed jib was trying to push the bow round one way and   the trysail abaft the mast was trying to thrust it the other. Although the trysail was larger, the jib was set farther from the mast and exerted more leverage – sufficient for the cutter to need some helm to balance her.

It took three or four minutes for Ramage to find the right amount of helm, then the Kathleen was lying with the seas rolling in on her starboard bow, lifting to them comfortably although occasionally slicing off crests which drove up over the bulwarks.

'She's snug enough now,' Southwick bellowed in his ear. 'It'll give the cook a chance to get something hot in the coppers!'

Ramage nodded, but he knew the sight of Sir John's flagship would put more warmth in his belly than anything even the most expert and patient of cooks could produce.

CHAPTER SIXTEEN

The gale lasted three more days. Below deck there was hardly a dry place in the ship: months in the hot sun had dried out and shrunk planking and this, followed by the working of the hull in the heavy seas, provided plenty of places for the water constantly sluicing over the deck to seep below in dozens of regular drips. Hammocks and clothing became damp, then sodden; mildew grew fast, like an odorous green cancer, fed by the humidity. And hour after hour the Kathleen pitched into a head sea, slowly – agonizingly slowly as far as Ramage was concerned – forereaching to the north-east.

Finally on Friday morning the wind began to veer to the south-east and ease slightly. It could be the gale blowing itself out, but, as Southwick pointed out to Ramage, it could also be the warning that another gale – from the Atlantic this time – was approaching. Both men feared that one of the area's notorious south-easters would trap the Kathleen in the great gulf between Cape St Vincent and the reefs of Cape Trafalgar. Hundreds of ships over the years had found themselves driven relentlessly into the gulf, unable to beat out against the wind to clear Cape St Vincent on one tack or Cape Trafalgar on the other, and usually ending up wrecked on the low sandbanks between Huelva, at the mouth of the Rio Odiel (from which Colombus sailed in 1492 on his first voyage to Hispaniola) and San

Lucar de Barrameda, at the mouth of the Rio Guadalquivir, from where Magellan sailed to circumnavigate the world in 1519. Those forty odd miles between the starting points for two of history's greatest voyages, Ramage realized, had seen the end of scores of others...

An hour before noon the cloud began splitting up to reveal patches of blue sky, and with fifteen minutes in hand Southwick appeared on deck with his ancient quadrant. Five minutes before noon a break in the sky allowed him to begin taking sights. Shortly after the bosun's mate rang eight bells, Ramage looked at him questioningly and Southwick said, 'Pretty sure of it, sir,' and went down to his cabin to work it out. A few minutes later, leaving the bosun's mate at the conn, Ramage joined him and as they crouched in the tiny, hot cabin, the Master pointed to the latitude he had calculated and at two crosses he'd marked on the damp and mildew-blotched chart.

'We're about here, sir – maybe a bit more to the west,' he said, a stubby forefinger confidently stabbing the southernmost cross, 'and there's the rendezvous.'

'Closer than I'd hoped.'

'Yes, sir, though there's this current setting south-eastwards, of course.'

'Very well Mr Southwick, we'll alter course for the rendezvous.'

Two hours after dawn on Sunday the Kathleen was hove-to near the Victory, a minnow in the lee of a whale, and Ramage was on board, explaining to Captain Robert Calder, who was Captain of the Fleet, that he had urgent news for the admiral.

Calder demanded to know what it was before taking him to Sir John, but Ramage, with a mixture of stubbornness and pomposity, refused to divulge it, since Calder had no right to ask. Further argument was stopped by a young midshipman arriving to tell Calder the admiral wished to see Mr Ramage in his cabin at once. Ramage hurried aft, hoping to leave Calder striding the flagship's well-scrubbed deck. Although this was the first time they'd met, he took an instant dislike to him.

The admiral's cabin was large and the canvas covering the deck, painted in large black-and-white squares, gave the impression it was a huge chess-board. Waiting with his back to the huge stern lights so his face was in shadow, Sir John stood in a familiar attitude, stooping slightly, his small head to one side and frowning, hands clasped behind his back, his eyes unwavering as he looked up.

'Well, Mr Ramage, the last I heard from Gibraltar was that you'd surrendered your ship and were a prisoner in a Spanish jail.'

His face was impassive despite the bantering note in his voice, and before Ramage could answer he continued, 'You've met Captain Hallowell? He is on board as my guest. Ben, this is the young man I was telling you about, Ramage, the Earl of Blazey's son. He has a certain facility for interpreting orders to suit his own purpose – I had almost said "whim". So far he's also suited the purpose of his superior officers. I trust,' he added, turning to Ramage, 'that happy state of affairs will continue; though I've never met a gambler who died a rich man in his old age.'

Ramage recognized the significance of a warning from the man famous as the Navy's strictest (and fairest) disciplinarian; and although he tried to fix a smile on his face he knew he looked like an errant small boy facing his tutor.

'I hear you lost the fair Marchesa to the Apollo,' Sir John added, as if knowing his warning had struck home. 'Still,

Captain Usher was an excellent host. And however cramped the Apollo, it was preferable to a Spanish prison cell...'

The old devil doesn't miss much, Ramage thought, and Calder walked into the cabin as he braced himself for the next shaft, but the admiral said conversationally as if to indicate there were no more rebukes to come (for the time being anyway), 'Well, what brings you here? Have you any news or dispatches for me?'

Ramage could not resist imitating the dry, even, unemotional way the admiral habitually spoke.

'News, sir. Admiral Cordoba had orders to sail from Cartagena with the Spanish Fleet by 1st February to make for Cadiz. He has twenty-seven sail of the line, thirty-four frigates and seventy transports.'

Hallowell jumped up from his chair with an exclamation of delight, ducking to avoid hitting his head on the beams, but Sir John remained impassive.

'You seem very positive, Ramage. How do you know?'

'I read Admiral Cordoba's orders from the Minister of Marine, sir.'

Because Ramage forgot Sir John knew nothing of his escape from Cartagena, he was startled by the effect of his bald answer.

Calder said immediately, without attempting to hide the sneer in his voice. 'Was it the Minister or the Admiral that showed them to you?'

Ramage ignored him, taking from his pocket the copy of the orders he had made in the gardener's hut, and his translation.

'You have a copy?' Sir John asked incredulously.

'Yes sir – this is the one I made from the original order to Admiral Cordoba, but I've also written a translation. I didn't have time to copy out all the polite phrases at the beginning, and the end,' he added, handing the translation to Sir John, who opened it unhurriedly and read it through a couple of times before passing it to Calder.

'I've no idea what you were doing in Cartagena. When did you leave?'

'On the night of 30th January, sir.'

'Do you think the Fleet was able to sail by the first?'

'Yes sir – it was as ready as any Spanish Fleet would ever be.' 'What did you do on leaving Cartagena?'

'I made for Gibraltar and arrived on the third. The Kathleen had been recaptured and was the only ship there and the Commissioner – he was the senior officer present, apart from the Governor – put me back in command of her with orders to look for you. We had a Levanter coming through the Strait and had to run before it, and then heave-to, so I was delayed making up for the rendezvous.'

Sir John nodded. 'Yes, we had trouble with that gale too. If it caught the Spaniards in the Strait, do you think they could have made up for Cadiz?'

'No, sir, definitely not.'

'You seem very certain, Ramage.'

'Yes, sir: it was one of the worst I've been in. Even allowing the Kathleen's only a cutter, I don't think anyone could have made up for Cadiz in that weather.'

'Hmmm,' growled Calder, 'how do you know this order' – he waved Ramage's translation – 'isn't a forgery? Or a deliberate attempt to mislead us? I can't see the Spaniards leaving orders around just for you to read.'

Ramage, still puzzled by Calder's blatant hostility, glanced at Sir John, but the admiral's face was still impassive.

'I don't know, sir. It could be a forgery, or it could be a deliberate attempt to mislead us.' Ramage kept his voice flat, and he sensed Hallowell – who must be considerably junior to Calder – was also puzzled not so much by the questions but by the tone of the man's voice.

'But you don't believe it's either?' asked Sir John.

'No, sir. Admiral Cordoba has replaced Langara and was staying in a house in Cartagena. The order was taken from a locked drawer in his desk. He hadn't the slightest reason to suspect anyone would burgle his house. And since the orders aren't missing he still doesn't know anyone has seen them, let alone that you now have a copy.'

'Who burgled the house, then?' demanded Calder.

'One of my seamen.'

'Why didn't you?'

The implication and tone was so insulting that Ramage flushed, but Sir John gave a slight nod which told him to answer.

'It was a question of burgling Admiral Cordoba's house at night, and picking locks. The seaman was formerly a locksmith by trade and I gather an occasional burglar by choice. He preferred to work alone. It would have been too risky to light a candle to read through all the papers in the house, so I waited in a shed in the garden with a light, pen and paper...'

Sir John interrupted: 'Ramage, you've obviously a splendid tale to tell. It'll sound all the better at supper, so join us at five o'clock. Let me have a written report as soon as possible.'

Ramage was just turning to go when Sir John said: 'You have no news of Commodore Nelson?'

'No, sir. They were worried at Gibraltar.'

'Very well,' and then he said, almost to himself, 'I'll be glad when Nelson joins us. If the Dons run into his frigates and transports... Calder, make a signal to the Britannia, Barfleur and Prince George – I've no doubt the rest of my admirals will also enjoy young Ramage's tale.'

As Ramage was rowed back to the Kathleen he realized that round the supper table, listening to the story of how

Admiral Cordoba's house came to be burgled, would be Vice-Admiral Thompson, Vice-Admiral Waldegrave and Rear-Admiral Parker. None, as far as Ramage knew, had been connected in any way with his father's trial. Each might have private views, but none had joined in the vendetta. And that, he realized, was probably why Sir John in his shrewd way had invited him to supper: they were all powerful men in the Navy and likely to become more so – and they (and Sir John, too, for that matter!) would be able to form their own opinion of 'Old Blaze-away's' son. The supper or, rather, the way he behaved and spoke during it, could be a turning point in his career. And he was so tired he had as much chance of shining in such company as a mirror in a mine shaft.

The supper was a complete success, and as soon as the cloth was removed and the brandy poured, Sir John told Ramage he would buy La Providencia as a dispatch vessel, and then insisted he began his tale by relating how he captured the dismasted Spanish frigate.

When Ramage described the explosion boat, Calder immediately interjected that it was a barbarous idea but was promptly squashed by Sir John, who pointed out that as far as the victims were concerned having the stern of their ship blown off by powder in a boat was far less dangerous to life and limb than having it blown off by the powder in the guns of a ship delivering a raking broadside.

The description of how Jackson produced a blank Protection and filled it in for Ramage's use led Sir John to comment, 'It's a pity the American Minister Plenipotentiary in London can't see that Protection. Have you still got it?'

Ramage had patted his pocket and Sir John said drily, 'Keep it – might want it again one day!'

As soon as Stafford's role as the burglar had been related, Hallowell slapped the table and exclaimed, 'Well, Sir John, that man deserves to be appointed Locksmith-in-Ordinary to His Majesty's Fleet!'

'Lock-picker,' corrected Sir John. 'But I think we'll leave him with Mr Ramage. If I had him on board the flagship I'd be forever worrying about the lock on my wine chest!'

When Ramage finished his story the Commander-in-Chief reached out and in a slow and deliberate move pushed aside the brandy glass on the table in front of him, and Ramage sensed his mood had changed.

'Tell me, Ramage, when you decided to tackle the dismasted Spanish frigate,' he said in a deceptively quiet voice 'did it occur to you that you were disobeying the Commodore's orders?'

'Yes, sir.'

'You mean it occurred to you before you did it, not after.'

'Yes, sir. Before.'

'It's becoming fashionable for a young officer to assume that if he disobeys orders and does something else, he gets promoted if he succeeds and court-martialled if he doesn't. That was what you were gambling on, eh?'

'No sir,' Ramage said frankly, 'because I didn't think I'd succeed.'

'Why try it, then? You don't need the prize money.'

Ramage, conscious the four admirals were watching him closely, knew it was no good lying. 'I still don't know why, sir. I think – well, the ship's company, the Marchesa, Count Pitti, they all took it for granted we'd do it.'

'Do you mean to sit there and tell me you let your ship be run by a woman and a bunch of ignorant seamen?' growled Sir John.

Hallowell said bluntly, 'With respect sir, I think it's to Ramage's credit that they had such faith in him.'

'Faith be damned, Ben; it only proves they're even more stupid than he is!'

'But Sir John,' said Admiral Waldegrave, 'surely it depends on the point of view. Ramage obtained this information. But one could argue that in using the American Protection, technically Ramage deserted from the King's Service and could be sentenced to death by the British under the Sixteenth Article of War. Yet at the same time if the Spaniards had discovered he was a British officer wearing seaman's clothes and carrying an American Protection while arranging for Cordoba's house to be burgled, surely they'd have shot him as a spy?'

'They could have and would have, my dear Waldegrave,' Sir John said grimly, 'and no one could blame them. But that has nothing to do with disobeying orders. Mr Ramage was under orders to get the Marchesa to Gibraltar by the safest possible route.'

'But I was on that route, sir,' Ramage said hopefully.

'Perhaps the Commodore's orders were loosely worded,' Admiral Parker said.

The Commander-in-Chief glared round the table. 'The first part of the Nineteenth Article of War lays down only one penalty – death. I'll trouble you gentlemen to recall the wording – "If any Person in or belonging to the Fleet shall make, or endeavour to make, any Mutinous Assembly, upon any pretence whatsoever…" It seems to me the whole bunch of you are making a mutinous assembly right in front of m' own eyes, on the pretext that young Ramage didn't disobey the wording of his orders! He simply disobeyed the spirit of them, which is worse.

'However, instead of making an order for his trial I'll give you a toast – gentleman, to young Ramage and his absurdly trusting ship's company!'

No sooner had they drunk to that than Captain Hallowell, who was a Canadian, said, 'And may I propose another – to his loyal band of temporary Americans!'

CHAPTER SEVENTEEN

Ramage woke next morning with a taste in his mouth as though he had been sucking a pistol ball and a head which throbbed like a drum beating to quarters. He shouted for his steward and regretted it a moment later as pain as sharp as a knife blade stabbed his temples. He'd certainly supped well on board the flagship, but wisely? Had he talked too much? Been indiscreet? Revealed too much about his thoughts? He didn't know; but he must have been quite drunk by the time he came back on board the Kathleen.

He suddenly saw a letter on his desk and as his cot swung reached out and grabbed it. Written orders from Sir John – at dawn the Kathleen would take up and maintain a position five miles ahead of the Fleet. He looked at his watch – it was 7 a.m., an hour or more after dawn. At that moment the steward came into the cabin and was promptly sent off to fetch the Master.

Southwick arrived looking cheerful but obviously tired, and seeing the surly expression on Ramage's face as he held the letter said, 'Good morning sir. Don't worry about that – we're in position.'

'But how – ?'

'When you came on board you mentioned something about orders, sir, and as you seemed a bit – er, tired, I took the liberty of taking the letter out of your pocket and opening it after you'd gone to bed.'

'Tired be damned,' growled Ramage, 'I was drunk.'

'You did mention, sir, that the admiral hoped to sight the Dons today.'

'Today or tomorrow. He thinks that if the Dons left Cartagena on time and ran into that gale, they'd have been swept even farther out into the Atlantic than we were, because they probably wouldn't have been able to heave-to. They should be working their way back to Cadiz now and we are stretching across their probable route...'

'Then with a bit o' luck we'll be the first to sight 'em!' The prospect clearly pleased the Master, who patted his stomach as if anticipating a good meal.

'Don't make any mistake this time, Southwick. Give me that paper on the desk – thank-you. I worked this out yesterday. Sir John has fifteen sail of the line and the Spaniards twenty-seven. Seven of them carry more guns than any of our ships. Wait until you see the Santísima Trinidad – she's enormous. It all adds up to fifteen British sail of the line carrying 1,232 guns against twenty-seven Spanish sail of the line carrying 2,308. Which gives the Dons an advantage of 1,076 guns. Nearly twice as many as us in fact...'

'Well,' Southwick said placidly, 'we're not outnumbered then.'

'What!' Ramage exploded. 'Don't be so – '

Southwick grinned. 'They'd have to be carrying 3,696 guns – don't forget one Englishman equals three Spaniards.'

'Men, not guns,' snapped Ramage. 'That kind of reasoning is ridiculous.'

The steward brought in an urn of tea and Ramage motioned him to pour a cup for Southwick as well.

'You're half-right, though,' he conceded. 'Men have to fire the guns.'

'I worked out that when we took La Sabina we were outnumbered about four to one, but it didn't seem to worry you.'

'It worried me all right, but' – he recalled the look on the admiral's face the previous evening – 'it worried Sir John even more. In fact – '

There was a knock on the door and Jackson burst in. 'Sail in sight, sir, on the starboard bow.'

Ramage glanced up at the tell-tale compass above his head.

'Hoist the signal "Strange sail" and the compass pendants. Beat to quarters, Mr Southwick.'

Southwick followed Jackson on deck while Ramage hurriedly washed and dressed. By the time he was on deck the signal flags for a strange sail and its compass bearing were streaming in the wind, giving their warning to the Fleet just in sight astern – the Kathleen was carrying out her task of increasing the Fleet's visible horizon by another five miles, like a giant telescope, signal flags taking the place of optical lenses.

Jackson, perched up the mast beside the lookout, shouted: 'Deck there! She's a frigate.'

'Mr Southwick, haul down "Strange sail" and hoist "Strange sail is frigate".'

A few minutes later Jackson called, 'Captain, sir – she might be the Minerve.'

She could be; the Blanche and Minerve were both with Commodore Nelson. But he wasn't going to take chances: the frigate could not see the Fleet to leeward yet and might have been captured by the Spanish, and now eager to snap up a small cutter.

Once again the familiar drum beat echoed across the Kathleen's decks and the drummer had just tucked his sticks into his boot-top and was unhitching his drum amid a rush of men to the guns when Jackson again hailed.

'She's the Minerve all right, sir, and she's flying a broad pendant.'

'Very well. Mr Southwick, warn the Fleet and signal its bearing for the Minerve – I doubt if she can see it yet. I'm going below to shave.'

By the time Ramage came back on deck, feeling a lot fresher, the Minerve was close enough for her bow wave to look like a white moustache at her stem. As she ran down towards the cutter, Ramage was reminded of the ridge and furrow flight of a woodpecker as she rose and fell on the overtaking swell waves. There was hardly a wrinkle in her straining sails, but almost every one of them had been patched several times. The sailmaker and his mates must have been busy. Ramage would have given a lot to know if the Commodore had sighted the Spanish Fleet at sea… An hour after the Minerve rounded up to leeward of the Victory, Jackson reported to Ramage that the flagship was signalling for the Kathleen's captain. As he stood in his cabin, the steward hurriedly brushing his coat, straightening his stock, and carefully brushing his new cocked hat, Ramage wasn't sure whether he was apprehensive or pleased. Either the Commodore considered he had disobeyed orders and Sir John had decided to take action, or – oh well, he'd know soon enough.

All the time that the Kathleen ran down to the Victory, and while he was being rowed over to the flagship, Ramage deliberately thought of other things: of Gianna, whether or not he had left out too much in his official report to Sir John, and which he now had in his pocket, and where Cordoba's Fleet was. He scrambled up the three-decker's side, acknowledged the regulation salutes made to him as the commanding officer of one of His Majesty's ships, and was just about to look round for the first lieutenant when he was startled at the sight of Sir Gilbert Elliot walking towards him, hand outstretched and a broad grin on his face.

'Well, young man, you didn't expect to see me here!'

Ramage saluted and shook the band of the former Viceroy.

'Hardly, sir!'

'And you nearly didn't, by God! We spent the night before last in the midst of the Spanish fleet!'

At that moment Ramage saw the tiny figure of Commodore Nelson leave the admiral's cabin and walk towards them.

'Ah,' said Sir Gilbert, 'my dear Commodore, you see whom we have here?'

'Yes, indeed. Well, Mr Ramage, you seem to have been busy since you left us at Bastia, eh? So have we. We've evacuated the Mediterranean, the Viceroy and I. And,' he added almost bitterly, 'we've left it a French and a Spanish lake. They can go boating without fear.'

The voice had the same high pitch, the same nasal intonation, but the man himself had undergone a subtle change. At Bastia Ramage had tried to define the curious aura about him, like the glow from a gemstone; but now whatever it was seemed even stranger. The one good eye – yes, he realized with a shock, it had the same look that Southwick's had at the prospect of battle.

'Don't mumble,' the Commodore said sharply. 'Sir John tells me that so far you've admitted disobeying orders, surrendering your ship, being taken prisoner and adopting a subterfuge to escape, playing the spy, burgling honest men's houses and reading their private letters – don't you call that being busy?'

'I thought you were going to call it something else, sir,' Ramage said frankly, relieved at the bantering note on which the Commodore ended.

'I gather Sir John has already expressed his views, so I've no need to add mine. But you took a devilish risk with the Marchesa. Never, never risk the lives of those you love or who love you, young man, unless you've written orders to do so.'

'But I – '

'If you don't love her, you're a fool. Don't assume a one-eyed man is blind, Mr Ramage.'

'No, sir, I didn't – '

'Now, now, Commodore, go steady for pity's sake!' interrupted Sir Gilbert, 'You're alarming the poor fellow more than the whole Spanish Fleet!'

'Were you frightened of being killed when the two Spanish frigates came alongside that night?'

The Commodore's question was so sudden that Ramage replied, 'No, sir, not of getting killed; only of doing the wrong thing,' before he had time to think... 'What d'you mean, "The wrong thing"? '

'Well, sir, what people would think if I surrendered.'

The Commodore gripped Ramage's arm in a friendly gesture. 'I think Sir Gilbert will agree with this advice. First, dead heroes are rarely the intelligent ones. It takes brains to be a live hero, and live heroes are of more use to their country. Second, and more important, never worry what people will think. Do what you think is right, and damn the consequences. And don't forget this: a man who sits on the fence usually tears his breeches.'

Sir Gilbert nodded in agreement. 'One assumes, of course, that the person to whom you give that advice is not an irresponsible fool, eh Commodore?'

'Of course! It's not advice I give everyone, and young Ramage only just qualifies for it! Well, gentlemen,' he smiled, 'you must excuse me: I am hoisting my broad pendant in the Captain. It'll be a pleasure to be back on board a seventy-four again – room for me to strut around, after being squashed up in a frigate. Though the discomfort was entirely alleviated by your company, Sir Gilbert.'

Sir Gilbert gave a mock bow.

'And Mr Ramage,' Nelson added, 'you'll find that the Kathleen's position in the order of sailing will be two cables to windward of the Captain. I'll signal your position in the order of battle. Keep a sharp look-out, watch my manoeuvres, and repeat any signals I might make so the rest of my division have no excuse for not seeing them. You'll be expected to read flags through smoke as thick as those clouds!'

Ramage had just returned to the Kathleen and the gig was being hoisted when Jackson, who had been put in charge of the signal book, reported excitedly, 'Flagship to the Fleet – number fifty-three, "To prepare for battle", sir!'

'Acknowledge it, then! Mr Southwark – our position is two cables to windward of the Captain – the Commodore's ship.'

'Aye aye, sir – they hoisted his pendant some time ago.'

Ramage looked at his watch. Five minutes past four on the thirteenth day of February – the eve of St Valentine's Day. It ought to have been St Crispin's, considering the odds, and he'd sit on the bowsprit end and recite Henry Vs speech.

As the bosun's mate's call trilled, followed by his stentorian 'D'you hear there! All hands, all hands, prepare for action! D'you hear there…' the Kathleen got under way again and bore up to windward of the Captain.

As soon as the cutter was in position, and while the men were placing match tubs and water casks, wetting and sanding the deck, carrying up more shot, rigging preventer stays, and completing what had become a ritual for them, Ramage called Southwick aft to the taffrail.

'We have to repeat all signals that the Commodore might make, so rig spare signal halyards in case any get shot away. We may have to take wounded men on board – get sails spread out below to put them on. A ship might need carpenters, so tell the carpenter's mate and his crew to have bags of tools ready. Hoist out the gig again and tow it astern out of the way. And remind me if I've forgotten anything – oh yes, both head pumps on deck.'

'Aye aye, sir,' said Southwick. 'Can't think of anything else for the moment.'

'Oh dear,' groaned Ramage as he saw the grindstone being brought up on deck. 'Must we have that damned thing scraping away again? Soon there won't be a cutlass, pike or tomahawk on board with any metal left...'

Southwick had managed to retrieve his sword when the Kathleen was recaptured and, remembering the flat he'd ground into it when preparing to board La Sabina and which he'd forgotten to grind out, said hurriedly, 'We'd better just make sure sir – and it'll give the cook's mate a chance to put a sharp edge on his cleavers!' With that he strode forward, the sheer delight at the thought of battle showing in his gait.

A mixture of tiredness and excitement had so far stopped Ramage pausing for a few minutes to have a good look at the Fleet, now lying-to in two columns. Even as he looked he saw three tiny bundles soaring up on the Victory's signal halyards and turned to point them out to Jackson, but the American was already watching with his telescope for the flagship's seamen to give the tug that would break out the flags. Suddenly all three streamed in the wind.

'Preparative – sixty-six, sir.'

Ramage nodded. 'To make sail after lying-to.' The order would be obeyed the moment the 'Preparative' signal was hauled down, and each of the sail of the line would get under way.

'To prepare for battle', then 'To make sail after lying-to'. What, speculated Ramage, would the next signal be? It was getting dark fast now; the Victory couldn't make many more flag signals tonight.

How many men in those ships – and in the Kathleen, for that matter – wouldn't live to see another sunset? What was Gianna doing – and, more important, thinking at this moment?

'You look like an owl who's just woken up... But why did you stay so long in Cartagena?... But, my love, all you've told me so far is that I've got to keep secret the fact you know a secret...' Would she ever understand that even as she had   a duty to Volterra, so he had a duty?

And the Commodore. Did he understand too much? Could he see too far into a man's heart? 'Were you frightened of being killed when the Spanish frigates came alongside that night?... What do you mean "The wrong thing"?... It takes brains to be a live hero...never worry about what people think. Do what you think is right and damn the consequences.'

That look in the Commodore's eyes – it was just like Southwick's in a killing mood. Was the Commodore a killer in that sense? Ramage wondered if he was himself. Walk up to a man and shoot him in cold blood... In the heat of battle, yes, but in cold blood?

Southwick, coming on deck for some fresh air as night closed down, was just in time to glimpse the nearest of the big ships as dark thumb marks against an ever-deepening grey backcloth. He was satisfied his own log was up to date, he'd checked that Jackson was keeping a correct signal log, and he'd had an hour's sleep. But he was irritated with the Commander-in-Chief's signal 'Prepare for battle' because it was obviously made much too soon, and had meant dousing the galley fire.

Southwick, who enjoyed his supper, had intended ordering a hen from his coop on the fo'c'sle to be killed and cleaned in anticipation, although he admitted in fairness to Sir John that it was a scraggy hen: plump birds were not to be bought in Gibraltar these days. But with the bird alive and uncooked for the lack of a galley fire he still felt empty – cold cuts from yesterday's roast were good enough for boys; but men needed hot food – it lined one's stomach for a cold night, Southwick always proclaimed.

Seeing the captain leaning on the bulwark looking at the Fleet, Southwick knew they both faced a tiring night: keeping station was going to be difficult Even before turning in he'd felt fog in the air: his right wrist ached and that was a sure sign. A couple of years earlier a blow from his sword had gone clean through a Frenchman's arm and the blade brought up so hard on the barrel of a gun that the shock had broken the bone. Although painful enough at the time, Southwick had since regarded it as a blessing in disguise – when forecasting the weather he put more stock in his wrist and an old piece of dried seaweed hanging in his cabin than all the mercury glasses he'd ever seen. Men laughed when he said he felt a night's fog aching in his wrist and damp on the seaweed. But he always laughed last later when he found them huddled on deck, the fog so thick it dripped off their noses.

Ah well, he thought, a fleet action at last. He'd served at sea all these years and never been within five hundred miles of one. He no longer feared death – that was one of the pleasant sides of growing old. Going over the standing part of the foresheet was inevitable one day – he'd lost count of how many times he'd stood by as the body of a shipmate, an old and valued friend sewn up in his hammock, had been launched over the gangway just above where the standing part of the foresheet was secured to the ship's side.

His thoughts were interrupted by Ramage, who walked over and said, 'Well, Mr Southwick, the Dons will have fog to help them, I saw a few patches to the south-east just before it began to get dark, and now the wind's falling light and it seems warm and damp...'

'Aye, sir, and I can feel it in my wrist: it'll be a thick night and plenty of bang bang – p'raps I ought to get some of the shot drawn from the forward guns?'

Ramage agreed: it was certain they'd have to be fired for fog signals during the night, and it would be better to have the shot removed now, in case it was forgotten later, and the fog signal ended up as a round shot through the Commodore's sternlights.

Half an hour later it was too dark to distinguish the big ships and Ramage had settled down to the tiring task of keeping in position using the shaded lanterns on the poop of the Namur, the ship next ahead of the Captain, when he noticed that occasionally they vanished for a few minutes as thin patches of fog drifted past. Each time he called to the men at the helm 'Watch your heading!' and the quartermaster standing at the binnacle peered down at the dimly lit compass.

But the Namur's lanterns had been out of sight for three or four minutes when suddenly he heard Commodore

Nelson's reedy voice shouting urgently from dead ahead, 'Ramage, you dam'd dunderhead, wear ship or you'll end up in Cowley's tap-room!'

Surprise paralysed Ramage for a moment; then fearing a collision was imminent, he leapt to the larboard bulwark and peered ahead for some sign of the Captain, but he could see nothing. Cowley's – that was the well-known inn at Plymouth Dock! He was about to hail the forward lookouts when the Commodore shouted again: 'D'ye hear me Ramage? Are you dreaming or dragging your anchors for the next world? Put y'helm hard up for Poverty Bay – let fly the sheets an' let's square the yards of those dam' Dons.'

Ramage jumped back with a curse as a bellow of rage from Southwick resounded through a speaking trumpet.

'Come aft, you drunken scoundrel!' the Master roared. 'Poverty Bay indeed! You wait until I've finished with you!'

At last Ramage realized what was happening – a drunken seaman sitting out on the end of the Kathleen's bowsprit was giving a passable imitation of the Commodore's voice… Ordering Southwick to stay aft and keep a watch for the Namur's lights, Ramage walked forward, still feeling shaky and foolish, only too aware of stifled chuckles from the other seamen on deck. Just as he reached the windlass a dark figure said, 'Captain, sir?'

'Yes, what is it?'

'Beg to report the lookout at the starboard cathead's drunk, sir.'

Ramage recognized Stafford's voice.

'Who's the lookout at the starboard cathead?'

'I am, sir,' Stafford said, giving a prodigious belch.

'Get yourself aft,' snapped Ramage, 'I'll give you Cowley's!'

He said it quickly in case he began laughing. Where the devil had Stafford heard the Commodore speaking? He hadn't realized the Cockney was such a good mimic and followed his unsteady walk aft until the man stood swaying slightly in the faint glow of the binnacle light.

'Why are you drunk?' Ramage demanded harshly.

'Dunno, sir – I only 'ad one nor'wester, and that don't do no 'arm normalally – I mean normally.'

He paused and, still swaying, made a tremendous effort to correct himself. 'I mean usuallilly, like I said, sir.'

'One nor'wester be damned,' snapped Ramage. 'More likely four due north. Mr Southwick, man the head pump – Stafford can refresh himself by drinking a couple of mugs of Cowley's special Cadiz Bay seawater and then stand under the pump for fifteen minutes until he knows whether he's a lilly or a lally!'

'Fetch me a mug!' growled Southwick, seizing Stafford by the shoulder and giving him a push forward. 'Man the starboard head pump,' he bellowed, in a sudden burst of anger, 'our Mr Stafford's going to dance more than one jig at Cowley's tonight!'

Ramage heard the pump gurgling as it began to draw, then its regular splashing. A few minutes later Stafford was violently sick, and Southwick came back to the binnacle still holding the mug. 'Can't understand him, sir. Been hoarding his tot, but I don't think it's because he's scared. One nor'wester, though!'

Ramage remembered the cool way Stafford had burgled Admiral Cordoba's house. 'No – he's not scared. Send another man forward as a lookout.'

Southwick's reaction was amusing: clearly he was more disgusted that Stafford should be drunk after only one nor'wester than of his actually getting drunk. But Stafford was being modest: in sailor's jargon, 'north' meant raw spirit and 'west' meant water, while a 'nor'wester' was a mug of half-water and half-spirit, which was clearly insufficient to provide the Cockney with enough inspiration for tonight's antics.

Just after nine o'clock – by which time a sobered Stafford, shivering with cold and thoroughly ashamed of himself, had come aft and apologized, and been sent below to change his clothes – they heard the boom of one signal gun and then another: the signal from the Victory for the Fleet to tack in succession, and the other flag officers repeating it.

'Belike the Captain'll run into a patch of fog now,' growled Southwick

'If she does,' said Ramage, 'it'll be the real Commodore, not Stafford shouting at us!'

The follow-my-leader turn after the order to tack in succession meant the Fleet was steering south-east. Unless they met the enemy or there was a sudden change of wind, it would stay on this course for the rest of the night. Somewhere ahead another fleet of nearly twice as many sail of the line was also under way, trying to make its way to Cadiz and being humbugged by variable winds and fog. The Spaniards would probably be uncertain of their position, desperately anxious to make a good landfall at daylight and, if they knew there was a British fleet near by, scared of their own shadows.

In three hours or so it would be St Valentine's Day. Ramage thought of his parents. They'd be in Cornwall, at St Kew, and by now would have dined and probably enjoying a game of cards. But for that damnable trial, he realized with bitterness, his father's flag might have been hoisted in the Victory, instead of Sir John's. The devil take such thoughts. It was now Southwick's watch and he decided to get some sleep.

CHAPTER EIGHTEEN

'From soon after midnight,' Ramage wrote in a hurried letter to his father, 'we heard the signal guns of the Spanish Fleet down to the south-west – so many that Cordoba was obviously having great difficulty in trying to keep his fleet together in this fog. Without doubt they were making up for Cadiz, and with the wind at south-west they have the weather gage, tho' I doubt 'twill do them much good since there's little more than a breeze which hardly shifts the fog patches lying between us.

'At first light the Culloden (one of our leading ships) made the signal for "Strange sail" and shortly after six o'clock reported them to be Spanish frigates, but the fog drifts about so much I don't know if they sighted us and warned Admiral Cordoba.

'Shortly after seven, two of our frigates made the signal for discovering a strange fleet, south by west, and the Victory ordered the nearest frigate to investigate. Soon after that, through gaps in the fog, we had our first glimpses of several Spanish sail of the line on both larboard and starboard bow, but unless we get a decent breeze it will be noon before we are up with them, as we are only making a knot or so.

'At a quarter past eight, Sir John signalled the Fleet "To keep in close order", although despite a foggy night it was already in almost perfect order of sailing in two divisions, and at twenty past eight he made my second favourite signal, number fifty-three, "To prepare for battle". This really repeated the same signal of yesterday and I think the Fleet was already prepared! Now we await my favourite, number five, "To engage the enemy".

'My Kathleens have long since breakfasted and are in great spirits; in fact I truly believe that if I told them I proposed boarding the Santísima Trinidad they'd give a cheer!

'At twenty past nine Sir John made only his third general signal of the day (I wonder how many Admiral Cordoba had made by then!), which was "To chase". A few minutes before then the wind had veered slightly and Sir John came round two points to starboard so we were steering due south.

'The fog began clearing very slowly (the sun was getting some warmth in it) and soon we could count twenty sail of the line in two widely separated groups rather than in two divisions, straggling and in no sort of order, steering right across our bow for Cadiz. This shows they must have been caught in the Strait by "our gale" and blown well out into the Atlantic.

'At ten o'clock one of our frigates made the signal for twenty-five sail of the line (we are fifteen, remember). Just then the wind veered again and Sir John came round to a course of south-south-west. It is now just before eleven o'clock, Cape St Vincent is eleven leagues to the north-east, and Southwick has just been down to tell me the fog has cleared, leaving banks of haze.

'I had always thought the prospect of a fleet action would be frightening; but I'm glad to say I am too busy (at the moment, anyway!) for fears or premonitions. I have only one regret – that I am not commanding a seventy-four manned by 500 of my Kathleens. Before long we'll be at the

Dons' throats, and I must put my pen away, but later I hope to add a few more pages describing a victorious outcome of our St Valentine Day's endeavours.'

On deck he found Southwick pacing up and down, cursing the haze. The Kathleen might be small – the smallest ship in the Fleet, in fact – but Ramage was proud of her appearance: although little more than a terrier among a pack of wolf-hounds, the ship and ship's company were ready for battle, yet somehow they looked – well, relaxed; there was no feeling of tension.

Besides each gun was a rammer, sponge, match tub and a stack of grape shot (each round looking like a rigid net bag packed with small onions) while the round shot were lying in fitted racks along the bulwarks, black oranges neatly spaced out on shelves. The boat was towing astern, head pumps were rigged and sprinkled sand made the dampened deck gritty underfoot.

The wind was still light and fitful, and each time the fog-soaked mainsail gave a desultory flap overhead it showered the men beneath with tiny water droplets. The fog condensing on the rigging had run down the shrouds, leaving dark puddles on the deck.

The crews were sitting or standing round their guns, chatting and looking as though they were waiting for a prize fight to begin. Stafford was at his gun: eyes bloodshot and face pale from the antics of last night but every movement showing he was brimming with his usual Cockney jauntiness. Near him Maxton's brown face was split with its perpetually cheerful grin. Jackson, acting as a quartermaster, stood by the helm ready to pass on orders to the men at the tiller. Rossi was gesticulating as he described something to the man beside him – an amorous adventure, judging from the way he moved his hands. The men listed in the general quarters bill as boarders already had their cutlass belts slung over their shoulders, although the cutlasses were hooked on to the bulwark, ready to be snatched up.

Over on the larboard beam the Captain was keeping perfect station on the ships ahead and astern and beyond Ramage could see most of the ships in the other division. The sun, weak as it was, tinged the banks of haze with a pink which brought out the colour of the sails. The sight of the two- and three-deckers trying to keep their sails full (but the tiny feathers of white at their bows showing how slowly they were going) was a splendid subject for a painter. The gun port lids, painted red on the inside, here now open and triced flat back against the ships' sides, making a checkerboard of red squares along the white or yellow strakes painted on black hulls which gleamed wetly, while the muzzles of the guns poked out like accusing fingers.

The haze softened the lines of the ships, and the tiny water droplets clinging to the rigging reflected the light like dew on spiders' webs. How could a painter capture the colour of those sails? The warm tint of umber with a little raw sienna or perhaps a touch of yellow ochre? (But no painter would want to spoil the effect by showing the dark, uneven blotches of damp along the heads of the sails.)

'Tuppence worth o' leg of beef soup and a penn'orth o' bread, that's wot I'd like,' he heard Stafford's Cockney voice declare to one of the other men. 'Minnie's place at the back o' me farver's shop – though I 'aven't bin there since the press took me up. Yus, I could do wiv that, but thanks to the Dons it'll be cold 'ash for us today.'

He spat over the side through the gun port and grumbled, 'This'll be the fourth watch me jaws 'ave over'auled this chaw o' baccy an' it's got abaht as much guts left in it as a bit o' sail clorf, s'fact.'

Southwick suddenly paused in his march back and forth across the deck and snapped at Jackson, 'The flagship's signalling!'

Jackson snatched the telescope. 'General – preparative – number thirty-one. Then compass, south-west.'

Southwick flicked through the pages of the signal book ' "Form line of battle ahead and astern of the admiral as most convenient…" '

He looked up to make sure Ramage had heard and grumbled, 'Unless we get a breeze those wine-swilling, fish-on-Fridays, priest-ridden gallows birds'll be in Cadiz, their yards sent down and everyone home for Easter before we form the line. Bah – chasing at a couple o' knots indeed!'

With that he banged the scabbard of his enormous sword against his boot. The sword intrigued Ramage and he'd watched how carefully Southwick had honed it the previous evening.

'How did you come by that meat cleaver, Southwick?'

'My father was a butcher, sir,' he grinned, 'but I bought this one at the best sword cutler's in London, Mr Prater's at Charing Cross. Paid for it with the first prize money I ever had. 'Scuse me sir – Jackson! Watch for – '

'Preparative's coming down, sir!' called Jackson.

'Very well.'

Ramage knew for the next minutes there'd be something of a free-for-all as the fifteen ships in two columns manoeuvred to form a single line, each captain determined to get as near as possible to the head of it, using the excuse that the position conformed with the admiral's signal as being 'most convenient'.

For all the polite but determined jostling the Fleet might be manoeuvring at a Royal Review at Spithead: a topsail backed here, lower yards braced sharp up there, a jib let fly for a minute or two, and quickly the two columns of ships merged into a single line nearly two miles long. The Captain was so close to the Namur that her jib-boom almost overhung the taffrail, and Ramage could imagine how the Commodore had been urging on Captain Miller, who commanded the Captain, and guess what Captain Whitshed was thinking as he looked anxiously astern from the Namur's quarterdeck.

'The Culloden's done it!' Southwick exclaimed. 'Trust Captain Troubridge!'

The Culloden had managed to lead the line, the Victory was seventh, followed by Vice-Admiral Waldegrave in the Barfleur, with Vice-Admiral Thompson and the Britannia eleventh. The Captain – hmm, thought Ramage, the Commodore's the thirteenth in the line – would it be his unlucky day? The fifteenth and last – 'the whipper-in', as Southwick called her – was the Excellent, commanded by Captain Collingwood.

Neither Ramage nor Southwick made any attempt to hide their excitement at the sight of the fifteen great ships in line of battle. Each knew he was watching one of the greatest sights of his lifetime; yet each saw it differently.

Southwick's professional eye noted whether each ship was the correct distance astern of her next ahead and that all her sails were drawing. The banks of haze into which they sailed from time to time were to him only simple problems in station keeping not, as Ramage saw them, delicate veils softening the ships' lines, giving them the same air of mystery and enigmatic beauty that real veils gave to an otherwise naked woman.

Nor would Southwick ever understand a thought passing through Ramage's mind – that the great two- and three-deckers were magnificent monuments to the muddled world in which they lived. The largest wooden objects ever made by man, and designed solely to fight the elements and kill the enemy, they were, nevertheless, among man's most beautiful creations.

A ship like the Captain was built of a couple of thousand oak trees grown in the clay soil of Sussex (from acorns, Ramage calculated, which would have been sprouting at the time Cromwell won his victory over the King at Worcester). She'd be fastened with about thirty tons of copper nails and bolts, and ten thousand or so treenails. Such a ship's lower masts probably came from America, from the forests of Maine or New Hampshire, where pine trees of the necessary diameter were still abundant, while the topmasts and yards were shaped from trees that grew on the shores of the Baltic.

The seams of her decks and hull would be caulked and payed with ten tons of oakum and four of pitch; even the paint would weigh a couple of tons. Ten thousand yards of material would have gone into her sails. (It was ironic to think the entire weight of the Kathleen was a lot less than that of the men in the Captain's ship's company and their gear, and the standing and running rigging and blocks.)

Yet the beauty of these great ships was similar to the beauty of a woman: there was no single thing that made them beautiful: it was the total effect of many, like the tiny individual marble chips that made up a mosaic. And the beauty of even a particular part was hard to define – the curves of a woman's lips might differ only slightly from her sister's, while the sweep of one ship's sheer varied only a fraction from another's. And yet, although the tiny differences defied description or explanation, one woman's mouth had the beauty her sister's lacked; one ship had a pleasing sheer and the other had not.

Each ship sat in the water with the same elegant yet solid, four-square sense of belonging to the sea as an

Elizabethan mansion house belonged on a gently sloping hill cradled among beech trees. Each hull had the symmetry of Grecian statuary – nowhere did the eye catch a straight line or harsh curve: from the end of the jib-boom one's glance travelled quite naturally down to the fo'c'sle and on to the waist and then up again to the taffrail, carried along easily by the sweeping sheer. The bow was bluff – yet the cutwater and the elegant beakhead and figurehead made it comely, not plump; although the stern was square the transom itself raked aft with the studied elegance of a cavalry officer's shako.

From this distance the stout masts, too, seemed slim and rakish, and it was hard to believe a mainmast was three feet in diameter at the step, and from the waterline to the maintopgallant truck was more than 180 feet. The forty or so tons of rope for the rigging made an ugly pile of coils in the dockyard, but when fitted aloft to the masts and yards it took on the tracery of Flanders lace. Yet however beautiful and powerful were the ships, they could fight only as well as the men in them. In that case, he thought, glancing along the line, the onus was now on the men because most of the ships had long since proved themselves in battle.

The Culloden, leading the line, had been with Howe at the Glorious First of June three years ago, when six French sail of the line had been captured and a seventh sunk. The third in the line, the Prince George, was with Admiral Keppel in 1778 when he fought Comte d'Orvilliers' fleet off Ushant, and with Rodney off the Saints in 1782, when five French sail of the line were captured. The Orion, fourth in the line, fought with Howe on the Glorious First of June. The sixth was also one of the newest as far as Ramage could remember – the Colossus had been launched within the past three years, while her next astern, the Victory, was well over thirty years old and had been Keppel's flagship at

Ushant. The Barfleur was Admiral Hood's flagship in Rodney's action, while the Egmont had been with Keppel at Ushant and in Admiral Hotham's action off Genoa a couple of years ago, when Captain Nelson in the Agamemnon had played a leading part in the capture of the Ça Ira and Censeur. She was followed by the Britannia, Hotham's flagship at the time, while the Namur had been with Rodney. The Captain had been badly cut up in Hotham's action and was followed by the Diadem, which had been with her. And the little Kathleen, Ramage thought wrily – well, she'd ventured a lot in the past few weeks, even if she hadn't achieved much…

Fifteen ships. Yet with the French Fleet at Brest probably waiting for the Spanish to join them for an attempt at invasion, the whole safety of England depended not only on the fighting ability of each of those ships but on the tactical ability of one man, Sir John Jervis. If he made one bad mistake this afternoon he might lose the war; one bad mistake leading to his defeat would leave the Channel an open highway for a Franco-Spanish Armada, for the Admiralty wouldn't be able to concentrate enough ships in time to do more than harry them. One man, one mistake: it was a heavy responsibility. Yet he wondered if it bothered Sir John. The old man was this very moment making the first moves in his task of destroying Cordoba's fleet simply because it was a duty for which a lifetime's training had prepared him. Ramage remembered his own father would want to hear about every move made in the battle and, knowing he would not be able to trust his memory, sent a man below to fetch a pad and pencil. Just as he sketched in the positions of the two Fleets Southwick asked: 'What d'you make of the Dons, sir?'

To windward, over the starboard bow, Ramage could see Cordoba's division of nineteen sail of the line, among them the Santísima Trinidad. If they'd ever been in any recognized formation it was now but a memory: they were like a flock of sheep being driven in for shearing, two, three and four abreast. They were running eastward, intending to cross ahead of the British line to join the second division, six sail of the line which were over on the Kathleen's larboard bow and now trying desperately to claw their way up to Cordoba's ships before the British line cut them off. Two flocks of sheep, in fact, trying to join up before a pack of wolves got between them, since it was through the ever-narrowing gap that the Culloden was leading the British line.

'What d'you make of the Dons, sir?' Southwick repeated and Ramage, lost in thought, realized he had not answered.

'They're paying the price for bad station-keeping during the night, Mr Southwick, and for relaxing because they thought they were near home,' Ramage said sourly, intending the lesson would not be lost but knowing he'd merely been pompous.

'You don't think it's a trap?'

'Trap? If it is, someone forgot to set it!'

'But might I – '

'Yes, you can ask why I think that. Cordoba probably has at least twenty-seven sail of the line – though we can see only twenty-five at the moment – against our fifteen. If he'd kept them together he could match them two to one against thirteen of our ships and still have one left to deal with our remaining two. Just think of the Captain, for example, being attacked by the Santísima Trinidad to windward and a seventy-four to leeward. Two hundred and four Spanish guns against the Captain's seventy-four.

'Instead of that, you can see Cordoba has nineteen up there to windward and six more down to leeward. And with a bit of luck we'll manage to get inbetween and stop them joining up.'

'Yes,' admitted Southwick, 'they've split themselves up nicely, Cordoba's letting us match our fifteen against six, or fifteen against nineteen. Sounds easy enough!'

'It isn't though – there's one big "if". If those two Spanish divisions do manage to close that gap, Cordoba will form his line of battle at the last moment right across our bows. All their broadsides against our leading ships – and we won't be able to bring a single gun to bear...'

'But d'you reckon Cordoba has a chance of doing it?'

'About fifty-fifty at the moment – it'll be a close-run affair. If the wind pipes up a bit, Cordoba's nicely up to windward so he'll get in first and bring it down with him. It might be just enough to turn the trick.'

Jackson said: 'Victory's hoisted her colours, sir!'

Ramage motioned to Southwick and the Kathleen's colours soared up to the peak of the gaff, and one after another the rest of the ships hoisted theirs.

Almost at once Jackson sang out gleefully, 'There she goes! Number five, sir!'

Two or three men started cheering and then the whole ship's company took it up. It was the one signal that they all knew by heart, 'To engage the enemy'.

Southwick sidled over to Ramage and said quietly, 'I think the men would appreciate a few words, sir.'

'A few words? What do you mean?' The idea irritated Ramage.

'Well, sir, a little speech or something. It's – well, customary, sir.'

'Customary in a seventy-four but hardly appropriate to us, surely? I said all I had to say when I came on board at Gilbraltar.'

'I still think they'd like it,' Southwick said doggedly.

Ramage saw the men had moved instinctively nearer their guns and were all watching him expectantly, and was unaware that to the men his lean, tanned face, and piercing eyes made him look like a buccaneer leader of earlier days. Then he heard himself speaking to them quietly.

'This may be the biggest battle you'll ever see in your lives, but our part in it is simply to repeat the Commodore's signals. We are just one of the crowd watching the prize fighters knocking each other's heads off.'

That'll cool them off a bit, he thought; then when he saw their eager faces he felt ashamed of such a sneer. Southwick's face, too, had that familiar taut look, eyes almost glazed and bloodshot with the prospect of battle.

Jackson, watching the Victory with the telescope, reported the order for a slight alteration of course, then exclaimed: 'There's another, sir! General, number forty.'

He fumbled through the signal book, and it was one Ramage could not remember.

' "The admiral means to pass through the enemy's line". '

'What? Check that again!' exclaimed Southwick.

Jackson looked through the telescope. 'It's number forty all right, sir.'

Southwick snatched the signal book and looked for himself. 'Yes, sir,' he said to Ramage. 'That's what it says.'

'Quite so, Mr Southwick. Don't forget we've only assumed that's what the admiral intended doing. He has to give the order and he's left it as late as possible in case the Dons did something unexpected. You don't want the Victory festooned with "Annul previous signal" do you?'

A moment later he realized it was an unfair remark but Southwick took it cheerfully, disregarding Ramage's words and thinking to himself it had taken Sir John a long time to come round to Mr Ramage's way of thinking.

CHAPTER NINETEEN

As Ramage looked through his telescope at the six Spanish ships trying to claw across the head of the British line to join Cordoba's division to windward he was reminded of two stage-coach drivers racing each other to a crossroad, one coming along the northern road, the other the eastern. And he knew from bitter experience the almost paralysing tension that must now be gripping each of the Spanish captains.

Ahead of them, less than three miles away, was the safety offered by their Commander-in-Chief and nineteen comrades; but approaching rapidly on their starboard side was the British line, led by the Culloden, intent on cutting them off.

Somewhere out there on the surface of the sea, he mused, is a spot unmarked by even a wavelet, and it's the crossroads, the point where an invisible line drawn along the course the British are sailing crosses a similar line along which the Spanish are steering. Whoever reaches that point first wins the race.

For a moment he felt sympathy for the Spanish captains. Even now each of them must be bending over the compass, taking a bearing of the Culloden and comparing it with a previous one. In a couple of minutes each will again bend over the compass and take yet another. And every successive bearing tells each captain how the race is going, a race which means all the difference between life and death for many of the men of both sides.

It's all beautifully and brutally simple: if the latest compass bearing shows the Culloden more to the north, the Spaniards know they are winning the dash for that unmarked crossroad; if more to the west, then the British are winning. And if the bearing stays the same, then they'll collide.

Even as he watched, Ramage was half-ashamed to admit his sympathy for the Spaniards was growing: he was sure they were losing and a little later he was certain.

Since Sir John had already hoisted signal number five, 'Engage the enemy', all the British ships were free to fire as soon as they had a target. At this moment, he mused, every gun in the Culloden is loaded; every gun on her larboard side is ready to fire. And from what he'd heard of Captain Troubridge, he'd be waiting until the last possible moment for the maximum effect, knowing the smoke of his first broadside (almost always the best-aimed) would then hinder his gunners by drifting to leeward and masking the enemy.

Spurts of smoke along the Culloden's larboard side; then distant thunder. He glanced at Southwick, who snatched Jackson's telescope. The battle of St Valentine's Day had begun. The spurts of smoke slowed and spread, merging into a low cloud drifting in the wind just above the surface of the sea.

Then a longer peal of thunder, and he saw the Blenheim streaming smoke from her broadside. Were they both firing at the same Spanish ship? The Prince George, third in the British line, fired her first broadside at the same instant the Culloden fired her second, and there was a brief interval as the noise rolled across the sea and the smoke began to spread before the Blenheim's second broadside.

So the six Spaniards had lost the race: by reaching that unmarked crossroad first, the British ships had been able to fire raking broadsides into the enemy's bows. Then through the smoke he saw the two leading Spanish ships turning away to starboard, to steer a parallel but opposite course to the British, and a distant rumble, followed by another, showed they were firing back as soon as their broadside guns could bear.

Suddenly Southwick, telescope still jammed to his eye, shouted excitedly. Yes! Both Spaniards had continued turning: instead of remaining on an opposite course they were bearing away, followed by the other four.

'Got their helms hard up for Cadiz!' yelled Southwick. 'That's half a dozen Cordoba can cross off the board!'

Again the Culloden, Prince George and Blenheim fired, and the smoke spreading to leeward hid all six Spaniards from Ramage's view.

'Sir!' shouted Southwick, though Ramage was only a couple of yards from him, pointing excitedly across at Cordoba's nineteen ships over to starboard. They too had given up trying to cross ahead: the leaders were turning to larboard, on to an opposite course to the British. In a few minutes they'd be passing down the Culloden's starboard side, and Ramage pictured men from her larboard guns' crews hurriedly crossing to reinforce those on the starboard side.

Swinging his telescope round to look at Cordoba's division, Ramage was surprised at the foreshortened and enlarged image, which revealed just how much the leading ships were crowded together, three and four abreast, so that their outlines merged together into apparently continuous tiers of open gun ports, the barrels like bristles on a scrubbing brush.

The red hull of the Santísima Trinidad (her white strakes broken at geometrically precise intervals by the four rows of open gun ports) was even more conspicuous, although ahead of her were the Salvador del Mundo and San Josef, both three-deckers, the San Nicolas and a seventy-four he did not recognize.

The five ships hid many of the others but apart from their lack of formation – or perhaps because of it – they looked formidable. Ramage was glad to lower the telescope and get them back in perspective, but several impressions remained – among them the San Nicolas' beakhead painted in scarlet and topped by the huge gilded figurehead depicting the saint after whom the ship was named.

He heard Stafford say, 'If yer 'ears a crunch, it'll be the Commodore usin' us as a fender between the Capting and the Santy Trinidaddy!'

And Stafford was likely to be only slightly wide of the mark: in ten or twenty minutes the Kathleen would be squeezed between the upper grindstone of Cordoba's line to windward, and the lower of the British to leeward. Still, if the Commodore wanted him to leeward he'd make the signal.

'We're going to 'ave the best view of the guillotining,' Stafford said with apparent satisfaction to one of his mates, 'an' yer know the chap that gets the best view? Why, the chap that's 'avin' 'is 'ead trimmed orf. That is, if they don't stow 'im keel down, so 'e don't see the blade coming.'

'Would you want to see it comin', Staff?' someone asked.

'Oh, yus, I don't like anythin' sneakin' up on me.'

'But that bleedin' knife don't sneak up on you. It drops fastern'n a master-at-arms spottin' a bottle of rum being smuggled on board.'

'Quick or slow, I still like to see what's coming,' Stafford said philosophically. 'Like when I fell orf a main t'gallant yard.'

'When you did what?' The man's disbelief was obvious.

'You callin' me a liar?' Stafford demanded hotly. 'I fell orf the t'gallant yard of the Lively – you can see her over there – 'bout three years ago. An' keepin' me eyes open did a lot o' good.'

'Why? Use yer eyebrows to 'ang on to an invisible 'ook?'

'No invisibual 'ooks in the Lively, mate. Nah, as I fell I looked down an' saw I wasn't going to be no trouble to the first lieutenant.'

'No trouble to the first lieutenant? What's he got to do with it?'

'My oath,' exclaimed Stafford, 'I do 'ave to spell it out fer the likes o' you, don't I? If I'd 'it the deck I'd made a nasty mess, wouldn't I, and it'd 'ave to be swabbed and it'd take a lot o' scrubbin' afore the first lieutenant passed it clean again.'

'But how did keeping yer eyes open stop yer 'ittin' the deck?'

'It didn't stop me 'ittin it. I just saw I wouldn't 'it it. Oh no, don't say it! Wot I mean is I saw I was goin' ter land in the sea. An' I did.'

Southwick, who'd obviously been as intrigued by Stafford's tale as Ramage, then snapped. 'All right, belay all that chatter now. You sound like a flock of gannets round a dead whale.'

At that moment he caught sight of the lanky figure of Fuller edging up to the taffrail.

'Fuller!' he bellowed. 'Where the hell are you going? Why have you left your gun?'

'My line, sir – I thought I'd see if I'd got a fish on it, sir.'

'Fish? Line? D'you mean to say you've got a fishing line trailing over the stern?'

With disbelief and rage fighting for possession of his face, Southwick banged the scabbard of his sword against his boot. 'So help me, Fuller, we're going into battle, not Billingsgate fish market! Get the – '

He broke off, catching Ramage's eye, and said, 'All right, all right. See if you've got a bite! Then get the line in and stowed out of the way.'

'It's a tunny!' Fuller shouted. 'Here, give me a hand someone or I'll never get it on board.'

Ramage turned quickly and said, 'Let him have half a dozen hands, Mr Southwick.'

Southwick's eyebrows lifted with surprise: he was obviously thinking, one man, yes, but six! But Ramage knew anything that kept the men occupied for the time being would do no harm. Even the dullest must realize that unless the Commodore made a signal very soon, they'd all be staring into the muzzles of nearly a thousand guns, and although it was accepted that sail of the line did not fire into frigates and smaller vessels, Ramage trusted neither Spanish marksmanship nor the officers' ability to control their men.

Conditions were almost perfect for gunnery: the wind light – sufficient to keep the sails drawing but not enough to heel the ships, and only a slight swell giving the ships a slow, even roll which would be no trouble to the gun captains, although if the Spaniards followed their usual habit of having soldiers on board, it might hinder them a little.

Unhurried, splendid in their precision, the fifteen British sail of the line continued their deadly game of follow-my-leaders – a game which would begin in earnest as the approaching San Nicolas, leading Cordoba's division, received the first broadsides of the Culloden and passed on to receive those of the Blenheim.

Each gun captain in the leading ships would be down on one knee, beyond the reach of the recoiling gun. The trigger line would be held slack in one hand and he'd be steadying himself with the other arm outstretched, peering through the open port, ready to give last-minute orders for training or elevating the gun as the target came into sight and watching anxiously for the officer-of-quarter's order to fire while the rest of his crew would be waiting, cursing, praying, joking or silent, according to their nature.

Everyone would be waiting for the moment when, with the gun aimed, the second captain would cock the lock and jump back out of the way of the recoil, and the gun captain would fire. The vital first broadside, he reflected, fired before the men were really excited, everything done by the drill book, and the decks clear of smoke. After that, officers-of-quarters usually had a hard time keeping control and almost inevitably men were soon injured by a recoiling carriage, and sometimes a gun burst because in the excitement and smoke it was accidentally loaded with a double charge of powder...

Still no signal from the Commodore for the Kathleen to change her position, so Stafford might well have a chance of seeing that guillotine blade dropping.

He could just see the stem of the Culloden. She was more than two miles ahead, and the height of her masts and those of the San Nicolas showed they were almost abeam of each other. He glanced at his watch – eleven-thirty exactly, three hours since Sir John signalled 'Prepare for Battle', thirty-three minutes since he ordered the line of battle, eighteen since 'Engage the Enemy', fifteen since the Culloden opened fire on the Spanish leeward division and six since they turned away...

Three dozen red eyes winked open and closed along the Culloden's starboard side. A moment later smoke spewed from the muzzles of the guns and then the rumble of her first broadside at Cordoba's division rolled across the great Bay of Cadiz like distant thunder.

Southwick suddenly recited a familiar piece of verse:

> 'From rocks and sands and barren lands
> Good fortune set me free,
> And from great guns and women's tongues
> Good Lord deliver me!'

'Especially great guns,' Ramage added. 'We've nothing to fear from the rest – at the moment.'

He had been conscious of angry voices nearby and suddenly Stafford staggered in front of him and fell flat on his back. As Ramage turned in surprise he saw Fuller rubbing his knuckles. A moment later Stafford was on his feet again and with fists clenched running at the Suffolk man.

'Belay that!' roared Ramage. 'Stafford, what's going on?'

' 'E 'it me, sir.'

'Fuller! Why did you hit him?'

'He was laughing 'cause I lost m' fish, sir.'

'Your what?'

'M' fish, sir – the one I had on the line. I lost it.'

Ramage's own fists tightened with anger until he remembered they were children at heart and had to be treated as such.

'Look, you two fools: there's the Spanish Fleet. It'll be half an hour before they're abreast of us. I can have a grating rigged and the pair of you seized up and given a dozen of the best – with the bosun's mate combing the cat between each stroke – and still have twenty minutes to spare.'

At that moment the San Nicolas' first broadside echoed across the water and, as Ramage watched, the smoke formed into a cloud slowly drifting to leeward towards the British line, menacing in its oily opacity. Suddenly it came alive as the rippling red flashes of the Santísima Trinidad's broadside flickered through it like summer lightning, followed by the noise of a thousand distant drums beating a long roll.

'My God!' exclaimed Southwick. 'So that's what a four-decker's broadside sounds like!'

Instinctively everyone looked at her target, the Culloden, just as Captain Troubridge's ship fired her second full broadside, flame darting from the muzzles of all her starboard guns. Once again the spurts of smoke fused into a thick yellowish-white cloud, blowing back on board the Culloden and completely hiding her hull for a minute or two.

Then Ramage could see her, the draught down her hatchways forcing the smoke to pour out of her gun ports again as if she was on fire. The men would be coughing and spluttering while hastily reloading and running out the guns. But there was little sign of damage from the broadsides of the San Nicolas and the Santísima Trinidad.

'Can you see anything sir?' Southwick inquired anxiously.

'Nothing that matters – just a hole or two in the topsails.'

'Cordoba's got a yaw-sighted lot of gun captains. Just think – a broadside by the biggest ship o' war in the world, and nothing to show for it!'

Ramage's eye was suddenly caught by a long trail of objects floating in the water between the Captain and Diadem. They were small and he had to hold the telescope steady to see them clearly. Hmm...dozens of casks, what seemed to be several small tables, scores of tiny crescents of wood – probably staves of barrels – and half a dozen curious white rectangles which looked like canvas berths. Obviously some of the leading ships in the line with a lot of gear on deck when the time came to clear for action had hove them over the side out of the way.

'What are they, sir?' inquired Southwick.

'Ammunition for the Navy Board clerks.'

The Master looked puzzled.

'Tables, casks, staves… Think of all the forms to be filled in to account for them.'

Southwick roared with laughter. 'If they've got any sense they'll report 'em as destroyed in battle. That always beats those dam' quill drivers! And that reminds me, sir, we've got some sails that want replacing. More patches than original cloths. If I hear as much as one shot whistle overhead, we'll get a couple of new jibs out of it!'

More broadsides – now the Prince George and Orion were firing and several Spanish ships replying; but as they were to windward the smoke hid them from the Kathleen. Within three or four minutes, as more ships opened fire, the broadsides became ragged, echoing all round the horizon like continuous thunder.

Occasionally Ramage sighted some of the Spanish centre and rear ships for a few moments as they sailed out of the banks of smoke. The San Nicolas was still at the head of Cordoba's division with the Santísima Trinidad on her starboard quarter and the Salvador del Mundo to larboard (and, Ramage noted, completely unable to fire even one of her guns because the Santísima Trinidad was between her and the enemy). Then close astern of the Santísima Trinidad was the San Isidro with the San Josef on her larboard side and unable to fire…

He pointed out to Southwick how Cordoba's failure to control his ships was halving the guns he could bring to bear on the British.

'Doesn't seem to make much odds anyway, sir. The Culloden's been fired at by five of 'em so far, including the Santísima Trinidad, without much sign of damage!'

Ahead of the Kathleen the battle now presented an in-congruous sight: on the larboard bow the centre and rear ships of the British line were sailing into battle through the smoke from the broadsides of those in the van, while over on the starboard bow the leading Spanish ships were sailing out of the smoke of battle in the opposite direction.

'The Commodore's signalling sir,' called Jackson. 'Our pendant, then one one five. "To take up station astern".'

For a moment Ramage was tempted to interpret the signal literally and bear away into the Captain's wake, ahead of the Diadem and Excellent, but the Commodore's meaning was clear: the Kathleen was to station herself at the rear of the line, astern of the Excellent.

'Very well, acknowledge. Mr Southwick, we'll take up our station one cable astern of the Excellent.'

The Master obviously shared Ramage's unwillingness to leave their present vantage point and took his time giving the necessary orders.

Suddenly Ramage saw the San Nicolas was no longer approaching head on, parallel with the British line. She had altered course at least a point to larboard. And the ship astern was this very moment following in her wake. If the rest did the same the whole Spanish line would soon be slanting away on an increasingly diverging course: the British would be going down the right-hand side of a 'V' towards the join (the rear of the Spanish line) while the Spaniards would be sailing up the left side towards the open end, the distance between the leading Spanish and the last British ship increasing every moment.

Because the Kathleen was still well up to windward of the British line Ramage could see this alteration of course quite clearly. But the San Nicolas was almost abreast the Victory: to Sir John it would be almost imperceptible; in fact with all the smoke it probably wouldn't be noticed at all.

He stared for several moments, and saw there was also no chance of the Victory seeing any signals from the Kathleen. But he also realized that since the San Nicolas was not yet abreast the Captain, the Commodore was bound to spot she had altered course away: her turn was gradually taking her out of range of the Captain.

Finally he snapped the telescope shut with a vicious jab. The copper of its tubes made his fingers smell. Lieutenants, he told himself, shouldn't question the actions of admirals, and as he was trying to thrust aside his doubts Southwick said: 'Puzzles me why we didn't tack in succession as soon as the Culloden was abreast the San Nicolas.'

Ramage was startled and gave a noncommittal grunt: the old Master's gruff comment echoed his own thoughts, which he'd drawn on a corner of the page with a question mark beside it. If Sir John have given that order as soon as the Culloden was in a position where tacking would take her up alongside the San Nicolas leading the Spanish van, each of the following British ships would have turned in succession in the Culloden's wake, so the second ship, the Blenheim, would have got alongside the second Spaniard, followed by the Prince George tackling the third and so on until both lines were sailing on the same course alongside each other, ship matched against ship. There was one other possibility.

'He might be going to order us to tack together.'

It was Southwick's turn to grunt

'With those leading ships turning away from us? We'd never get near 'em.'

And again Ramage was forced to admit perhaps his own fears weren't groundless: Southwick was making the same point.

'Trouble is,' Southwick grumbled. 'I'm dam' sure that with all this smoke they can't see what's happening from the Victory.'

Waiting until the two lines were abreast of each other – when the San Nicolas leading the Spanish van was level with the Excellent at the rear of the British line, and the Culloden at the head of the British line level with the last Spaniard – and then ordering the Fleet to tack together was standard and meant the whole line attacked at the same time. But it depended on one thing: that both lines were on opposite and parallel courses or, if not, that the ships farthest from the enemy had a chance to get up to their opposite numbers in the enemy line.

'Look,' Southwick said, 'the San Nicolas has gone round even more, and I bet the Santísima Trindad's going to follow in her wake. They don't want to fight: mark my words, sir, they're quitting!'

Ramage opened the telescope reluctantly, feeling like a child in bed who'd heard a strange noise in the night and was curious yet frightened, uncertain whether to look and confirm his fears or hide his head under the sheet.

There was no doubt: the San Nicolas' turn was part of some plan Cordoba had devised; it wasn't because she had sustained too much damage, or her captain was scared of British powder and shot. The ships bunched up astern had turned in her wake now, and were being followed by the rest. The Spanish line was becoming half-moon-shaped where they turned, but the trouble was they were turning after they'd passed the Victory, hidden from her by the smoke. Those ahead of her, which Sir John could see, hadn't reached the point on the bulge where they turned...

Yet what on earth could he –

'Flagship's signalling sir.' called Jackson. 'General – number eighty. "To tack in succession". '

In succession, not together! That proved Sir John could not see Cordoba's van. And as far as Ramage could see – for the Kathleen was still to windward of the line, still bearing away slowly to get into position astern of the Excellent – the Culloden was well past the last ship in the Spanish line... Tacking in succession meant the Culloden would turn and might with a bit of luck and good seamanship get alongside the last ship, but the Blenheim and those astern of her would tack and find no opponents...

Ramage felt there was some terrible flaw in his reasoning as he drew another sketch of them tacking in succession; some simple factor he had overlooked which would be the key to it all, which would reveal Sir John's real intentions. He then drew a diagram of them tacking together, and put a question mark beside that, too.

Southwick had no such doubts about Sir John's intentions.

'You're sure it's number eighty?' he snapped to Jackson.

The American nodded but sensing the questions had a greater significance which was lost on him looked again. 'Yes, sir, eighty it is.'

'Give me the signal book a moment,' and as he looked up the number he growled, 'Watch in case they run up "Annul". '

Turning to Ramage he said, 'It's right, sir, that's number eighty. But d'you think there's been a mistake? I was expecting "Tack together". '

Ramage said nothing: he glanced at his watch – eight minutes past twelve – and then looked at the leading Spanish ships, an idea forming in his mind.

'But sir,' Southwick expostulated, 'they'll all escape if we tack in succession!'

'Wait and see if the Victory hoists "Annul".'

'But the Culloden's already coming round,' wailed Southwick. 'All we're doing is grabbing the tip of the rat's tail when we've got his whole body dam' nearly alongside!'

'That'll be enough, Mr Southwick,' Ramage said shortly. There was a chance Sir John had some trick up his sleeve, but he was beginning to doubt it: with a given wind a ship could sail only at a certain speed and in certain directions: likewise there were only four aces in a pack of cards.

CHAPTER TWENTY

By now the Kathleen was in position astern of the Excellent and at the end of the British line, the puppy following the huntsmen. From ahead the continuous rumble of broadsides, and the Kathleens watched the Blenheim brace her yards round and tack in the wake of the Culloden. Ten minutes past noon and the Culloden was doing her best to catch up with the rearmost Spanish ship.

Almost weeping with frustration, Ramage glared at the mass of ships forming the van of Cordoba's division: an almost solid wedge, the San Nicolas still leading, with at least seven more ships in a tightly-packed group tucked in astern, two and three abreast, the rest scattered astern along the bulging line.

'One thing about it,' Southwick commented, 'they sail like haystacks drifting to windward...'

'Flagship sir,' said Jackson, 'number forty. "To pass through the enemy's line".'

Fifteen minutes past noon. So Sir John intended the Culloden to try to cut through Cordoba's line, splitting it in two.

'He'll never do it,' Southwick said quietly. 'We'll never catch up with 'em in this wind. And only the Culloden and Blenheim have tacked – thirteen more to go!'

With maddening slowness, the Prince George, Orion and Irresistible came round one after the other in the light breeze, and then as the Colossus began turning, her foretopgallant mast bent in the middle and began to fall – so slowly, so gracefully, that it took a moment for Ramage to realize it had been shot away, bringing with it the foretopmast. Then the foreyard and foretopsail yard slewed to one side and fell to the deck, a confused jumble of wood, cordage and sails, leaving her unable to tack. Her captain obviously decided to wear round to get out of the way of those astern because almost at once Ramage could see through the telescope that her mizzen topsail was beginning to shiver.

'Wind's backing a bit sir,' Southwick reported. 'Due west now.'

And it was falling even lighter. Ramage doubted if the British ships were making much more than a knot. But even allowing for the lack of wind, he was surprised at the slow pace of battle. Action between single ships – his only experience so far – was much faster, more clear cut: the difference between a game of draughts, perhaps (with the two players able to move in only one of two directions) and chess, where concentrating on the diagonal moves of the bishop, for instance, left you open to the dangerous jinking hop of the knight's move. And at the moment Sir John was playing chess with more than half the board covered with smoke.

Fifteen minutes to one o'clock. His feet ached; he felt sick with hunger. And, like the warning of violent toothache to come, was the nagging question of why Cordoba was now steering to the north-west. It was taking him away from his lee division and, more important, away from Cadiz. It was a ruse: he was sure of that. The San Nicholas and Santísima Trinidad and the rest of the van would soon be abeam. But more important was that the Culloden,

Blenheim and Prince George still had not caught up with the rearmost Spanish ships.

For ten minutes he paced up and down the starboard side, rubbing the scar on his forehead from time to time. His pistols – he'd found the box and his clothes still in the bread-room where he'd bundled them as the Kathleen was captured – were tucked in his belt and made his ribs ache. He pulled them out and gave them to Jackson. Not wanting to talk to Southwick, he sent him below for a quick meal and was grateful when the steward brought up some cold chicken, which he ate with his fingers as he walked.

Slowly Cordoba's van ships drew abeam and farther away. It was nearly one o'clock and the Victory, next in line after the damaged Colossus, still had not tacked – the Colossus was probably in her way – but the Culloden seemed to be gaining a little on the Spanish rear ships and drawing well ahead of the Blenheim.

The steward came with a bowl of water and a napkin, and Ramage rinsed his greasy fingers. Pointless, perhaps, since he might be a pulpy mass of flesh and blood before the hands of the clock reached the next hour. What made him think of that? He shivered and tried to thrust aside his earlier wild idea, assuring himself that of all the ships in the British Fleet, the Kathleen was the safest: none of the Spaniards would attack her.

As he wiped his hands and gave the napkin to the steward he glanced over the man's shoulder and his stomach shrivelled.

Instead of the Santísima Trinidad, San Nicolas and the rest of the leaders being almost broadside on, he found himself staring at their starboard bows: in the few moments he had been occupied washing his hands they had put their helms up, turning towards the Kathleen and obviously intending to pass very close round the end of the British line, probably raking the Excellent (and the Kathleen too, since she'd be in the line of fire) in the process.

Ramage felt he was looking down on the chess-board and could see the next half-dozen moves with unnatural clarity: unless Sir John signalled at once for the eight ships forming the rear of the British line to tack together and head them off, there was nothing to stop Cordoba's ships running down to join his other six ships to leeward as soon as they rounded the Excellent's stern, and with his fleet united once again, Cordoba could then resume his dash for the safety of Cadiz. And the banks of smoke were certainly hiding the whole manoeuvre from the Victory.

Ramage snapped: 'My compliments to Mr Southwick: would he come on deck at once. Quartermaster, edge us up to windward but I don't want it to be too noticeable.'

The idea – fantasy, almost – was gripping him more strongly. Was this how a man worked himself up before committing suicide? The thought made him feel dizzy.

Jackson saw him rubbing his brow and looking anxiously at the ships ahead, and guessing he was looking for signals from the Commodore, from Admiral Thompson in the Britannia, or Sir John in the Victory, the American watched carefully with his telescope. And almost at once a string of flags fluttered from the flagship.

'Minerve's pendant, sir, and' – Jackson glanced at the signal book, – 'and the Colossus', "To take in tow".'

Ramage, who had instinctively walked towards Jackson in anticipation of the order 'Tack together', spun on his heel to hide his anger and disappointment and looked yet again at Cordoba's leading ships. They now had the wind about three points abaft the beam – almost their fastest point of sailing.

Southwick clattered up the companionway, his sword scabbard clanking, and even before Ramage turned to speak, exclaimed, 'There! They're doing it! I knew they would!'

He looked ahead, saw the Victory and the eight ships astern of her still had not tacked, and added viciously:

'Nothing can stop those fish-eaters unless we all tack together! So help me, that I should live to see the day! Just look at them – coming down like a flock of sheep and not even a dog to give 'em a fright by barking! Why, if that leading ship yawed a couple of times at least half a dozen of 'em would run aboard each other!'

Ramage clenched his fists. The idea, plan, fantasy, dream – he wasn't sure what to call it – was becoming clearer: the significance of Cordoba's move and its danger to the British fleet was making him think so fast he was momentarily surprised when he looked up to find the Kathleen and Cordoba's van still sailing on their respective courses. Nothing had happened – except in his imagination: he was still alive – yet in his imagination, he had, a few seconds earlier, died along with every man on board the cutter.

Perhaps through the smoke the Victory's next astern had glimpsed Cordoba's change of course; perhaps even now Commodore Nelson was trying to signal to the Victory. But the facts were clear enough: Sir John was in grave danger of being defeated by smoke, the light wind – and time. Whatever he might order to be done now, it would still take time for ships to move from position A to position B. And Ramage knew he had to face up to one other unpleasant – and for himself probably fatal – fact: that there was only one chance of giving Sir John time. Yet…he turned violently and he paced up and down, watched by Southwick and Jackson.

His face was drained of blood, leaving the tanned flesh yellow: concentration and the horror of his knowledge made him clench his teeth so the jawbone was a hard white line, the muscles tight knots beneath the skin. His eyes were no longer deep-set but sunken, as though he was in the last stages of a grave illness. Both Southwick and Jackson knew their captain was alone in some private and desperate hell, and they felt empty and angry at their inability to help him.

Ramage felt the fingers of his right hand almost breaking as he squeezed some small object and, coming back from a long way off, tried to focus his eyes on it: Gianna's ring, still on the ribbon round his neck. He thrust it back inside his shirt and as though waking from a dream realized the gulls were still mewing in the Kathleen's wake; the guns were still rumbling ahead; a weak sun was doing its best to shine through the haze; and several of the ship's company were still laughing and joking. And Southwick was standing in front of him, pointing, a puzzled look on his face.

The Captain had begun turning to larboard out of the line and away from the enemy. There was not one signal flag flying. It was as if she was out of control – except her sails were being trimmed. And she kept turning.

'She's leaving the line and wearing round!' Southwick exclaimed incredulously. Ramage realized at once the Commodore's intention. But the Captain was a mile farther away than the Kathleen: a mile she'd take twenty minutes to cover. And unless Cordoba's leading ships could be delayed for twenty minutes, she'd arrive too late.

The fantasy which had become an idea now became a necessity if the Commodore was to succeed, and Ramage felt fear. Swiftly he sketched on the pad, did some calculations in his head, and then turned to Southwick. He could not look the old man in the eye as he said in a strangled voice barely recognizable as his own: 'Mr Southwick, I'll trouble you to tack the ship and steer to intercept the San Nicolas.'

Turning away quickly, not wanting to see Southwick's face, he looked back at the Captain. After wearing round, she'd come back through the line astern of the Diadem and ahead of the Excellent. Then (alone and, he guessed, not only without orders but in defiance of them) the Commodore would steer for the leading – nearest, anyway – Spaniards.

Southwick had given the necessary orders to put the Kathleen about on the other tack before fully realizing the significance of what Ramage was planning to do. Once he did understand he felt humbled that someone young enough to be his son could make such a decision with no apparent fear or doubt. He was pacing up and down with the same relaxed, almost cat-like walk as if he was on watch, and occasionally he rubbed that scar.

Without thinking, Southwick spontaneously strode up to Ramage, looked at him directly with his bloodshot eyes, and said softly with a mixture of pride, affection and admiration: 'If you could have lived long enough, you'd have been as great an admiral as your father.'

With that he turned and began bellowing orders which steadied the Kathleen on her new course with Cordoba's leading ships approaching broad on her larboard bow, the British line stretching away on her larboard quarter, and the Captain just passing clear of the Excellent's bow and breaking away from the line.

There was nothing more to do for a few minutes and Ramage leaned back against the taffrail looking for the hundredth time at Cordoba's ships. Only then did he picture the physical results of his decision, and as he did so the real fear came.

It came slowly, like autumn mist rising almost imperceptibly in a valley; it went through his body like fine rain soaking into a cotton shirt. And Ramage felt he had two selves. One was a physical body whose strength had suddenly vanished, whose hands trembled, whose knees had no muscles, whose stomach was a sponge slopping with cold water, whose vision sharpened to make colours brighter, outlines harder, details which normally passed unnoticed show up almost stark. The other self was remote, aloof from his body, aghast at what was to be done, appalled that he had planned it, yet knowing full well he had ordered it and coldly determined to see to its execution.

And then he remembered watching the Commodore and realizing the little man often had the same look in his eye that Southwick had when he was in a killing mood. And he remembered wondering then whether he could himself kill a man in cold blood. Well, the wondering was over. Now he knew he could kill sixty men in cold blood, sixty of his own men, not the enemy, and the realization made him want to vomit.

He found himself looking at a coil of rope: fear made him see it with such clarity that he might never have seen rope before in his life. Every inch or so was flecked with a coloured yarn – 'The Rogue's Yarn', a strand put in when the rope was made up in the Royal dockyards, so if it was stolen it would always be recognizable as Navy Board property. Had he – and Southwick, and Commodore Nelson, and perhaps half the commission and warrant officers in the Fleet – a Rogue's Yarn woven into their souls that set them apart from other people, that let them kill their own men and the enemy without compunction?

Yet when he looked again at the Spanish ships and knew he had less than half an hour to live, the fear ebbed away as silently as it had come. Slowly he realized fear came only when death was a matter of chance, a possibility (or even probability) yet beyond a man's certain knowledge or control. But now, because he knew for certain he'd be killed as a result of his own deliberate decision – thus removing the element of chance – he accepted its inevitability and unexpectedly found an inner peace and, more important, an outward calm.

Or was it really just cold-bloodedness? Perhaps – it was hard to distinguish.

Jackson had saved his life – and despite his loyalty and bravery, Jackson must die. Southwick, who cheerfully obeyed every order from someone a third of his age (and a tenth of his experience, for that matter) had been told a few moments ago that he was in fact sentenced to death – and merely expressed genuine regret that Lieutenant Ramage would not live out the day because otherwise he'd have become as great an admiral as his father. Poor father – John Uglow Ramage, tenth Earl of Blazey, Admiral of the White, would also be the last earl: his only son was also his only male heir, so one of the oldest earldoms in the kingdom would become extinct. Poor mother, for that matter. He closed his eyes for a moment and pictured Gianna but opened them almost at once: if anyone could make him change his mind...

Then there was Stafford, the Cockney locksmith who'd prefer to watch the guillotine blade drop, should he ever be strapped down on 'The Widow', instead of being blindfolded. Bridewell Lane wouldn't see him again. Then the rest of those with him at Cartagena – Fuller of the fishing line; the young Genovesi, Rossi; the cheery coloured seaman Maxton; and Sven Jensen... And the Kathleen herself; she lived, had a will of her own, had peculiar little quirks her captain had to understand and pander to, who responded with all her wooden soul when sailed properly, but became dead in the water the moment anyone ignored for a moment the precise set of her sails or used her helm with a hard hand. Matchwood – he was consigning her to matchwood, shattered flotsam to be cast up piece by piece at the whim of wind and current for month after month and probably year after year along the Portuguese, Spanish and African coasts. Men speaking many languages would seize those pieces of her timbers and carry them home to burn on their fires or patch their homes and never know whence they came.

He found his eyes fixed on a few square inches of deck planking at his feet: he saw each hard ridge of grain standing proud above the tiny valleys where the softer wood between had been scrubbed away over the years by countless seamen. He saw the grain, the knots, the very texture of the wood with a new clarity, as though for all his life without realizing it he'd been looking through a steamed up glass window which had been suddenly and unexpectedly wiped clear. He saw the wrinkling of his soft black leather boots marked as white lines where salt had dried in the creases. He felt the downdraught of the mainsail and glanced up to realize he'd never before really seen the texture of the sail. Nor, as he looked over the larboard bow, the gentle pyramiding of the sea. Nor the deadliness of a group of five or six enemy sail of the line, one of them the largest ship in the world, the biggest thing the hand of man had ever created to float on the sea, and intended only to kill.

The sight brought him back to the immediate present and the limited future. The Kathleen was close enough now for the hulls of Cordoba's leading ships to be outlined above the line of the horizon, and for a moment their size and slow progress took Ramage back to a childhood episode: crouching muddy, nervous and excited in the rushes at the side of a lake, his eyes only a few inches above the water, watching swans returning to their nests nearby with their cygnets: rounded, majestic, splendid in their graceful movements, yet each with hard, wicked and spiteful eyes, ready to savage anything in their path – particularly a small boy lurking in the rushes.

The San Nicolas was still leading, forming the sharp end of the wedge with the Salvador del Mundo on her larboard quarter and, beyond, the San Josef. On the nearest side of the wedge the Santísima Trinidad was on the San Nicolas' starboard quarter, with the San Isidro astern of her. The San Nicolas was the key, and he was thankful, although she was an 84-gun ship, she was next but smallest of the five.

He felt inside his shirt for Gianna's signet ring, ripped it from the ribbon on which it hung, and slipped it on to the little finger of his left hand. It fitted perfectly since it was a man's ring and Gianna normally wore it on her middle finger. Curious, he thought, that a family heirloom of the Volterras, handed down from generation to generation, should leave its Tuscan home to spend the rest of Eternity with him at the bottom of the ocean eleven leagues south-west of Cape St Vincent. She was and would be with him in spirit: thank God not in the flesh.

Gloomy, morbid thoughts but excusable. He almost laughed at the thought that he was really solemnly apologizing to himself. When Southwick had walked away from Ramage he'd wished he'd shaken him by the hand. He couldn't because the ship's company would have seen and guessed it was a farewell. It wouldn't have made them do their jobs unwillingly, but his years at sea had taught Southwick that men fought like demons when there was a chance of survival, but a condemned man rarely if ever tried to fight his way off the scaffold. A man tended to bow to the inevitable – which, he chuckled to himself, was inevitable.

The Master, giving his orders through force of habit, had time to reflect that secretly he'd always dreaded the time when he'd be too old to go to sea. He hated houses, hated gardens, hated even more the thought he'd end his days anchored to one particular house and one particular garden, and would only leave it when he was carried off in a plain deal box (he'd specified that in his will; the usual expensive coffin with bronze fittings was a sinful waste of good wood, metal and money).

After taking up some bearings on the San Nicolas he'd deliberately stayed near the mast. Mr Ramage was leaning back against the taffrail with that look in his eyes that told Southwick he was taking a last look far beyond the horizon into a world of his own. Probably thinking of the Marchesa. Aye, they'd have made a handsome couple, he thought sadly. Now it'd be left to some young fop to lead her to the altar.

That lad – Southwick found it easy to obey his orders yet think of him as a lad – had been born with all the advantages possible: son of an admiral, heir to an earldom, clever (except in mathematics, which he freely admitted), humorous and with this extraordinary and quite indefinable ability to lead men. With only a few years at sea, barely past his twenty-first birthday (if in fact he'd yet reached it) he'd inherited his father's enemies in the Service and so far had beaten them.

So far – and this was as far as the lad would go. Now he was going to sacrifice his life (to the King's enemies, anyway) in a manoeuvre which would probably fail – through no fault of his – and almost certainly not be appreciated, except by his father and the Commodore. Courage, Southwick thought as he bellowed through his black japanned speaking trumpet at a skylarking sailor, was an inadequate word to describe what's needed to sentence yourself to death.

Jackson fingered the two pistols Mr Ramage had given him and wondered whether to continue holding them or just put them down somewhere. They wouldn't be needed now – and he'd known that long before Mr Ramage had yanked them out of the band of his breeches and started drawing on a pad of paper.

The American had begun to guess how it would all end when Mr Ramage interrupted old Southwick's meal, and knew for certain a moment later when the quartermaster was told to edge up to windward. Jackson was surprised how long it took old Southwick to hoist in what Mr Ramage intended to do. Jackson supposed it was because Southwick was old; too set in his ways – which was why he was still Master of a ship as small as the Kathleen – to anticipate someone might do the unexpected. And Jackson realized he'd learned that lesson from Mr Ramage. 'Surprise, Jackson – that's how you win battles,' he'd once said. 'If you can't surprise the enemy by stealth, you can always surprise him in front of his very eyes simply by doing something completely unexpected!'

Well, old 'Blaze-away's' son practised what he preached, though this'd be the last time. Jackson felt no regrets as he looked at Cordoba's ships with the knowledge they would probably kill him and the rest of the Kathleens within the hour. He'd felt no regrets the day he left Charleston as a boy in a schooner trading to the West Indies; no regrets as the coast of South Carolina had finally dipped astern below the horizon. That was nearly twenty-five years ago, and he could still picture it. No regrets either, when he'd been pressed into the Royal Navy, despite his American citizenship. And he knew that given the chance of going back now and steering a different course so that he wouldn't risk dying this Valentine's Day, he wouldn't change anything.

Ramage's feet now ached so much they throbbed and his boots seemed a size too small. The night of fog left him tired, his eyes strained and burning as though the eyelids were dusted with fine sand. At sea the emergencies nearly always came when you were physically at the end of the rope, rarely when you were fresh. He was so tired everything around him had an air of unreality. He felt he was using the Kathleen as a hideous mask to frighten the Spanish. Or – and the thought almost made him giggle – like a frightened little man using stilts to make himself ten feet tall. He thought how in a thick mist the boulders on the Cornish moors looked grotesque and huge, yet in sunshine seemed rounded and small. Mist...grotesque and huge... The words seemed to echo as he repeated them. Mist, fog – smoke! Even the sail of the line looked grotesque (and still did) with banks of smoke from the guns drifting over them – particularly the Culloden when the wind blew the smoke of her own guns back on board until the draught down the hatchways made it stream out of the ports again. But the Kathleen's guns couldn't make enough smoke.

Then he remembered himself as a young midshipman, one of a group secretly burning wet gunpowder to smoke out the rats and cockroaches in their berth. (It had resulted in them all being mastheaded because they'd forgotten the smell of the smoke would drift, and a Marine sentry had promptly raised the alarm of fire.) The idea grew in his mind. But how to make a screen of smoke large enough to hide the Kathleen, using only wet powder? Perhaps the braziers used to dry and air below deck? Light them, toss in some chunks of pitch and then wet powder? It might work with the braziers up on the weather side so the wind blew the smoke across the ship. Anyway it'd probably puzzle the Spaniards long enough to make them hold their fire for a few minutes – and that alone made it worth trying.

And need all the men die? There might be a chance for some of them. Piles of lashed-up hammocks on deck – they'd float and support men. So would all the spare wood the carpenter's mate had stowed below. The lashings of the spare gaff stowed alongside the mast must be cut so it would float clear. He called Southwick and Edwards, the gunner's mate, and gave them their instructions.

Then, as the details of his plan gradually took shape, he realized he wanted a dozen men who were nimble, good with cutlasses, and who'd fight until they were cut or shot down. Who should he choose? Out of the whole ship's company it was only a question of eliminating the less nimble since everyone met the other requirements. Well, it boiled down to choosing a dozen men to die with him, so first he decided on Jackson and the five who'd been with him at Cartagena.

He told Jackson to hail the five with the speaking trumpet, and picked another half-dozen from those at the guns. As soon as they were all grouped round him he gave them their orders.

'It'll be out of the frying pan into the fire,' he concluded as he dismissed them, but he noticed they walked with jaunty strides, obviously delighted at having been chosen. The poor fools, he thought. Yet perhaps they weren't – he was honest enough to admit he was glad he was going to lead them because he'd no wish to stay in the frying pan.

'Do we stand a chance, sir?' Jackson asked quietly.

'Of telling our grandchildren about it? No, none. Of doing the job – yes. At least an even chance.'

Jackson nodded. 'I'm glad she isn't, for her own sake, but the Marchesa'd like to be with us, sir, and Count Pitti.'

'Yes,' Ramage said shortly, instinctively feeling the signet ring with his thumb. He had to say it to someone, if only to – well, he felt an aching guilt towards his Kathleens.

'Jackson, if there was any other way' – he glanced back at the British line, but except for the Captain steering towards them, it was sailing on, drawing away, although a couple more of the leading ships had tacked – 'I'd try it but there isn't…'

'We know, sir, but none of the lads'd change places with anyone walking down St James's.'

Ramage looked at his watch. They'd tacked only a few minutes ago. It seemed an hour. His mind was racing and the men were working fast: already the braziers were being hoisted up on deck, and there was a stack of hammocks round the forehatch with others being arranged in piles along the centreline.

The secret papers: he'd forgotten to get a lead-lined box made. He'd use a canvas bag and a roundshot. Jackson would have to put the signal book in at the last moment and then throw the bag over the side. Down in his cabin once again he glanced round as he put the papers in the bag. Few cabins in a ship of war could have such memories for a captain. He shut the top drawer and opened the second. Gianna's silk scarf was lying there where he'd put it when he came back on board, neatly folded. He picked it up, intending to tie it round his waist, then decided neither smartness nor the custom of the service was important now and knotted it round his neck, tucking the ends under his stock. If he'd brought her any happiness, then now he was going to bring her an equal amount of grief.

Then he was back on deck, looking at the San Nicolas. As she and the rest of the leading ships drew nearer he saw they were farther apart than he first thought.

'The right ship's leading 'em, sir,' commented Jackson as Ramage drew yet another plan showing the position of the ships, this time to help him calculate the best angle of approach.

'Right ship?'

'Haven't you noticed, sir? She's named after the same saint as you!'

The San Nicolas – no, he hadn't realized it and said with a grin, 'Since she's leading this undignified rush for Cadiz, Jackson, I'll trouble you not to mention it!'

Jackson laughed. 'Well, sir, let's hope he decides to look after you and not the Dons!'

The San Nicolas, Ramage reflected: an 84-gun ship of about two thousand tons compared with the Kathleen's 160 tons. Why, the Spanish ship's masts and yards alone would weigh as much as the whole of the Kathleen, while the nose on the figure head of St Nicolas must be about thirty feet above the waterline. The jib-boom end would be all of sixty-five feet high – and that was the height of the Kathleen's mast... Oh, the devil take it, he told himself angrily, guessing dimensions won't make the San Nicolas an inch smaller or the Kathleen an inch larger.

'Any signals to the Captain from the Victory, Jackson?'

'Can't see the Victory for smoke, sir; but nothing hoisted in the Captain: no acknowledgements: just her colours.'

Southwick said, 'Captain Collingwood won't leave the Commodore unsupported for long, orders or no orders. We'll soon see the Excellent following the Captain.'

'I hope so.'

'Did you expect the Captain to quit the line, sir?'

'Yes. At least, I hoped she would!'

'But the Commodore left it a bit late,' ventured Southwick.

Ramage shrugged his shoulders with feigned indifference. 'Late for us; but he's probably just got time to head them off – particularly if we can cause a delay. He won't have time to get in among the leaders, though.'

'He'll go for the Santísima Trinidad?'

Ramage nodded. He knew instinctively that if there was any choice that the Commodore would tackle the largest ship in the world, and by chance she was to leeward of the rest and so nearest to the Captain.

Then Ramage looked at the Spanish ships, at the Captain, at the British line and at the sketches on his pad, and suddenly he knew his plan was not only futile but absurd. Despite what he'd just said to Southwick he knew that even if the Kathleen did manage to delay the Spanish van for fifteen or twenty minutes, the chances of the Captain catching up were slender. But, more important, even if she did she wouldn't be able to head off all those ships: each one of them had a heavier broadside: all of them would rake her time and again before her own broadsides would bear.

And he knew that even now he could wear round the Kathleen on some pretext or other and return to her proper position, astern of the Excellent. But he was still looking at his sketch of the Kathleen superimposed on the San Nicolas when he realized that, despite what the pencil lines told him, he had to go on because if he turned back now, for the rest of his life he'd never be sure whether it was logic or fear that made him give up.

Once he'd decided to go on he was angry with himself for the alternate bouts of fear and calm, confidence and uncertainty. And then he also realized that although the Commodore might have had similar doubts (though hardly similar fears) he'd nevertheless quit the line and was going to try, and that was all that mattered. If the Kathleen could give him an extra fifteen or twenty minutes, they might make all the difference between complete failure and a partial success...

And he must put a term to idle thoughts and daydreams: the San Nicolas was coming up fast, and there was no room for mistakes. Edwards had the braziers ready, lashings holding the four legs of each one against the ship's roll, and they were half-full of old shavings and scraps of wood and chunks of pitch, a few screws of paper tucked in the bottom ready for lighting.

Ramage's dozen men were arming themselves with a variety of weapons. Jackson had a cutlass in his hand and a butcher's cleaver – presumably borrowed or stolen from the cook's mate – swinging at his belt from a line through the hole in the wooden handle. Stafford had cut down the haft of a boarding pike so that he had in effect a three-sided dagger blade on a three-foot handle, and he was practising swinging a cutlass with his right hand and lunging the pike with the left. He'd arrived at the old main-gauche, Ramage realized, without ever having seen the shadier side of knightly combat. Maxton, the coloured seaman, had a cutlass in each hand and was slashing at an imaginary enemy with such fast inward swings that Southwick commented to Ramage, 'He could cut a man into four slices before anyone saw him move.'

'He was born with a machete in his hand,' Ramage replied, remembering Maxton's comment at Cartagena. 'He learned to swing a blade cutting down sugar cane.'

Still the San Nicolas ploughed on. The nearer she came the less graceful she appeared: the cutwater could not soften the bulging bow, the bow wave was no longer a feather of white but a mass of water being shoved out of the way by the brute force of a ponderous hull. Her sails were no longer shapely curves but overstretched, overpatched and badly-setting. The beautiful lady in the distance was proving on closer inspection to be a raddled woman of the streets.

But there was no mistaking that raddled or not the San Nicolas had teeth: the muzzles of her guns were dozens of stubby black fingertips poking out of the ports. In a few minutes he'd be able to see details of the gilt work on her bow and figurehead. She was about a mile off.

Stafford was teasing Fuller again. 'Wotcher want wiv that pike?' he demanded. 'Use a rod and a big fish 'ook, mate; yer won't need bait. Just cast yer 'ook so it 'itches in their breeches!'

Fuller grunted an oath and continued chopping the pike haft to shorten it.

'Fishes could teach you a thing or two.'

'Ho yus! Reely brainy, fish. So brainy they bite your 'ooks. Takes brains, that do.'

'There's more brain in a cod's head than your whole body, y'clacking picklock!'

'Belay that,' Southwick interrupted. 'Keep it for the Dons.'

He then walked over to Ramage with his sword. 'Perhaps you'd care to use this, sir. It's served me well.'

It was enormous. Ramage could visualize a bearded Viking waving it with two hands as he leapt on shore from a longboat. But as he drew it from the scabbard he realized it was beautifully balanced.

'I'd appreciate it, Mr Southwick,' he said, 'and I hope I'll put it to good use.'

The Master beamed and slipped the shoulder belt over Ramage's head.

As the San Nicolas came on, Ramage noted thankfully the rest of the leading group were instinctively closing in astern of her. And in behaving like driven cattle crowding together behind their leader to pass through a gate, they were increasing his chances of creating confusion.

'A cast of the log if you please, Mr Southwick. Jackson, pass me my pistols. Quartermaster, what is you heading?'

Ramage wanted to know the Kathleen's exact course and speed, and after looking at the Captain he glanced at his sketch. Southwick stood beside him, studied the pencil lines and shook his head.

'The Commodore won't make it.'

Ramage shrugged his shoulders again and pointed towards the British line. The Excellent had already quit the line and was following the Captain.

'Perhaps not. But we don't seem to be keeping a very sharp lookout, Mr Southwick. I trust we haven't missed any signals?'

'Bit difficult to know where to watch,' Southwick said sourly. 'So dam' much going on!'

'You merely have to watch; I've got to think and plan as well!' flared Ramage.

'Sorry, sir.'

'So am I,' Ramage said hurriedly. 'We're all a bit jumpy. Well, I'd better say a few words to the ship's company: time's getting short. Muster 'em aft, Mr Southwick.'

CHAPTER TWENTY-ONE

As he stood balancing on a carronade waiting for the men to gather round him Ramage wondered how much his face had revealed in the past half an hour. Had it shown the slight doubt which had swelled into something approaching paralysing fear? Did it even now betray the tingling exhilaration which was beginning to grip him like drunkenness?

He was surrounded by a sea of eager, excited and unshaven faces: the men were stripped to the waist and most of them had rags tied round their heads to stop perspiration running into their eyes. They looked tough – almost wild – eager and confident. And they were silent. There was just the occasional creak of the tiller and the slopping of the sea under the counter as the cutter pitched slightly. A few gulls wheeled and mewed astern, as if trying to attract the cook's mate's attention and tell him it was time a bucket of rubbish was emptied over the side.

'I told you earlier,' he began, 'that we'd only be spectators at the ringside. Well, I was wrong: we're going to be one of the prize-fighters and – '

He paused, surprised at the men's burst of cheering and, realizing the men liked the boxing metaphor, quickly rephrased what he was going to say.

' – and I just want to make sure you know where we land our first punch. Well – you can see the Dons are trying to make a bolt round the end of our line. It looks as though Sir John can't see for smoke. Anyway, you all saw the Commodore leave the line to head them off, and it's touch and go whether he can get in among the leaders in time.

'That's where we come in. There they are – you can see 'em all bunched up, with the San Nicolas leading.' He gestured over the bow and saw he had little time left.

'Well, I'm certain that if we can do something to stop the San Nicolas or make her alter course suddenly, the rest of that lubberly bunch astern of her will get so confused they'll run aboard each other. If we can cause enough confusion to delay 'em just ten or fifteen minutes that'll be enough for the Commodore and Captain Collingwood.

'So this is what we're going to do. Most of you have served in a ship of the line. You know her weak spot – the jib-boom and bowsprit. Knock them off and nine times out of ten down comes the foremast.

'We've got one punch and that's where it's got to land. You can see we're heading for the San Nicolas. She can only fire her bow-chasers at us, and frankly they don't scare me. At the last moment I shall turn to larboard – like a boxer stepping back to deliver a punch – and then suddenly turn to starboard, slap across her bows. If I time it right our mast should snap off her jib-boom and with a bit of luck her bowsprit should catch in our rigging.

'What happens after that is anyone's guess. My guess is that for a few moments before her stem hits us our whole weight will be hanging on her bowsprit, and she'll start dragging us along. But the minute she does hit us, she'll start to roll us over – and as we go we'll be pulling even harder on the bowsprit. I'll tell you later whether we sink before the bowsprit gives way!'

Again the men cheered. A glance forward showed he had at the most two minutes left to explain what he wanted.

'Now whatever happens, one thing's certain: as we hit the San Nicolas there'll be a few moments before anything happens. During that time the dozen men I've chosen will try to get on board her and cut every sheet, halyard and brace they can reach. It won't be easy but it shouldn't be impossible because they won't expect to be boarded. In fact they'll be expecting to watch us drown.

'Jackson – step over there and the rest join him. There – they are the twelve, and they have absolute priority in boarding: the rest of you must give 'em a hand if need be. After that, you're all welcome to join the party!'

They laughed and there was a chorus of 'Rely on us, sir!'

'Fine. But no needless risks. If you can't board the San Nicolas, try and save yourselves. Those hammocks piled up there will float and there'll be plenty of wreckage. Grab anything for the moment and hang on. Don't give up hope, however long you have to wait.

'There'll be a lot of smoke and a lot of noise, and there's a danger you'll mistake each other for Dons. So' – Ramage was glad he'd just remembered – 'the challenge is "Kathleen" and the reply...' Damn, he couldn't think of anything.

'Nick!' shouted a seaman.

'Very well,' Ramage grinned, 'the reply is "Nick". Not "Old Nick", if you please!'

'Kathleen!' bawled a man.

'Nick!' roared the rest.

Ramage held up his hand.

'The rendezvous – the San Nicolas' quarterdeck!'

Again the men roared their approval.

'And remember this: every halyard, every brace, every sheet you see – cut it! don't go for the Dons first, go for the sheets and braces. With them cut, the ship's helpless and then you can tackle the Dons. And make a noise – that's what frightens 'em. Shout and slash – and challenge!'

'Shout and slash!' The men bellowed, 'Kathleen, Nick! Shout and slash!'

Again Ramage held up his hand for silence.

'Very well, men, time's getting short. He glanced at the San Nicolas and to the men's delight exclaimed, 'It's so short we're up to the bitter end! Right, don't hang around gossiping!'

With that he jumped down and beckoned to Edwards.

'Get those braziers lit. Are the bags of powder properly dampened?'

'Aye, sir, I've been trying some over a candle flame, like you said. Reckon I've got just the right dampness now.'

'Carry on then!'

The San Nicolas' starboard bow looked like the side of a large house viewed a hundred yards off. With the telescope Ramage looked again at the Spanish ship's bowsprit and jib-boom, together more than eight feet long and jutting out from her bow like an enormous fishing rod. The inboard end, the bowsprit, would be some seventy feet long and probably three feet in diameter, but much of its length was inside the ship: coming in over the stem at a sharp angle, it was held by the heavy knightheads, passing down through the deck to butt up against its step just forward of the foremast. The jib-boom, the thinner extension of the bowsprit, was probably fifty feet long and a little over a foot in diameter.

The whole of Ramage's plan was based on one essential fact of ship construction: because the foremast of a ship of the line, made up of four sections one above the other, was set so far forward, its main support forward came from stays leading down to the bowsprit and jib-boom. Destroy the outer end of the jib-boom and you could be fairly sure the jerk on the foreroyal stay would bring the highest, the foreroyal mast, toppling down, while smashing the whole jib-boom would probably bring down the topgallant mast as well. Breaking off the bowsprit where it passed over the figurehead would carry away the stays holding the foremast and foretopmast. In other words the whole mast could go by the board.

This defect in ship design was why every captain feared a collision; particularly feared that while sailing in line ahead at night or in fog he would get too close to the ship next ahead so that his jib-boom or bowsprit struck the other ship's taffrail.

It was all a gamble, and Ramage knew it was useless calculating whether or not the puny Kathleen could do the job – that's why he had chosen his dozen men. But because of the enormous bulk of the Spanish ship, the sheer heights involved made even the dozen men's ability to board her a matter of chance. The top of the Kathleen's bulwarks forward were ten feet above her waterline, and amidships only seven feet. Again Ramage cursed himself: there was a time when thinking merely wasted valuable minutes and acted like a powerful magnifying glass on your doubts. There were times – and this was one of them – where you copied the bull and not the matador: you put your head down and charged.

The braziers suddenly began to blaze as the kindling caught fire and set the men down to leeward coughing and spluttering. Ramage's dozen men, led by Jackson, grouped round the larboard shrouds gripping their odd collection of cutlasses, half-pikes, tomahawks and butcher's cleavers.

The San Nicolas was almost dead ahead, looming so large Ramage forced himself to look away.

'I shall luff up for a moment, Mr Southwick, then turn to starboard. As soon as I give the word let fly all the sheets and halyards. Make sure they're overhauled and ready to run.'

To the quartermaster he said: 'Steer directly for the San Nicolas.'

He tucked his pad inside his shirt; pulled out the pistols, checked there was enough powder in the pans and jammed them back in his belt; then bent down to undo the strap over the sheath of the throwing knife inside his boot.

By the time he looked at the San Nicolas she was only eight hundred yards or so away.

'Edwards! Smoke, please!'

Edwards bellowed down a hatch and men came scrambling up with wooden cartridge boxes, each going to a particular brazier. At the one farthest forward Edwards took the bag of powder from the box, slit the corner and gingerly shook some of the damp, caked gunpowder on to the burning brazier. At once thick clouds of oily yellow smoke billowed up.

Edwards ducked up to windward and looking aft called: 'How's that, sir?'

'Fine, Edwards. Carry on with the rest of them!'

The men promptly extracted the bags, slit the ends and began shaking powder into the braziers. Within a minute billowing smoke covered the whole ship and Ramage ran to the weather side to get a clearer view as the acrid fumes set men coughing and gasping.

'Quartermaster – come here and pass on my orders: the men at the helm will have to cough and bear it!'

A red eye winked at the San Nicolas' bow, then another, as her bow-chasers fired and the puffs of smoke drifted ahead of the great ship. There was a sound like the tearing of canvas – the noise of shots passing close overhead. He counted the seconds – the Spaniards must have reloaded by now, but they did not fire. Perhaps they were confused at the sight of the cutter. From where he stood the smoke pouring up from the braziers hid the mainsail and he guessed it probably went high enough to hide the topsail as well. The rolling bank of yellow smoke, caught by the wind, was already obscuring the horizon to leeward.

Southwick walked up through the smoke, handkerchief over his mouth and nose, eyes redder than usual, and coughing.

'We must look a fantastic sight, sir! I bet the Dons wonder what the devil's gone wrong with us! I heard a couple of shots go overhead but that's all.'

'They haven't fired again.'

Southwick looked ahead. 'She's a big bitch.'

Ramage grunted.

Southwick pointed over the larboard quarter.

The Captain, every inch of canvas drawing, was well over half-way between the British line and the Santísima Trinidad. As they watched, a hoist of flags broke out and fluttered from the Captain's signal halyards.

'Jackson – signal book!' Ramage shouted, training the telescope. 'Quickly – our pendant, numeral twenty-three! Mr Southwick, have it acknowledged. Well, Jackson? Hurry, man!'

'Twenty-three, sir: "To take possession of the enemy's ships captured"!'

Ramage laughed: the Commodore was a cool fellow to have time for jokes. Cool enough, he suddenly realized, to know the signal would be a tonic for the Kathleens.

'Mr Southwick – pass the Commodore's signal to the ship's company!'

There was no time to comb the book for a witty reply; in fact both the book and the other papers in the weighted bag ought to have been sunk by now.

'Jackson – put the book into the bag and heave it over the side!'

'Now hear this!' Southwick bellowed through the speaking trumpet (so loud, Ramage thought wrily, they'll hear in the San Nicolas), 'now hear this – an order from the Commodore to the Kathleen. We've got to take possession of all the enemy ships we capture! So no skulking off to the spirit room and getting beastly drunk just because you capture a two-decker: leave a couple of men in command, then use her boats to go over and take a three-decker! Leave the Santísima Trinidad for me personally!'

Few of the men could see Southwick but through the smoke came a volley of cheers mixed with happy roars of 'Kathleen, Nick! Kathleen, Nick!'

Southwick grinned at Ramage, who merely nodded. He'd been watching the San Nicolas as the men cheered. No condemned man cheered the hangman when he recognized him. Fortunately the Kathleens didn't recognize him, and they cheered.

Yet the Spaniards too had been overconfident: the San Nicolas' anchor cables were already led out through the hawse and bent to the anchors – a thing usually done when the harbour was in sight because at sea the ends of the cables were stowed below. The carving of the St Nicolas figurehead was beautifully done, rich with gilt and flesh tones, even if the rest of the ship was shabby.

The last five hundred yards.

'Jackson – are you all ready there?'

'Aye aye, sir!'

'Stand by the sheets and halyards, Mr Southwick!'

'Aye aye, sir.'

Now for it. Time was slowing down. Keep calm. Speak slowly.

'Quartermaster, half a point to port,' he drawled.

'Half a point to port it is, sir.'

The slight alteration of course brought the San Nicolas round to fine on the cutter's starboard bow, ready for the last-minute turn, and Ramage had to run forward to see her because of the smoke pouring from the braziers. Both ships were on almost opposite courses and as far as the Spaniards knew apparently going to pass each other to starboard and fifty yards apart.

And the smoke streaming up from the braziers along the Kathleen's entire length was drifting off to leeward in a huge, ever-advancing bank into which the Spanish ship was heading. From the San Nicolas she must seem to be on fire from stem to stern.

Four hundred yards. Less, perhaps. With one foot on the forward carronade slide Ramage watched the two-decker ploughing on – enormous, relentless, implacable – and seemingly invulnerable. The sea curving up and over in thin feathers of water at her bow was pale green. Groups of men on her fo'c'sle were looking down at him. Both bow chasers flashed red and spurted smoke. Somewhere overhead he heard wood splintering.

This was a fish's view of a fat angler on a river bank, the bowsprit and jib-boom jutting out like the rod in his hand. So much gilt and red and blue paint on the headrails. Popping of champagne corks – yes: Spanish soldiers kneeling and resting their muskets on the rail as they fired. She was pitching slightly in the swell waves – just enough to make aiming difficult. And they could see little to shoot at anyway because of the smoke. Only him, he suddenly realized: everyone else was farther aft. The foredeck felt lonely.

Three hundred yards. The San Nicolas' standing and running rigging a complicated cobweb against her sails and the sky. St Nicolas' features discernible, and he did not seem very saintly: a lot of pink paint on his cheeks – he looked as if he drank too much wine. Grape for the Saint, grapeshot for Nicholas.

Again the double flash of the bow-chasers: a dragon winking bloodshot eyes. So close the shot passing sounded like tearing calico. He could make out the seams in her hull planking. Greyish patches on the black paint where salt had dried. They must usually keep a canvas cover over the figurehead – or paint it once a week.

Two hundred yards. Plenty of popping now but he didn't hear the ricochet of musket balls. The double crack of the bow-chasers – they can't depress them enough now to hit the hull, but pray to God they don't hit the mast

A Spanish officer waving his sword like a madman – twice over his head, then pointing at the Kathleen. Over his head again – curious fellow: maybe he's trying to inspire his men. The great bulging sails so badly patched – seams stitched too tight and uneven so the material crinkled.

One hundred yards. He'd never smash that great jib-boom: it was like the trunk of a great pine tree sticking out over a precipice.

Perhaps the jib-boom but certainly not the bowsprit.

Waiting for the executioner's axe to fall after you've put your head on the block must be like this. For God's sake do something. Wait. Seventy-five yards. Wait, wait, wait! All right – turn round…

'Mr Southwick! Ready at the halyards and sheets?'

Acknowledged. Then he remembered he'd already asked that. Ten seconds to go. Memory pictures sped through his head: Gianna, mother, father; the tower of Buranaccio in the moonlight when he rescued Gianna; Southwick's excited bloodshot eyes; Jackson's grin and Stafford's imitation of the Commodore.

Turn again. Calmly. Loud enough for the man to hear.

'Quartermaster! Helm hard a'port!'

The Kathleen's bowsprit began swinging to starboard towards the San Nicolas. Slowly, oh so slowly. Too slowly! No, perhaps not. Anyway, too late to worry...

No – he'd timed it perfectly! The Kathleen's foretopmast stay would hit the outer end of the San Nicolas' bowsprit.

'Mr Southwick! Let fly halyards and sheets!'

Beside him the banging of a blacksmith's hammer on the anvil: musket balls hitting the barrel of the carronade. Musket balls aimed at him. Poor shooting.

Without looking up at the San Nicolas he turned and ran through the smoke to join the boarding party at the main shrouds. Several of the men, including Jackson, were already waiting half-way up the ratlines, looking ahead as the Kathleen's sharp turn began to bring the San Nicolas into view, poised for the desperate leap to board her. He prayed no one would jump too soon and fall into the sea between the two ships. Splashing water – the San Nicolas' bow wave!

He hitched round the cutlass belt so Southwick's sword was out of the way, hanging behind him like a grotesque tail, and as he rammed his hat hard on his head there was the crack and snap of splintering wood and a jolt shook the cutter: God! She'd managed to get closer than he'd expected before her topmast stay hit the San Nicolas' bowsprit A crash aloft – he didn't bother to glance up: the stay had torn down the topmast.

A momentary spasm of fear in case the rest of the mainmast should go, tearing down the ratlines on which the boarders were perched. The shrouds vibrated, twanging with the strain; a seaman losing his grip fell, arms and legs flailing, hitting the deck a few feet away with a grunt which could have indicated unconsciousness or annoyance.

Then chaos: a great black bulging shape suddenly towering above him in the smoke – the San Nicolas' bow. A moment's silence then her stern smashed into the Kathleen's side just forward of the mast, biting deep into the planking with a shock which nearly knocked him down. A nightmare of noise – wood cracking and crunching; ropes whiplashing as they snapped under enormous strain; water splashing, surging, gurgling; men shouting with almost maniacal voices, insane cries of 'Kathleen! Kathleen! Kathleen!' – cries coming, suddenly, and almost unbelievably from above him, from the San Nicolas.

And slowly the Kathleen heeled: the San Nicolas' bow was rolling her over as it rode into her hull, pressing her down under the massive curving forefoot.

A rope swung past. Without realizing what he was doing he leapt up and out and grabbed it, managing to hold on with desperate energy, to find himself swinging over the water and the wreck of the cutter like a pendulum.

On an upward swing he had a momentary glimpse of Jackson and other boarders scrambling through the lower rail. As he swung down again he saw below him the Kathleen's gashed hull impaled by the San Nicolas' stern.

By flexing and stretching his legs he tried to get sufficient momentum to swing high enough to reach the anchor cable, but even as he began soaring up on the final swing the whole anchor came adrift and fell into the water with a splash and tearing of timber. He just managed to twist round in time to get a leg astride the lower rail with a thump which drove all the air out of his lungs. For a few moments, gasping for breath and trembling with excitement, he sat helpless, watching Jackson and Stafford just above him dodging through the main rail.

Then he began climbing up after them and saw below the San Nicolas' jib-boom hanging down, smashed into three pieces. With a curious detachment he registered the fact he'd succeeded in doing what he'd set out to do. He glanced down at the Kathleen – she was lying on her side like a stranded whale, the underwater section of her hull dark green with slime and wood and speckled with barnacles. And one of the flukes of the San Nicolas' fallen anchor had pierced her hull and the strain on the cable was helping to hold her so she did not roll over completely.

His brain was racing and even as he climbed he realized the Kathleen would fill in a very few minutes and, if her shrouds could take the strain, her dead weight pulling down on the San Nicholas' bowsprit might break it off short and bring the mast with it. Then...but there was no more time to think: Jackson and Stafford were screaming at him and gesticulating upwards.

Already the San Nicolas' splintered foreroyal and topgallant masts were hanging down and now the foretopmast was bending forward like a bow. Even as he watched it suddenly split like a bamboo cane and slowly toppled down, bringing the yard and topsail with it. For a moment he thought it would crash on him, but the weight of the yard slewed it round so it plunged over the larboard side.

Yet the wreck of the Kathleen was still being thrust through the water by the sheer bulk of the San Nicolas. Some Kathleens were standing on the side of the hull – which was almost horizontal – and quite unhurriedly (or so it seemed to Ramage) grasping various pieces of the Spanish ship's severed rigging and beginning to climb up hand over hand to get on board.

Ramage scrambled up on to the platform and in a moment was with Jackson, Stafford and several others crouching close against the beakhead bulkhead waiting for a hail of musket fire from the Spanish soldiers who before the collision had been firing into the Kathleen from the rail just above. But there was not so much as a face at the rail. Smoke which bit into the lungs and seared nostrils was still drifting from the Kathleen and when Ramage leaned cautiously over the head-rails and looked aft he saw a few Spaniards on the fo'c'sle at the bulwarks looking down to see what was happening under their bow.

At once he realized the beakhead bulkhead was hiding the group of Kathleens: no one realized they were on board. For the next few minutes the Spaniards' efforts would be concentrated on clearing away the wreckage of the mast and yards – and any moment the Kathleen would sink. If her last plunge snapped off the bowsprit, his task would be complete. So for the moment, he realized thankfully, there was nothing more the Kathleens need do: it'd be better to wait hidden on the beakhead platform. The Spaniards were already in complete confusion. If they showed any signs of sorting themselves out the Kathleens could discomfort them again with all the advantages of surprise.

He gave orders to Jackson and to Stafford. The Cockney beckoned three men and climbed down to the lower rail and, out of sight of the Spaniards, began hauling other Kathleens on board as they swarmed up the hanging ropes and wreckage. Each man, soaking wet and shivering, then joined the group huddled against the bulkhead.

Anxiously Ramage watched. Of his 'Cartagena Sextet' Rossi was missing. And there was no sign of Southwick. Finally he could wait no longer.

'Jackson – go down and help Stafford. See if there's any sign of Mr Southwick.'

How long before some Spaniards came along the gangplank to the bowsprit – the 'Marine's Walk', as it was called – and discovered them? Ramage told two of the men with half-pikes to stand guard and, as soon as anyone set foot on it, dispose of them quickly and silently with a sharp upward jab.

Spaniards shouting like men demented, stern voices of authority swamped by yells of confusion and panic, the slopping of water under the bow, the steady thumping against the hull as waves caught the wreckage of the masts and yards hanging over the side – and even as Ramage absorbed the impressions, he sensed the ship slowly beginning to swing to larboard, up into the wind. He felt dizzy with relief – the San Nicolas, leading the Spanish van, was out of control!

With the Kathleen athwart her bow, her great topmast and yards over the side dragging like an anchor, and the wind still filling the sails set on the other masts with nothing forward to balance them but the single sail left on the remains of the foremast, her stern was being forced round, throwing her bow up into the wind. And unless the Spaniards quickly braced the yards hard up to stop the wind getting forward of the beam, every sail would soon be a'back. Then, given the normal ration of confusion, the San Nicolas would quickly gather sternway and begin to drive astern through the rest of Cordoba's ships which were following close in her wake. Ramage could scarcely believe that the little Kathleen had achieved so much.

Gunfire – close astern, too! Peering round between the headrails he saw the Captain approaching – she was perhaps six hundred yards away, smoke from her guns streaming to leeward. Almost at once another broadside (which from its noise could come only from the Santísima Trinidad) echoed across the sea.

Someone tugged his sleeve and he turned to find Southwick grinning at him, the white hair plastered down over his ears and forehead making him look like a bedraggled but happy old English sheepdog just emerging from the village pond.

Ramage gripped his shoulders. 'Are you hurt?'

'No, sir! The mainsheet took a turn round my leg and I couldn't get free, though.'

'Standing in a bight of rope, Mr Southwick,' Ramage accused him with a grin. 'How many times have you rubbed down a man for that?'

'Aye,' Southwick admitted, 'and I'd still be down there if it hadn't been for Stafford and Jackson.'

'What did they do?'

'Came down again and cut me free. I was a bit rough with them because I thought they'd quit you.'

Ramage laughed. 'No, we're taking it easy, the Dons don't seem to have spotted us and they're doing quite well without our help – for the moment, anyway.'

Astern the rumble of guns was louder and closer. Still the San Nicolas' bow continued swinging slowly to larboard, and a moment later noises like giant hands slapping wet cloth showed her sails were being taken a'back.

Southwick grinned at Ramage. 'No, they don't need our help!'

More Kathleens were climbing up on to the platform. The cutter, still on her side, was almost completely submerged: air escaping through hatches hissed and whistled out in great spurts and bubbles, like a sea monster gasping in its death throes.

Southwick pointed at the shrouds hooked over the bowsprit. 'Can't understand how they're holding. Wouldn't believe it if I wasn't seeing it myself.'

Suddenly they both jumped with fear: without warning the huge bowsprit snapped like a carrot a few feet ahead of the figurehead. Ramage recovered just in time to yell 'Duck!'

Then came the crackling and groaning of a massive piece of timber splintering like a tree falling under a woodsman's axe, and the whole foremast and foreyard slowly toppled over the starboard side, part of the foresail draping across the fo'c'sle and the rest hanging down in the water, hiding the wreck of the Kathleen like a pall.

'Anyone hurt?' demanded Ramage.

There was no reply.

The gunfire was nearer: much nearer. In fact he was sure a British ship was firing into the San Nicolas' stern because all the shouting in Spanish came from aft.

Then a whole broadside shook the ship.

'My God!' growled Southwick, 'She's being properly raked!'

'Look sir,' Jackson exclaimed.

The Salvador del Mundo had put her helm up and was passing along the San Nicolas' larboard side and even as they watched Stafford yelled from across the platform, 'The Excellent! Cor, just look at 'er. Just like she was at Spithead!'

Captain Collingwood's ship was passing close along the other side of the San Nicolas and a ripple of red flashes sent the Kathleens crouching once again in a tangled heap against the bulkhead as the Excellent's full broadside hit the San Nicolas. The whole ship shook as the heavy roundshot thudded into her timbers, and the little iron eggs of grapeshot sounded like metal rain, clanging as many ricocheted off metal.

Then the Excellent was past. The San Nicolas did not reply; instead, through the bulkhead, the Kathleens could hear the chilling, almost demented screaming of badly wounded men.

On the larboard side yet another Spanish ship was passing, keeping in the wake of the Salvador del Mundo.

The Excellent began bracing up her yards, obviously intending to pass across the San Nicolas' bows to engage the other two ships.

Suddenly a thump shook the San Nicolas as though she had run on a rock. Ramage and Southwick glanced at each other, mystified. There was a sudden silence: the shouting stopped for several moments – even the wounded were quiet – and then began again with many voices raised in near panic. Ramage looked down to see the Kathleen had vanished – she'd obviously sunk when her shrouds tore away the San Nicolas' bowsprit – and then scrambled up to peer over the bulkhead across the fo'c'sle. First he saw why the Spaniards had not spotted the Kathleens or anyway left them alone: in falling, the various sections or the foremast had swept the fo'c'sle clear, tearing guns from their carriages or overturning them, wrecking the belfry, shattering the fore-bitts and smashing some of the deck planking. Torn sails, some hanging over the side, hid more damage. Then he saw the reason for the thump: the massive stern of the San Josef was jammed hard up against the San Nicolas' larboard side, her huge red, gold and red ensign flapping languidly against the main shrouds.

Ramage dropped down again.

'What did you see sir?' Southwark asked excitedly. 'What was it?'

'Somehow we've run aboard the San Josef – or she's run aboard us! I can't make out how she got there, but her transom's tucked hard up against our larboard side at the main chains. The Captain's lost her foretopmast but she's closing on our starboard quarter – it looks as though the Commodore's going to lay her aboard us!'

The men began to chatter among themselves.

'Quiet, you fools,' hissed Southwark. 'There are five hundred or so Dons still on board this ship!'

Ramage realized that if the Commodore really did board, the San Josef might send over men to help the San Nicolas – it'd be easy enough: they merely had to jump on board.

'Listen, men. There are enough of us to help the Captain's boarders. I know most of you aren't armed, but we'll split into two parties. My original boarders will go first and make for the quarterdeck. Mr Southwick will lead the rest of you – you'll find plenty of the Dons' muskets and pikes lying around. And once you get aft keep on shouting "Kathleens here!" otherwise you'll find yourselves shot or run through by the Captains.

'Mr Southwick – while my party makes for the quarterdeck, I want yours to keep along the larboard side to cover the San Josef. If she sends men over it'll be up to you to stop them.'

With that Ramage climbed up the bulkhead for another look. The San Josef was still jammed against the San Nicolas; the Captain was four hundred yards off and bearing down for the San Nicolas' quarter.

He dropped down to the platform again and, remembering he still had Southwick's sword, began to take off the belt, but the Master stopped him.

'You'll be leading, sir. I'll find a cutlass.'

Ramage protested but saw Southwick wanted him to keep it.

'Now, where are my men?'

Jackson, Stafford and the others crowded round him.

'Right – all of you against the bulkhead. The rest stand by to give us a leg up: we want to surprise 'em. Now, no shouting until I shout "Kathleens". We may get quite a way aft before they spot us coming.'

Again the San Nicolas shook to the sound of an enormous thump. One of the seamen gave Ramage a leg up. The Captain's bow had hit the San Nicolas' starboard quarter: her bowsprit was right across the Spanish ship's poop, her spritsail yard hooked up in the mizzen shrouds. Already the Captain's boarding parties were grouped along her bulwarks ready to jump, and there were soldiers among them – he remembered she was carrying a detachment of the 69th Foot. As Ramage called down to Southwick to warn the men of the soldiers, there was a cracking of musket fire from the troops in the San Nicolas and Ramage saw several of the Captain's men fall.

'Right men, up you come. Give me a shove, blast you!'

The man heaved up so hard Ramage pitched right over the rail and, before he could get his balance, fell flat on his back on the fo'c'sle, the hilt of Southwick's sword knocking all the breath out of him. More of the Kathleens came up over the rail and Jackson was kneeling beside him.

'You hit, sir?'

'No, I tripped. Come on!'

In a moment Ramage was on his feet leading the men in a wild dash across the fo'c'sle, scrambling over the thick folds of the foresail, pieces of masts and yards and tangled cordage. Right aft he could see British seamen's cutlasses glinting as they scrambled from the Captain's spritsail yard on to the San Nicolas' mizzen rigging. Spanish soldiers were shooting up at them and sailors stood ready with boarding pikes. Then a rattle of musket fire from the Captain cut down several of the Spaniards.

Meanwhile the bow of the San Josef was swinging and she'd soon be lying right alongside the San Nicolas.

Suddenly he realized he was empty-handed: Southwick's sword was bumping the back of his legs – he hadn't hauled the belt round. As he ran he dragged at it, grabbed the hilt and by drawing it over his head managed to get it clear. He tugged a pistol from his belt and cocked it with his left thumb. Three Spaniards suddenly appeared from behind a gun they'd obviously been skulking there out of the way – and ran aft yelling to raise the alarm. Jackson flung his half-pike like a spear and the farthest fell, a rag doll tossed on the floor, making the two others turn.

One with a pistol in his hand was by then a couple of yards from Ramage and aimed straight at his face. Forgetting his pistol, Ramage desperately swung Southwick's sword but saw the man's index finger whiten as he squeezed the trigger.

The sword cut into the man's shoulder as Ramage waited for the flash from the pistol's muzzle which should have killed him. Then he saw the Spaniard had forgotten to cock the pistol. Clutching his wounded shoulder, he spun round and as he fell the third man, cut down by Stafford, collapsed beside him. Stafford paused to pick up the pistol and followed Ramage.

Now he was abreast the mainmast. Drifting smoke hid much of the ship and several Spaniards were still standing to their guns and staring at the Captain, oblivious of the Kathleens running past.

Then Ramage was abreast the boats stowed amidships and running along the narrow gangway, dodging round more Spanish seamen who were still watching the bulk of the Captain, which was too far aft for them to train round their guns. He saw a British officer – Edward Berry, just promoted and serving as a volunteer in the Captain – dropping down from the mizzen rigging on to the quarterdeck, a couple of dozen men following him. At the same instant a surge of Spaniards from the larboard side suddenly swept across the quarterdeck almost overwhelming Berry and his boarders.

The sharp clinking of sword against sword, the popping of pistols and muskets, more smoke, wild shouts –

Ramage's own! A Spanish face in his way. The great sword swung and the face disappeared, but before Ramage could recover from the swing another man lunged with a cutlass. Ramage fired his pistol almost without aiming and the man screamed and fell to one side. As a third lunged with a pike Ramage tried to ward him off with the sword and an instant later Stafford's cutlass slashed into the man's side

Ramage ran half-blinded with excitement but seeing more men jumping on board from the Captain. At last the quarterdeck ladder – and a Spanish officer, backing down it with a British seaman above lunging at him, turned to jump and fell to Jackson's cutlass.

'Kathleens here!' Ramage bellowed up to the quarterdeck, 'We're the Kathleens!'

''Bout bloody time!' bawled the seaman and started back up the ladder to rejoin the fighting.

But pistols were firing in the captain's cabin and instead of going up the ladder Ramage ran under the half-deck to find a dozen or more Spaniards shooting aft into the cabin through the closed door. Jackson, Stafford and several others had followed him and as Ramage roared 'Kathleens! Come on the Kathleens!' the Spaniards turned, throwing away their pistols and swinging cutlasses and swords. There was no conscious thought, only instinct: parry a stabbing blade here, slice at a screaming Spaniard there, jump back to avoid a lunging cutlass point, sidestep and reach over to parry a wrist-jarring slash which would have split open Jackson's skull. A man in magnificent uniform and garlic-laden breath leapt forward with his sword but before Ramage could parry a blade flashed, the sword dropped from the man's hand and he fell. Glancing round, Ramage just had time to see Jackson grin and realize the Kathleens were standing amid a pile of bodies when the cabin door, riddled with pistol shot, suddenly burst open and a wild-eyed, smoke-begrimed seaman leapt through, cutlass in his hand, pausing a moment before attacking them.

'We're English!' yelled Stafford. 'Watch 'art, yer crazy loon!'

The strident Cockney voice stopped the man as effectively as a bullet, but he was flung aside by more men so Stafford repeated his yells. Then the Commodore was standing there, hatless, sword in one hand and pistol in another. He stared at Ramage for a moment, said with a grin of recognition, 'Ah! At least you obey my orders!' and ran past to get to the quarterdeck ladder.

Ramage followed but realized the fighting up there had stopped. Berry and his men were already herding the Spaniards over to the starboard side where they could be covered by muskets from the Captain's decks.

Commodore Nelson spoke a few words to Berry, pointing to the San Josef now lying alongside the San Nicolas, and Berry shouted for his men.

'Mr Ramage!' called Nelson, 'I think we'll have that fellow as well!' and began running to the San Josef.

Without waiting for more orders, Berry's men and the Kathleens made a mad rush across the quarterdeck, the lithe little Commodore among the leaders, The San Josef's bulwarks were considerably higher than the San Nicolas' and both Ramage and Nelson leapt into the main chains together. Nelson slipped, Ramage grabbed his arm until he regained his footing, and just as they began climbing a Spanish officer appeared above them on the quarterdeck, calling down that the ship had surrendered. Nelson gave a yell of delight and Ramage felt relief. Then there was a sudden flash at the gun port below and Ramage felt himself swirling slowly down, down, down, into a deep black well of silence.

CHAPTER TWENTY-TWO

The drum was beating in rhythm with his heart, the drum would never stop beating, forever sending the ship's company to quarters and to death. Heart of oak, are our men... Tat-tat-tat, tat, tat-tat... Ramage tried to scream at the drummer to stop but no words came. The beat was regular and loud: it throbbed in his ears, in his temples, in his chest, and as he twisted his head to get away from it he felt himself spiralling upwards, weightless, dizzy and frightened. He opened his eyes and saw Southwick's blurred face creased with anxiety. Slowly it began to revolve like a top and Ramage shut his eyes again.

'Mr Ramage!'

'Wha's it, Southwi'?'

'How do you feel, sir?'

'Wha' happen'?'

'You were shot at through a gun port after the San Josef had surrendered.'

Throb, throb, bang, bang; the band round his brow was tight and Southwick's face began to spin again. Ramage clutched his head and felt cloth: strips of cloth wound round like an Indian's turban.

Southwick seemed to be whispering from a long way off. Ramage opened his eyes again to find Southwick's face close, beads of perspiration welling up through the bristles. Southwick unshaven? It was all very puzzling: he wasn't in

297

his cabin in the Kathleen. Ramage started to sit up but Southwick's face spun again.

'Easy sir, easy, you're on board the Irresistible. The Commodore's hoisted his broad pendant in her.'

'But why aren't I – '

'You remember, sir,' Southwick said soothingly, 'you remember we boarded the San Nicolas and then the Captain – '

'Yes, I remember.'

It came back slowly at first, not facts but pictures: the Kathleen steering for that great cliff face that was the San Nicolas; the impact and the cutter dragging athwart the Spaniard's stem; then that mad dash along the San Nicolas' decks then the Commodore and climbing the San Josef's main chains and a Spanish officer shouting down they had surrendered. Abruptly the pictures stopped.

'What happened next?'

'Next to what, sir?' Southwick was puzzled.

'After that damn' Spaniard said they'd surrendered?'

'You were shot at through a gun port. They didn't know below that the ship had hauled down her colours. If you'll excuse me a moment, sir.'

With that he bellowed to the sentry at the door. Ramage winced, the pain blotting out Southwick's words.

'You fell, sir,' Southwick continued.

'I'm not surprised.'

'No, I mean you fell into the sea between the two ships.'

'Why didn't I drown, or get crushed?'

'Those two again. Jackson and Stafford. They went down after you.'

'They're mad. No wonder I feel sick. I must have swallowed half the bay of Cadiz.'

'You did, sir. I flung them a rope but it took time to get a turn under your armpits. When they got you on deck we thought at first you'd gone. I've never seen anyone look so dead.'

'You'd better send for those two.'

'Well, if you'd wait a moment, sir.'

Ramage felt too weak to argue.

A knock at the door but the person did not wait for an answer. Ramage tried to turn to see who it was but again his head spun.

'Well, Mr Ramage,' said the familiar sharp, nasal voice, and the Commodore was standing at the foot of the cot. 'Well, Mr Ramage, you have a thick head – fortunately!'

'At the moment it feels a bit thin in places, sir.'

'It is, too! Now you'll have two scars on your starboard beakhead, a bullet wound to add to the sword cut. And a good thing, too, the ladies love it. Take my word for it, if you're going to get wounded, a handsome scar they can admire is worth more than the handsomest face in the room! My own little souvenir of the battle, for instance, won't count for much. I have a most unromantically bruised stomach!'

Ramage laughed and felt he had been hit on the head again.

'But seriously, Ramage, only a criminal idiot would have tried to do what you did with the Kathleen. Fortunately for me, the wicked sometimes prosper. You succeeded and I've achieve a little notoriety for having captured two of the Fleet's four prizes.'

'I'm glad, sir.'

'I know you are,' Nelson said warmly. 'But I said notoriety, not credit. I've not yet seen the Commander-in-Chief, and since I acted with as much authority as you did, both of us might be in a scrape. But whatever happens, Mr Ramage, if it ever lies in my power to render you a service…'

Ramage was struggling to find a suitable reply when Nelson added, 'And I'm glad to tell you that you'll be sent home in the Lively frigate with Sir Gilbert Elliot.'

'No!' exclaimed Ramage. 'I mean, if you please, sir, I'd prefer to stay with the Fleet!'

'But why?'

'I – well sir, I'd like to see my ship's company are all right.'

'Mr Ramage,' Nelson said gently and with a smile, 'you have no ship, and therefore no ship's company. And the Service is well able to take care of the survivors.'

Ramage felt too weak to explain, and knowing the Commander was right he shut his eyes with weariness and pain.

'I'll call on you again,' the Commodore said sympathetically, and left the cabin.

'What was the butcher's bill?' Ramage asked Southwick several minutes later.

'Incredibly light, sir. Twelve dead. Edwards, the gunner's mate, wasn't seen from just before we hit the San Nicolas – I think a shot from her bow-chaser may have got him – and eleven seamen. Six of those never got on board the San Nicolas and five were killed in the fighting. One of those was Jensen, who was with you at Cartagena, hit by one of the San Josef's sharpshooters. Only four wounded – yourself, Fuller and two ordinary seamen.'

'We were lucky,' Ramage said soberly. 'God knows, we were lucky.'

'You were careful, sir,' said Southwick.

'Careful?'

'I've been – well, sir, I know it's a bit unusual, but the ship's company asked me to tell you – as discreetly as possible you realize, sir – they appreciate the care you took to lessen the loss of life.'

'If only you – ' he exclaimed, then said, 'no, thank them, Southwick. But from the moment we tacked towards the San Nicolas I never expected any of us to survive.'

He took a deep breath. 'That's the care I took,' he added bitterly; 'Instead of more than sixty dead, I killed only a dozen.'

'No, sir, don't take on like that. You aren't fair to yourself. We've got to fight; some of us'll get killed. The men know that. They thought all along after we tacked that they'd be killed. They knew you thought they didn't guess: but they did realize, and they kept cheerful for your sake, sir. And they're right to thank you.'

'I suppose so,' Ramage said. 'But I'm too befuddled – '

The door opened and the chubby and bespectacled surgeon came in. 'Goodness gracious, Mr Southwick – I must ask you to leave. Our patient looks worn out. Really, really, really! All my work undone by fifteen minutes of chatter, chatter, chatter!'

Southwick looked alarmed and stood up to leave. Ramage winked as the Master turned to the door.

Next day while Ramage fretted in his cot, irritated by the constant attention of the surgeon (who was quick to spot the Commodore's particular interest in his patient), Sir John Jervis' ships were becalmed with the Spanish Fleet still in sight – 'In great disorder,' Southwick reported gleefully.

The day after that the British Fleet spent several hours trying to weather Cape St Vincent against head winds, and finally Sir John decided to bear away for Lagos Bay, just to the eastward of Cape St Vincent, and in the evening the Fleet and its prizes anchored.

Ramage, allowed to sit in a chair, had just started writing once again to his father – hard put to read what he'd

written in the first letter, which had been soaked in seawater
– when Southwick came into the cabin.

'From the Commander-in-Chief,' he said, handing
Ramage a sealed letter addressed to Lieutenant Lord
Ramage, formerly of His Majesty's late cutter, 'Kathleen'.
'I've signed for it. One's gone to every captain.'

Ramage read the letter and then wondered if it was
identical in wording to the others. Not a mention of the
Commodore, either by name or the rôle of the Captain.
Nor Captain Troubridge and the Culloden, Captain
Frederick and the Blenheim, nor Captain Collingwood and
the Excellent.

Dated 'Victory, Lagos Bay, 16th February, 1797', it said:

Sir,

No language I am possessed of can convey the high
sense I entertain of the exemplary conduct of the flag
officers, captains, officers, seamen, marines and
soldiers embarked on board every ship of the Squadron
I have the honour to command, present at the
vigorous and successful attack made upon the Fleet of
Spain on the 14th inst. The signal advantage obtained
by His Majesty's arms on that day, is entirely owing to
their determined valor [sic] and discipline; and I
request you will accept yourself, and give my thanks
and approvation to those composing the ship under
your command. I am, Sir,
Your most humble servant,

J Jervis.

Southwick was watching him closely and said, 'It's going to
cause trouble, sir.'

'How do you know? Have you read it?'

'No, sir, not yours; but Captain Martin gave me a sight of his before he read it to this ship's company. He was pretty angry – reckons it's an insult to the Commodore.'

'Well, it mentions no names, so there's no favouritism.'

'No, but I heard by a side wind from the Victory that Sir John's official letter to the Admiralty doesn't mention captains or ships either.'

This seemed so improbable that Ramage grunted his disbelief.

'It's true, sir, the whole Fleet knows by now that Sir John wrote one letter, then Captain Calder read it and, being a spiteful man, said if the Commodore was given any praise it'd encourage others to disobey orders. So Sir John wrote another, mentioning no names at all.'

Calder! Ramage knew at once the story was probably true: it was common knowledge Calder was more than jealous of the Commodore. (And that, he suddenly realized, probably accounted for Calder's hostility towards him: he probably thought he was one of the Commodore's protégés.) Surprising that Sir John didn't see through such spitefulness.

There was a knock on the door and the Commodore himself walked in.

'Sitting up and taking nourishment, eh?'

'Precious little nourishment in this, sir,' Ramage said, waving the letter.

'Oh well, words on paper count less than actions, Mr Ramage,' Nelson said banteringly. 'In the battle the Prince George expended 197 barrels of powder, the Blenheim 180, the Culloden 170 and the Captain 146. The Captain fired more shot than she would have had on board – when we had no more round or grapeshot for the 32-pound carronades my men began using 9-pound roundshot. But when the official letter is published, I doubt if you'll see the four ships named even once. Yet does it matter, really? Those whose opinions any of us value will soon get to know, and who cares about the rest? Remember, if you don't fret and expect justice, you'll probably hoist your flag eventually and live to a ripe old age!'

'I hope you'll guarantee that in writing, sir!'

'I've just told you not to expect justice! But seriously, Ramage, it's more important to forget the profit and loss account in a battle and think of the total effect on the enemy.'

'I don't see the difference, sir.'

'Well, Sir John's despatch will delight the Press; the politicians will gleefully announce in Parliament that a British Fleet of fifteen sail of the line met twenty-seven Spanish sail of the line, gave them a good trouncing and captured four at no loss to themselves. They won't reveal – won't even realize – the most valuable and significant part of the victory.'

'But – '

'It's the men that matter, Ramage, not ships. The finest and largest fighting ship in the world is useless if her captain and crew are frightened of the enemy. The worst and smallest fighting ship is invaluable if her captain and crew believe they will win. Good heavens man, you tackled the San Nicolas with the Kathleen, didn't you?

'Remember that, and then think beyond the horizon: this is the first battle the Spaniards have fought against us in this war. In sheer numbers they had nearly twice as many ships and twice as many guns – and that doesn't take into account most of their ships were larger. They had the weather gage, and they fought knowing they had Cadiz to leeward as a refuge for refitting. Yet they lost – decisively!'

'And,' Ramage said, 'they lost knowing that their admiral was useless, their broadsides counted for very little and that one British seventy-four boarded and captured one of their eighty-fours and then did the same to a 112-gun ship!'

'Precisely,' Nelson said. 'When the rest of the Spanish Navy hears the details of the battle, there'll hardly be a single man, whether cook's mate or admiral, who won't secretly believe deep inside him – and that's where it matters, that's where the fighting's lost or won – that one British ship equals two Spanish. The first battle of the war has given them indisputable evidence.'

'So from now on,' Ramage said, 'the Dons are likely to feel beaten before they set sail!'

'I hope so!' Nelson said soberly. 'I hope every man, from the King and the Minister of Marine downwards, will think twice before sending the Spanish Fleet to sea – and then order it to stay in port. That'll give us a chance to deal with the French and the Spanish ships a chance to rot.'

The Commodore took an envelope from his pocket, gave it to Ramage, and said he would return later.

Ramage took the envelope but, preoccupied with Nelson's words, did not open it at once. If the Spanish Fleet had reached Cadiz safely (and they might have done but for the gale which blew them out into the Atlantic, allowing Sir John time to catch them as they struggled back) they might have gone on up to Brest, driven off the British Squadron blockading the French Fleet and let it out, and sailed for England...

But they met a gale, then they met Sir John's Fleet. And they lost four ships. Yet at least two of those ships, Ramage realized with a start, would not have been captured by the Commodore unless the Kathleen had delayed the Spanish van by ramming the San Nicolas...

It'd taken him all this time to realize that. Southwick had known and the men had known – he recalled Southwick's message from the Kathleens. But Lieutenant Nicolas Ramage had not known. And yet in a way he had. Not by thinking of it as a complete sequence of events: he hadn't steered the Kathleen for the San Nicolas with the idea of trying to defeat a Franco-Spanish Armada against England. He'd done it to slow down Cordoba's van. But, he realized, the greatest archway ever built was made of small bricks and rocks, and each one of them depended on the others, and they all depended on one, the keystone.

He broke the seal of the letter. It was from one of the Admiral's staff. The Lively frigate was leaving for England with the Commander-in-Chief's dispatches for the Admiralty, and Lieutenant Ramage was to return in her – as a passenger – if he was well enough to be moved. In view of the fact the frigate was well below her complement, Lieutenant Ramage was to name twenty-five of the best men from among his former ship's company and send them on board with the Master. For Lieutenant Ramage's personal information, the letter added, another frigate was leaving the Fleet shortly for Gibraltar and then returning to England with the Marchesa di Volterra, and if Lieutenant Ramage wished to write…

Which meant, he realized with a joy which drove away all thoughts of the pain in his head, he'd be waiting to welcome her to English soil. And if the Spring arrived at St Kew before an Admiralty letter bringing him orders, they'd walk together among the blossoms and the fresh green grass, alone for, the first time without the threat of urgency of war tapping them on the shoulder.

DUDLEY POPE

GOVERNOR RAMAGE RN

Lieutenant Lord Ramage, expert seafarer and adventurer, undertakes to escort a convoy across the Caribbean. This seemingly routine task leads him into a series of dramatic and terrifying encounters. Lord Ramage is quick to learn that the enemy attacks from all angles and he must keep his wits about him in order to survive. Fast and thrilling, this is another highly-charged adventure from the masterly Dudley Pope.

'All the verve and expertise of Forester'
– *Observer*

RAMAGE'S CHALLENGE

The Napoleonic Wars are raging and a group of eminent British citizens have been taken captive in the Mediterranean by French troops. The Admiralty traces their location and sends the valiant Lord Ramage to effect their release. As Ramage and his crew negotiate the hazardous waters off the Tuscan coast, they soon begin to doubt the accuracy of their instructions. Ramage comes to realize that in order for his mission to succeed he must embark upon a fearful and highly dangerous escapade where the stakes have never been higher.

Ramage's Challenge is another action-packed naval adventure from the masterful Dudley Pope.

DUDLEY POPE

RAMAGE AND THE GUILLOTINE

As France recovers from her bloody Revolution, Napoleon is amassing his armies for the Great Invasion. News in England is sketchy and the Navy must prepare to defend the land from foreign attack.

Lieutenant Ramage is chosen to travel to France and embark upon the perilous quest of spying on the great Napoleon. His mission is to determine the strength of the French troops – but his discovery will mean the guillotine!

'The first and still favourite rival to Hornblower'
– *Daily Mirror*

RAMAGE'S PRIZE

Lord Ramage returns for another highly-charged and thrilling adventure at sea. Instructed with the task of discovering why His Majesty's dispatches keep unaccountably disappearing, Ramage finds himself involved in a situation far beyond his expectations. Based on true events, *Ramage's Prize* is another gripping story from Dudley Pope.

'An author who really knows Nelson's Navy'
– *Observer*

DUDLEY POPE

THE RAMAGE TOUCH

The Ramage Touch finds the ever-popular Lord Ramage in the Mediterranean with another daring mission to undertake. He soon makes a shocking discovery which dramatically transforms the nature of the task at hand. With the nearest English vessel a thousand miles away, Ramage must embark upon a truly perilous and life-threatening course of action. With everything stacked against him, he has only one chance to succeed…

RAMAGE AT TRAFALGAR

Lord Ramage returns to fight in the most famous of Britain's sea battles. Summoned by Admiral Nelson himself, Ramage is sent to join the British fleet off Cadiz where the largest battle in naval history is about to take place. Finding himself in the front line of battle, Lord Ramage must fight to save his own life as well as for his country. The result is a thrilling, hair-raising adventure from one of our best-loved naval writers.

'Expert knowledge of naval history'
– *Guardian*